PR.

It's one of those stories that is hard to put down. This may be my first book I've read by Croft, but it won't be my last.

— AMY'S BOOKSHELF REVIEWS

It was a surprisingly pleasant coming-of-age ride late bloomer style. I would recommend it to anyone who is open to a different perspective of werewolf fiction and who can identify with the awkwardness and anxieties of finding our own path in life.

— KAIAH OSEYE, AUTHOR OF DESTINY AND FATE

I enjoyed this story, its a debut novel for Jeanine and a great start.

— JEANNIE ZELOS BOOK REVIEWS

This isn't your typical werewolf book. I find so much of the genre to be saturated with overly alpha, domineering, unrealistic males. This story felt so much more realistic. It was refreshing to get that in a werewolf story. Applause for Jeanine Croft.

— MELISSA MITCHELL, AUTHOR OF THE DRAGONWALL SERIES

ALSO BY JEANINE CROFT

Winterly

JEANINE CROFT

THORNE BAY

First published in the United States of America in August 2018 by Jeanine Croft.
Second edition published 2020 by Jeanine Croft.

Names: Croft, Jeanine, author.
Title: *Thorne Bay* / Jeanine Croft
Summary: "Evan Spencer throws a dart at a map and heads to Alaska looking for change. She discovers herself in the company of wolves, and the change she was looking for comes at a cost when she falls in love with a werewolf."

ISBN-13: 978-1720123972

Cover design by Jeanine Croft

For Josh. I love you.

A SONG OF DEATH…

Past blurring streaks of malefic shadows, I ran for my life. The monstrous trees watched coldly as I fled, stretching their sharp fingers out to gouge at my face and tear at my dress. They whispered low, lifting their roots out of the ground to trip my feet. I fell and stumbled and sprinted and whimpered in terror, sure I could feel hot fetid canine breath on my shoulders; sure I could hear the excited grunts of wolves snapping violently at my heels.

How long had I been running? How much longer before they gave chase? Then came the signal I'd been dreading. A long, ominous howl rent the hush. A dooming knell. Panic surged viscous and frigid through my veins. The answering calls followed swiftly after, excited and frenzied—a baleful chorus of awful wolf-song.

It had begun.

1

TEA AND CROTCHES

"We should probably go to the beach later," said Mom, turning her face up to the Florida sun. The early light lovingly burnished the dark russet shades in her hair.

I shrugged my shoulders noncommittally, my knee bouncing underneath the table, as I watched an excited black Labrador running into the water in pursuit of its frisbee.

It was still early and not many people were on the beach yet, mostly just the diehard joggers and the fishermen on the pier. The waves were no more than ripples brushing the sand with languid strokes. The humidity had already plastered my hair damply to my neck.

"It'll be your last swim for a while," she went on, her smile indolent.

"I'll have you know—" with amusement "—there *are* beaches in Alaska, Mother."

Mom favored me with a deadpan expression. "Better pack your drysuit then."

I snickered. God, I'd miss my mother. How had I, a solitary moth, come from such a beautiful social butterfly? A question I pondered often.

We were sitting in our usual seats at The Turtle. The cafe, like the beach, was largely empty at this early hour. I had hung my apron up for the last time yesterday afternoon, and it was disquieting to realize that I would no longer be slogging around these wobbly tables for middling tips. And, tragically, I would no longer get to perv on Andy anymore.

All my raunchiest fantasies featured Andy. Only in my daydreams did I have the confidence to manhandle him like a drunken cheerleader—my fists balled in his shirtfront to yank him down for a passionate snog. Afterward, I'd shoot him a flirty wink and then master the perfect pirouette on my six-inch heels before walking out and leaving him absolutely gobsmacked and hopelessly in love with me (a toothless Mr. Horvath cheering me on all the while). Obviously it would be the best kiss of his life, and obviously (in this fantasy at least) I'd be wearing the type of sexy black barely-there dress I'd never have the guts to wear in real life, and his eyes would, all the while, be glued to my backside as I made my grand exit. Then he'd rush out after me and—

"Can you hear me, Major Tom?"

"Hmm?" In an instant, the daydream dispelled like fractured glass. I turned a guilty flush toward Mom who was waving her hand in my face.

"Where'd you go?"

"Nowhere interesting," I lied. "Was just 'floating around my tin can', ya know?"

"Uh-huh. Well, you had a really strange look on your face."

I hurriedly misdirected her with a pithy response. "You mean the look of abject terror? Yeah, moving across the country will do that to a girl."

"Actually you were smiling like a lunatic. So either you're really excited about dog-sledding and woolly long johns…or you're thinking about finally proposing to Andy."

God, she knew me way too well. "I've already bought the engagement ring," I joked.

"And his one-way ticket to fireside paradise."

I waved my hand dismissively. "Nah, I'd planned on restraining him with some pink fluffy cuffs and shoving him in my suitcase."

"Don't forget to poke breathing holes in your luggage then." Her smirk no doubt mirrored mine, but after a moment her gaze turned serious. "You are excited about the move, though, right?"

"Excited. Nervous. I can't tell one from the other most of the time." Both made me feel light-headed. Admitting to my mother that I was afraid was easy, but to Gramps I never could. He'd just tell me that I could "find sympathy in the dictionary between shit and syphilis". I dropped my gaze to the insipid bowl of grits in front of me, finding it poignant that my life, till now, sort of resembled it—colorless and unappetizing. I'd also discovered an intrusive little hair squatting in my porridge, and it certainly wasn't mine. *Gross.* "Flight's booked," I went on, pushing the bowl aside, "I'm going. Gramps did say I should figure my shit out." Actually, he'd told me to pull my head out of my ass and do something with my life, but I wasn't going to split hairs.

"Yeah, but you can do that just as well here as in Alaska."

"And miss out on all the excitement in Thorne Bay? Never!"

She gave a snort and leaned back, aware that I was sublimating my anxiety with humor. "Just playing devil's advocate."

"Besides, I have a better chance of 'adulting' properly if I do it on my own. Away from here." It was always way too easy to run to my mommy or hide in my room with *Carmilla* and *Frankenstein*, and all my other favorite gothic horrors. "Anyway, I thought you were onboard HMS *Alaska Bound*? Kinda sounds like you want me to change my mind."

"I am onboard," she replied, "and this will be good for you, but I'm still going to miss you, kiddo. A part of me will never be ready for you to leave home. That's the part of me that wants to keep you here under my wing and convince you to travel the world another time."

"But if I don't do this now something tells me I'll suddenly wake up when I'm sixty and be suffering under the misconception that 'seeing the world' means borrowing my mother's car to go to Publix for tampons."

"You probably won't need tampons by then, dear," she quipped.

"Poligrip for my dentures then." Glancing over to the booth nearby, to where Mr. Horvath was reading his paper, I spied his dentures propped predictably in his water glass.

He was one of the regular patrons and that toothy water glass was my old nemesis. Every time I served his breakfast, I half expected the creepy teeth to jump out and nip my fingers. That was about as exciting as my days ever got over here—either tripping on Mrs. Goldstein's poodle or spilling Mr. Horvath's denture water down my shirtfront. All of it was so familiar and dull as dishwater. Except, of course, for the few perv-worthy halcyon days when Andy was around helping his parents in the cafe.

The snarling water glass gave me the heebie-jeebies. "There are scarier things than moving to Alaska."

"True. What's the worst that could happen?"

"Umm, I get eaten by rabid wolves?"

"Well, there is that," she chuckled. "By the way, how many times did you throw that dart at the map?"

With a guilty smirk, "Why would you think I threw it more than once?"

She shot me a knowing look. "That many, huh?"

I answered with a noncommittal shrug. On my first attempt, the dart had landed in the Sahara. Then in the middle of the Amazon jungle on the second try. I wasn't brave enough to tempt fate by ignoring the little arbiter of my destiny a third time, so to Alaska I would go.

"Well, just don't leave because of Gramps. Do this for the right reasons, okay?"

I nodded, but nothing short of being mauled to death by Goldstein's poodle was going to keep me from pulling anchor and heading north. When I'd told Gramps two weeks ago that I'd just go ahead and throw a damn dart at a map and go wherever it landed (except the Amazon and the Sahara) if it meant I didn't have to listen to his nagging me about my future anymore (or lack thereof), I'd never imagined I'd actually call his bluff. Nor had he. But my wrecked nerves were well worth it just to prove him wrong.

My flight was booked, my bags were packed, the logistics were finalized, and all arrangements had already been made with Alison and Owen. The countdown had commenced. In twenty-four hours I'd be in Ketchikan. Though the dart had actually landed in Ketchikan, my journey would end in Thorne Bay. That was where Mom's old college friend, Alison, lived with her husband, Owen, who, I'd been told, was a very colorful character. They were the owners of the hunting Lodge I was going to spend my summer working in.

"I know your grandfather's a tough old nut," Mom continued after a while, "but he means well. You know, when I was your age I wanted to be an actress, but he told me that wasn't a 'real job'. So I ditched drama school and gave up the dream. Got a business degree instead."

"An actress, huh?"

"Yup." Her eyes flashed mischievously as she took a sip from her coffee mug. "I guess now we'll never know whether or not Chris Hemsworth could've been your father."

Snorting into my ice tea, I patted her hand condescendingly. "Okay, cradle-snatcher."

She winked. "Men like older women."

"I'm sure they do," I rejoined, "until they hit their mid-life crisis and trade their ole lady in for a gold-digging twenty-something twinkie. So unless you're sporting Texas curls and plastic boobs, you got no chance, Mama."

Mom winced. "You're too young to be this cynical, Ev."

I knew I was. Kids from broken families usually were. "I call it like I see it." And I'd seen my dad do it enough times. But a subject change was in order before Mom got it in her head to start talking about my fath—

"Have you spoken to your father lately?"

Dammit! "Nope," was my terse reply.

"He might have wanted you to—"

"Hang out in Cape Town and play third wheel to his fifth wife, what's-her-face?" I knew exactly what she had been going to say. "I'll give that tempting idea a pass, thank you very much." My mouth dropped at the corners.

"Okay, fine." Mom held her hands up placatingly and let the matter drop.

If my dad wanted to speak to me, he could bloody well pick up a phone and dial my number for a change. The perfunctory Sunday phone calls, since Mom and I moved to Florida a few years back, had by now retrograded into yearly Christmas and birthday calls.

Anyway, I was twenty-one now. Too old to fake interest in my absentee father. And he, likewise, felt the same about me—the mediocre daughter with the two failed degrees and the crumby dead-end waitressing job (oh wait, I was officially unemployed now).

At least my stint in the cafe had diluted some of my introversion and given me a little financial freedom. I'd even saved enough Benjamins to pay my own way to Alaska. Not for a minute had I entertained the idea of letting my grandfather defray the cost of my flight, even though that was technically the consequence of losing the bet. Yeah, he'd bet me a plane ticket that I didn't have the guts to go. Ha!

By now the eggs on Mom's plate were ice cold, the golden yoke having bled across her toast ages ago. Like me, she'd become lost in her own thoughts. But we were both startled from our reveries as the object of my earlier fantasy, Andy himself, materialized at our silent table with his usual, easy charm. My heart danced at the unexpected sight of him—I'd been so cruelly starved of his presence. A whole two days!

"Morning, ladies," he drawled, his voice smokey and rich.

Marry me! "Hey, Andy." That I even got his name out without breaking out into hives was miraculous. Realizing that I was still waving awkwardly, I grimaced and quickly dropped my hand, abruptly knocking my ice tea over onto his shorts. "Omigod! I'm so sorry!" I half sobbed, beyond mortified. At that moment I would have given anything for a sinkhole to appear under my chair.

"It's fine," he said, trying to reassure me with a polite smile that I suspected really meant, "I actually prefer my shorts to look like I've pissed myself, so thanks."

Despite the location of his unfortunate wet spot, he chin-wagged with my mother a little while longer, dabbing periodically at his shorts with a napkin as I squirmed in my chair. Alas, there was no sinkhole to the rescue. Finally, though, with a languid wink, he left us, removing himself a safer distance away from my clumsy hand to head toward another table where two of his equally hot friends were seated

I dropped my forehead against our table with a groan and glanced to the side to see that Andy's friends were now laughing at the stain over his crotch. The fact that he was still grinning good-naturedly made me feel even worse about what I'd done.

Mom gestured for our server to bring the check over, and then she snuck me a knowing wink. “Whoa, you’ve got it bad, kid.”

“Jeez! Why don’t you speak a little louder, I don’t think he heard you.”

“Have you got the pink cuffs here?” she whispered loudly, leaving thirty dollars on the table. “It’s now or never.”

“Hilarious, Mother,” I groaned, my skin mottled as we stood to leave.

From Andy’s table, I could feel the hot pressure of male gazes following as I passed. Thankfully, though, I managed not to trip and fall on my face as I left the cafe for the last time.

2

THAT TALL DRINK OF WATER

It always astounded me that, even after a sprinkle—hardly even a shower at all—Floridians suddenly lost the ability to stay between the lines. The wipers had barely swiped a drop from the windscreen when we'd found ourselves crawling southbound along the freeway.

"Damn rubberneckers," Mom grumbled as we passed the accident on the northbound side of I95.

Once we'd made it to the airport, we hurried to the counter to check my bag in with only minutes to spare. The woman tagging my luggage was giving me squinty eyes as she transferred the heavy bag to the conveyor belt. "I can't guarantee your bag will arrive on this flight," she said with a disapproving sniff.

"No worries." As long as it got there eventually and in one piece, I didn't care.

"Boarding starts in twenty minutes." She dismissed me promptly and nodded to the next person in line. Clearly, there was a carrot up her backside that she'd failed to dislodge this morning. That or someone had crapped in her porridge.

With a tight smile, I left her to her sour disposition, shoving my driver's license into my back pocket.

"This is only goodbye for a little while!" Mom said, her chipper words sounding discordant as she sniffled bravely. "No tears."

"Sure," I scoffed, wiping at the tears spilling warmly onto my cheeks. "I love you, Mom!" There was a raw lump in my throat that had been swelling painfully throughout the drive to the airport. "I swear, one day I'll pay you back for wasting all the money you've spent on my—"

I was instantly enveloped in one of her fiercest hugs. "Don't think about that now, Ev. I'm considering it an investment. Make the most of life and have fun." And then she pulled away to fix me with a stern and watery look. "But not too much fun…" she clarified meaningfully. "Don't forget what I said about always using condoms."

"Mom!" I grimaced with a laugh, my face turning puce.

"I'm just saying! And remember, I'm just a phone call away if you need me, okay? Say the word and I'll hop on the first flight to Ketchikan."

"I know." She was the only stable and loving fixture in my life. Struggling for composure, I took my backpack from her arm. "Is it too late to change my mind?"

"Yes"—with tongue in cheek—"I've already rented your room out to Hugh Jackman."

"Mmkay." I checked my watch. "I'll call you when I get to Ketchikan." With a last, trembling wave, I hurried off before I did change my mind. Or missed my flight. Gramps would love that, I thought derisively.

Goodbyes were brutal. Mom's teary face nearly crumbled my resolve altogether when I turned to glance back one last time, so I determined not to look back again. Figuratively too. She would have been proud of that. My feet ate up the drab linoleum as I followed the signs for my gate with eyes still dimmed by tears. The TSA line was, thankfully, short, so I was able to breeze through security. The officer studied my puffy eyes stoically as I shoved my laptop back into my backpack. Once I'd pulled my sneakers back on, I raced for my gate.

By the time I got there the last of zone four was trickling past the ticket scanner. Before I knew it I was buckled up, listening to the deep hum of the engines as they idled. I was really doing this! It was heady and surreal—taking control of my life. The knots of tension in my gut were alternately loosening and tightening, as if still unsure of which emotion—fear or excitement—held primacy. I knew I should be fearful for leaving my safety net for parts unknown, but it was impossible not to let the latent power of the engines, and the sight of the other planes hurtling down the runway, act like a counterpoise to meekness.

As the 737 was pushed back from the gate, I quietly said goodbye to the suffocating humidity and to the ninety-degree morning heat already scorching the sun-bleached tarmac now that the rain had passed.

Moments later the G-force suddenly pushed me back against my seat as the jet surged into the takeoff roll. We were speeding down the longer of the parallel runways, the lofty control tower flashing briefly past my little port side window.

That restrictive doubt and fear that was always a constant heavy weight around my neck, like an engorged python, seemed to fall away as we gained altitude. I'd forgotten how much I loved flying. Surely this wasn't the wrong decision if I was feeling so weightless, despite the positive G's?

I peered down past the wing as we banked and watched the coastline falling away, my lungs seeming to expand further than they had in a long time.

As the oceanside mansions of Palm Beach Island, and even *Mar-a-Lago* itself, became indistinct and the clouds swallowed us up, I pulled my sketchbook from my backpack. Drawing was one way to exorcise self-doubt...and negate my grandfather's sullen prognostications that I'd be running back to my mother, tail between my legs, within the week. I scoffed at the thought.

It was a balmy forty-three degrees Fahrenheit when I landed in Ketchikan. From the moment the 737 had descended through the clouds I'd been struck with the sprawling beauty of the granite mountains bestrewn with towering Sitka spruce, cedar, and hemlock. The air was so crisp it stung my lungs as I left the terminal. But arriving in a strange place all alone was vastly intimidating. There was no one waiting to welcome me. A stab of loneliness suddenly chilled that part of my heart where most of my courage was hiding. After a quick call to my mom, both to borrow some of her confidence and to let her know I had landed safely, I hoofed it to the ferry dock, bought a ticket and boarded the ferry with a small handful of other pedestrians, an Air Alaska van, and a sedan.

It was a three-minute ride from Ketchikan International across the choppy narrows. I bypassed the bus stop and taxis to brave the wind since Thorn Aviation was only a short walk from the ferry terminal and parking lot. Alison had explained in her email that I'd be taken to Thorne Bay by Bear Lodge's private floatplane… because how else did anyone get around. By boat or by air, I'd been warned. Those were my only options from now on.

Initially, the thought of such isolation had given me pause, but the dart had pointed and I had agreed to go where it willed me. There was nothing for it now but to make the best of this pilgrimage of self-discovery.

The floatplane terminal was packed with tourists, which was to be expected since the first cruise ship of the season had only just docked in town for a few hours. Timidly, I glanced around, chewing one side of my lip and then the other as I searched the crowd for a face I'd never laid eyes on—my pilot.

I knew only that his name was Matt Mitchell, but nothing else. Not his age or any distinguishing features. Nevertheless, I scanned the foreign faces deliberately, looking for epaulets and Ray-Ban aviators. Unfortunately, no one here seemed to fit the *Top Gun* mold.

Standing around like a lost fart in the wind, I re-positioned my green beanie a little more snugly around my ears, hoping that none of the locals were judging my thin-blooded proclivity for dressing like an Eskimo. I had definitely underestimated how much I took the tropical heat for granted. I could already feel my skin objecting to the cold, stretching and splitting into Death Valley mud cracks.

I was wearing a maroon wool-lined *Fjällräven* jacket and a thermal base layer underneath, but still, my bones were chilled. Conversely, most of the locals were in nothing but light flannels and jeans and rubber boots. I could easily pick out the tourists because I looked just like one.

I ran my tongue over my lips and pulled a granola bar from my pocket, peeling the wrapper down with frozen hands as I continued dragging an abstracted gaze around the terminal. Abstracted, that is, until my gaze suddenly stalled over one man in particular. I was so completely fascinated by the tall stranger that had prowled into the terminal, from the waterside, that I clean forgot about my snack and instead feasted unblinking eyes on the most beautiful man I'd ever seen.

He moved with such marked fluidity amongst the bleating sheeple that it was almost impossible *not* to notice him. And then he was gone! The crush of humanity instantly swallowed him up.

I strained on the tips of my toes, looking, nearly sobbing with bereavement, trying to catch sight of him again, but, despite his height, he'd melted into the crowd. Well, I told myself as I expelled the reverential breath I'd been holding in, at least he hadn't caught me gawking like a creep. Not in a thousand years would I have imagined it possible for any man to outshine Andy. But the stranger had done that easily. He'd made my Andy, who had always seemed to me the paragon of male perfection, look like nothing but a pug.

I fanned my hot cheeks, inwardly sneering at my dramatic reaction to him. I returned my attention to my neglected granola bar, instantly devouring it like a starving chipmunk. And now that I was no longer distracted by the stranger, I found myself growing nervous, waiting for my overdue pilot. My worry escalated further and further the longer I waited. What if I was forced to spend the night in the terminal?! What if—

"You Evan?"

I spun around to face the resonant voice that had spoken my name, my cheeks still engorged with half-masticated chunks of soggy granola (crumbs probably cleaving to my chin). Tall as I was, my eyes collided instantly with a very wide male chest. Blinking rapidly, I slowly dragged my gaze up to stare bemusedly at the tall drink of water who was regarding me with a waggish grin. The beautiful stranger I'd spied earlier!

Of course *he* would turn out to be my pilot; of course he'd chosen *this* moment to approach me, just as I'd stuffed my face; and of course he had the most mesmeric eyes I'd ever beheld.

3

FLYING BEAVERS

"Evan Spencer, right?" the stranger asked again, his mouth quirking slightly. He had dressed his athletic frame in the ubiquitous flannel of his brethren, paired with scarred jeans and scuffed, dark Blundstones.

I still hadn't answered him, only continued to gape blankly, my tongue suddenly as articulate as a watermelon, and my cheeks still stuffed with granola. Thankfully, though, he was not only gorgeous but seemed to understand my rapid blinking—Morse code for, "Help, I'm pathetic!"

"I'll take that as a yes."

"Yeth!" My hand belatedly flew up to ward off flying granola, but it was too late. Out came the chunky deluge. I was horrified! With one dry and painful swallow, I choked the granola down like a mouthful of sand and finally managed to utter something intelligible. "Sorry!" My cheeks flooded with humiliation.

"Don't worry, I've been hit with worse." Topaz eyes glittered with humor. They were the most vivid and lightest of Gulf Stream hues—not quite green and not quite blue. Too intense to stare into for long. "I'm Tristan Thorn, your chauffeur."

I diffidently lowered my gaze to his waiting palm. Unlike my fumbling lips my hand was at least functioning reliably today, and without any input from me, it obediently slipped into his. His handshake was confident and warm, just firm enough that he didn't crush my fingers. I almost wished it had been a 'wet fish' sort of handshake because then I would have been far less intimidated.

"H-hi, Tristan." Where was Matt?

"You look disappointed," he said, grinning.

It took me a second to clear my head of the fluff that had collected there when our palms had met. "I was told…um…" *It's really not that hard, Ev, just take your goddamn foot out of your mouth.* "I, uh, expected a Matt."

"Well," he replied, apparently not in the least offended, "I'm afraid it looks like you're stuck with a Tristan instead."

Poor me. Smiling, I surreptitiously wiped at my mouth on the off chance there were any unsightly wet crumbs still loitering there.

Ordinarily, I'd have been thrilled to spend any time in the company of such a superior specimen (preferably without having spat on him first), but right from my initial glimpse, there'd been something primal and sylvan underlying my fascination. It seemed to evade my senses, yet it pawed restlessly at the fringe of animal instinct. Something about him seemed…not altogether safe. If he did pose a threat, however, I figured it was only to my flustered lady bits. He didn't strike me as a sociopath. But, then again, I'd never met a sociopath…

I shifted uncomfortably under his scrutiny, fiddling with the straps of the backpack on my shoulder, wishing he'd look elsewhere. Mom would have told me to fake confidence, so I forced myself to meet his gaze and resolved not to hide my own on the floor again. "How'd you know I was Evan by the way?" Technically I was an Evangeline, a silly name that bore no familial significance. A name I disliked enough to assume a male byname instead.

Tristan's one brow winged facetiously before he shrugged and dragged his eyes dubiously over my copious layers. "You looked…a little lost."

He had no idea just how lost I was.

He, however, looked confident and fresh, and so divinely rugged it made my eyes water. Was it any wonder I'd found my way to the Last Frontier—the last place on earth where men were men and sheep were scared… Wait, did that make me a sheep?

His thick, wind-blown hair lay like dark coffee, in perfect disorder, curling slightly at his ears and nape. I followed the angle of his jaw and then up toward that engaging dimple at his left cheek, watching, enthralled, as it deepened under his growing amusement. He'd clearly noticed my gawking.

"If you're gonna be staying a while, you'll wanna get yourself some Ketchikan sneakers."

"Umm…" I looked down at my white fashion sneakers, bewildered.

"No," he said, chuckling. After searching the crowd, he gestured over to a lady in sturdy grey rubber boots. "*Those* are Ketchikan sneakers." Then he swiftly bent down to grab my duffle, turning around only briefly to acknowledge a greeting from someone who'd called out to him. "What's your shoe size? I'll get you some on the next mail run."

"Size eight." I blinked bemusedly.

He nodded and, without further ado, left me to trail behind him, my bag slung over his wide shoulder like a boar destined for the hearth fire, the flock of tourists scuttling meekly out of his way.

"After you," he said with a chivalrous wink, pushing the double doors open for me.

I preceded him through the glass doors and then followed him down the wooden gangway to the float plane dock where about ten De Havilland Beavers were basking under the grey sky. Earlier, I'd read a tour brochure at the counter, so I was confident I'd correctly identified the distinctive lines of this flock of floating planes.

"Good thing you came in today. We had a freak windstorm this time yesterday. Peak gusts were at 112 knots! You'd have been stuck in Seattle for the night."

"An Alaskan hurricane?!"

"Pretty much," he said, readjusting the duffle onto the other shoulder. "So what accent is that?"

"South African." I watched as surprise lit his eyes. "I was born there," I explained, "but I've lived in West Palm Beach for the last five years."

"South African? You're a long way from home." He whistled, ostensibly impressed by the distance. "D'you miss it?"

I shrugged. "Well, home has always been where Mom is. What about you? Have you always lived in Alaska?"

"Born and bred under the northern lights."

My gaze strayed admiringly over his rugged frame and untamed hair. "Raised in the wild, huh?"

He shot me a comical look. "Sure."

He looked like he'd been an Eagle Scout, so it was no stretch of the imagination to picture him living off the land and off the grid like a pioneer in a bear coat trapping rabbits for fur and meat, reading by candlelight, and swimming under waterfalls. It was all very romantic, the thought of such glorious subsistence living. Minus the rabbit-skinning. "I'm not gonna be heating my bath-water over the fire am I?"

He snorted. "We have electricity in Thorne Bay, don't worry."

"I'm not worried," I said proudly. "I've watched a few Alaskan survival shows."

"Sounds like you've done your research then."

"Yup," I said, grinning facetiously, "learned most of my survival skills from *The Jungle Book.*"

"That's cute." His lips parted enigmatically as he smiled. A sharp smile.

By this time we'd drawn up alongside a blue and white seaplane, Thorn Aviation emblazoned on the fuselage. But I hardly noticed the plane, still reeling from that keen-edged smile of his, and a little flustered by the fact that I'd just glimpsed a pair of unsettling canines. Or had I imagined that?

"The weather's been holding up," he said, all business now, as he stowed my luggage in the back of the plane where a stack of parcels and boxes had been placed, "but we're supposed to get fog later. You'll find the weather's unpredictable here." There was a glint of mischief in his eyes as he continued, "It changes like a woman's mood—all pretty smiles one minute and dancing a temper the next."

"Excuse you, I'm pretty mild-tempered."

Whether he heard me or not I didn't know. His forehead creased suddenly as he looked past me toward the horizon.

I followed his gaze to see a looming cloud bank in the distance.

He took a moment to scroll through his phone. "Damn—" shaking his head "—forecast just changed. It's moving in a lot faster." After he'd shoved the phone back in his pocket he held his hand out for me, helping me from the pontoon dock onto the floats, up the steps and then, from the rear door, into the cockpit.

I self-consciously pulled the beanie from my head and tried to smooth the static from my long, mousy mane. I hated my hair. It was so dull and lank and dead straight.

"Do you get airsick?" Tristan asked suddenly.

"Uh, good question." I hadn't really been in a little plane before, but I did well enough in commercial jets.

"Here." He passed me a small, blue envelope.

Inside, I discovered a folded sick bag. "Gee, thanks."

"I can't have you destroying the upholstery."

"Just my dignity." I rolled my eyes.

"I just got the interior refurbished."

I looked around the cockpit, taking note of all the switches, circuit breakers and instruments on the panel that he was currently fiddling with. A robust and exoteric blend of masculine spices infused Tristan's cockpit—old charts, sun-warmed leather, and avgas. "Well, it's a pretty swish interior, I wouldn't want to defile it with half-digested granola."

"Not like you did my shirt…"

I groaned, flushing with mortification. "Thanks for the reminder."

"Anyway," he drawled, stroking the dash with a cheeky wink at me, "you wouldn't have thought I'd hit a bird two months ago, eh?"

"What?!"

"Yeah" —nonchalantly flicking switches, twisting knobs, and positioning levers— "a gull came straight through the windscreen on your side."

Visions of bird guts and feathers flew morbidly across my imagination. "You're shitting me!"

"I shit you not!" he yelled over the sudden roar of the old radial engine. "But that bird sure shat itself!" The propeller blades had instantly blurred into motion. He slipped the green David Clark on and handed the second headset to me. "Don't worry, lightning doesn't strike twice…or so they say."

"Well, *they* sound like idiots," I muttered into the microphone.

Our repartee was subsequently suspended as Tristan taxied out into the waterway. "Ketchikan Radio," he said, the transmission followed by a blur of information I only caught in spurts. "VFR to Thorne Bay…two souls onboard…an hour and thirty on the fuel…"

I watched him scanning the harbor traffic, his attention focused as a large ferry chugged by—the same one that had brought me across to this side earlier.

A static, monosyllabic response instantly droned into my ear cups a moment later, but the unfamiliar tinny voice spoke too fast for me to follow.

“Ketchikan area traffic, One Tango Alpha departing harbor east.” That said, Tristan turned a wide excited grin to me. “You ready?”

I answered with a grin of my own, eyes following as he opened the throttle wide. The engine roared as we plowed through the chop. Suddenly we were airborne, the beaver freeing herself of the little whitecaps, pulling her wings ponderously through the air. The widening of the narrows seemed to foreshorten the distance between the beaver and the glister of the vibrant blue water below.

“This is incredible!” I finally tore my eyes from the stunning view. “So you work for Bear Lodge too?”

“Nope, Alison and Owen are good friends and since their plane broke down this morning, I offered to take you on my mail run.”

He seemed so nonchalant about the broken plane. “Well, that’s…comforting.”

That dimple flashed again. “The salt water's pretty corrosive. Something's always breaking. Good thing I love turning wrenches just as much as flying.”

Honestly, I was too exhilarated and loopy from the jet-lag to dredge up much worry about corrosion or rivets popping off wings. “But this plane’s safe, right?”

“This old girl has the sweetest temper, don’t worry.”

“So she’s yours?”

“Sort of. My brother and I own and operate a fleet of ten amphibian Beavers and three Bell helicopters. Our company,

Thorn Aviation, does a lot of charter work, tours, and general utility work like pipeline survey, mosquito spraying. That sort of thing. And—" gesturing with a thumb toward his cargo "—we just got the mail contract too. But any time Bear Lodge's beaver is AOG, we help them out regardless. Ali and O are good people."

"AOG?"

"Aircraft On the Ground—as in down for maintenance."

"Ugh, I can see I'm going to have a steep learning curve here."

"Nah, unless you find Sex on the Beach to be unfamiliar territory, I think you'll catch on quickly."

There was no mistaking his bar humor, but, like the repressed freak I was, I'd gone and pictured actual sex. With him. On an actual beach. And since I'd not yet voted my cobwebbed hymen off the island, the word somehow held a mystical sort of power over me.

Unfortunately, Tristan hadn't missed the heat flushing into my cheeks. "Um, it's a type of cocktail," he said, his left eyebrow climbing a little higher than the right. "Just so we're on the same page here, that's vodka, peach schnapps, cranberry and orange juice. Not some sort of lewd suggestion." Then he frowned thoughtfully. "Wait, you are going to be working at the Bear and Beaver, right?"

"I am, yeah." That was the name of the bar that was partly affiliated with Bear Lodge. It was doubtful I'd be serving Sex on the Beach there, but one never knew.

"So have you had one?" he asked.

"Had what?"

"A Sex on the Beach."

"Pfft, of course," I said with a comical wave of my hand that I hoped conveyed my worldliness and sophistication. I'd also watched plenty of Sex And The City reruns. That, surely, made me urbane enough to handle a flirty conversation with him, didn't it? I just wished I could flirt as well as Carrie did with Mr. Big.

"I hear it's all the rage down in Florida."

"What is?" I said, grinning, "Sex on the Beach or…sex on the beach?"

"Don't try to corrupt me, Evan"—grinning like a jackal as he stared out over the water—"I'm already as pure as the driven snow. And, anyway, you'd have to buy me a drink first. I'm old fashioned like that."

"What's your poison, Mr. Thorn," I asked, chuckling.

"Anything but a Sex on the Beach."

"Are you sure? The fact that you know your Sex on the Beach mixology, tells me you know way too much about girly drinks."

"We all have our dirty secrets, Evan."

And I'd have given anything to know what his were. The provocative edge in his tone inferred that I had only scratched the surface of this man's character. The brief, piercing look he'd shot me had dared me to look closer.

Midway through the flight, Tristan allowed me to take the yoke and pedals, instructing me with patience as he explained how each flight control moved the corresponding aileron or rudder. He was all calmness and quiet capability. A rugged bush pilot with a dimpled smile so perilous I feared for my heart.

I would have thought the flight from Ketchikan to Thorne Bay Seaplane Base would have taken longer than it did (or maybe it only seemed too short) but I was enjoying Tristan's company too much to worry about kamikaze birds.

By the time the floats skimmed the crystal waters of Thorne Bay, I imagined that the Evan of yore was falling away, her hangups sloughing off like cruddy, old skin with every cleansing inch of water that rushed up over the floats. I wondered about what awaited me in Thorne Bay and what sort of people could live all the way out here. Most of all, I wondered about Tristan.

4

RUMORS

Owen Hodge was physically exactly what I had envisioned him to be—an archetypal outdoorsman, replete with rubber camo boots, a military green, moleskin jacket, and rubber hip waders. In spite of his incredibly active 'sporting' lifestyle (if hunting could be termed as such), he had a well-established, protruding six-pack, the kind of gut a person inevitably achieved from dedicated 'beerthletics'.

Once my feet were firmly planted on the dock, he took my hand in his massive paw and shook it vigorously. I had to tilt my head right back just to meet his eyes. Tristan, who was himself an alpine giant, was soon treated to the same enthusiastic greeting.

"Welcome to Thorne Bay, Evan." Owen grabbed my bag from Tristan, grinning indulgently at me.

"Population now three hundred and one," said Tristan.

"You guys have a good flight?"

"Amazing!" I replied, watching Tristan's shirt stretch across his broad back as he began securing the aircraft to the cleats on the dock.

I was so busy fervently hoping that this would not be the last time I saw him that I was unaware Owen had noticed my blatant ogling. When he hemmed none too subtly, I looked up into his knowing grin. He had definitely interpreted my breathy "amazing" as being in reference to Tristan's back and not the flight. *Busted!*

"Tristan, m'boy, you gonna join us for dinner?" He shot me a sly wink. "Alison's got some caribou steaks marinating."

"I'll take a rain check," Tristan replied, transferring his gaze only briefly to Owen. "Got plans with the family."

"That's too bad." Owen glanced at me and shrugged, as if to say, 'hey, I tried.' "The ladies will be disappointed."

My face burned with mortification as I was treated to an avuncular nudge of his elbow. *Real subtle, man.*

Tristan, meanwhile, was tying a clove hitch to the wooden rail, thankfully too absorbed by his post-flight ritual to notice my pained looks.

I caught myself wondering about his family. *Please don't have a wife!* But of course a guy like that couldn't possibly be single. His partner was probably disgustingly fabulous too.

"Thanks again for delivering the package safely." Owen gave my back a cheerful slap—just in case Tristan was in any doubt as to which package he was referring to.

"It was my pleasure." Though he answered Owen, his eyes were fastened to mine. This, of course, only seemed to amuse Owen more.

Mercifully, before Owen could embarrass me any further, we finally left the dock. When Tristan was satisfied the Beaver wasn't going anywhere without him, he joined us in the parking lot. Owen had by now dumped my duffle into the bed of his white and tan F-350.

Once my seatbelt was secure, the driver's door opened and the truck dipped momentarily under Owen's weight. Soon after, my passenger window slid down as he jabbed a finger on the control at his door, bellowing his goodbye across me. His wave was punctuated by the obnoxious sound of the foghorn under his hood. "Tell Dean I'm ready to talk numbers!" he added, shifting the truck into drive.

"He'll be glad to hear it!"

I offered Tristan a small wave as we pulled out of the lot, which he acknowledged with an enigmatic half-smile. A momentary pulse of igneous green suddenly flickered in his eyes, catching me off guard. But when I blinked again it was gone. Just how jet-lagged was I really? Intrigued by what I thought I'd seen, I studied his tall figure receding in the side mirror at my door as the distance stretched between us. As if disturbing canines hadn't been weird enough…

Tristan stood watching us all the while, seemingly preoccupied, with his hands stuffed into his pockets. Eventually, though, we turned onto Main street and he disappeared from view altogether.

"Don't worry." Owen had caught the direction of my gaze and mistaken my woolgathering for angsty yearning. "You'll see him again."

"But I…I wasn't—"

"Say no more." Those shaggy brows quirked meaningfully at me.

I rolled my eyes. I hadn't come here to chase tail. In fact, I hoped Tristan did have a girlfriend and ten beautiful, illegitimate kids as well! But if that really was the case then Cupid over here wouldn't have been playing matchmaker, would he?

Attempting to distract him from his mischief, I asked, "How long's the drive, Mr. Hodge?"

"Please, call me Owen. We should be there in about half an hour. I don't like driving too fast since we get a lot of meeses on this road."

“Meeses?”

“Moose.” He then chuckled at his own pitiful joke. “Those bastards pack a punch. You gotta watch those moose knuckles…”

Oh boy.

As Jason Aldean’s twangy crooning poured from Owen’s stereo twenty minutes later, I couldn’t help but snort as my new boss began country rapping along with *Dirt Road Anthem.* The off-key serenading continued on my left as the last of the sunlight spilled across the North Pacific Ocean that soon appeared on my right. Before I knew it we were turning off the asphalt onto a dirt road that shortly brought Bear Lodge into glorious view.

It looked almost like one of the ski resorts we’d stayed at in Lake Tahoe last year, with its timber logs and stone facade. It was situated on a picturesque, lakefront property of about twenty acres, or so Owen informed me as he killed the ignition and offered to take me on the grand tour.

The main building consisted of about ten luxurious suites, one of which had been vacated that morning and the guests flown, by Tristan, to Ketchikan just before I’d arrived there. The room was immaculate and already awaiting occupancy. Well, *that* or a Travel Magazine photoshoot.

The romantic lighting complimented the white wainscoting and russet cedar floors. In the marbled bathrooms hung luxuriant, fluffy towels and the king size bed was draped in ivory bedding that bore a surplus of downy pillows, all expertly arranged. It was all sumptuous and perfectly deserving of the five-star quality, as far as I could tell, that Bear Lodge boasted.

Too bad these weren’t the crew quarters. Pretty sure Gramps wouldn’t have financed that anyway. Not that I’d have let him, even if he wasn’t as tight as a camel’s ass during a sandstorm. Which he was.

Further along the tour, I was shown the dining room and restaurant, fitness center, reception area, and the cozy lounge with its library overlooking a massive fireplace. Beyond the large windows lay the undulating, heavily-forested mountains.

The bar, where I would soon be employed most nights, was a few yards south of the property and connected to the lodge itself by a winding, conifer-lined, pebbled pathway. Although the trees along the path were festooned with solar lights, the light pollution was appropriately muted.

For those guests that sought to be further isolated, there were ten private chalets interspersed amidst the woodland that encompassed the vast estate, but they were all currently occupied and so I was denied a peek inside.

This was definitely not your average rustic getaway because Bear Lodge catered more to the affluent members of society, seeing that each chalet went for a cool seven hundred a night! I'd have thought Owen would have been more bumptious and snooty, considering what Bear Lodge was—pure luxury—but he was exactly the opposite: unpretentious and jocular. Although his humor ran to the coarse side he was overall harmless and good-natured.

My room was, comparatively, very modest, as, presumably, were all the other plebeian accommodations tucked away from the main building.

Owen, after heading back to his truck to grab my bags, helped me carry them up the small set of stairs and left me to my unpacking, promising to come back for me later. Their house was a few miles up the road, separate from the lodge, and I'd been invited for dinner.

I hope they're seitan steaks, I thought with a groan, but somehow I doubted that.

To my everlasting relief, however, Alison had marinaded a few squares of tofu for me, having found out earlier, from my mother, that I preferred my sustenance to be of the non-sentient variety. She and I hit it off instantly. But that was to be expected since I'd been born a generation too late (hell, more like a century), and I usually got on with the baby boomer generation. My music preferences alone attested to that.

Poor Owen hadn't been able to get a word in edgewise as we made our way through almost every topic imaginable. No subject was taboo by the third glass of Prosecco! Sadly, not even my pitiful love life.

"So Owen tells me you've taken a shine to Tristan," she said, grinning shrewdly.

I tucked a hair behind my ear and threw Owen a bit of a dirty look. "Did he also tell you how unsubtle he was?"

"Ha! He's as subtle as a Mack truck."

Owen rubbed his protuberant belly and shot his wife a suggestive wink. "Engineered to last, baby. Just call me Mack Lovin'."

"Case in point." She shook her head.

He raised his rum glass to Ali, smirking. "Cheers, sweetness."

"You should come with a warning label," I muttered.

"You'll thank me one day."

"Pretty sure I won't," I countered.

"I just don't see the need to pussy-foot. You women seem to think we men can smell what y'all want."

"Hmm, maybe Tristan can." Ali shot me a conspiratorial grin. "He seems like a perceptive guy."

"I'm not pussy-footing!" I interjected, embarrassed. "And there's nothing to smell." Unless, of course, my pheromones gave me away? Ugh, could a girl not just partake of a cheeky ogle without everyone alerting the bloody media?! "Anyway, I barely know the guy."

Owen's answering look was completely dubious. "I know when someone's twitterpated, I got eyes."

"Well, obviously you need glasses."

"You young people—" rolling his eyes as he adjusted the logs in the fire pit "—always wasting time and playing games."

"That's half the fun!" Alison reached over to top my glass off again. "Except some of you men are as thick as bricks when it comes to flirting."

"Hmph. Just grab the bull by the balls, I say." He emphasized his statement with a passionate shake of his fists. "What have you got to lose, eh?"

"My front teeth?" I snickered, imagining what would happen to someone daft enough to grab a bull's balls. "Seriously, my problem isn't that I play games. I'm just…not socially adept. I literally scare men off without even trying to." They always seemed to interpret my shyness as frigid reserve. That was when I wasn't humiliating myself by spilling ice teas over crotches or hacking granola at handsome strangers. I didn't mean to be either clumsy or reserved, but such was the case, unfortunately.

Owen gave a dismissive shrug. "Strong women usually do scare off the riff-raff, remember that."

Ali nodded. "He has a point."

Owen's smile grew mischievous as he leaned over to me. "Ole Tristan didn't look scared to me."

Just the mention of his name summoned all the blood back to my face. "Doesn't he have a girlfriend?" There it was. I had finally asked.

"Not sure." Ali shot a sidelong glance at her husband. "Reckon he's seeing that Nicole character?"

I got the distinct feeling that she didn't care for whoever this Nicole person was.

"Hmph." Seemed like Mack Lovin' had had enough of discussing Tristan's love life. "Ask Dinwiddie," he said, ironically, "she knows everything."

"Do you guys see a lot of him?" I tried to inject as much

nonchalance into the question as possible, but I was afraid I was being as subtle as Owen.

"No, not really," she answered. "They're pretty private. Like to keep to themselves mostly. Rumor has it their family was here long before this place was a logging town."

"Oh?" I said, hoping she'd elaborate. There was so much about Tristan that intrigued me and no amount of gossip would satiate my growing fascination.

"The town was named after old Manley Thorn. Think they were originally Thorstensens during the gold rush, but somewhere along the line the name got changed."

"Scandinavian?"

"Maybe."

"His brother's real antisocial," said Owen, changing the subject.

"Until recently," his wife added.

"Hmm, yeah. Dean's been trying to get me to sell him some land—ten acres adjacent to his own property. The cabin's a little rundown though."

"Yeah, we really ought to just get rid of the place." Owen stroked his beard thoughtfully. "Too many damn wolves up there anyway, scaring off all the game. No point in keeping it."

"True, but with us gone Sarah will be their closest neighbor. Poor Dean."

"Poor Dean?" I asked.

Ali and Owen glanced meaningfully at each other, but it was Alison that answered. "Sarah Dinwiddie's…a bit nosy."

"Woman's a damn gossip," Owen grouched. "Face like a squeezed teabag, if you ask me."

Ali gave a long-suffering sigh before she addressed me again. "Anyway, there's no love lost between her and the Thorn brothers. Folks around here tend to be wary of that family."

"It's like cancer, these rumors." Owen gave a belch of disgust.

"And that damn Dinwiddie woman's the worst of the shit-talkers."

"She's not that bad," Alison argued. "If we sell the place at least there'll still be a few hundred acres between her property and theirs."

"What kind of rumors?" I was very intrigued now. Thorne Bay was proving to be a lot more interesting than I had anticipated.

She gave a noncommittal wave. "Just nonsense really. People will always distrust what's different. And since Dean's family don't exactly…" She was clearly searching for a diplomatic way to finish her thought.

"Since they don't exactly act normal?" her husband interposed unhelpfully.

"No, that's not what I was gonna say." Ali swatted his arm playfully before continuing. "They just don't try to fit in. They're pretty isolated up there except for Sarah and her husband living nearby. I hear they've been trying to buy her land up too."

"Ha! She'll stay there forever just to spite them."

"Since when is being reclusive grounds for suspicion?" I asked, baffled.

"You gotta admit, it's all very mysterious—a bunch of young folk living isolated in the woods, keeping mostly to themselves."

"Dinwiddie's convinced they're a bunch of Branch Davidians," Owen said, chuckling, "running around buck naked and getting up to all sorts of hoodoo mischief. I'm telling you, the woman's a damn nuisance."

"Huh." On the whole, Tristan had seemed pretty normal to me. Abnormally handsome, sure, but that was no crime (my odd hallucinations about sharp teeth and glowing eyes were long since dismissed as jet lag).

Owen chuckled, wriggling his brows comically at me. "As for

you, you're fresh meat, so you'll quickly get the tongues wagging too!"

I gave a solemn nod of my head, oblivious to his teasing. *People will always distrust what's different.* Ali's words hit very close to home. Yeah, I knew all about being different.

But just how different were they exactly?

5

THE WILDLIFE

The furious peal of my alarm jolted me awake, and my head jerked up instantly from the unfamiliar pillow. This rude awakening was punctuated by a disgusted moan as I realized that I was still fully clothed, having literally collapsed on top of my bedding the minute I'd locked my door last night!

I dragged myself, bleary-eyed, out of bed and shed my clothing, tripping over my jeans and shoes as I made my way to the bathroom. It was under the feeble spray of the shower head that I began thinking about Tristan. Again. My inconstant heart had already abandoned Andy, and the featured hero in this morning's fantasy far exceeded the previous one in both height and beauty. I traced Tristan's chiseled features in my mind's eye, his face as vivid there as if he was standing in the shower next to me.

His eyebrows were inhumanly straight and sat low over thick black lashes and smoldering cyan eyes. It was such a piercing male stare even in the privacy of my thoughts that my anxious hands came up swiftly to cover myself as the sudden, disquieting sense of being watched came over me.

Get a grip, Ev! Ignoring the odd sensation, I put my hands to better work, lathering my hair with shampoo as my mind resumed the pleasurable pastime of dwelling over Tristan's face.

After I'd rinsed my hair, and squeezed the water from my eyes, a slight movement in my peripheral drew my gaze to the floor beside the toilet. I froze.

My palsy, though, was short-lived. I began shrieking wildly, like Janet Leigh in *Psycho*. Ripping the shower curtain from its rail, I flew from the bathroom still soaking wet, nearly slipping and cracking my skull open on the tub. Once in the safety of my room, I spun around to see that the object of my horror had turned to watch me—a monstrous wolf spider. It leered openly.

The little pervert soon followed my wet trail, scuttling eagerly from the bathroom to perch itself in the doorway, the better to fix me with those eight hairy eyeballs. Whatever wildlife lurked nearby, I was pretty sure there was not even a damn cockroach in the acreage when I was done screaming. No woman had ever scrambled into her underwear faster than I did at that moment.

Spiders I preferred out of sight and out of mind. Preferably out of my bedroom too. Thankfully, the little peeping Tom turned out to be quite a cooperative prowler because, after I'd opened my door for him, and with a little leery guidance on my part, he vacated the premises like a considerate evictee.

With the spider crisis now sorted, I could concentrate on the day ahead. I was supposed to be acclimatizing myself today, and weathering the jet lag, but I'd come here with a purpose, so I decided to pay Alison a visit in her office and beg for a mission. My orientation would only be starting tomorrow, but I wanted something to do today.

I expounded this all to Alison thirty minutes later and she suggested I take her SUV into town for a drive. If I was feeling energetic, she said, I could go run some errands for her too. That way I could also visit Thorne Bay Market and stock the little pantry and mini fridge in my room with essentials. If I happened to see any spider deterrents whilst shopping, I'd be purchasing those in bulk.

"I'd also get some bear spray if I was you," Alison suggested, tapping her bottom lip with her pen.

"You do realize we have bears in Florida?" *Not to mention gators and snakes and spiders.* Hell, there were even panthers down there. I didn't want her to think I was some clueless urbanite. "I don't plan on getting close enough to the wildlife to use pepper spray."

"Trust me"—her brow curved a smidgen higher as she placed the GMC keys in my hand—"the wildlife's a lot bigger in Thorne Bay, and nine times out of ten you won't see each other till its too late."

For a one-horse town, the store on Shoreline Drive was rather impressive from the outside, only insomuch as there were no tumbleweeds drifting past the glass doors. Not exactly a ramshackle building selling bait, snacks, and sundries, but commonplace all the same. My attention, though, was very quickly diverted from the red corrugated facade toward the black truck in the parking lot with a Thorn Aviation decal on the back window.

I maneuvered the white Yukon carefully into the parking space beside it. Earlier, when I'd passed the port, I'd seen One Tango Alpha docked beside the post office. The sunlight blinking off the windscreen had seemed to wink suggestively at me. It knew exactly who I was looking for.

And now that I'd killed the ignition, the silence only tautened my nerves with expectation. Was he inside?

I had no idea what sort of car he drove, so I had no way of knowing if the truck was… *Jeez! Stop being such a stalker, Ev.* I shook my head, irritably. *Who cares if he's here or not? You do*, a voice within taunted knowingly. "Shut up," I growled at myself, hopping down from the running board and slamming the door for good measure. That's what I got for spending too much time in my own head—annoying inner monologues.

With one last look at the F-250 over my shoulder, I reached a hand out for the door. But it unexpectedly swung open even as my fingers touched the handle and I jumped back with a squeak of surprise as a tall woman emerged briskly from the store.

"Damn *cheechakos*," she barked.

I stammered a small apology and sidestepped to let her stalk past me, which she did, glaring as though I was the bug guts bespattered across her newly cleaned windscreen. Blocking the doorway was hardly cause for rudeness, but I let it go. Despite her terse manner, I couldn't help admiring her physicality. She was stunning. The sunlight gilded her hair lovingly like a halo. Her manner, though, was anything but angelic. And here I was in ridiculous thermal leggings and a mundane blue hoodie.

Right on her heels came two other women, both of whom—except for brief and perfunctory nods—were watchful as they passed me by. Neither rude nor friendly, yet absurdly curious, twisting their necks around to look back at me.

Was there something on my face? The thought precipitated my hand self-consciously to my chilblained cheeks. Or did I smell funny? I backed up toward the entrance, my gaze trailing them as they approached a black Escalade where they promptly began unloading their brown paper shopping bags into the back. Each one of them had a very commanding presence. Especially the scary blonde who fired off another sharp scowl at me.

"You coming in?" came a familiar voice from the doorway that I was blocking yet again.

I'd completely failed to notice the three people waiting at the open door, the blonde had so starstruck me. Tristan, of all the men to catch me acting like a gaping twit, stood propping the door open with a boot. Dark walnut waves had settled at his temples and a lazy smile was lifting one corner of his mouth. His impressive, flannel-clad torso was hardly obscured by the two cases of Alaskan Spruce IPA he was holding. He inched the door a little wider, no doubt wondering why I was still standing there, dumbstruck.

"Thanks," I mumbled, slipping past the intimidating trio. It was clear that they, the women included, were all leaving together. Was Blondie his girlfriend? *Ugh! Please, God, no!*

The striking couple standing just behind Tristan had been observing us curiously, almost knowingly, as I'd slunk away. They'd probably already determined that I was the village idiot. Worse still, I'd been on the verge of blurting out a "toodle-oo", I was that maniacal. And that would have been catastrophic! No one ever said toodle-oo anymore except maybe my grandmother, a woman who still sent faxes, for God's sake, and still referred to her couch as a Davenport!

Managing a wan smile, I gave a diffident wave goodbye as I hurried into the first aisle. Once safely out of sight, I dropped my face instantly into my hands. The heat from my cheeks was like a furnace against my cold palms. I could have cried, I was that frustrated with myself. Why was I such a *fidiot*?!

"Evan?" Tristan's woodsy scent enveloped me like smoke and earth as he unexpectedly drew up beside me.

Crap! I began blinking furiously as though there was an irritant in my eye, and then, pretending I'd loosed it from my cornea, I forced my gaze up and plastered a pseudo smile of surprise on my face. "Tristan! Hey!" God, he looked so good in green! I added a few more watts to my creepy smile, just in case he wasn't already convinced I belonged in an asylum.

At some point, while I'd been wallowing in my discomposure, Tristan had relinquished the cases of beer and now stood before me with his hands casually shoved in his pockets. "You ran off so quickly, I didn't get to introduce you to my friends."

"Oh, I…just…" *Need a checkup from the neck up?* "I assumed you were in a hurry, so…" Blondie, at least, had definitely seemed as though she was. That or she'd just taken an instant disliking to me for whatever reason.

"You know what they say about assumptions?" He waited for half a beat before saying, "Don't make them."

"True," I sighed. It just hadn't occurred to me that he'd want to pause for a chitchat, never mind introduce me to his friends. Sadly, whatever magic had come over me when we'd first met, when I'd actually made him smile with my rare wit, had long since evaporated. Might as well be my boring self now because he was both unavailable *and* tragically out of my league. Something told me that the pissy blonde she-devil was the same girlfriend that Alison had speculated about last night. Nicole, was it? "I've made a few too many assumptions today already."

"Uh-oh." He folded his arms, amused.

"Yup. This morning's assumption cost me a shower curtain."

He cocked his head like a shepherd. "Oh?"

"But I reckon most people *assume* they're alone when they take a shower."

His brow at first creased and then instantly relaxed as I expounded my hideous wolf spider encounter and once again lamented my ruined shower curtain.

He chuckled. "*That* isn't the type of wolf you should worry about."

I narrowed my eyes. "Lest I stumble into any more hairy situations, what other Alaskan wildlife should I be worried about?"

"In the shower?" His left eyebrow crept a little higher.

"Especially in the shower," I replied, trying to keep a stern face.

"Thankfully, the 'wildlife' you really want to worry about is gonna be out of doors." That had sounded entirely too ominous, more so because his grin had disappeared suddenly. "Trust me," he went on, "there are some pretty interesting species here in Thorne Bay."

"Like Bigfoot?"

My attempt at humor appeared to have missed its mark. He gave not even a twitch of the lips. "Something like that."

6

BIGFOOT

The silence quickened hotly between Tristan and I. I wanted to grimace when *Let's Get It On* began streaming through the market. *Real funny, Marvin.* I was struck with the fidgets again. "So…were *all* those people your friends?" Mostly, I was curious about the blonde.

"Some of them." His face seemed to harden suddenly. "I'm sorry about Nicole. She's a little short on manners."

So the blonde had a name! And lo and behold she *was* his girlfriend! Why else would he feel the need to apologize for her? Cold dismay rushed into my gut as the truth settled in. "Ahh," I said with a weak smile, "so that's not how the natives usually greet us…*cheechakos*, was it?"

"Nah, over here we usually welcome newcomers with Sex on the Beach."

"Is that right?" I tapped my lips thoughtfully. "I'll have to file a complaint with the Thorne Bay officials since I never got mine."

"They'll be horrified by the oversight." His eyes darkened. "No woman should ever be denied Sex on the Beach."

Swallowing my reserve, I said, somewhere between a whisper and a croak, "Depends on who's serving it."

His lips twitched. “Some backwater pilot probably.”

Yes, please.

Then, noticing the shopping list I was fiddling with, he leaned in (for a hot second I thought, rather irrationally, that he was pulling in for a kiss) only to reach a hand behind me to take a basket from the stack nearby. “You’ll need this.” He appeared to have no intention of handing the basket to me, only nodded toward my list expectantly.

I lowered my gaze to the list, feverishly aware that his eyes were moving curiously over my flushed cheeks. “Um…I need… mustard.” Good thing I hadn’t chosen the condom and ‘personal lubrication’ aisle to hide in. My mortified heart would not have withstood that much strain—flirting with Tristan was heady enough as it was without being surrounded by condoms. And then, mind veering off tangent again, I wondered if there was, in fact, a condom aisle here.

“The condiments are this way,” he said.

My head snapped up in shock. “Pardon?” Could he read minds now?

He gestured from my list to the condiments aisle. “Mustard’s over there.”

“Right,” with an awkward cough. Not condoms, then. My mind seriously needed ripping from the gutter.

“Tristan?” Nicole appeared suddenly. Her arms were folded in front of her chest expectantly. “Aren’t you gonna be late?” The prickliness in her tone made me flinch. The other four soon appeared behind her, as if on cue, and her already elevated eyebrow rose even higher. “We’re waiting,” it seemed to say.

“Nicole, this is Evan.” His mouth compressed into a hard line. I never wanted to be on the receiving end of that look—he was frightfully intimidating when he wasn’t smiling. “She flew over with me yesterday.”

"Hi," she said curtly, inspecting me from head to toe. Clearly, though, she was deeply unimpressed.

It was a shame she was proving to be so catty because she really was beautiful. Unlike her personality. She was willowy and tall, her features delicately formed. Her nose, however, gave her haughtiness away instantly. It was long, like a Saluki's, and turned up naturally at the tip. If she'd been smiling, it might have left a better impression than cold arrogance. Her full lips were currently pursed into a moue of impatience.

Ignoring her less than enthusiastic greeting, Tristan continued to introduce me to the rest of his friends. The two women standing next to Nicole, Leeann and Alex, greeted me reservedly.

"This is Lydia," he said, lifting his chin toward the fourth woman.

Her smile, at least, was genuine as she shook my hand.

"And that gorgeous bastard," Tristan went on, nodding to the leonine man beside Lydia, "is James."

Inundated as I was by the symmetrical beauty they all possessed, I felt increasingly aware of my physical inferiority—the only donkey at The Royal Ascot. Lydia and James, I decided, had to be twins, they were both golden-haired and their eyes shared the exact same tawny hue.

"Evan just arrived from Palm Beach yesterday. She's gonna be working at the Bear and Beaver for a while."

"That so?" James transferred a curious smile from Tristan to me. "Well, it just so happens that that's my favorite bar, Evan."

Nicole gave a derisory snort.

"So what brings you here?" He asked, ignoring the peanut gallery.

"I—"

"Ugh, I'm leaving." Nicole shot me an evil look as though it was my fault James was talking to me. If looks could transmit syphilis, hers would have done it that instant. I shouldn't have given two peppered shits about her rudeness (after all, she didn't know me from Adam), but I did. And later, when all the delayed comebacks would suddenly rush into my head, I'd be irritated for letting her make me feel two inches tall.

Tristan spared her a curt nod. "Fine. Just don't harass any more tourists on your way out."

Grimacing slightly, I tried not to resent being called a tourist.

With a black look at me (as though I was holding Tristan hostage or something), she finally left the aisle. I for one could breathe easier now. Alex and Leeann followed swiftly in her wake.

"So why Thorne Bay?" James tried again.

"I was promised girly cocktails." From the corner of my eye, I watched Tristan's mouth twitch again.

The twins peered curiously between us, but Lydia's scrutiny seemed the more penetrative. "It's a far cry from Florida. Hopefully, you'll be happy here," she said, her tone oddly grave and discordant considering her words.

"As long as the Peeping Toms stay out of her bathroom," Tristan remarked, "she might be."

"Peeping Toms?" This from James.

"Of the eight-legged variety," I answered helpfully. "I almost got a spider hickey this morning."

He gave an unaffected shudder. "Aside from spiders, I'm partial to all the beasts of the forest."

Lydia rolled her eyes.

"Speaking of which," I said, "I hear there are some very interesting species roaming the woods here in Thorne Bay." I looked conspiratorially at Tristan, who'd as much as hinted at Sasquatch earlier. But this time my innuendo fell far short of the mark. All three of them seemed to tense up as though I'd said Lord Voldemort's name. I felt instantly foolish. Man, these Alaskans had moods like their weather—capricious!

"We better get going." Lydia aimed a pointed look at Tristan and the shopping basket in his hand.

"You still have to warm the engine up," he answered dismissively. "Go on, I'll be out in a minute."

They said their goodbyes and reluctantly left us. The bell over the entrance signaled their exit as it had done Nicole's. Tristan and I were alone again.

"Are you flying today?" I asked him, my hand closing over a carton of soy milk.

"No, Lydia is, but James and I are catching a ride into Ketchikan to run some errands."

By now we'd finally migrated to the condiments aisle. Tristan was pretending not to notice the three nosy old ladies who were blatantly staring. Strangely, no matter which aisle we were in, we attracted the attention of whoever was loitering there. Animal magnetism, I told myself. He had it in spades. I was hyper-aware of him every second I was in his company. The small hairs on my skin seemed to stretch themselves out toward him, desperate for contact, his scent enveloping me with that dark tang of wildwood spice that was all his own.

I'd have been in heaven if not for the intrusive gazes that were all narrowed warily at him. "What's with the staring? I feel like I'm about to hear banjo music," I muttered under my breath.

"Don't worry, it's not quite Deliverance, USA," he said, shrugging, "and clearly not backwater enough *not* to stock the fake hippy milk." He shook his head with mock disappointment, easily deflecting my curiosity about the dodgy rumors, as he gestured to the soy milk in my basket.

"It tastes pretty good, you should try it." I had not missed the suspicious way in which he'd eyed my milk.

"I'd rather just take your word for it." He towered over me as he studied the other items on my list.

Why hadn't he left with Lydia and James? Or his girlfriend for that matter. Moreover, why was he still here talking to me?

"The canned goods are over here." He motioned for me to follow him. When we got to the right shelf he pulled a can down and chucked it inside the basket. "What's after tomato sauce?"

"Well, technically I wanted ketchup," I said, grinning, and reached into the basket to retrieve the can so that I could deposit it back on the shelf. "Across the pond ketchup is referred to as tomato sauce."

His expression turned dubious as he considered that fact. "Yeah, they do a lot of things the wrong way around on that side of the world."

"Mmkay, well, we're not the ones that misspell aluminium." I made sure to enunciate the extra vowel as we left the canned goods aisle.

"You mean aluminum, don't you?"

"Negative. Al-oom-in-ee-um. You left out the extra 'i' there." My tone was smugly didactic. "Live it. Learn it. Love it."

Very slowly, deliberately, Tristan leaned in, his head slightly canted as though listening intently. "Hear that?"

My brow furrowed bemusedly. My ears strained to hear above the sound of the blood rushing excitedly through my veins. "Hear what?"

"The sound of how wrong you are." He smirked, leaning away again. "It's deafening."

I gave his arm a playful nudge. "No, that's the sound of your feeble excuse dying a horrible death."

"Agree to disagree."

"Not a chance."

"Well, Miss Spencer, a wise man knows not to argue with a woman."

"That's because," I rejoined, "you know that all we women

need to do is flash some boob and that puny, male logic crumbles."

"That doesn't sound like much of a threat, Evan." He was trying valiantly not to laugh. "I may start an argument after all..."

The air grew instantly thick with delicious tension, his gaze lingering with male fascination. Though his eyes never strayed lower than my mouth, my female intuition was very aware of which area of my anatomy his imagination had wandered to. Unfortunately for him, I was not one to arbitrarily flash my bits.

Without warning, though, like the jarring of a scratched record, the sounds around us suddenly obtruded the steamy haze that had enveloped us moments before.

He widened the space between us, taking a cautious step back as his nostrils flared. "I better get going." He promptly handed my nearly empty basket to me, my skin sparking at the touch of his fingers.

He threw me a suave two-fingered wave and my chest deflated in bitter disappointment as I watched him turn away. This time the bell over the door chimed more like a lonely knell as he left the store.

There was no denying Tristan's effect on me. I could barely think rationally when under that intense gaze. I'd been so oblivious to my surroundings until the moment he'd left my side. As it turned out Thorne Bay Market did indeed have a condom aisle. And I was standing in it.

It was well after dinner before I returned to my neck of the woods, my circadian rhythm already discombobulated by the sunlit 'night'. Unlike yesterday, though, the lowering sky was cast in sullen shades that consequently deepened the shadows of the hinterland, imbuing it with an unnatural and feral twilight. Overhead, the ravens called stridently from their aeries, their cold voices the creepy *pièce de résistance* of an ominous darkling forest.

The sound of the keys in my fumbling hand seemed discordant in the hush that followed after the ravens stilled. Unexpectedly, the leaves rustled sinisterly behind me. My blood froze instantly. Eyes wide and furtive over my shoulder, I scoured the darkened woods, blindly jamming the key at my door.

"Who's there?" I whispered.

Of course, if Sasquatch had been hiding in the shade, I doubted I'd have gotten a friendly answer. Thankfully, there was no reply. Another panicked jab and the key slid home. The lock finally snicked open and I rushed into my room, hastily slamming the door shut and locking it behind me.

Later, however, I convinced myself the sound had been nothing more than a scuttling mouse. Or my neighbor, the giant wolf spider. Even a spider was preferable to Sasquatch!

The first hint of dawn washed into my room at four AM. I was already awake, being as I was still on east coast time, nervously listening to whatever was now snuffling loudly outside my door, but I was too chicken shit to look.

Sunlight, though, was always a good counterpoise to creepy sounds in the dark. When the sun was up in full force, albeit still cloaked behind a benign layer of grey stratus, I finally deemed it safe enough to venture outside again. Dew still clung to the porch and the steps, and the air was like nothing I'd ever smelled before. My lungs were filled with the cleansing taste of the glaciers, the woodland, and incoming rain. A light drizzle began to fall seconds later, hardly even rain at all. It was as if the heavens had descended from the mountains and I was walking through suspended specks of sweet spring water.

The sight of the odd spoors beside my bottom step, however, quickly dispelled the diurnal magic. Instantly wary, I lifted my gaze to the silent trees. Nothing. Just a lonely owl and the sound of the wind soughing whisper-soft through the boughs and needles.

Satisfied that there was no mythical beast glaring at me through shadowed boles, I knelt carefully beside the baffling spoor. The prints were neither canine or ursine, seemingly too large and protracted to be the former—clearly some plantigrade beast—and yet not quite the right shape to be the latter either. So what then? Bigfoot? *Impossible!*

A chill of agitation fluttered up along my spine, throwing fine hairs up in its wake. If this had been made by a grizzly, which I still doubted, it was no beast I cared to encounter. It was monstrous.

Resolved to identify the culprit, I positioned my foot beside one clearly defined print for a size reference and snapped a picture of it with my iPhone. My shoe size was likely average for a girl my height, but the paw prints were a lot larger than my meager size eight. The drizzle, meantime, began to fall harder, which meant that the prints were already rapidly disappearing.

"Damn." Reluctantly, I yanked my attention away from the strange impressions fading in the mud and continued on toward the main building. Melissa, one of the bartenders I'd briefly met when Owen had given me a tour of the place, was supposed to be training me today and I didn't want to be late.

Maybe someone up at the lodge would be able to identify the odd spoor.

7

NUTS

"Heads up," Melissa whispered to me, filling a glass with ice. "Mr. Eisen just walked in."

I looked up to see the old curmudgeon approaching the bar as his heavily botoxed wife seated herself at their usual table by the flat screen to watch the U.S. Open. He was a decent enough tipper, but not much else endeared him to me.

His wine had to be served at a certain temperature, had to be decanted a particular way, and left to breathe a specific amount of time before he'd drink it. Even then he'd wipe fastidiously at the clean wine glass despite that I'd polished it under his watchful gaze. Mr. Eisen would have probably whinged about how the damn grape pickers had handled the fruit before extraction and barreling if he could have. Asinine was what he was.

As if his fussiness wasn't heinous enough, he had a wandering eye too. This was only my third shift, but I'd pegged him for a perv on day one when he'd lowered his small eyes to my meager chest, staring so hard I feared he'd burn holes through my shirt. More often than not he'd lurk at the bar each night eating all the peanuts from the bowl, messing half of each handful onto the floor because he was too busy staring at Melissa's breasts to worry about his aim. I only hoped, for housekeeping's sake, his poor aim didn't extend to his bathroom habits as well.

"You serve him please!" I entreated as I poured myself a club soda, turning my back to the approaching perv. "I'll do anything."

"No way, it's your turn."

"C'mon, I'm still the FNG." The frigging new guy. That surely counted for something?

She waited for me to take a long gulp from my glass and then, with deadpan precision, said, "Fine, but you're picking up his nuts."

"Whoa!" I choked, wiping my mouth as Mr. Eisen loomed closer, "there's no need to bring his nuts into this."

Melissa, like Tristan, had been completely unexpected—I'd never imagined I'd meet any quality people in God's Nowhere, let alone anyone quick-witted, young, and fun. She was a lithesome six foot twenty-seven year old with shoulder-length honey-wheat hair, cobalt eyes that lightened to green at the center, and had a wacky sense of humor that was strangely reminiscent of my mother's. It was no wonder I loved her already. I didn't normally love so quickly or too easily.

She was only moonlighting as a bartender because her day job didn't quite pay the bills yet. Photography, she'd told me, was her first love, aside from her husband, Matt. He was the Bear Lodge floatplane pilot that I'd been expecting that first day in Ketchikan when Tristan had turned up instead.

Mr. Eisen had, by now, reached the bar counter. We greeted him dutifully as he planted himself on a stool, Melissa with her usual peppy cheer and I with my signature diffidence, holding a tray guardedly across my shirtfront. Melissa chuckled at his stale jokes, pretending to listen intently as though his nasally voice wasn't tearing at her eardrums. I gave a spiritless roll of my eyes as he began intoning his usual instructions to her, like the self-proclaimed sommelier that he was.

Eventually, he slunk off back to his perpetually surprised-looking wife. I bent my narrowed eyes over the counter to inspect the mess he'd wreaked on the floor. "Fair is fair," I mumbled with a sigh. It was my job to clean his nuts tonight. I sniggered at the thought, taking the brush and dustpan from the storeroom before heading off to sweep up the tainted nuts.

"So Melissa…" I said once I'd done cleaning up.

"So Evan…?" She was steaming and polishing glasses, watching as some of the lodge guests and two Forest Service guys trickled out into the night.

"I need to start jogging again." I hadn't jogged since I'd left home and I could already feel the effects of my lack of exercise. I was tall and when I didn't workout, my back inevitably began to ache. "Is it safe to jog here? I don't wanna run into a pack of ravenous wolves." Then I thought about the simian-like print I'd found outside my door a few days ago. "Or Sasquatch," I subjoined.

"I'd worry more about the bears." She bent down to grab more vinegar for the steam water. "Have you got bear spray?"

Unable to help myself, I quickly rolled a tea towel and then flicked it across her backside as though we were a couple of teenage boys in a locker room. "That's for the ice you dropped down my bra earlier!"

She eyed the towel suspiciously and held up her hands. "Truce!"

I flung my damp weapon to the side as proof of our ceasefire. "And yes," I finally answered her question, "I have my trusty bear spray back in the room." The same can that Alison had insisted I buy.

"Good, and make sure you get someone to go jogging with you. Also," she went on, beginning to number these caveats on each finger, "don't wear headphones or run at dusk. Or dawn for that matter."

“So basically don't go running at all.” I sighed loudly, my shoulders sagging a bit.

“Such a fatalist.” She shook her head. “You can go running, just be smart about it. And make a lot of noise, you don’t wanna scare a brown bear during hyperphagia.”

“Hyper-what?”

“It’s like a feeding frenzy. Most of the hiking trails tend to keep clear of the known food sources, like salmon streams. But you just never know.”

“God, I love when you get your nerd on! It’s so sexy!”

“Right? You should see me do an oil change on the Chevy.” She wiggled her brows.

“Not sure I could handle that much sexy. So—” batting my lashes sweetly “—d’you wanna come running with me tomorrow morning?”

“Can’t,” Melissa said with an apologetic grimace, “I’m heading to Coffman Cove. I’ve been commissioned to do a school photoshoot.”

“Oh.” Even if my crestfallen expression didn't evince as much, I was happy for her. “Guess I’ll go on my own then.”

“Strength in numbers, Ev. Try and find a running partner.” She then pursed her lips mischievously. “What about Chris? He needs the exercise.” She was convinced that one of the Bear Lodge servers had the hots for me. Love hearts practically bled from his eyes every time he looked at me, she’d said.

“I’d rather cuddle that damn spider than run with Chris,” I replied with a shudder. He was a nice enough guy, but I was not interested in anything beyond friendship with him. He seemed the type to misinterpret any platonic overtures a girl might make. “Anyway, his idea of getting sweaty probably entails exercising his bicep with beer curls.”

“I bet that's not the only way he’d like to get sweaty with you…”

"Ew!" I covered my ears like one of the three wise monkeys. "Please stop talking."

"And," she continued, wrestling my hands away from my ears, "he probably made those weird prints outside your door the other day to scare you, hoping you'd go spoon with him in his room."

That was another thing she was adamant about. I'd showed her the blurry picture of that weird footprint, but she'd shrugged it off as just a hoax. She'd promptly decided that Chris was the mastermind behind it—apparently, he was something of a prankster.

"What about the snuffling sounds?"

"He was heavy breathing at your door all night."

"You're a sick woman. Now you owe it to me to come jogging."

"I get enough exercise running my balls off between both my jobs."

"Your lady balls?" I scoffed. "Classy." I headed off to clear some glasses.

When the door opened unexpectedly, admitting a chilly gust, I looked up from where I'd been wiping a table top. Half expecting to see the Eisens again, I nearly swallowed my tongue when Tristan strolled in instead.

He gave me one of his signature crooked smiles and a sexy nod of hello before he beelined it to the bar, oblivious to the chaos he'd just unleashed in my chest.

My heart was doing backflips in my throat again. *Stop drooling, Ev. Play it cool.* I gathered as many abandoned beer glasses as I could carry, watching as Melissa poured him a draft of some local IPA. *Don't be so creepy, he has a girlfriend. Well, we don't know that for sure. Ugh, now you just sound pathetic. Yeah, and desperate. Oh, piss off, all of you!* Seriously, if anyone could hear half the crap my inner legion and I squabbled about, they'd shove me in a nuthouse! *Or call the priest.* Yeah, I thought, that too.

I watched as Tristan's hand delved languidly into the same bowl of nuts Mr. Eisen had been slobbering over earlier.

Should I go over and talk to him? I wavered nervously. *Do it!* I shook my head. *No way!* What witty remark could I offer? *Just go over there. Remember, when in doubt...tits out.* With my bottom lip between my teeth, I strode over and leaned across the counter next to him (with what I hoped looked like confidence), depositing the glasses safely out of sight behind the bar. That done, I placed an elbow on the granite and faced him. "Pardon me, sir, but have you considered how many dirty old hands have rifled through those nuts?"

Tristan's lips twitched slightly as he lifted a single salted peanut, twisting it this way and that so as to study it carefully. He regarded me from the corner of his eye as he popped it into his mouth. "Adds to the flavor."

"But think of all the sweaty places all those filthy hands have been."

"That does sound disturbing," he said, reaching for another helping. "I generally have a healthy aversion to sweaty nuts."

"Well, no one likes sweaty nuts."

He turned to face me fully, a broad smirk curling his lips. I now had his full, keen, and undivided attention (and Melissa's for that matter). "Evan, are you trying to turn me off my nuts?"

"No, I just hate to see a man nibbling on contaminated nuts."

"Should I assume you have a nut fetish?"

"I did till I escaped the nuthouse."

"I feel a few bad nut puns coming on."

"Negative." I shook my head, innocently. "The only ones I can think of just now are…salty."

"Now you're pecan my interest." He tilted his glass to his lips, turquoise eyes spotlighting me over the rim. "Do tell."

"I walnut," I said, folding my arms smugly.

He snorted and raised his glass to me. "Nut bad, Spencer. Well played."

"That can't be the extent of your punny nut-isms," I said, chuckling.

"Afraid so."

The sound of his thumb brushing softly over stubble, as he languidly stroked his jaw, seemed to reverberate over my own skin. It was mesmerizing. I was hardly even aware that Melissa had, by now, skipped off to serve a newly occupied table.

I was loath to let the moment pass just yet. "You sure? Even a bad pun will do." Unwittingly, my voice had turned husky. And hopeful. "Any pun."

"Any big bad pun, huh?"

"Any," I murmured, nodding.

His smile lengthened wickedly. "All right." He leaned in a little closer, his eyes darkening. "In the forest, late at night, you feel something watching from the shadows…"

Unprepared for his sudden sexy change of demeanor, and the smoldering tone of his voice, my arousal spiked—puncturing my heart and sending a rush of feverish blood straight to my belly. I unwittingly licked my lips and dropped my eyes to his mouth. "This already sounds like a campfire ghost story, not a pun." Actually, anything he'd have said just then (even a bible verse) would've sounded like word porn to me, his sex appeal was that potent.

"But this isn't a ghost stalking in the dark. It's something big. Something tangible. It has teeth. It bites."

I swallowed the saliva pooling in my mouth, thrilled by that hungry stare.

"You can't see it, but you know it's there. Watching you. A monster."

I nodded ponderously, distracted by the hypnotic timbre of his voice—low and sensuously masculine.

"What is it, d'you think?" He leaned in a fraction closer, our noses almost touching.

Amber flecks seemed to glint brighter in amongst the greens and blues of his eyes. It took me a moment to snap out of my sudden trance. When he asked the question again, I dragged my eyes down to his mouth as though reading his lips might better help me parse his words. "Hmm?"

"What do you call that monster you can't see, Evan?"

"I-I don't know." What the hell were we even talking about?

Strangely, there seemed to be shadows in his smile as he finally leaned away. "A *where*-wolf, Evan."

"What?" I was still too muddled by that seductive little interlude that I'd completely forgotten about puns. If this was how he told jokes then I wasn't sure my heart could take any more "big bad puns" before leaping out of my chest at him.

"A monster you can't see—a where-wolf." As if he hadn't just thrown my hormones into turmoil, he nonchalantly reached for his glass. "You're welcome."

While I was struggling to douse the fire in my loins, Tristan finished off the last of his beer and aimed a furrowed glance at the door. The humor effectively and suddenly deserted his mouth.

Curious, I followed his gaze, but there was no one there. No ghosts in the darkness and no stalking monsters. When I turned back to face him—or rather his chest now that he was standing—he was peering down at me so intently that it robbed me of all breath.

After a long look, he finally gave a brief, salutational quirk of his lips—hardly even a smile—and then left my side, making his way over to the oxblood chesterfield in the corner by the fireplace.

I was still musing over Tristan's sudden withdrawal when the door flew open, as if from a gust, and a stranger prowled in, stomping dirt from his boots.

What the hell was in the water here in Thorne Bay? This man was just as beautiful as Tristan. He appeared as tall, if not taller. His features were sharp and alert and his hair was a windswept, autumn gold. Nearly brown but not quite. From this distance I couldn't tell what the colors of his eyes were, only that they were dark. The tail ends of black tattoos, disappearing beneath the sleeves he'd rolled up over his corded forearms, only added to his already feral mien.

By the pricking of my thumbs, something wicked this way comes...

His eyes flickered over me a moment, narrowing disapprovingly before he seated himself on the recliner under the antler chandelier next to Tristan.

That look very nearly crippled my meager confidence. I wanted desperately to sniff my armpits for the source of his instant dislike of me. Did I smell bad? No wonder Tristan had withdrawn so quickly.

Since Melissa was closest, she detoured and greeted the stranger familiarly, her bright red lipstick accentuating her winsome smile and cute dimples. "The usual?" she asked, to which both men nodded.

I had a hunch that he was Tristan's brother. They looked enough alike. Yet for all their striking good looks they were both still so ineffably peculiar and so unlike anyone I'd ever seen. What it was that set them apart had nothing to do with male beauty and everything to do with some impenetrable energy that seemed to stir the adrenaline in my blood. From the first day, my awareness of Tristan had been tinged with something dark. Even now my gut twisted with both lust and sobering disquietude, but, with the arrival of the stranger, the latter now outweighed the former. Even Melissa, who was the most gregarious person I knew, seemed uncharacteristically wary around the brothers.

The firelight flung carnal hues across their features, augmenting and disfiguring the shadows that were cast on the wall behind them so that when they moved their heads together to speak lowly, there appeared behind them formidable black giants crouched in quiet collusion. It was an unsettling and sinister impression. Evidently, I needed to stop reading horrors before bedtime. And stop believing that Sasquatch was hiding in the woods behind my room.

"Mel, do I stink?"

My question furrowed her brow as she came around the bar. "No. Why?" Then she surreptitiously sniffed herself. "Do I?"

"Never mind," I muttered. "Who's that with Tristan?"

Melissa tilted a pint glass under the beer faucet and pulled the lever. "That's Tristan's brother, Dean."

I bit my under lip admiringly, ignoring the strange thrill of warning at my nape. I told myself that, like Tristan, Dean would make an awesome addition to my fantasy bank. Although, if I was being honest, I found my gaze was more fatally drawn to Tristan. "Whatever's in the water here in Thorne Bay needs to be bottled up and shared amongst the lesser men of the world," I sighed, giving Melissa a playful nudge.

Both men, I belatedly noticed, had instantly swiveled their heads around to gape at me—Tristan in bemusement and Dean with a comical frown.

What the... Had I spoken too loudly?! *No, impossible!* Panicked, I purposefully knocked a glass over and then swiftly ducked down behind the barrier next to an empty growler to escape those perilous sets of eyes. And to clean up the broken glass. I had definitely whispered the comment quietly to Melissa, who was now snickering heartily as she finished pouring beer, so how had they heard me?

Shaking her head at me as I cowered, disgruntled, on the sticky floor, Melissa finally left to deliver the drinks.

Once I had dredged up enough courage, I scrambled out from behind the bar straight to the kitchen under the guise of discarding shards of glass. The rest of the evening I spent avoiding them. And, at the risk of anything else inadvertently reaching their bionic ears, I abstained from all talking in general. But that didn't mean they returned the favor. Occasionally, I'd feel a prickle at my nape—the press of eyes settling over me—which did nothing to negate the blood rushing wildly into my cheeks.

I looked at my watch impatiently and groaned at seeing that my shift would not be over for two more hours. How would my little heart sustain such masculine scrutiny with any degree of calm? It just wasn't possible.

Thankfully, it wasn't long before Owen made an appearance, and the three men sat together and spoke at length. When my boss left forty minutes later, I thought for sure the brothers would leave too, but no such luck. The pair ordered another round and then chatted quietly amongst themselves a while longer. I knew this because, no matter what I'd resolved, I still peeked under my lashes now and then. But only when I couldn't feel the prickling of eyes on my heat-stained cheeks.

Eventually, though, the Thorns and their prickling eyes finally left. I quickly ducked into the back kitchenette to hide again. When I eased my head around the corner a few seconds later, to assure myself the coast was clear, I released a pent-up breath.

"Talk about nuts…" said Melissa, raising a stern brow at me. She'd witnessed every bit of my eccentric behavior the last hour. "What was that all about, huh?"

"I don't know what you're on about."

"Uh-huh." She shook her head dubiously and flicked my thigh with a tea towel for good measure. "Don't even go there, you little hussy." Even though she was smiling, there was an appreciable dose of gravity tightening her eyes. "I mean it."

"And where is *there*, exactly?" Although I might flirt with Tristan, I was no home-wrecker. I hoped she didn't assume I was hankering after forbidden fruits. Well, I was, but that didn't mean I meant to do anything about it.

She surprised me with another answer entirely. "In all seriousness, Evan—" and she did look as serious as a heart attack "—be careful there. Hot they may be, but trust me, you want nothing to do with that lot or their freaky cult."

8

CREEP

Melissa's warning replayed itself in my head throughout the next week.

So now Tristan was doubly off limits—first for having a cranky girlfriend who looked more than capable of wiping the floor with me if I so much as looked at her the wrong way (or Tristan for that matter), and secondly for being some creep in a cult. I'd sensed something hairy about him, that was undeniable, but I'd never have guessed he was some would-be Manson!

Tristan just didn't look or act anything like a damn cultist, not that I'd known any personally. I just couldn't imagine that of him. The Hodges sure hadn't been wrong about the wagging tongues, but I just wished they'd elaborated a little more about the exact nature of those rumors I'd been warned about.

Unfortunately, no matter how hard I stared at the ceiling it offered no illuminating answers. I had some free time on my hands, I should've been doing something epic and productive. I was in Alaska for God's sake. Instead, though, I was lying on my bed brooding. The sound of a Darth Vader's sudden heavy breathing, alerting me to a new text message, was a welcome diversion.

It was from Mom. "Any more spider dramas?"

"Thankfully not," I typed. "No more creepy spiders perving on my nakedness."

"Speaking of nakedness, Chris Hemsworth stayed over last night. He's gonna be your new step-daddy. Thought you should know."

"You're outta control, cougar. TTYL. Gotta run." *Literally.*

The treadmill in the gym had been a good enough substitute thus far—like eating hardtack when all I craved was a fresh cookie—but I needed a decent run. And seeing as it was my day off, I decided to go for a brisk jog. Outside.

I yanked my fluorescent orange runners on and secured my hair into a high ponytail. Then, heeding Melissa's warning about not wearing earbuds, I shoved my phone snugly into the pockets of my leggings. Listening to loud music over the iPhone speaker would serve me well enough as a bear deterrent. But my primary defense, in the unlikely event that I still managed to sneak up on any hyperphagic bears, was the bear spray resting in the opposite pocket at the side of my thigh. I felt a little like Lara Croft actually.

With Portishead streaming from my left thigh, sadly disrupting the mellifluous eagle calls, I left my room and began jogging along the incline toward the tree-lined main road.

A part of me missed the cypress trees, pale beaches, and the lazy mangroves back home, but the distant slate blue of the sleeping mountains, the glorious stretches of purple fireweed blanketing the roadside, and the trees soaring sharply into the sky of this northernmost state definitely all had their own dark allure. As far as I was concerned, this vista was by far the more dramatic one. Though the tropical waters were unquestionably beautiful, Florida seemed so tame by comparison.

The crisp Alaskan air filled my lungs with its sweet, piney redolence, I pushed myself harder and further. Three miles in and not even the stitch gnawing at my side could slow me down. I felt free and—

"Hey there!"

At the unexpected greeting, I shrieked like a strangled cat and fell ass over teakettle down the slope.

Leaves shot up and blurred around me as I tumbled down into the gully that ran parallel along the road. I was slammed against pine cones, roots and rocks before finally plowing into a pile of dead leaves at the base of an unyielding tree.

Gingerly, I pushed myself up and settled back against the knurled bark as Tristan's alarmed shouting registered through my dazed mind. He'd already rushed from the cab of his truck and clambered down after me. The volume of my phone had been turned all the way up, and my mind deeply lost in thought, so I hadn't even heard the diesel engine pull up alongside me until he'd yelled over the music and, subsequently, sent me rolling down the slope.

"Shit, Evan, I'm so sorry!" He'd reached the bottom almost as soon as I had and was now looking me over assiduously, his sleeves rolled up over his sinewy forearms. No tattoos there to mar that perfect, golden skin. "Are you ok?"

"I think so," I groaned, turning the blaring music off. "Here I was stressing about bears when, all along, it was the sneaky Thorn at my side I really needed to worry about."

"Funny," he replied distractedly, his brows knitting in consternation as he looked me over. "Are you hurt anywhere else?"

I'd already taken a mental inventory of all my aches and pains, especially the sharp throbbing at my ankle. "Just my ankle and a few scratches, I think." I gave an involuntary hiss as I tried to move my foot.

He transferred his gaze to my foot and I winced as he began prodding it gently. "What's with the loud music anyway? I thought jogging outdoors was about enjoying the peace of nature."

"I was trying to scare the bears away," I explained, a bit defensively.

"Don't forget the wolves," he added. "And the giant spiders." There was no lip twitching this time, but I clearly detected the swift glint of amusement beneath his lashes.

The mention of spiders had my eyes popping wider in dread. I threw a suspicious glance about the forest floor, lifting my hands safely into my lap, suddenly convinced that I'd see another wolf spider wiggling its brows suggestively at me from some nearby mossy log.

"You shouldn't be out here alone," Tristan muttered, hooking a steely arm carefully under my knees and the other behind my back with the obvious intention of lifting me up.

"What are you doing?!" I was at once thrilled and terrified to be in his arms. I reeked of sweat and last night's onions and garlic! *Omigod, I'm sweaty garlic girl!*

He paused, still crouched beside me, his piercing gaze inches from mine. "Pretty sure it's obvious what I'm doing."

"I can walk!" I gave a nervous little laugh.

He shot me a pointed look. "Hobble, you mean."

The very next second I was airborne as he hoisted me up carefully and with very little effort. Ignoring all further protests, he cradled me like a skittish bride.

"It's okay," he said as I stiffened, "I've watched *An Officer and a Gentleman*, this is how it's done. Trust me."

"Yeah, but Richard Gere never ran the poor woman off the road."

"Everyone's a critic."

Moreover, Richard wasn't a man of questionable, extracurricular activities that involved cultish shenanigans.

Unaware of my dark thoughts about him, Tristan grinned

down at me unrestrainedly, baring those sharp white canines in the process. Was it mandatory, in this cult of theirs, to file their teeth into long points? I also wondered if he had some hidden falsies somewhere that he used to disguise those disturbing teeth in case he scared any *cheechakos*. Likely so because they weren't always so sinister looking. My widened glare was fixed warily to his closed mouth all the while he easily scaled the hill as if I was nothing but a featherweight, which, compared to him, I supposed I was.

The left door of his black Ford was still wide open when we got up to the road, the hazards blinking patiently. He deposited me in the driver's seat and promptly began to inspect the scratches on my hands and arms before removing the running shoe from my swelling foot and handing it to me for safekeeping.

My stomach tensed with anticipation as he unexpectedly straightened up, looming over me to grab his Tervis cup from the center console at my back. God, he smelled heavenly, but I didn't want to think about that because then I'd have to consider the rankness of my own scent. *Eau de Sweaty.* It was very confusing to have my libido revving in one direction as my head balked cautiously and skeptically into another. I wasn't even sure if I was relieved or disappointed when he, just as quickly, leaned away again, too busy playing doctor to comment on my schoolgirl neurosis. Or my stench.

Careful of keeping the ice back with one hand, he emptied the water out of the cup and poured the ice onto a microfibre cloth he'd grabbed from the back seat. He then positioned his boot on the running board and rested my injured foot onto his bent knee before placing the makeshift ice pack at my ankle. In the meantime, I kept myself busy fidgeting with the laces of my sneaker as I studied the granite contours of his gorgeous profile.

There was not a man in the world that unsettled me more than he did. Not even Dean, who was probably even better looking. It was a very powerful sexual allure that held me spellbound by Tristan. Which was inexplicably odd considering his awful canines. He intimidated me with his half-smiles and sphinx-like demeanor; unnerved me with his piercing looks, and unsettled me with his enigmatic silence. When he wasn't sharing a joke with me I had no bloody idea what was going on in his head. Despite my ever increasing lust for him, I couldn't stop thinking about Melissa's warning either. Maybe the soundness of my judgment had been fatally impaired by my raging hormones. He could very well be in a toothy cult. Why shouldn't I heed my friend's warning? And now I was completely alone with him.

"Relax, I won't bite," he said without looking up from my foot.

I gave a humorous laugh and watched his mouth flatten at the sound.

All my dire speculations had me tensing uncomfortably, which Tristan hopefully ascribed to the sprain and not to the fact that he made me so nervous. If he'd have heard the conversation between myself and the pesky voices in my head he'd have thought us a bunch of space monkeys talking to each other through the toaster. I sounded bananas even to myself. Thankfully, he was blissfully unaware of my thoughts and merely continued his careful ministrations, his expression thoughtful and his fingers impossibly warm where they touched my foot. In fact, I barely felt the ice at all.

"Good news is it's not broken," he said, "but you won't be bartending for a while. Or running."

"I'm fine," I said, feeling a *Monty Python* quote coming on, " 'tis but a flesh wound.' "

"Stop flapping your gums, you're distracting me." Even so, I could tell he was amused by the perfect British accent I'd nailed.

I watched a lot of BBC. "I'm fine, Doc. Honestly. How about

you sign my discharge papers and let me pay my bill?" I was sure he had better things to do than play nursemaid to me.

"Payment, huh?" He stroked his chin with some deliberation. "What kind of payment?"

"How do your…um…other patients—" I licked my lips and swallowed "—normally pay you?" My heart was beating like a thing deranged, rattling my ribs excitedly from the inside.

"That all depends on the patient…" His smile had become perceptibly darker and edgier.

"Sex on the Beach it is." Where I got the courage to say that I didn't know, but I instantly berated myself for flirting with the devil. After all, his was the type of smirk that promised wicked things and I was, as per usual, hopelessly out of my depth here.

My comment seemed to have ignited his eyes. Strange flecks of yellow began pulsing around his dilating pupils. It was hypnotic to watch. The forest grew still as he held my gaze. I could feel the air thicken as he leaned in a fraction closer. He was going to kiss me!

Yes! No! Fuck! Argh! I panicked. "I should go," I said abruptly, dispelling the moment. I fumbled desperately with my shoe, a jolt of pain stabbing my ankle as I finally yanked it on.

He, meanwhile, slowly set the ice aside and moved away, bemused, but said nothing at first. His dark brows edged a little lower and his eyes followed my movements as I hobbled down from his truck. Alternately wincing and gasping, I limped off into the sunset (well, there was a sunset somewhere in the world) like an unsteady (and horseless) John Wayne.

"Where the hell are you going, Spencer?" His surprise was almost comical. Almost. And his tone implied that I'd gone off the deep end, space monkey style.

I affected a precarious little pirouette and faced him. "Walking back." *Duh.*

"You can barely do even that properly." He gave me a flat

look and rested his forearm casually on the top of his open door. "Also, you're going the wrong way."

"Right." I swiftly changed direction, cursing myself.

His eyes probed me uncomfortably as I hobbled past him. "C'mon, you maniac, get in the truck."

"I'm fine." Wait, how many times had I already said fine? *Who cares, he's right. You're acting like a maniac. Take the damn ride.*

"Women always say they're fine especially when they're not."

His logic was unappreciated. I still made no move back toward him.

"This is ridiculous," he said tersely, getting into his truck and slamming the door. He fired the ignition and the truck began to crawl forward. His elbow was resting in the open window, his expression unreadable as he halted beside me.

I waited expectantly.

So did he. His diesel engine growled angrily into the silence.

"What are you doing?" I asked warily.

"You give me no choice but to follow you like a creep." He gave a shrug of annoyance.

Whoa. In the space of two minutes, I'd gone from damsel in distress to *persona non grata. Yes, because you're a nut job. Get in the goddamn truck.* I sighed and headed around the hood to the passenger seat. He'd proven his point.

He leaned over to open the door for me. "I'm not gonna shove you in the bed of my truck and bury you in the woods if that's what you're worried about." He waited till I'd climbed in and shut the door before he said, "I left the chloroform at home anyway." How could he be both irritated and charming all at once?

"Also, your fingerprints are all over my foot now," I said as the truck began to accelerate forward. It wasn't exactly a grin that lit his face, but his hardened facade cracked just enough that I still felt gratified to have almost put the smile back in place.

"The question is, can latent prints be lifted from dead bodies?"

"Pretty sure they can be." I slitted my eyes at him. "I should warn you—"giving my little can of bear spray a warning pat "—I'm packin' heat."

He raised one hand from the steering wheel in surrender. "I'm only here to help you, not molest you."

"For the record," I said, feeling suddenly chagrined for allowing stupid rumors to make me doubt him, "I know you won't hurt me." Of that, at least, I was now certain. The way he'd cared for and touched me had been nothing less than altruistic. *God, make up your damn mind. Do you feel safe with him or don't you?* But I didn't have an answer because I did and I didn't. Because I sensed both safety and danger in him, two opposing forces—perhaps logic and instinct—pulling me off axis.

He glanced over briefly to notice me chewing my lip indecisively. "But?"

"But what?"

"You tell me. There's obviously something still bothering you."

Was I really about to broach this sensitive subject? Yes. I had to know. "I heard…I heard a really weird rumor. About you."

"It's not a rumor," he said, his face deadpan.

"It's not?!" *Oh, God.*

"No, I really am the reigning Backgammon champion in Thorne Bay." He shot me a lopsided smirk.

"Whoa, watch out," I chuckled, momentarily relaxing. "That's truly impressive, but I was referring to the rumor about…you know…you being in a cult. Is that true?"

"You're right, that is weird."

My brows rose expectantly.

"As if I wouldn't deny it either way," he scoffed.

"Uh…"

“The answer—” sighing “—is no, Evan. We're not up there sacrificing virgins or dancing around fires. Or whatever the hell I’m rumored to be doing these days.” His lips compressed into a hard line.

“I haven’t even thought about what being in a cult might actually involve, to be honest.”

“A lot of my…extended family can be a little hermetic. But it's really not as sinister as some folks like to think. A lot of busybodies up here get tickled by gossip, that’s all. So whatever you don't want the whole damn town knowing, you should probably keep to yourself. Fair warning.”

“So no creepy blood sacrifices then?”

“No blood sacrifices,” he affirmed. “At least not for many years now…”

“What a relief,” I muttered, distracted by his profile.

The sea-foam in his irises appeared iridescent as the sunlight slanted through the trees and onto his face. Even when his features were relaxed and calm, as they were now, his eyes always hinted at turbulence beneath. In fact, I suspected they could rival the Bering Sea when roused to temper.

I almost wished I hadn’t asked about the gossip because now I seemed like just another nosy scandalmonger. “Well, I didn’t really buy into any of that garbage.”

“Hmm,” was all he offered in reply. Not a convincing sound by any means.

An uncomfortable silence fell between us. He was ostensibly lost in thought and I’d already said too much, there was no chance I’d risk putting my injured foot back in my stupid mouth.

But, sadly, the universe wasn’t done playing with my emotions just yet. Radiohead’s very distinctive guitar distortion crescendoing over the speakers suddenly drew me into the plaintive lyrics, each word hitting a thousand tender nerves. How poignant—here was the soundtrack to my life right now.

From the corner of my eye, I tried to read his guarded features. I would have given anything to know what he was thinking, and whether or not he was listening to the words too. Was he thinking that I was a creep? A weirdo? That I didn't belong here?

All too soon we were parked outside the staff barracks, and before I'd even curled my fingers on the handle, Tristan was at my door to help me down from his truck.

"Thanks for babysitting me."

"It was the least I could do for causing the sprain in the first place."

My smile faltered slightly. Of course he'd felt duty bound to help me. "You, sir, are a scholar and a gentleman." Who was almost certainly happy to be rid of me. *Yup, you as good as compared him to Charles Manson, he's probably never going to come near you again.*

Once my apartment door was unlocked, I stood at the threshold, trying to think of some witty parting remark that would make him forget all about my John Wayne moment, or that I'd made him feel like some deviant. "Did you sharpen your teeth?" I blurted nervously.

"What?" He cocked his head, baffled.

My inner logic had already slapped me hard across the face in disgust. "Nothing," I quickly muttered. This was probably going to be the last time I would ever be alone with him again. Or see him. I felt like crying all of a sudden. *You idiot!*

"You should go elevate that foot and put some ice on it," he instructed, turning to head back to his truck.

"Okay." I gave a two-fingered salute. Actually freaking saluted him. Cringe.

"See ya, Evan."

"Bye, Tristan."

"Oh, and stick to treadmills from now on, okay?"

"Sure," I said sheepishly. "Don't worry, you'll have no more complications from me."

He climbed in, shut the door, and snapped the seatbelt on before regarding me through his open window. "I think," he said after a heavy pause, "it's too late for that." And then he was gone in a plume of leafy detritus.

9

WEIRD NOT TO BE WEIRD

The week following my sprain was spent mostly supine on my bed like an invalid. Alison had turned out to be one strict nursing supervisor.

As predicted there was complete radio silence from Tristan, apart from the card he'd sent with a carton of soy milk (which had been cleverly wrapped in a bandage and tied off with a neat bow). That was something at least, I'd thought then, but when the second week crawled by without word (not that he owed me words) my sham indifference cracked into full-blown crazy. Was it cabin fever or Tristan fever?

The 'something at least' turned out to be nothing at all. He remained torturously elusive weeks after. Nor could I blame the man for it—why wouldn't he avoid me like the bubonic? Since the moment I'd met him I'd been nothing but a gawky disaster. Worst of all, I'd actually asked him if he was in a bloody cult!

Being in my own head during my boring convalescence also meant that I'd been rehashing my John Wayne moment over and over again, *ad nauseam*, and I was now mortified that that should be Tristan's last memory of me. That one day, when he was eighty and watching *True Grit*, he'd suddenly have a flashback of that sweaty garlic girl (whose name he'd long forgotten) hobbling off down the road like a maniac rather than drive with him. That same screwy girl with those strange ideas about cults. There had also been that panicky moment where I'd sabotaged what would almost certainly have been a first kiss; he probably thought he'd dodged a bullet, but I was filled with regret.

Whatever I was doing, whether pouring a beer or brushing my teeth, it never failed—at the oddest moments, with or without an audience, I'd either give a random snort of disgust or facepalm myself. Sometimes both. This had earned me lots of strange looks lately. By now, most people probably assumed that I suffered from a severe case of Tourette's.

But, as Gramps would say, I could crap in one hand and heap *wishes* onto the other, and see which hand filled up first—it was useless to obsess or wish myself back in time to have a do-over. Thankfully, though, by the end of week four (not that I was counting), I stopped looking for him every time the door opened.

I was in my room folding clothes like the exciting and worldly woman that I was (not), music blasting from my portable speaker as I worked. My shift with Melissa wouldn't start until later this evening, so I was taking advantage of my morning to do some laundry and other very grown-up chores.

Shouting along with the lyrics, I rocked my body to the beat knowing full well how ridiculous I looked doing the Sprinkler, but that was fine because I didn't mind being ridiculous on purpose. And in private. It was when I did or said stupid shit inadvertently, in front of gorgeous witnesses, that it rankled.

When my phone began to ring, mid-Sprinkler in fact, it automatically cut the music off. Mom usually called this time of day, so, without checking the screen, I answered. "You naked with

Chris Hemsworth again?" I asked her, still breathless from dancing.

Only it wasn't my mother. "Um, should I be?"

"Uh…" My cheeks instantly began to burn. How the hell did I get myself into these cringe-worthy situations with Tristan? "You mean you're not?" I injected a good dose of disappointment into my response, so as to mask my humiliation. When in doubt, salvage with humor.

"So we're back to talking about my dirty little secrets, huh? Girlie cocktails I'll own, but Chris Hemsworth isn't one of them."

"That's not what I heard," I joked in a sing-song voice. I halted all panty-folding to give the phone call the concentration it deserved.

"Well, there was that one time…but it'll take a few drinks before I'll confess to all the nasty details."

"Yeah right, I bet it'd only take you two girlie drinks to spill your guts, Mr. Thorn."

"Ahh, so you *do* know it's me. I was worried there for a minute."

"Oh, I know exactly who I'm speaking to." *Woman, be cool!* I smacked my brow with a grimace of disgust.

"How's the ankle?" he asked in a solicitous change of tone.

"You mean my cankle?" I sighed. "It's fine."

He chuckled again. "I hope you don't mind, but I got your number from Owen."

"No, that's fine." *Argh! I forbid you from saying fine ever again!* I lifted my eyes to the dresser mirror and flipped my reflection the bird.

"I just spoke to him actually and he mentioned that tomorrow's your day off?"

"You were speaking to Owen about me?" I nibbled at my thumbnail as I waited breathlessly for the answer. Knowing just how subtle *Mack Lovin'* could be, he probably volunteered my hand in marriage along with my number.

"Yeah, he gave me your social security too and I passed it onto my cult leader."

"Oh snap." I felt my lips curl instantly. Without meaning to, I caught myself picturing his smile (not the sharp smile), and the sexy way he'd sometimes angle his head, almost imperceptibly, whenever he made a wisecrack.

"Too soon for cult jokes?" he asked.

"No, I was laughing on the inside."

"Right." The way he protracted the vowel only broadened my goofy grin. "Well, I *was* gonna invite you up for a helicopter ride, but now I'm not so sure."

"Seriously?" My fingers were probably leaving indents on my phone. "No way!"

"So that's a yes?"

"Yes, I'd love to go!"

"Okay, but you'll actually be required to laugh at all future jokes no matter how questionable."

"Done." Whoa, I hadn't scared him off yet? Progress. I gave my reflection a thumbs up and an enthusiastic nod.

"Pick you up around six AM?"

"Are you asking or telling me?"

"Wasn't sure if you'd mind getting up at the ass-crack of dawn since you might've had plans to sleep in. The hangar's a bit of a ball ache to get to, so we have to leave early."

"Negative, I don't need any beauty sleep," I lied. There was no amount of sleep capable of beautifying me anyway. "I'm in."

"Great. I'm taking two glaciologists up to Glacier Bay National Park tomorrow. Picking them up in Juneau just after ten, so skids up at seven thirty."

"Hmm, business *and* pleasure."

"Figured you'd want to dodge some birds and see a few glaciers with me."

"You figured right." I'd help him scrub porta-potties if it meant spending time in Tristan's company.

"Text you tomorrow morning when I'm about five minutes out."

"I'll be ready at six."

"See ya then."

"Bye!"

As soon as the line went dead my music flared back to life. I began twerking my celebration dance on top of my mattress. My folded clothes were soon reduced to nothing but a crumpled mess around me. When the song ended, I collapsed onto my clean laundry and reached over to retrieve the card I'd placed on my bedside table.

I still hadn't removed the bow from the soy milk either. In fact, my bedside had become a little Tristan shrine of late. *That's not freakin' creepy at all.*

His words, as I imagined them in his voice, always made me smile each time I reread his note (and I did that at least twice a day).

Evan found this dodgy box of mystery milk at the market. Made me think of this weird girl I know, and her strange addiction to pretend milk :) Hope it tastes better than it looks. At the very least, you can use it to elevate your foot...or feed it to your pet spider.

Tristan.

P.S. I like weird.

. . .

Screw flowers and chocolates, I thought. Sure, it would have been adorable if he'd sent those instead, but totally unimaginative. Although I wasn't sure how I felt about him thinking I was weird. Then again, according to John Lennon, it was weird not to be weird.

~

"Ugh, he's not in a cult." I raised my eyes to the ceiling, sighing my annoyance and wishing I could keep a straight face around Melissa.

"Did David Koresh tell you that himself?" she retorted. "Well, then, it must be true."

I threw a balled up sock at Melissa. She was sitting on my bed fiddling with her camera equipment. She was supposed to be helping me decide what to wear today but was failing miserably at it. Instead, she reminded me to pack my pepper spray in case I found myself kidnapped and married off to a psychotic polygamist with a harem of teenage wives.

I purposefully removed the bear spray from my backpack and set it on the dresser to make a point. "It's staying right here."

"Fine, it's your creepy wedding," she quipped with a shrug, implying that it was more like my funeral.

"Focus, woman." I laid out the two options for her to consider. "The red sweater or the green?"

She had arrived at Bear Lodge much earlier, four AM to be exact, to shoot some sunrise landscapes over the lake, and had popped over a few minutes ago knowing I would already be up shaving my bits, spraying the pits, and generally freaking out about this date that wasn't a date.

"I heard Mrs. Dinwiddie saying that she saw Dean running naked through her backyard last week." Melissa folded her arms and winged her eyebrows meaningfully at me. "And I'm pretty sure Mrs. Thatcher said the same about Tristan once."

"Melissa—" I threatened her with another sock "—Thatcher's half blind. It was probably her drunken husband stripping in his shed again."

She waved her hand impatiently and got back to the topic, much to my annoyance. "Look, I like Tristan just fine. He's not a bad tipper. Maybe he's not in a cult exactly, but you can't tell me there isn't something weird about that whole family. Doesn't Dean give you the heebie-jeebies? They live in a compound, for God's sake. C'mon, Evan, that's freaking weird."

"Uh, look who you're talking to."

"Point taken." She threw herself back against my pillows. "Actually, you suit each other." She aimed a careless finger at the deep red cable-knit. "Wear that one. That way the sheriff can find your dead body in the woods a lot easier."

"Green it is." I slipped the oversized emerald green sweater on over a white base layer and dark blue skinny jeans before inspecting the ensemble in the full-length mirror behind the door.

I had elected to wear my hair in a messy bun on top of my head and I thought I looked casual in an *I'm-not-trying-too-hard-but-don't-I-look-cute-anyway?* kinda way. Satisfied, I turned back toward the bed, feeling almost sick with nervy anticipation. But the incoming text distracted me instantly and, squealing happily, I dove for it even before Darth Vader had stopped his creepy breathing.

I knew exactly who it was. So did Melissa, whose humorous little snort barely registered in my delirium. As oblivious as I was to my surroundings, and utterly engrossed in Tristan's text (informing me he was ten minutes out), I didn't realize that Melissa was aiming her lens at me. Not until I heard the shutter going off in rapid succession.

"Woman—" I narrowed my eyes at her "—I hope that's a practice shot you intend to delete later."

"Sure." The Mona Lisa smile she offered me completely belied her words. She gathered her things up, having noticed the time, and hugged me goodbye. A moment later she was at the open door, preparing to head out. But she unexpectedly halted at the threshold to rifle through her large handbag. "Ev, before I forget…"

Something was already sailing at me through the air even as I said, "Yeah?" The instant I caught the object, Melissa bolted from the room, shutting the door firmly behind her. Within my uncurling fingers lay a little, square Trojan packet.

"Safety first!" she yelled from the other side of the door, cackling as she sprinted down the stairs and out of earshot of the less than savory epithets I was shouting at her.

Moments later, I heard the bold thudding of footsteps mounting the stairs. Likely Melissa, I thought, returning because she had just realized she'd given me the last of her willie-warmers or something. Also, it hadn't been ten minutes yet, and I hadn't heard Tristan's truck. So I ripped the door open and, without even checking first, hurled the Trojan at her with a vengeful, "Ha!"

But my exclamation diminuendoed like the last note of a flat tire.

"I told you, Evan," said Tristan, grinning as he inspected the condom packet that had hit him square in the chest, "you gotta buy me a drink first."

10

PREDATORS

"Oh. My. God." When I saw Melissa again, I'd bloody choke her with that damn condom! I covered my face with my hands, horrified. The urge to cry was almost as strong as the urge to laugh. Well, that was bound to happen, wasn't it? I couldn't seem to go a full second without mortifying myself in front of this man. "That was…for Melissa," I finished lamely.

"I won't ask."

"Probably for the best," I muttered, stepping outside to lock my door.

When I had dropped my key into my backpack, I turned to find Tristan already waiting at the passenger door for me. He was wearing a blue flight suit that did nothing to repair my tattered self-composure. There was nothing in the world hotter than a man in a flight suit, I decided.

The day he'd driven me and my bum foot home I'd barely noticed his truck, but I took the time now. It was a modified black King Ranch with mud splatter thrown up over the fender wells. There was a winch below the brush guard and a large aluminum toolbox in the truck bed and a tank of jet fuel with a fuel hose attached. A very masculine truck indeed.

"No more cankle," he remarked, nodding at my boot as I hopped into the passenger seat.

"And no more dignity." The heat of humiliation was still cooking the proverbial egg on my face.

"Which reminds me…" He dropped the foil packet casually into my lap. "This belongs to you." He then closed my door firmly and walked around to his side wearing a shit-eating grin.

"You know," I said, glaring at the little silver square, and forgetting to filter my thoughts, "condom is right up there with all the other cringey words like *moist*—" I grimaced "—and orifice and coitus."

He snorted. "Then I'll be especially careful never to use all four in one sentence."

"Yes," I said, admiring his long fingers on the wheel, "feel free to use euphemisms."

"Like what? Wet, hole, and porking? Yeah," he chuckled, "those are *so* much better."

I shuddered. "You left condom out."

"Does prophylactic sound any better to you?"

"I prefer the term 'French letter', thanks."

"Come again?" His brows twitched.

"French letter sounds way better than condom."

"Sounds just as dirty to me."

I chucked the French letter into the backseat and dropped my hands to fidget in my lap. "Nice try, Tristan, but you're not ruining French letter for me."

"We'll see." He shot me a fleeting look, which I caught from my peripheral.

Would we see? Why did that sound like the most delicious threat ever? I swallowed my heart back down from where it had somersaulted into my throat. "By the way, thank you for the card and the hippie milk."

"You're welcome." He gave a long-suffering sigh. "Can't believe I'm encouraging your weird milk fetish."

"Yet you claim to like weird." The proof of which was written in bold, black ink in the card on my bedside table.

"I do."

"And you think I'm weird?"

"Very."

"Oh." My brow puckered with uncertainty.

"Extraordinary, remarkable, exceptional—take whatever euphemism you want, Evan. The point is you're different. Why would you want to be *ordinary*." He said the word with heavy distaste.

"Not ordinary, just normal would be nice for a change."

"Normal is boring, and people die of boredom every day."

"No, more people die of excitement. Boredom is safe."

"Well, would you rather die being bored or die doing something amazing?"

"I'd rather not die period." But he was right, it was why I was here at all—taking chances and making changes. "So can I assume that you're weird too?"

"You may."

"Really?" I eyed him skeptically. No way did we share *that* in common. I'd had acne in high school and might as well have been a leper. He'd have been the complete opposite—the quintessential football god with an entourage of half-dressed, giggling pom-pom brats. I promptly shared these thoughts with him.

"Nah," he answered, "I was homeschooled. Trust me, there's no euphemism for the kind of weird that I am." His expression was deadpan as he scanned the road and the trees either side.

"Then may I just say that the weird in me respects the weird in you."

To that, I received only an enigmatic little smile. He was completely at ease after that, casually drumming his fingers on the steering wheel, watching the scenery as it passed by his window. By comparison, I couldn't seem to sit still, looking anywhere but directly at him.

The backdrop was incomparable, the conifers looming beneath a cerulean sky, cloudless and brisk, the likes of which we seldom saw down in Florida except in winter mostly. But he was by far the more magnetizing view and I found myself ignoring the beauty of nature in favor of his.

Unexpectedly, his eyes shifted sidelong toward me, catching the unmistakable detour that my gaze had taken over the slope of his mouth. Hurriedly, I looked away. When he pulled over suddenly, parking on the shoulder, my heart lurched into suspenseful overdrive. I imagined him suddenly pulling me over onto his lap for a passionate kiss, but the fantasy was snuffed almost instantly. He'd spotted a turtle sunbaking in the middle of the highway, and—as if he wasn't perfect enough already—climbed out to rescue it. Once he'd removed the little thrill-seeker to the side of the road in which its mobile home had been pointed, he climbed back into his truck and we set off again.

Was there anything in the world sexier than a nature-lover? No, there was not.

When we eventually got to the Thorn Aviation heliport an hour later, I was to find that Tristan had, the evening before, already preflighted and fueled the aircraft (a sleek-looking, four-bladed, dark blue helicopter with pop-out floats). So it was now just a matter of him steering the dolly out of the heated hangar with the tug and parking the bird on the big yellow 'H' painted over the square pad. On the whole, this all took no more than five minutes.

"Jeez," I said, gaping at the dark trees and wild terrain that hemmed the pad and hanger, "this place is in the middle of nowhere."

"Everything in Thorne Bay is in the middle of nowhere," he

answered, shoving chocks either side of the dolly wheels. "Although, technically," he added, "we're not really in Thorne Bay anymore." He climbed onto the skids and made quick work of checking the oil levels of the engine and transmission (with a running commentary of what he was doing) and then fastened the cowlings back up before jumping down from the high skids.

"So do you live close by?" I asked.

"Yup, my cabin's not too far from here."

"Your compound, you mean." I was imagining high, barbed wire fences and massive alsatians patrolling the perimeter.

"Exactly." He shot me a flat look.

"And where does the rest of the cult reside?"

"Hereabouts."

"So where is *here* exactly?" I gave my phone a little impatient shake and held it high over my head as if that might magically improve the signal. It didn't.

Tristan shook his head and gave an amused snort as he watched my antics. "We're about halfway between Coffman Cove and Big Lake."

"Is that where Alison and Owen's hunting cabin is?" The one that Dean seemed so eager to buy.

"Yeah." He was scanning the trees with a distracted frown.

When I looked out to see what he was searching for, I saw only a handful of squirrels bickering in the branches and a thrush rifling through the leaves on the ground.

"Their property abuts my brother's." His voice was lower now, his nostrils flaring toward a nearby thicket.

Disconcerted, I raised my nose to do the same, sampling the breeze like a dog. Nothing. I opened my mouth to address his strange preoccupation, but he placed a finger against his lips in warning. Then he purposefully eased me behind him, so that I was positioned between the helicopter and himself while he glared keenly into the woods up ahead.

"Tristan?" Unnerved, I sidestepped just enough to lean out and study his face for cues.

"Shh." His shoulders became rigid. No part of him moved except where the wind ruffled his hair and lightly compressed his flight suit to his abs. He was so attuned that, were it even possible, I'm sure his ears would've been pricked forward to whatever unheard decibel he'd detected. It was uncanny.

The waiting attenuated my nerves, each one seeming to snap discordantly in the hush. When the bushes nearby began to rustle ominously I felt my pulse jolt with fright. Something large was moving within them. The next second a colossal bear emerged from the trees. It began sniffing the air with its long, mobile nose before emitting a low, pernicious moan.

"Fuck." Tristan's muttered curse only exacerbated my fear.

That was not a word anyone wanted to hear from their pilot—ever. I was pretty sure Captain Sully hadn't even dropped a fuck into the black box when he'd lost his engines.

"Tell me that's just a black bear," I said under my breath. Black bears were at least more tolerant of humans and not as aggressive as their larger counterparts. However, the grizzled white-tipped hair on its shoulder hump and the grisly stare suggested otherwise.

He shook his head. "A brownie."

I felt my gut clench as the grizzly's ears flattened. It swung its head from side to side and pawed restlessly at the ground with long, nasty-looking foreclaws.

Even if my legs hadn't already turned into soup I wouldn't have bolted—only an idiot would try to outrun a predator.

"Should we play dead?" If I lived through this, I promised myself, I'd never leave home without my bear spray again.

"Won't work," Tristan answered. "She's decided we're prey."

"She?" I hadn't even thought to look lower than those alarming jowls and that large head swinging threateningly from side to side, never mind the bear's plumbing! Didn't he have a rifle stowed in the baggage compartment? At this point, it was fight or flight, but no way in hell would we be "skids up" before the bear came crashing through the plexiglass. Both shitty options.

Armed or not, I hoped Tristan had a plan because this bear was a monster—at least five feet from her pads to her shoulders! My heart wilted when she suddenly stood on hind legs, her menacing grunts growing louder as she moved closer.

Tristan, though, appeared deadly calm. He leaned his body forward imperceptibly and balled his fists as he growled low. Actually fucking growled. My skin crawled violently. I staggered backward, recoiling from it, the sound rumbling across my cold marrow like a sharp clap of thunder.

For her part, the bear appeared just as disturbed by it because she instantly halted her charge. For a moment, it seemed that she was sizing up a rival predator, two sets of eyes locked in silent battle. To my everlasting shock, the bear withdrew. Slowly, she took a step back, followed by another, and then another, moving further and further away, groaning in frustration each time Tristan edged toward her.

I respired deeply as the grizzly cautiously retreated from view. My relief was such a physical force that it nearly precipitated me right into Tristan's tense back in a paroxysm of hugging and hysterical weeping. If not for the fact that his feral growl was still ringing in my ears, or that he was still disturbingly frozen and silent, I might not have resisted the impulse at all.

"Are…are you o-okay?" I tried to walk around him, but he moved forward abruptly, denying me a view of his face.

"Just give me a minute." There was a guttural, forbidding rasp to his voice.

After a moment he headed off to inspect the tree line where the bear had withdrawn. Cowed by his demeanor, I stayed frozen on the helipad. Until the flash of red on the inside of his hand caught my notice. I rushed to his side and reached out for his right hand.

But he flinched away before I could touch him. “Don’t,” he warned me tersely.

It didn't matter, though, because I’d already seen the deep gouges in his palms. “You’re bleeding! Did you scratch yourself?”

Had that been from clenching his fists? If so his blunt nails should have left shallow half-moon indents in his flesh. Not bloody gashes. Who the hell was he? Wolverine?!

“Yeah” —his canines flashed sharply— “I scratched myself.”

My breath hitched fearfully. “Tristan, you’re s-scaring me.” A primal sense of foreboding gripped my heart.

There seemed to be blood seeping lightly from his gums, staining his teeth a grisly copper. His irises had lightened somehow, eerie flecks of gold flickering within the green—now a feral pulsing green! It was all I could do to suck air into my trembling chest. I was as silent and motionless as I’d been when the grizzly had first appeared, sensing, as before, something savage in my midst.

It was as if I’d opened a cocoon and caught something at the last stage of a macabre chrysalis. Then I blinked and the moment passed.

His pupils narrowed back to normal proportions. The preternatural yellow dimmed from the green. “Sorry.” He shook his head and the last vestiges of menace volatilized from his face as if it had never been. Beneath his sealed lips, I could see his tongue running over his teeth.

“Your teeth…they…” My own head was shaking with disbelief. How to explain what I’d seen without sounding crazy? “They’re so long!”

“The better to eat you with?” he mumbled. His joke, however, fell abominably flat. He must have realized as much by my silence because he shrugged and dragged his hand self-consciously through his hair. "It's just a family trait. I told you I was weird, Evan." His face hardened. "Don't make a big deal of it."

Obviously, I was more traumatized by the bear than I had initially realized. Men didn't just go around growing fangs. Nor was it possible for eyes to glow or change color (not to the extent that his had). This guy was a dark horse. *Dark something, all right.* Moreover, how the hell had he managed those creepy sound effects? "What happened with the bear?" I asked him. "How did you scare it off?" But that was a stupid question, bloodied fangs would scare anything off!

"Haven't you heard?" He shot me a measured look. "I'm the bear whisperer in my cult." That said, he loped off toward the helicopter, grabbing an oil rag from the baggage compartment to wipe the blood from his hands.

More stupid jokes? I followed him, having till now forgotten all about the wounds on his palm. "Don't you have a rifle or something?"

Tristan looked up from studying his palms and met my insistent gaze. "Or something," was all he finally replied, close-lipped.

I returned his piercing stare. We stayed like that for a long moment, his thoughts obscured behind a stony facade and hooded eyes. For my part, I was still trying to correlate this version of Tristan with the one I'd seen and heard moments before.

Without warning, he closed the distance between us with a slow, purposeful stride, towering over me without actually allowing any parts of our bodies to touch.

I should have been terrified. I should have demanded he take me home. No, I should have *run* all the way home. Yet I knew not to run from a predator. There was hunger in his gaze. A hunger that my blood answered not with a prey's fear but with swelling, quicksilver heat. It was an uprush of staggering desire so overwhelming and inexplicable that I promptly dropped my gaze, utterly shaken by my own reaction to him.

Instead of risking another glance up at him, I took his hands gently in mine to distract myself from the probing of his eyes, and to inspect the wounds I'd seen, trying valiantly to ignore the wild clamor of my racing heart. This time he let me look.

Running a finger curiously over his palms, I was taken aback to see nothing more than shallow half-moons already scabbed over. *What the...* "Nothing makes sense anymore." Not him, not his strange physiology, and certainly not my reaction to him. "I think—"

"Don't think so much," he murmured huskily. "Not everything has to make sense."

I shook my head, bewildered. "I could've sworn I saw..."

"Do you think I'd hurt you?" He closed his fingers over mine and angled his head lower and closer.

My breath hitched expectantly as his lips paused just above mine. "You just told me not to think."

"Then what does instinct tell you?"

"That you're other than what you seem," I whispered. "But you won't hurt me." Somehow I knew that. In fact, he'd saved my life.

"Can that be enough for now?" The heat of his breath fluttered sensually against my mouth.

"You don't want me to ask any more questions about what happened here?"

"No, unless you want me to lie and tell you I moonlight as Sasquatch once a month."

I would have chuckled if my loins weren't on fire for him. I shook my head. "I'll waive the questions, for now, just tell me no lies."

"Deal." The unveiled hunger in his gaze pressed down on me,

a mesmeric heat, and his fingers tightened perceptibly, holding me in place in case I meant to retreat from him. I didn't. I had no will to.

The deliberate and sensual way his eyes glided down to my parted lips was evidence enough of his intent. He meant to devour me! And I wanted it badly.

11

MICROWAVES AND POTATO CHIPS

The shrill ringing of Tristan's phone instantly dispelled our moment. As Tristan slowly backed away, his earthy spice and warmth subsided with him.

Now there's a goddamn phone signal?! I groaned in silent frustration as the amatory haze ebbed from my blood.

He answered the call as calmly as though he hadn't just survived a near mauling by a vicious bear or left my legs unsteady with that near kiss. I turned my face to the wind to cool my cheeks and listened to Tristan's deep voice as he spoke into the receiver. This, however, didn't mean I couldn't feel the heavy press of his gaze on my back.

By the time the call ended, I felt composed enough to face him again, resisting the urge to shoot his phone a dirty look as he returned it to the breast pocket of his flight suit.

"We better get going," he murmured. "C'mon, I'll help you with your lifejacket."

This time, when he moved back into my personal space, he was all business. His arms enveloped me only long enough to secure the lifejacket strap about my waist. His fingers lingered no longer than was necessary. My fingers, comparatively, were restive and my body enlivened.

"I'm sorry about scaring you earlier," he said. "That bear came out of nowhere. Usually, my control is ironclad, but with you here I…" He seemed discomposed by the rest of the thought. "I'm not used to having so little control of myself."

I wasn't quite sure yet who'd disturbed me more—him or the bear. Then that almost-kiss had completely thrown my blood chemistry out of whack. Now my brain was high on a hormonal Molotov cocktail of adrenaline and lust. "The way you scared that bear off…" I said, just as lost for words. "Shit! Tristan, are you even human?"

He gave a light snort. "I'm something of an expert on predators."

Whereas I happened to be something of an expert on movie quotes. "Speaking of predators, you do realize that you missed out on quite possibly the most perfect Schwarzenegger moment ever." When he only blinked in confusion, I couldn't resist saying, in probably the worst Arnie imitation ever attempted, "Get to da *choppah*!"

My accent couldn't have been all that awful, I reasoned, since the lightbulb over his head finally flickered on. "Shame on me." His expression was anything but ashamed. "I obviously spent way too much time outside as a kid."

"Uh-huh, think of all the great film references you've missed out on. I feel sorry for you, actually." I sniggered, relieved that we were settling safely back into our usual badinage.

"The pitfalls of a misspent youth," he said, gesturing for me to climb into the chopper.

Once I was in my seat Tristan helped me fasten my shoulder harness and seatbelt, our fingers brushing together momentarily. I pretended not to notice the searing contact that galvanized my hands promptly into my lap. Instead, I studied the circuit breakers overhead till he shut my door and disappeared from view to do his final walk around.

Fungus. Gym socks. Scoliosis. I replayed these prosaic words over in my mind as a means to relax, but even this unsexy mantra did nothing to deter my hyperactive libido.

Finally, he climbed into the cockpit with me and began going through his pre-startup checks. I'd never felt so aware of a man in my life.

"You ready?" he asked.

I cracked my knuckles with counterfeit bravado. "I've never been more ready."

"That's what she said..."

Chuckling, I gave him a mordant round of applause. "Nice." I'd walked into that one.

"I don't care what you say, everyone loves a he-said-she-said joke."

Stop being so freaking adorable!

His eyes shifted to the digital gauges right before the turbine began to spool audibly. There came a rapid-fire series of ticking sounds. Seconds later, the engine belched loudly into life, the subsequent roar vibrating steadily through the cabin. The four blades began moving counterclockwise, turning ever faster until I couldn't distinguish one rotor from the other. They had all become one large, blurry disc beating loudly overhead.

"Headset on!" he instructed over the clangor of the engine, shoving his helmet over his head. He then hit the power button on my Bose, so that the noise-canceling suddenly cocooned my ears.

This ship, he'd said, was primarily used for government contracts and utility work, hence the cargo hook I'd seen dangling from the underbelly.

"Here we go," he warned, raising the collective pitch.

There was nothing on earth like watching as the skids levitated off the pad as we got underway. Hovering was by far one of the strangest sensations that I had ever experienced. It felt inherently wrong, yet thrilling, to be floating five-feet off the ground as the furious thudding of a giant guillotine whirred overhead.

The plants and long grass at the edge of the pad were by now almost horizontal, flattened by the colossal force of the downwash. Even the nearby trees weren't immune. The branches were waving furious limbs as if caught in a gale. Tristan raised the collective lever even higher, lifting us vertically into the sky like a thundering helium balloon.

"This is incredible!" I yelled, white-knuckling the upholstery.

"Oh, this is nothing…"

That sounded ominous. I whipped my head around to catch the mischievous curve of his smile beneath the black visor. It was really too bad that his helmet concealed most of his face. As he inched the cyclic stick between his legs forward, the rotor disc, likewise, tilted toward the horizon, and we began accelerating into forward flight. My eyes flew wide as we cleared the tall hemlocks that enclosed the pad.

"This is your first time, right?" His voice was smoky and rich as it filtered through the intercom.

"Yup, you're my first."

Tristan's grin broadened, but thankfully he withheld whatever wicked comment I knew was sitting on the tip of his tongue.

"How high are we?"

"About a thousand feet," he replied as the helicopter leveled off. He diligently scanned the horizon like a hawk, answering the many questions I posed with patience. None of which, by tacit agreement, touched on the abnormalities of earlier.

Even with the deep drone of the rotors and the engine, there was a profound silence at altitude. Alaska had the type of beauty that stole even your thoughts away till there was nothing left but immense soul-staggering awe. The fjords winked with prismatic light, throwing the lush archipelagos in stark and variegated relief. The landscape stretched out toward granite ridges tinged indigo with distance. For a moment, I almost forget that Tristan and I weren't the last two people on earth.

I wish we were! Then he'd have no choice but to shag me senseless—for the sake of humanity's survival, of course.

"Beautiful!" It was too underwhelming and colorless a word to do the view any real justice. Like the man beside me.

"Most things in nature that are beautiful are deadly," he said. "Alaska will quite literally take your breath away if you're not careful and don't give her the respect she's due."

"Tristan," I said after a silence, chewing my under lip, "there's something you should know."

"What's that?"

"You look like a giant fly in that helmet."

He gave a snort. "Ladies and gentlemen, this is your captain speaking. I regret to inform you all that your in-flight entertainment has now been suspended indefinitely due to a particularly rude passenger who has, at this time, infiltrated the cockpit to abuse and distract the crew."

"But aren't *you* the in-flight entertainment, *Lord of the Flies*?" I rejoined.

"You do realize I could make you airsick, right?"

"Then I give you fair warning—I won't be cleaning my breakfast off your gauges if you get too cocky with that stick of yours."

He gave a genuine bark of laughter. "I've had to clean worse off my instruments, trust me."

"I don't wanna know." I knew he was talking about bird guts, in part, but there was definitely something salty about our repartee. It kept my cheeks stained with vinous heat.

"Not that I don't love talking about my stick, Evan, but I'm kinda curious about why you really left Palm Beach for Thorne Bay."

I peeked at him from the corner of my eye, deciding to tell the truth. "Because I threw a dart at a map, and it pointed north. So here I am."

He glanced at me briefly, clearly unsure of whether or not I was pulling his leg. "Seriously?"

"Would I lie to you?"

"I can smell a lie, so I wouldn't if I were you."

"In that case yes, I'm serious."

"I think you just became the coolest person I know."

"Or am I crazy?"

"As a box of frogs," he agreed. "So no college?"

"That's just it, who the hell knows what they want to do at eighteen, never mind twenty-one." I sure as hell didn't.

"I did." He shot me a sidelong, teasing look.

"You always knew you wanted to do this?" I said, gesturing to the cyclic between his legs.

"Wiggle sticks? Yes, ma'am."

"Then teach me, Sensei," I said with a flat look. "What's your secret to vocational enlightenment?"

He shrugged. "Just follow your nose."

"Wow, that's deep. You read that in a fortune cookie?"

"Nah, it was on a bumper sticker I saw once, right next to 'I had a life, but my job ate it.' "

I chuckled. "That seems kinda poignant."

"Yup." He adjusted the altimeter and then resumed a serious tone. "So how long are you staying around for?"

"Until I have a clue what to do with myself, I guess. My grandfather decided that I should be a lawyer or a politician. But I've dropped out of college twice, which is why he doesn't really talk to me now except to lecture me."

"Politician?" Tristan's lips compressed in disgust. "You're way too honest to be a politician."

"You mean I have no filter."

"Which has been extremely entertaining thus far." If his visor hadn't been down over his eyes, I was sure I'd have seen him wink at me.

"And you? Are you always honest?"

"We've established that I try to be, but I'm not above using Jedi mind tricks to avoid questions I don't want to answer."

"I had no idea you were such a nerd."

He flashed me another grin. "I'm an aerosexual, of course I'm a nerd." Then, with an imperceptible Obi-Wan Kenobi wave of his left hand, he said, "Tell me all your deepest, darkest secrets."

His Jedi mind trick wasn't all that compelling, but, since I was in a confiding mood, I obliged him. "My secret fear is that I'll disappoint my family, especially my mother. I'm so scared of making the wrong decisions, so for a while there it seemed safer not to make any at all." I didn't want to look back twenty years from now and regret all my mistakes. "I guess your mind trick worked after all."

"The Force is strong with me." The dimple appeared again, where it always did. The *force* of it occasioning all kinds of wild fluttering in my chest.

"Next you'll be telling me you're my father." And actually, he did look a little Darth Vader-ish in that helmet.

Thankfully, he seemed appropriately appalled by the idea. "Firstly, I wasn't a promiscuous seven year old. Secondly, and more importantly, I don't have a single paternal, or fraternal, feeling toward you, Evan. Anyway," he grumbled, steering the conversation back on track, "loads of people more than twice your age still have no idea what they want to do."

"I'd rather not be so directionless."

"Directionless or adventurous? Are you a *glass-half-empty* or a *glass-half-full* kinda girl?"

"Hopefully whichever is more predisposed to making fewer mistakes."

"That's boring. How'd you think penicillin was discovered?"

"Um…"

"Not on purpose, that's how."

"Oh jeez." I was starting to see where he was going with this.

"Microwaves too—another awesome mistake."

"Let's not forget potato chips," I said, rolling my eyes.

He gave a smug nod. "Exactly. I rest my case."

"Which is what exactly? That my life struggles can be quantified in microwaves and potato chips?"

"Patience, young grasshopper, I'm getting to that." The Shaolin smirk climbed higher on his face. "You threw a dart and had the courage to follow through, so that tells me you're the adventurous *glass-half-full* type. I'd say the dart's lead you in a pretty awesome direction so far."

Yeah, and I'd met him into the bargain.

"I reckon your life's purpose is yet to be revealed, so stop worrying."

I was surprisingly stirred by such simple logic and chewed it over as another cluster of islets rushed by the chin bubble beneath my feet. He seemed to have me quite figured out, yet he was all but a mystery to me. There was so much about his elusive character I still needed to figure out. There was a part of him so much like dark matter—some inexplicable and invisible shadow crouching just behind his eyes, but it had no name that I could define it by. It was the part of him that dwelled on the dark side of the moon.

"Enough about me," I said at last. "*Quid pro quo*, Mr. Thorn."

Just like that, the light mood in the cockpit shifted into grey, and his jaw tensed with obvious wariness.

12

JUST FRIENDS

"Let's focus the spotlight on you." My tone was positively saccharine with smugness.

"Let's not," he said.

"Just your garden-variety questions, I promise." If he'd been watching me he'd have seen the lie pulling mischievously at my lips. "Got any sister wives hiding in your closet?"

"So much for garden-variety."

Sighing, I realized that peeling his layers was going to be more like pulling teeth. *But speaking of closets…* "Secretly gay?" My *gaydar* said otherwise, but I couldn't resist.

"Negative," he sighed. "Just boringly heterosexual."

Amen. "So where do your parents live?"

"They're over in Haines Junction in the Yukon Territory." This time he didn't leave me hanging, likely sensing, correctly, that I was going to be tenacious about my onion peeling. "My father and Dean have an uneasy relationship. Too much sordid history between them. I followed my brother out here when he left home. Don't really speak to my old man if I can help it."

"Oh." I knew what that was like. "I'm sorry."

“I’d rather you weren’t sorry for me,” he said behind his inscrutable visor. “There’s no such thing as a perfect family.”

“This I know,” I said wryly, regretting the loss of his good humor. And I had barely gotten past the first layer. “Your parents still married?”

“Yeah, but not happily. My father, whether he’ll admit it or not, never got over his first love—Dean’s mother.”

“Mine are divorced.” It was almost five years ago to the day that Mom and I left Cape Town and moved all the way to Juno Beach to be near her parents. “Dad was never around…but he sure ‘got around’, if you know what I mean.”

“Hmm.” He seemed to mull that over broodily.

A terminal silence prevailed after that, so I diverted the subject safely to aviation. The hour and a half it took us to get to Juneau flew by as we bantered. By unspoken agreement, we avoided all touchy subjects the rest of the flight. It was like the ‘bear incident’ (which was how I had begun to think of it) never actually happened and, sadly, the same could be said about that unfulfilled kiss.

“Welcome to the capital,” said Tristan, banking left to cruise directly over the Gastineau Channel. He directed my gaze to the first peak looming up ahead to our right, Hawthorne Peak, and then explained that the towering land mass to our left was Douglas Island.

Downtown Juneau sat nestled at the base of a colossal snow-capped massif. The steep mountain slopes rose up like giant batters on all sides of the vibrant city. Mount Juneau and Roberts Peak (from which a steady progression of trams crawled to the summit) guarded it on one side and the channel snaked like a moat alongside the other.

The sunlight had, by now, become diffused behind a sheer veil of grey cirrus that stretched overhead across the vivid panorama. It was muted enough that Tristan lifted his dark visor up out of the way and, instead, replaced it with the amber one behind it so that I could now see his face clearly. *Much better.*

There was no longer as much opportunity to shoot the shit now that we'd entered a hive of activity. There were cruise ships, yachts, eagles, gulls, and helicopters wherever I looked, and the common traffic advisory was blowing up with radio chatter. Even so, Tristan still managed to point out various attractions to me as I gaped and nodded.

"There's no road to Juneau," he said. "The only way in is by sea or by air."

We'd made such good time getting here that Tristan decided on a detour over Taku, one of the world's few advancing glaciers. Then we were off to Mendenhall Glacier so that I got to see it lolling out like a jagged, blue tongue into a lake of icebergs.

Shortly afterward, we beelined it to Juneau International, and landed on the general aviation ramp beside another helicopter. Once the fuel order had been placed, we headed over to the pilot lounge to grab a coffee.

"The weather's a lot trickier here than in Ketchikan." Tristan then explained that the Fairweather Ranges (ironically named) and the Boundary Ranges tended to funnel the lower pressure and moisture in from the Bering Sea and Gulf of Alaska, which meant that the visibility here could drop in a matter of minutes. "I had to spend the night on an ice field this time last year because the visibility dropped so suddenly," he went on, "and we were socked in with dense fog till later the next day."

"Where'd you sleep?"

"In one of the dog camps."

I'd always wanted to go dogsledding. "Then you must not mind dogs very much, although I guess you didn't have much of a choice that night."

"I love dogs, actually." One corner of his mouth curled enigmatically. "But I'm rather more of a wolfman, to be honest."

I could feel my brow furrowing curiously, bemused by the strange expression he wore. "So you spooned some huskies that night because you got caught in the fog. Sounds like you dodged a bullet."

"Yup, there were two helicopter accidents last year due to low vis."

"First the bird through the windscreen, and now I have to worry about fog? I'm not sure I'm getting back in that chopper with you, Tristan."

"Nature's unpredictable and fickle." That wicked grin lit his face again. "Which is why mother nature is a woman."

I rolled my eyes and followed him to the flight planning room. I leaned in to peer over his shoulder at the computer screen as he diligently checked the weather.

Mistaking my nearness for meteorological interest, Tristan began explaining what each graph meant and how it pertained to our flight for the day. When I stifled a yawn, however, he stopped himself and chuckled apologetically. "I'm boring you, aren't I?"

"No," I deadpanned, "I love talking about the weather. You make it sound so exciting." And I promptly ruined that claim with yet another unladylike yawn.

"Well, what would you rather talk about?" The crooked smile was back in place as he closed the internet tab.

Considering the possibilities, I followed him over to where the leather recliners faced the tv. But neither one of us spared Fox news any attention.

There was really only one thing I was dying to discuss. "Back at the hangar—"

"Look, the bear gave me a death-stare and all I did was return the favor. I don't know how else to—"

"No," I interjected, cheeks scarlet, "I mean…what happened *after*." When he'd almost kissed me.

His gaze narrowed thoughtfully as realization dawned, ostensibly aided by the telltale blush spreading over my cheeks. "You mean what *didn't* happen." His eyes dropped momentarily to my mouth.

I gave a small nod, biting my under lip uncertainly.

"I shouldn't have put you in that position, Evan."

Telling myself to woman-up, I gathered up every ounce of steel in my bones and said, "What if…what if that's a position I'm not opposed to being in again?" I wet my lips and the movement drew his gaze again.

After a lengthy silence, in which my heart palpitated so nervously that I was sure he could hear it, Tristan released a pent-up sigh. "You *should* be opposed. I like you too much to drag you into my world."

"Your world?" I felt my forehead pucker in consternation. "Because we're separate species?" I scoffed.

"You have no idea."

"A kiss can't possibly be all that complicated?"

"But it is," he said quietly. "Because I'll want more." He dragged his fingers tiredly down his jaw. "After the bear I wasn't thinking straight. For your sake, Ev, all I can offer is friendship."

"Friendship," I said woodenly, wondering if Nicole was at the root of his sudden change of heart. Yanked from the brink of a kiss and then unceremoniously friend-zoned all in one morning? This man was giving me such whiplash. "For my sake?"

"Yes. I hope I haven't ruined that friendship already?"

"No." With effort, I blinked away tears. "Of course not."

This time I almost welcomed the interruption when his phone suddenly rang into the uncomfortable silence. The glaciologists were here. I felt sure the brittle smile on my face would shatter at any moment, but, thankfully, it held. If Tristan could school his features so well then so could I. With an easy smile, he introduced me to the scientists (as well as a woman from the Forest Service). Once airborne, I laughed and bantered with them as though my heart wasn't black and bruised. The morning slipped by without further incident. We flew from one waypoint to another, fending off bugs, trudging through muskegs and marching up glaciers. We dutifully gathered ice samples and measured permafrost until the weather forced our retreat.

All throughout, I'd tried my best to act the happy idiot, but Tristan's penetrative gaze appeared to find every crack in my smile. The undercurrent between us was thick with tension. There seemed to be a looming presence pacing hungrily between us, pawing the ground restlessly. The dark matter—all the unspoken and invisible shadows between us.

"Just friends?" Mom's tone was dubious.

"Yeah." I was lying on my bed, the phone on the pillow beside me as I watched the anarchy of moths and bugs leaping at the light pouring from my window.

It was black as dog's guts tonight. The moon was blotted out by the cloud bank that had followed us back from Juneau. The Full Thunder Moon, it was called—or would be in three days. The brief fulmination that followed the distant rumbling seemed to reinforce that fact. Or foretoken something ominous. Tristan had said that thunderstorms were incredibly rare here—guess I must have brought that phenomenon up from Florida with me.

"Hmm," Mom continued after a loud yawn, "he sounds confused." It was almost midnight in Florida. "If all he wants is friendship then why the hell did he almost kiss you?"

"That's what I'm saying." I suspired loudly. "He implied his life is complicated."

"Definitely a woman. That Nicole person you told me about?"

"Yeah, maybe. I don't get it, Mom, she seems like she'd be

nothing but high maintenance." And he seemed too smart to be seduced by a pretty face with an attitude problem.

"Well, Ev, then it sounds like it's not your problem." Another yawn.

"And it sounds like you should go to bed."

"I am in bed."

"Goodnight, Mom," I chuckled.

After one more "I love you" she finally signed off. It was just me and the music of the nighttime after that. And the storm brewing outside.

Tristan's card was now stowed away in my journal for safe-keeping.

"P.S. I like weird," he'd said.

I sighed. "But not enough, evidently."

After I'd reread it once again, I set it aside and opened the page it had bookmarked for me. A drawing of Tristan that I'd sketched from memory. What I'd felt for Andy, back in West Palm Beach, I realized now, was a tepid infatuation compared to the napalm that Tristan excited in my veins.

My journal was filled with poems and sketches of all sorts, including landscapes, but I loved best to draw faces and hands. His face still needed some finishing touch-ups before it did any justice to the man himself. Overall I was pleased with the result. Especially the shape of his eyes. They wanted only some azure shading around the pupils and they'd be perfect. *Or yellow*, came a whisper of premonition.

I'd chalked up the color change to a trick of the light—suppressed it more like—and convinced myself he'd been hiding unusually sharp canines behind some falsies that may have fallen out during the bear scare. Maybe he was really self-conscious about it. Maybe he had severe gingivitis too and that accounted for the bleeding. I just didn't fucking know anymore.

Sighing, I forced those tricky puzzles from my mind and

shaded his eyes a little more till I was satisfied I'd replicated them to the best of my ability—even adding the gold flecks.

As for my eyes… Leaving the sketch on my bedside, I moved to stand in front of the bathroom mirror to study the unremarkable features of the girl that stared back at me. I decided my mouth was too demure by half to be considered pretty, but at least my hazel eyes were flecked with enough green to make them interesting. Larger than average, they were probably my best feature, and the limbal rings were darkly prominent where they outlined each iris. My face was symmetrical enough, I thought, but not beautiful. Nothing like Nicole's celestial features.

In the midst of this critical study came the sudden confident rapping of knuckles against my door. My heart lurched into an excited gallop, convinced of who was at my door. "Tristan!" it clamored loudly.

13

JUNGLE JUICE

"Chris," I said, instantly tightening my smile in case it fell right off my face. "Um, hi."

"Hey, neighbor." He was wearing a vintage Star Wars shirt, looking hopeful as he shifted nervously on his feet. "A couple of us were…uh…gonna go hang out at the cove. Wanna come?" The last was asked with a thumb thrown over his shoulder towards his truck.

I was about to decline, but my phone forestalled me with a text message.

"Was that Darth Vader?" He perked up with excitement.

I answered with a distracted nod.

The text was from Melissa. "Guess who just showed up at Forse Cove!"

"Sorry, Chris, one sec." I held up a finger before turning around to type my reply. "Who?"

"Come and see for yourself," she replied smugly. "Is Chris there yet? I told him to drag your hermit ass over here."

What was the alternative? Stare at my ceiling and brood all night? No, thanks. I pocketed my phone and turned back to my neighbor. "I'd love to go."

"Try the jungle juice." Without waiting for a yes or no, Chris unscrewed the top off a flask he pulled from his back pocket and poured a generous shot into my Solo cup. "You'll like it," he promised, watching as I took a wary sip.

It was a fiery concoction of battery acid and rum that I tried not to spew back in his face. I thanked him with a gag and a grimace and undertook not to be too irritated with how close he was standing next to me.

Gary, Chris' pervy friend, chose that moment to sidle up to me and fling a sloppy arm over my shoulder. I promptly removed it. When Chris and Gary (or was it Larry?) became momentarily distracted by a tall brunette strolling past us, I surreptitiously emptied my red cup into a nearby bush (which might have made me guilty of herbicide) and then filled it with water instead. Water, I thought proudly, that was cleverly disguised as vodka.

Melissa, having noticed the turfing of the battery acid, shot me a covert grin. Of Tristan, however, I had seen nothing and I was beginning to think she'd lured me out under false pretenses. But apart from Gary's (or Larry's) boomerang arm, it was actually turning out to be a pretty awesome night. I'd already planned on getting a ride home with Melissa, who was the self-proclaimed designated driver, because Chris was already well-lubricated on firewater.

It was a beautiful night and only a handful of Thorne Bay denizens were out to appreciate the gibbous moon floating high over the water. It mantled the ripples with bands of silver. It seemed to me an otherworldly moon with its strange halo of diaphanous clouds. I was suddenly stuck with sentiment, thinking about all the amazing things that had happened since I'd left Florida. If someone had told me, at the beginning of the year, that by

July I'd be watching an Alaskan moon rise over the bay with my new friends, I'd have never believed them.

Melissa nudged me suddenly, distracting me from the view, and gestured over toward a group of people that had appeared around some rocks. My stomach instantly twisted with disappointment as they neared and the moonlight caught each of their faces. Dean was one among them, but not Tristan.

This brother was, admittedly, something to look at, and so I took the opportunity to study him because he was by no means a lesser exemplification of male beauty. As though he'd felt my scrutiny, Dean turned to look right at me, instantly putting the kibosh on my curiosity. Sighing, I shifted my attention half-heartedly to Chris who had been telling me a joke I'd hardly heard.

"Whoa," Melissa whispered with another poke at my ribs, "he can't stop looking at you."

"Gary?" I asked distastefully.

"No"—she made an impatient sound—"Dean."

I looked over at Tristan's brother, and then just as quickly snapped my head back around to my friend. "Shit! What the hell for?"

She sniggered into her cup so that all I could see was the knowing hike of her brows. "You know why."

With a blank stare, I tilted my cup of pretend vodka to my lips.

"You're a hottie, Ev. Shit, I stare at you all the time and I'm straight."

I hadn't meant to dispute that with a fit of coughing, but somehow I'd managed to snort up a lungful of water. Clearly, I struggled with compliments. As I bent over gasping for air, Melissa gave my back a patronizing pat, laughing unrepentantly. When I raised my watering eyes back up it was to see Dean's mouth curving slyly as he watched me make a mess of myself. He wasn't the only one who'd witnessed me inhaling my drink—Tristan had joined the group.

My stomach somersaulted excitedly as I met his eyes, but instead of walking over, as I'd half-expected, he only acknowledged me with a cursory nod and continued talking to the blonde standing beside him. Nicole.

Standing? Pfft. There was far more clinging and leaning than actual standing on her part.

My throat constricted as he bent his head to her, those blood red lips practically wrapping themselves around his ear as she whispered. *Next thing she'll be tonguing him, the tart.* But that was unfair of me. If she really was his girlfriend, which seemed very likely now, then she had every right to do all manner of things with her tongue. Bile settled bitterly into my gut.

Nicole must have sensed me watching too, or had noticed Tristan 'greeting' me earlier, because she fired one helluva stink eye in my direction. That was interesting. Was her touchy-feely display more a means to mark her territory than to show affection? Either way, watching them together had turned my gut and instantly soured my good mood. But I didn't want to make Melissa and Matt leave early on my behalf, so I pulled my big girl socks up and resolved to ignore the couple.

My only consolation was that I'd not seen Tristan smile at her even once, nor had he returned her embraces; the canoodling was all, admittedly, pretty one-sided. Still, I decided then and there that Tristan was off limits and I was *not* going to be doing any more sketches of him. My diary would, from now on, be a Tristan-free zone. And so, figuratively, would my shower be.

Sometime during my lovelorn looks and inner monologues, I'd lost track of Melissa's whereabouts. The sneaky little wench had vanished by the time I dragged my eyes away from Tristan to look for her. I waited for what felt like an hour (but was likely only five minutes), studiously avoiding Tristan while my poor ears were being filled with Chris' nattering. Melissa was probably off snogging Matt's face off in the dark somewhere, and getting pine needles in unfortunate places. She'd be back soon, I hoped, and then we could finally go.

Surely five minutes was enough time for them to 'do it like they do on the Discovery Channel'? I was tired of removing Gary's hand and listening to Chris' verbal diarrhea, so I figured I was fully within my right to call in the friend card. My thumbnail was hooked impatiently behind my eyetooth as I pressed my phone to my ear, waiting for the ringing that never came. It went straight to voicemail.

I turned my back to Chris, not that he could hear me over Gary's horrific belching anyway. "Mel, you deserter," I hissed after the tone had beeped. "You've literally left me to a pack of drunken wolves!" Then I jammed my finger at the screen and hung up.

"Not all of us *wolves* are drunk," a voice drawled from behind me.

I squeaked as I whirled around. How had I not seen or heard Dean sneak up on me? The man was built like a brick shit-house, for God's sake. "Sorry, didn't see you there…" *Eavesdropping.*

"Evan, is it?" His dark eyes and wily grin were strangely hyena-like.

"Yes." I only barely stopped myself from appending that with a 'sir'.

Chris had made himself scarce as soon as Dean had joined us, unlike Gary who held his ground and stood swaying dangerously between us. But Dean's cold glare finally seemed to blast through the booze fog in Gary's brain. With a pained little hiccup, he eventually staggered off, probably to go find Chris or pass out in a bush. Hopefully a bush with nettles and fire ants.

He took my cold hand confidently in his, his palm like a furnace. "I'm Dean."

I know. I nodded, pulling my hand safely away.

"Can I refill your water for you, Evan?"

"This isn't…I'm actually drinking…" I dropped my gaze into the red cup. *Busted.*

"It's okay. I'm not much of a drinker myself."

What? You don't drink the blood of newborn babies? Better not, I decided. Even Tristan was somewhat sensitive about the cult jokes lately.

"Like to stay in control."

Like his brother. What was it with these Thorn brothers and their control freak tendencies?

"So my little brother's caught your eye." It wasn't a question.

Little brother? There was nothing "little" about Tristan.

Dean, I noticed furtively, was looking sternly between Tristan and I.

Here I'd thought I'd been sly about my unreciprocated mooning. I couldn't very well deny it because my stupid blush incriminated me instantly. In cases such as these, I determined, silence was the only answer. Damn, he unnerved me. "We're just friends." The word tasted like lemons.

"Relax," he said, eyeing my fidgety hands. "Look all you like, it's nothing to me."

"Gee, thanks," I finally mumbled. *What a jerk.* He was right, it was no business of his where I bloody looked.

"What *does* concern me, however, is the way that *he* keeps looking at *you.*" Yup, that definitely stuck in his craw. "Neither of you are fooling anyone with your *friendly* looks."

"And that's a problem because Nicole's his girlfriend?" I asked, forcing restless eyes up at him.

Dean smirked. "Nice try. You should ask him that."

"He seems a little busy." That awful lump from this morning

rose into my throat as I recalled the moment he'd nearly kissed me.

Dean's brows pleated. "He's not so much busy—" with an impatient sigh "—as obligated."

"What does that mean?"

"I wouldn't worry about it, Evan." His lips compressed as though talking had become a nuisance. "He'll either make it your business or he won't."

Was Nicole preggers or something? Was it *that* kind of obligation?

"And I don't have to warn you not to get on Blondie's bad side," Dean said, throwing a nod at Nicole, "because it's too late for that."

Yeah. I was already there. "Does she even have a good side?"

"Nope," he said candidly. "And, unfortunately for you, you've already established your rank in the pack."

"Huh?"

"The pack of 'drunken wolves'," he answered.

Ugh. I'd almost forgotten that he'd heard me.

"So guess where timidity gets you in the hierarchy." When I made no answer he took a step closer. "Want some advice?"

Okay, creepy-hot-guy-who-I-barely-know. "Uh, sure."

"Keep your eyes up," he warned, the words almost too low to hear. Then he backed away, eyes flashing with amusement.

At first, I thought the smirk was at my expense, but when I followed his gaze I was confronted by Tristan's. There seemed to be a silent argument raging across the space that lay between them—the crossfire in which I stood.

Nicole had also noticed that she no longer held Tristan's fulminating attention, so she promptly added her black scowl to theirs.

Yeah, this is getting weird. "Sooo, I'm gonna go find Melissa." I offered Dean one of those awkward smiles I was good at, wished him a good night, and then turned to scuttle away while ignoring Tristan altogether.

"Evan…"

I glanced over my shoulder. "Hmm?"

"Melissa's over there." He gestured to the makeshift parking lot.

"Uh, thanks." I removed my hoodie and tied it around my waist, finding it suddenly too uncomfortable and hot against my skin. "Seeya."

"Seeya," he mimicked.

I found Melissa exactly where Dean said she'd be. "Don't you answer your phone anymore?"

"Battery died." Her brows arched inquisitively. "Are you okay? You look flushed."

That she could tell how hot and bothered I was, even in the dark, only exacerbated the color further. "I'm fine, let's just go."

Melissa looked past my shoulder, grinning.

Since I could still feel two heavy gazes on my back, I had no need to see for myself what amused her now.

"Hot damn, girl. You just got eye-poked by two hotties."

"Jeez, Mel, shut up!" Remembering their bionic hearing, I pulled her away, trying to smother her words with a desperate hand.

"Sure you wanna leave?" She easily dodged my frantic hands. "I think they want to know you biblically."

"Shh!" I then begged Matt to leash his woman, but he only chuckled and shrugged in surrender.

"Someone wants a bit of the ole in and out," Mel went on. "Some lust and thrust."

"I'm gonna kill you!" As soon as she got me home I would literally strangle her.

When she began to sing *Sexual Healing* I sprinted after her toward the car, ready to tackle her if necessary. Maybe after I'd smacked her around a bit, we'd have a serious talk about the girl code.

A fatal urge drew my gaze to Tristan one last time. He wore a strange look of determination that, for some reason, heated my cheeks still further and distracted me all the way home. A look that had held a dark, unfathomable promise.

14

THE PATIENT WOLF

I had just closed my door as the storm, that had been hovering broodily in the northwest, finally rolled in. The sound of it was strangely soothing. A remembrance of home. After my mother, the storms were what I missed most about Florida.

It was late, I realized, checking my watch as I trudged into the bathroom, but luckily I wasn't working until tomorrow evening, so I could afford a lazy sleep in.

Not till I had almost scoured the enamel from my teeth did I relent and gentle the strokes of my toothbrush. But it wasn't the cloying taste of Chris' jungle juice, still clinging to my tonsils, that had me feeling so splenetic. It was the fact that I was *still* thinking about Tristan. I uttered a groan of disgust and spat the toothpaste rudely into the basin.

The unexpected knock on the door startled me suddenly. I hoped it wasn't Chris again. I wasn't in the mood to fend off drunken flirtations. Simply ignoring the knock was an option that briefly crossed my mind, but my lights were still on and Sia's lyrical rasping filled my room. All proof enough to any determined visitor that I hadn't yet gone to sleep.

I marched impatiently to my door and yanked it open. My

ready rebuff died instantly on my lips. "Tristan." I stood there gaping at him, stunned.

"Saw your lights on…" he said, rubbing agitatedly at the back of his neck as though he'd been drawn to my light like a moth, knowing he might be burned.

I opened my mouth to speak, but when nothing sensible struck my tongue I merely closed it again. Clearly, I had no talent for accurately guessing who was behind my door.

"I'm kinda disappointed." He cocked his head ruefully. "No welcoming condom confetti this time?"

"I'm all out of condoms." I folded my arms over my chest. *And humor.* It was late and suspicion had rapidly replaced my shock. Despite what I'd said this morning, I wasn't feeling any inclination toward friendship. Not now. Not for a man who'd nearly kissed me despite the reality of a scary girlfriend who was very possibly pregnant.

The deluge was, meantime, coming down in slanting sheets as the wind drove it hard, throwing fine droplets into the air to settle at his lashes. Each tiny bead gleamed mesmerically like citrine under the outside light.

"Um, it's raining," said Tristan archly, giving a sexy flick of his head to clear his sodden hair from his eyes.

I girded my loins and told myself he wasn't all that sexy really, but lying to myself was about as effective as a knitted condom. Damn his pretty eyes! I could feel the ice calving off my cold resolve every second he remained standing patiently at my door, looking all wet and sexy. "I see that. What's your point?" I asked him tartly. He was partly under the eave, so I didn't feel too bad about making him stand outside.

"My *point* is that I'd like to talk to you."

"That's why you're skulking out here?" I peered over toward his truck, expecting to see Nicole there, but the passenger seat was blessedly empty. "To talk in the rain?"

He lowered his gaze pointedly to his drenched jeans where most of the water struck him slantways. "Preferably not in the rain." Then he moved in closer beneath the eave to lean a muscled shoulder on the doorframe. "And, for the record, Spencer, I'm not skulking. I come bearing gifts." He then produced a pair of rubber boots he'd been concealing behind his broad back. "Ketchikan sneakers. Better late than never."

"Thanks." I resented the smile nudging the corner of my lips. And I resented the fact that he looked as good wet as he did dry. I would have looked like a drowned sewer rat if it had been me standing where he was. "I didn't realize Thorn Aviation does midnight deliveries too." I took the boots from him and placed them just inside the doorway.

"We don't."

"Then what do you really want, Tristan?"

"Now there's a loaded question." He dropped his gaze fleetingly to my lips before releasing a sigh. "For now, just to use a towel please."

"Fine." Despite myself, I was intrigued by his sudden appearance. I bit the inside corner of my lip and I stepped aside, holding the door open for him to enter. "But you could've just Jedi mind tricked me, you know."

Out came that skewed smile to shake my foundation yet again. "Inviting me in should be your choice, not mine. Although I promise to be the perfect gentleman."

I narrowed my eyes at him and said, "What's that saying about *gentlemen* being nothing more than patient wolves?" I closed the door after he'd stepped across my threshold.

His eyes darkened appreciatively. "A wolf will never waste his patience on something not worth having."

"And how might this wolf behave if she lets him in?"

"Unpredictably," he admitted.

"Then I won't ask about those sharp teeth."

The green seemed to brighten in his eyes. "Then I won't tell you what I'll do with them."

"I warn you, Little Red Riding Hood got the better of the wolf in the end."

He gave a lift of his shoulders. "Depends on which variant of the story you tell—the sanitized version or the original."

Wise-ass. He was right though. Originally Little Red had been devoured in her grandmother's cottage. I had a feeling he'd just countervail whatever I threw at him (not a man to play chess with, obviously), so I gave a roll of my eyes, held my tongue (since his folktale knowledge evidently eclipsed mine), and pointed to the bathroom. "Help yourself to a towel."

He left his muddy boots at the door and prowled into my bathroom, but instead of grabbing the fresh towel I'd expected him to use, he reached into the shower and, from the towel bar on the wall, lifted the one I'd used earlier. I angled a narrowed look overhead, from which I imagined the universe was smirking down at me. My earlier promise of keeping even my shower (where I often thought of him) a 'Tristan-free' zone seemed to taunt me now. Because there he was, in my shower. *Very funny.*

Actually, the thought of Tristan, even a fully clothed Tristan, in my shower was enough to enkindle my *nether-verse.* Taking a bolstering breath to quell my hormones and clear my head, I headed over to the mini fridge. "Can I get you a drink?" I called out to him, deciding to be hospitable.

"Sure," he replied, emerging from my bathroom a little dryer.

Apart from soy milk, which I knew he distrusted, there was little else to offer him but wine, so I grabbed two stemless glasses and, opening the bottle on my countertop, poured us each a glass of my favorite Malbec.

When I turned around, a glass in each hand, it was to see him standing by my bedside, his head lowered and his eyes skimming curiously across my open journal. Specifically at the sketch of his own face! *Aargh!*

What kind of congenital twit would leave her diary lying open as if it was nothing but a grocery list?! My sketches were like glimpses into the private vaults of my mind and heart. There were all kinds of weird drawings and doodles in there that I wouldn't even have allowed Mom to see.

There was a pensive crease to his brow, but it vanished when he finally lifted his eyes from my most private pages. Inscrutable as ever, he moved casually toward the chair beside my dresser and sat down with a nonchalant arm thrown behind his head, scrutinizing the room as though he hadn't just seen himself in my pencil sketch; seen me naked, figuratively speaking.

"That for me?" He looked meaningfully at the glass in my hand (that I miraculously hadn't dropped) as I continued to stand there scarlet-faced.

Making a tiny, strangled squeak of confirmation, I inched forward and held his glass out to him in such a way as to avoid his fingers touching mine. The crimson liquid sloshed up the sides as I trembled. It looked like we were going to pretend that he hadn't just sort of inadvertently invaded my privacy? Which was fine by me.

"Thanks." He took it, clinked his glass against mine, and then lifted the rim to his lips, locking our gazes as he tasted the wine.

I cleared my throat nervously. "So this is just a friendly visit?" Were midnight calls ever *just* friendly?

"I don't know, to be honest. I just kinda found myself here." His mouth tightened with self-deprecation, and his eyes bored into mine as though willing me to understand something. "Does that make sense?"

"Not really."

"Maybe you're right." That humorless half smile materialized to taunt me.

It seemed that nothing between us made sense. Mostly our 'relationship' was based on a confusion of *halves* and *almosts*—almost kisses and half smiles. It was exhausting. He was mercurial and so infuriatingly mysterious about himself. Well, I wasn't going to play games with him. He could lead this little 'visit' wherever he wanted and I would try to hold my cards close to my heart until he bared his.

He regarded me quietly. "What are you thinking about, Evan? I never know what's going on in your head unless your filter fails you."

"Good," I said, "because I never know what the hell *you're* thinking about either." *Like right now.* Too bad his filter never failed him.

"I was just thinking we should go for a walk down to the lake. It stopped raining."

Tristan had so commanded my attention that I'd not even noticed the storm's passage. All I heard now were the insects chirping outside. "What about the bears?" I asked.

"I think I've proven I'm pretty handy around bears."

"Right," I scoffed, "the *Bear Whisperer*." He still hadn't explained his frightening metamorphosis—the canines especially.

He ran his thumbnail absently over the stubble between his chin and under lip—up and down, lost in thought. Finally, he said, "So, d'you wanna go? For a walk, I mean."

I did, despite that nighttime walks in the Alaskan wilderness seemed insanely reckless, but I knew I shouldn't, for reasons beyond the dangers that the forest posed. Being alone with him in the dark did *not* seem like a good idea. *As opposed to alone in your room where there's a bed at hand?*

He should never have come to my room tonight! Even if Nicole wasn't terrifying—which she absolutely was—I was no home-wrecker. And even if I was one, Nicole's home was not one I'd ever choose to wreck; not unless I was suicidal. That chick had *bunny boiler* written all over her. Had he seriously not watched *Fatal Attraction*?

Anyway, the point was that we were here alone, which wasn't a safe situation to be in, at least not in the 'biblical' sense. But at least in my room, unlike the seductive shadows outside, the lights were obtrusive and glowering.

"I think we'd better not," I finally answered. At which point I plonked myself onto my bed, trying to look comfortable. Belatedly, though, I realized what this maneuver might infer. I didn't understand the male mind all too well, but what if, in man code, my sitting on the bed like this was an invitation for him to occupy *Vagistan*?

Tristan's eyes had followed mine, taking in the rumpled bed.

My heart leapt with panic. I wiped a clammy hand on my knee and watched as his mouth compressed. What was he so irked about? Did he think I was going to throw myself at him? *As if I had the guts.* "Relax," I said to the floor, panic making my voice sound harsh, "I'm not about to jump your bones."

He purposefully rose from the chair, dominating the small room with his height, and carefully set his glass on the dresser. My eyes flew wide as he prowled to the window beside my bed.

"It's not *your* self-control I'm worried about," he murmured, watching me in the reflection of the glass.

"Then why are you here?"

He pushed away from the windowsill and came to stand next to me, pausing, as if my nearness would inspire an answer.

Too close! Yet, at the same time, he wasn't close enough. My eyebrows were buried in my hairline, I was sure of it, and my bones felt like hot custard under that gaze. My blood had instantly left my face and drained away to *Vagistan.* I swallowed noisily, running my tongue over my parched lips as he studied my mouth again, a furrow pinching the skin between his brows.

"I've been asking myself that same question for a while now," he said. "A man doesn't just randomly show up on a woman's doorstep in the middle of the night, Evan. Not unless he… unless *she's* gotten under his skin."

I held myself so still that even my heart paused to hear his words.

"And a woman," he went on, "doesn't just sketch a man's face into her journal unless it means something, right?" When I only blinked mutely, he continued, "Or does it mean nothing, Evan? I'm trying to make sense over here, help me out."

"Friendship. That's all you said it could mean."

He gave a curt nod. "Can I ask you something?"

I offered a slow nod.

"If you had a secret that was so colossal that it kept you from opening up to someone because you know they couldn't possibly accept you for who you really are, would you even try to get close? What would be the point, right?"

I hadn't expected a theoretical question. "I honestly don't know, Tristan. What type of secret is this, hypothetically?"

"The dangerous kind. The type that isn't only yours to share. The breed of freaky that alienates everyone *normal*."

"But if it kept me from loving…?"

"And trusting," he added. "How do you trust someone enough to get really close. Close enough for them to hurt you? You can't love properly until you trust, right?"

Could a person love without trusting first? Was it like the chicken and the egg? Which came first? "I guess not. I don't have a simple answer, but, for what it's worth, I think life's all about taking risks." Geez, this seemed like a heavy discussion to be getting into at this late hour.

"A risk isn't worth taking if it means possibly hurting someone who gets too close."

"Follow your nose. Make mistakes. Isn't that what you told me?"

"If I had a normal nose I might follow it."

"I thought you said *normal* was boring."

"It is, but most people hate what's different. They fear different. I've never wanted to be normal till this moment, Evan." He touched me with nothing but his eyes, exotic green caressing my face.

"I don't want you to be normal."

His gaze held mine as if he meant to peer into my soul. "What would you have me be then?"

"Just yourself."

"Then I have one last question for you."

Oh boy.

"Do you believe in monsters?"

15

EAU DE WEREWOLF

Do I believe in monsters? "If by monsters you mean psychopaths and sickos," I said, "then yes. I believe the world is full of monsters."

He heaved a sigh. "No, I was referring more to myths and legends."

"Like vampires?"

"Yes. Think they exist?"

"I wish."

"Really?" One brow was lifted dubiously. "You like glittery teenage boys?"

"No." I pulled a face. My literary needs were satisfied only by the Stoker, King, and Rice versions of the genre rather than the fluffy, sparkling types. "I'm more of a Lestat de Lioncourt kinda girl."

"Who?" he asked, looking puzzled.

"Only the most seductive, terrible, and unapologetic being in modern literature."

He raised a brow that implied I had questionable taste in literature. "So you don't actually believe in vampires?"

"No, I do. People can literally suck the life out of each other. It's despicable and—"

"Again," he said, chuckling, "not what I meant." He lowered himself onto the bed beside me, not close enough to send my heart into a panic, but it certainly didn't calm me to be sitting within reach of him. So caught up in that strange fire pulsing behind the green of his eyes, I almost didn't hear his next words. "I wonder what you'd do if I turned into a monster right now."

"If you grew fangs and turned into a bat I'd hang you in my shower." *Le sigh.* My shower was exactly where I wanted him.

"No," he said, biting back a smile, "something hairier."

"Sasquatch?"

"A werewolf."

"What would I do?" I repeated thoughtfully. "Probably hope to God that bear spray works just as well at repelling werewolves."

"It does," he replied, mouth quirking. "We hate the stuff as much as the bears do."

"So you're a werewolf, are you? Well, that explains everything."

Tristan folded his arms behind his head and leaned back against the headboard to gauge my reaction. Although his mouth was curled with humor, his gaze was strangely alert.

"Now that you mention it," I said, deciding to play along, "I did catch a whiff of wet dog when you walked in."

"That's just my cologne."

"Attract the bitches does it?" *Like Nicole.*

He shrugged.

"I bet fleas on the crotch isn't fun though."

"Fleas," he replied with a smirk, "are never sexy."

"But a werewolf on the loose is serious business." I tapped my bottom lip contemplatively. "A girl might worry about her virtue."

"I would if I was her."

My voice lowered to match his, deeply affected by the intoxicating sexual tension waxing between us. "What's a girl to do?"

"That's what I'd like to know."

"I could call animal control."

"You could, but werewolves are cunning. And fast."

"And has this wolf—" taking a bolstering sip of my wine "—been neutered perchance?"

Tristan's grin darkened provocatively. "No, I don't let just anyone near my *undercarriage*, Evan."

Don't look at his crotch. Don't look at his crotch. Don't look at his...

"I'm glad we got that outta the way," he murmured languidly, moving closer. "It's never an easy subject to broach."

"Neutering?" My pulse spiked at his nearness.

"Werewolves."

"Uh-huh." I snapped my eyes shut for a moment to exorcise the lust from my brain. "Um, Tristan?"

"Yes, Evan?"

"Can I ask *you* something now?" Not that I hadn't enjoyed his attempts at lightening the mood with sexy werewolf humor, but it was time to get down to brass tacks before the flirting lead anywhere else.

He bent a knee and angled his hips toward me, resting his hand between us, next to mine, so that our fingers were nearly touching. "What do you want to know?"

"Is Nicole your girlfriend?" I asked, my eyes pleading for him to discredit the idea.

There was a heavy silence in which he appeared taken aback, ostensibly having not expected that to be my question. But when the pause stretched a little further, attenuating awkwardly, I decided he was trying to figure out how best to answer. And *that*, in and of itself, told me all I needed to know.

"Never mind," I muttered crossly, "you pretty much just

confirmed it." So why the everlasting fuck had we nearly kissed?! "Go home, Tristan."

"Wait, I haven't confirmed anything." His voice was hard. "And I wouldn't be here now, alone with you, if she was my girlfriend."

"Does *she* know she's not your girlfriend?"

"She knows exactly how I feel, Evan." Another long sigh.

I scooted away a little and folded my arms in an "I'm listening" posture.

"Her father and mine," he began, "sort of had an understanding."

Since he seemed to be battling with how best to word his odd explanation, I decided to help him along. "What, like an arranged marriage or something?" Although I'd meant it ironically, his face colored the instant I said the words and I suddenly realized I'd hit closer to home than either of us had expected. "Omigod! You *are* in a cult!"

His eyes flashed with irritation. "I'm *not* in a goddamn cult and she *isn't* my fiancé. And for your information lots of respected religions still practice arranged marriages, thank you."

"So you're not in a cult," I allowed dubiously. "Is she pregnant then?"

"No." His jaw tightened as if I'd just lampooned him.

"So what's this 'understanding' between your father and Nicole's?"

"It's an alliance," he gritted out impatiently.

"Sounds like an arranged marriage to me."

"Evan," he growled, "it's complicated."

"No, it's ridiculous is what it is." My jaw was clenched so hard I was sure my teeth would crack. "God, it would have just been easier if you *were* a damn werewolf!"

His laughter erupted unexpectedly. Just like that the heat of choler evaporated from his eyes. It was like a contagion, drawing a grudging smile from me. I tried to suppress it, but, in the end, I gave up and joined in his mirth.

"Be careful what you wish for," he said when his laughter had finally wound down. "Truth is sometimes stranger than fiction."

So he wasn't engaged or even dating Nicole and nor was she pregnant. Could that be enough for me? "Well, whenever you're ready to share your *truth* with me, Tristan, I'll be ready to listen."

He seemed to want to say something, but his mouth flattened in protest.

I gave a loud sigh. "Just promise me something, please."

"Depends on what it is."

"Promise me that the next time you knock on my door it's because you're absolutely sure what you want from me."

"I promise."

"Good." I nodded, pulling my hair over my shoulder to twist the strands nervously. By now he'd finished his wine, so there was really no longer any need for him to stay. "So what now?" I asked, little knowing just how reactive those three little words would be.

"Now?" One corner of his mouth lifted. His pupils began to widen, the green around them becoming lambent with something that both thrilled and scared me. "Isn't every promise sealed with a kiss?"

I squirmed nervously as he watched my mouth with keen, male interest. What was it about having a pair of gorgeous eyes glued to one's lips that made a person want to lick the dryness away. Mine were parched and stained red with wine—the color of lust. The instant my tongue flicked out over my bottom lip he leaned in, as though that was the invitation he'd been waiting for. Deliberately he moved. Slowly.

I had only a moment to suck in a breath, my muscles coiling

expectantly as his mouth slanted over mine. The spark that had vibrated between us all night suddenly roared as he closed the contact. My heavy lids fell over my eyes, the kiss too intense to sustain all my senses at once. My sight now extinguished, all other sensations flared.

At first, the pressure of his lips was light. All he seemed to want to do was sample and savor with silky, intoxicating caresses. Patient and seductive. When I finally opened my mouth to him he deepened the kiss. My skin puckered in eager welcome where warm fingers glided over my nape and into my hair. The weight of the other hand settled at my hip as his tongue met mine in a masterful orchestration of thrilling strokes. I sighed into his mouth and wrapped my arms around his neck to anchor myself to his solid warmth and rigid plains.

No sooner had I locked my arms in place than I was flat on my back with Tristan's chest flush and heavy against mine. Our fevered contact escalated then. His movements became rougher, his stubble teasing and abrasive. All the while my fingers relished the contours of his broad back and the feel of the shifting muscles beneath his shirt. I arched into him, my breathing raspy as he maneuvered his way down my neck with hungry purpose, alternately sucking and pulling my flesh carefully between his teeth. I would have bruises there come morning, for sure, but I'd wear them gladly. I wanted him to brand me that way. I wanted to belong to him.

After a long sultry moment, it suddenly occurred to me, in the confusion of my own furious desire, that his clever thigh had somehow parted my legs and was firmly settled against the achiest, hottest part of me. Just like that, a momentary frisson of vestal fear jolted my eyes apart. But he did nothing more than lazily graze his teeth over my flesh and lavish gentle kisses at the hollow of my neck. I relaxed again and my lids fluttered drowsily to my flushed cheeks.

The delirium built like the pressure of a swelling balloon as he shifted his weight fully between my legs, his hips flush with mine, the glorious friction spreading red heat through my flesh like bold wine. Tension coiled almost unbearably at the junction of my thighs, like a tornado gaining momentum. Wanting both to tear his clothes out of the way and keep a barrier safely between us was frustrating.

No matter how much my body wanted his, my head was screaming for me to slow down. To stop. And I would, I promised myself. *Eventually.* I just wanted to taste a little more.

The hem of his shirt gave way to my gliding fingers. I dragged my nails up along his flanks, momentarily startled by the growl that reverberated approvingly in his chest. My fingers tentatively found their way to the front of his jeans where the sexy 'pathway to heaven' disappeared behind his button and zipper. Where his erection pushed almost painfully at my thigh. A strong hand instantly moved to restrain me, lifting my hands up and securing them over my head.

Instinctively I bent my knees so his weight centered more tantalizingly between my thighs. A small moan of pleasure slipped from my lips. I clamped my thighs tightly around his hips, restive and needy, urging him closer with my calves. My head was a maelstrom of foggy lust, my back arching in some primordial tempo I was barely aware of.

Without warning, he ripped himself off me and abruptly pushed away from the bed like a panicked animal from a fire. I sat up cautiously, straightening my clothes as I wondered what I'd done wrong to make him stop.

"It's late." His voice was raw and he'd turned his head away from me. "I'd better go." Tristan backed away slowly as though I'd just caught him with his hand in the cookie jar. *My* cookie jar.

"Uh-huh." Was I agreeing? Or was that an objection? My

brain was still coming out of its stupor. “I’m sorry.” Wait, what was I apologizing for?

“You’re sorry?” Tristan regarded me keenly. Silently. But not with his usual calm. I could tell he was as affected by the kiss as I was, his breathing as unsettled as my own. Before I could work myself into a decent fluster, he brought his lips directly back to mine, kissing me again. Hard. Though it was nowhere near chaste, this one was succinct and purposeful, not meant to incite or rekindle. “That’s too bad,” he said with force, “because I’m not.” Then he gently pulled at the strands of hair that were caught at the corner of my mouth and tucked them behind my ear. “I really have to go now.” He winked, moving away again. “I did, after all, promise to be a gentleman.” He strode confidently toward the door despite the protuberance in his jeans.

Now who’s walking like John Wayne? I smiled, placing cool fingertips over lips that were still hot and swollen from the aftermath of that stunning kiss.

His eyes dropped knowingly to the hand I held to my tenderized lips. “Sleep tight, Evan.” He withdrew and shut the door silently behind him.

Half an hour later, well after the growl of his truck had diminuendoed, my fizzled brain was still trying desperately to reboot itself. I lay on my back hugging my pillow fiercely, my face buried into the cotton so that the feathers could swallow up my happy squeals.

He’d tasted of rain and forest and something else I was unable or unequipped to recognize. The scent of man and cedarwood still clung to my body. Everywhere that he’d trailed his fingertips along my body still hummed with aftershocks, like living memories. I’d never felt this way before—floating, soaring and heavy all at once. Totally blind drunk in the best and most delicious way.

"Sleep tight, Evan." The words he'd left me with still hung in the air because I was unable to let them slip away just yet.

"Good night, Tristan," I said softly, heaving an almighty sigh of contentment. But if he thought I was going to "sleep tight" tonight, he was seriously delusional. *That* was one goodnight kiss destined to keep me awake till dawn. A kiss that had forevermore put paid to talk of friendship. Friends didn't kiss friends like *that*.

16

A GIRL AND HER MOP

No longer was Darth Vader the harbinger of my text messages. At least, not from Tristan. His were now alerted by an excited minion voice—it was the sound of how deliriously happy I felt every time he texted me. It had been an agonizing two days since he'd left me panting in my room.

Strangely, he had no personal social media accounts, so I couldn't verify whether or not he really was in Juneau today. No 'Bragbook' check ins or cockpit selfies. I had only his word that he was doing some or other pipeline patrol flying up north. Trust in the male species was not something that came easily to me. My mother's marriage and subsequent dating had jaded my outlook on the idea of love and monogamy. Maybe Tristan was different. Everyone else in Thorne Bay certainly thought so, if rumors could be believed.

Just as I turned my hair dryer off, wondering what to wear for my shift tonight, the glorious sound of a laughing minion was heard over the music. I snatched my phone up to read Tristan's text.

"What are you wearing?"

My eyes popped wide with excitement, my fingers blurring

over the keys to type a response. "Still deciding." But my finger hovered over the little 'send' arrow, hesitating. On second thought, I decided to delete that amateur response altogether. "My favorite bloomers," I wrote instead, snickering to myself, "and my fluffy pink flannel nightgown."

"…" That was all I got in response.

I beamed at the blank text he'd sent, imagining his horrified face.

"I have no words," he said at last. "That's way too much sexy for me to handle."

"Don't make me laugh, you're making my curlers fall out and my mud mask crack."

"Mud mask?! Now you're talking dirty."

"Wow, punny," I replied with a chuckle. "Are you wearing that tight little flight suit again? I can't resist a man in uniform."

"Duly noted."

"Especially when he's wearing *Wet Dog Eau de Cologne*." I added a drooling emoji and fired the text off with giddy speed.

"Stop flirting with me!"

I burst into laughter, my heart swelling in my chest. "You in Juneau for the night?"

"Guess again."

I frowned. Did that mean…? Was he back in Thorne Bay? I waited to see if he'd write anything else, but the missing ellipses at the bottom of the screen indicated that he wasn't typing a long response but was waiting for me to say something. Or maybe he was already busy with something else. His texts always left me wanting more. In an effort not to appear the horny teenager, I resisted the urge to reply and forced myself to set the phone patiently aside. Hopefully I, for once, would leave him unfulfilled and eager for more.

Since there was every possibility I might see Tristan tonight, or so his text had alluded, I applied some mascara and opted for my favorite emerald blouse, pairing it with dark skinny jeans. I'd trudge over to the bar in my new Ketchikan sneakers, since it'd rained earlier, but once at the Bear and Beaver I'd swap them out for a pair of comfy, yet pretty, green pointed-toe flats.

Feeling suddenly confident and sexy, I faced the mirror for a little female powwow. "Okay, Ev," I said sternly. "Are you ready to lose the V-plates?" Taking a deep breath, I gave my reflection a bolstering smile. "Yes." It felt good giving myself permission for…whatever happened tonight. I turned on my heel and left my little apartment with the giddy anticipation of this night being the most epic one of my life.

"Shotgun not mopping!" Melissa grinned smugly as I sauntered into the bar.

"Ugh, fine." I headed over to the storeroom to shed my boots and get the mop.

My nose filled with Murphy Oil Soap, tobacco, and leather as I dragged the mop absently across the hardwood floor. The Bear and Beaver had the look and feel of a colonial big game hunter's lair, apart from the pool table and the TV mounted on the wall, and I could almost picture Allan Quatermain sitting broodily by the fireside with his rifle. There were antler chandeliers hanging from the ceiling and disgusting taxidermied corpse heads staring from the timber walls, their glassy eyes creepy and lifeless. There was even a twelve-foot bear standing on hind legs in the corner, it's frozen snarl like an eerie snapshot of the grizzly that had nearly attacked Tristan and I last week. On the wood paneling beside it hung a large salmon, life-like as though leaping from its mount. Amidst all these 'trophies' were other grim hunting paraphernalia—pelts hanging like tapestries, photographs of middle-aged dentists beside bears and wolves, hunting books and magazines on shelves, and an antique shotgun mounted over the fireplace. The pool table notwithstanding, it was a shrine of violence and dead things. I wasn't sure I could bear working here much longer.

"Ev," said Melissa, leaning over the bar top as I ran the mop around the tall chairs, "did I ever tell you my mop story?"

"No. Do I want to hear your mop story?"

"Of course you do." She smirked and wriggled her eyebrows at me. "Have I mentioned Laura before? Your predecessor."

"Uh-huh."

Melissa's smile turned devious as she nodded. "Oh, Laura was a horse of a different color. One time I arrived here an hour earlier than I usually did so I could scarf a meal before my shift. The place was pretty dead."

My gaze meandered to the sightless caribou head nearest the bartop. "Hmm."

"Laura was suspiciously AWOL. I checked the kitchen and the bathrooms. Nothing. There was really only one last place she could be."

"The storeroom," I guessed.

"Yeah, so that's exactly where I headed." Melissa was biting her lip to keep from grinning wickedly. "But when I opened the door…" She dropped her head to her forearm and began hooting with laughter.

"What happened?" I shook her arm. The suspense was infuriating.

"Lusty Laura was riding that handle—" pointing to the mop in my hand "—like it was American Pharaoh and she was winning the Kentucky Derby!" She slapped the granite counter enthusiastically. "I mean she was literally—"

"I get it, Mel!" Horrified, I dropped the mop. "Spare me the details."

"A closet paraphiliac, that Laura." Mel had laughed so hard

that her eyes were moist with tears. Still chuckling, she wiped at them.

"There's a word for that?" The mop received a glare as I stepped over it. "Gross."

She rolled her eyes as I pushed her out of the way to lather my hands at the bar sink. "Don't worry, Ev, I threw the old mop out that same day."

"You've ruined mopping for me."

"Now you know why I never do it." She rescued the mop from the floor and dropped the head into the bucket, holding the handle out to me. "Be strong, Ev. Get back on the horse, you can do it."

When Def Leppard's sexy guitar riff sounded over the speakers a few minutes later, Mel turned the volume right up, since the bar was still empty. If ever there was an appropriate time to straddled one's mop, this was it—Joe Elliott in my ear, telling me to "shake it up". Mop in hand, I gyrated my hips provocatively as we both belted out the lyrics and swished our hair with glam metal flair. "Pour some sugar on meh!"

Unable to resist the lure of the mop, and spurred on by the second chorus, Mel took her turn, wielding it like an epileptic jockey.

Once the song was over, however, and the volume once more reduced to a dignified decibel, Melissa stowed the mop. Still out of breath, she leaned on the bar next to me. "So when does lover boy get back?"

"Tonight, I think."

With a pointed look, she gestured at my crotch. "I hope you landscaped."

"Um, a little." *Sort of.*

"Evan!" Her look of dawning horror—having guessed rightly that my garden had been left to flourish wildly—was utterly sobering.

"A little goes a long way," I argued.

"Not there, it doesn't." She aimed an accusing finger at my groin. "Unless you just like *hairy veils*."

I grimaced. "Well, when you put it that way…"

"Trust me, less is more," she advised. "And I do mean *less hair*, not less effort. It's all about the *Bald and the Beautiful*, if you're picking up what I'm puttin' down."

"I'll just trim—"

"Trim?! Hell, woman, take it all off!"

"Well, I'm not sure he even wants to go *that* far south of the border so—"

"Lemme stop you right there, Ev. Make no mistake, the guy's hot for you. That much you can take as gospel. The only question is, are you sure you know what you're doing?"

"Pretty sure I can figure it out," I answered, looking at my crotch. "But I'll try not to circumcise myself."

"I don't mean your hedges." She rolled her eyes. "I hope you know what you're doing with Tristan."

"I really like him, Mel."

"I know. Shit, I'm not gonna lie, *I'd* even drink his bathwater." She poured me a club soda—my usual drink—and set it down on the coaster for me. "But that whole *Addams Family* vibe is weird. Just weird. So be careful there."

I was growing tired of empty warnings. Why couldn't she just be happy for me? "I can be the Morticia to his Gomez."

She gave a perverse smile, but the sound of a diesel engine as it purred to a stop outside forestalled her before she could offer another eye-rolling comment (something like "He's more of a Cousin It than a Gomez Addams."). She peered past my shoulder through the window. "Speak of the devil," she said under her breath.

My heart leapt as I followed her gaze to the window. Tristan's black truck had pulled into the parking lot. With an excited squeal, I saluted Mel—who was shaking her head amusedly—and raced off to the bathroom to hyperventilate into a bag while I checked my face for any smudged mascara or whatever.

As I stared at the neurotic girl in the restroom mirror moments later, I tried not to berate her for being so gutless for hiding in here. "Just be yourself," I told her. *Are you sure about that?* "On second thought…" *Ugh.* I pulled my hair free of its braid and fluffed it out. Then, changing my mind, I lifted the massy locks up into an untidy bun and gave a nod of finality. It seemed as good a time as any for a Yul Brenner speech. "I see pride. I see *powah*. I see a bad-ass *mudder* who don't take no crap offa nobody!" My sorry excuse for a Jamaican accent was anything but *irie*.

With a fierce stare at my reflection, I readjusted my bra. But this was instantly ruined by the sound of a flushing toilet. One of the stall doors, that I'd assumed to be unoccupied, opened abruptly and out walked the cleaner lady. Muttering unintelligibly under her breath, whilst affording me a wide berth, she warily scurried from the bathroom with her cleaning caddy.

"Good night, Gosia!" I said, snickering to myself. I sucked in a hearty lungful of confidence (and Pine-Sol fumes) and finally marched from the ladies room.

While I'd been scaring the help, Tristan had been talking to Melissa at the bar. Out came that smoldering dimple as soon as he spotted me. He stood directly from his barstool and, once I'd reached his side, bent his head to plant a warm kiss lightly on my lips. "I wondered where you'd run off to?" His eyes glittered enigmatically.

"She was just making sure she had no nuts in her teeth," said Melissa, taking a handful of the peanuts from the bowl on the counter. "Those little suckers get into the most inconvenient places."

He considered her wryly. "Are you speaking from experience?"

"I plead the fifth."

"Always with the nut jokes," I said, rolling my eyes at them.

Shaking his head, he turned back to me. But it was still Melissa to whom he directed his next question even though it was my face caught beneath his gaze. "Tell me, Melissa," he said with a languid grin, "is the cleaning lady Jamaican?"

"Jamaican?" There was bemusement in her voice.

My face blanched. *No!* There was no way he'd heard me all the way from the washroom.

"No," Mel answered. "Gosia's from Poland."

"That's what I thought," he said after a knowing pause.

17

THE SOCIETY OF SOCIOPATHS AND LONERS

I missed Florida. Missed the heavy black clouds that would roll in abruptly from the west, churning overhead as though the sky was boiling. Sometimes, if the light was just right, the reef water seemed to glare a mystic aquamarine beneath a darkening sky. The same storm was now brewing in Tristan's eyes.

It seemed I'd blinked and some unseen hand had swept in to slap the grin from Tristan's face. One minute he'd been making arcane references about the Polish cleaning lady and then, the very next second, the storm rolled in with startling speed. I forgot all about his uncanny hearing, disquieted now by the shadows gathering over his changeable, lambent eyes. Eyes that had flown to the door in readiness. Readiness for what?

I wasn't kept waiting for long. With the force of a cold north wind, Nicole swept in. On her tail came Alex and Leeann, trailing like obedient spaniels. Her eyes spat venom as she passed me by.

Whoah. I'd be sure to avoid *ever* being alone with that one. She'd probably drown me in the toilet if I was stupid enough to find myself in the washroom alone with her.

Dean strutted in soon after with a handful of others, Lydia and James included. Without warning, or a backward glance at me,

Tristan suddenly stalked off to join his brother. Very few words appeared to be exchanged, but one brother's jaw was rigid with anger and the other's mouth was curled up sardonically. James quickly stepped between them, diffusing the tension with a few back slaps and a careless smile.

"That's weird," Mel said beside me.

"What is?" Tristan's moods?

"Them. The Society of Sociopaths and Loners."

"Rude," I admonished quietly.

"I mean I guess it made sense to see them at the cove, they live up that way. Not that they mingled with us plebs. Well, except for you. But they *never* just hang out."

"That's not true, I've seen Tristan and Dean here with Owen."

"For no other reason than the land Owen's selling them," she countered.

"They own an aviation company, Mel. They wouldn't be successful if they were as bad as you say."

"Tristan, James, and Lydia, I grant you, are the only ones with personalities. They're also the only pilots from Thorne Bay. Dean rarely flies—he'd probably scare the customers away. The rest of their employees are Ketchikan based *normal* folk with *normal* lives. The others over there—" she gestured to the group, shaking her head "—I never see unless they're rushing in and out of town for supplies. I'm telling you, this is odd behavior for them."

Listening with only half an ear, I watched the group as I used to watch the popular kids in school—from the sideline with the rest of the misfits and rejects. I clearly didn't fit in here either.

I tried not to stare, but I could no sooner look away from a pride of lions in my living room than from this strange and dynamic family. Every look and touch seemed layered with subtle meaning as though I was watching a film in another language, yet unable and unwilling to catch the subtitles for fear I'd miss the vital nuances.

I also kept watching in hope that Tristan would call me over to him; blow me a kiss; sneak a wink, for God's sake. Anything to reassure me that I wasn't invisible. But I was. He never looked over even once. I'd been so nervous all week about seeing him that I hadn't even considered he might actually ignore me.

His friends, on the other hand, were *not* making any effort to hide their interest. Every now and then I'd catch a different pair of eyes regarding me, except the green ones I pertinaciously sought, as though I was carrying some sign around my neck and they were trying to make sense of the words.

"Girl, you're in trouble," said Melissa, fanning herself. The first round of drinks had been poured and she was back behind the bar with me.

I looked askance at her.

"Before the others walked in I thought he was gonna impregnate you with that stare of his."

"Zip it!" I whispered furiously, now more than ever convinced of Tristan's superhuman hearing.

"So no more talking about your *ladyscaping*?"

"Shh." I swatted her backside. "I'm serious, you lunatic."

The horror that was pasted over my face must have finally registered because she clamped her lips shut after that and gave a skeptical shrug that suggested I'd lost both the plot and my sense of humor. Our voices weren't really loud enough to carry anywhere, especially over the classic rock, so I understood why she thought I was being overcautious.

The more time I spent with Tristan, though, and the better I got to know him, the more fascinating he became. Not the fascination of a woman for a beautiful man (at least not entirely), but the sensation of a girl falling deeper into a rabbit hole—a dark sense of curiosity I'd willingly surrendered to. I knew that what I might find at the bottom would likely make little sense and only confuse me more, yet still I was drawn inexorably to those crouching shadows. The answers to his secrets were lying in that fathomless darkness; not once, however, did I consider that I was falling to my death.

When the second round was ordered, I volunteered a little too enthusiastically. Melissa smiled knowingly as she placed a beer glass on my full tray. While she was making quick work of the rest of the drink orders, I gingerly walked my leaden tray into their midst like a mouse beneath nine tigerish smiles and adamantine gazes. Only Tristan's gaze remained veiled with impassivity.

From Nicole's corner, I perceived prickling stabs of antipathy. Painfully aware of my movements, I placed the drinks down carefully on the hightop nearest Tristan, cleaving to his presence, however cold it was. There was every chance I might drop the whole tray if I tried to dispense their orders individually, shaky as my hands were. Let them figure out whose potation was whose, I decided, suddenly eager for escape.

"Hello again, Evan." Dean's greeting couldn't have sounded more predatory if he'd tried.

My dislike of him had, by now, overshadowed whatever sex appeal he possessed. His eyes were the color of smoked cedarwood, very unique, and beautiful if not for the ruthlessness I detected there.

"That's an interesting scent you're wearing," he remarked, offhandedly. His tone was uncomplimentary, so I didn't delude myself that he was being kind. His friends were all listening in, their sharp eyes glinting with unrestrained humor.

"I'm not wearing any perfume," I replied uneasily, noticing the way his nostrils gave an imperceptible flare.

Ignoring my answer, he shifted a meaningful gaze to his brother. Tristan met his brother's look with a defiant glare, but there was an unmistakable flush tinging his neck that intrigued me.

What the hell…? I resisted the urge to sniff my pits, mortified by the thought that he was implying I smelled bad.

Dean's insinuation, whatever it was, had stirred some chuckling within the group. Only Tristan, Lydia, Nicole and I remained unamused.

Once the tray was empty, I hoofed it back to the bar with my tail between my legs before Nicole could leap from her chair and scalp me. I told Melissa I was done serving that lot. Otherwise there was a very good chance I would be hocking a few good loogies into Nicole's vodka tonics tonight if I continued to serve her. That one was itching for a fight, she'd made that very clear.

I might be a maniac who spoke to herself in weird accents in public bathrooms, but I was no classless bimbo to engage in catfights; moreover, I had way too much self-preservation. Nicole had a few good inches on me and looked like a wiry spitfire that could easily wipe the floor with my bloody nose. I, on the other hand, had more freckles than courage. Mom would have said that it takes courage and dignity to turn down a fight. Well, if that was true I had plenty of courage.

I looked up from the chore of wiping condensation rings from an empty table. Tristan might not be watching me, but his brother still was. "Don't you eyeball me, boy!" I wanted to say but didn't dare. Damn, if only I was as ballsy in real life as I was in my head.

The least I could—and did—do, however, was return his brazen stare, but he, of course, only grinned and maintained the infuriating contact until I lowered my sheepish eyes in defeat. I had never been all that good at giving the ole hairy eyeball anyway.

"Stop flirting and get to work," Mel said, slapping my backside as she passed with her empty tray.

I forced a smile, hoping Melissa didn't see the telltale reddening of my eyes. Under the guise of taking dirty glasses to the kitchen, I rushed to escape out the back door where I had every intention of indulging in a good cry. The night air brushed a cool touch against my face as my eyes dimmed with hot tears. My heart ached with the undeniable fact that Tristan was ashamed to be with me. Why else would he have ignored me the moment his brother and friends had arrived? Discarded like yesterday's nachos after only a week.

"Aww, Ev." Melissa materialized at my back and wrapped me in a tight squeeze. "What's the matter?"

"I'm just being stupid," I said, sniffling. "He only kissed me once, it's not like we're—"

"You're not stupid!" She stepped around to face me. "What did those assholes say to you?"

"Nothing. That's the problem—Tristan hasn't said one word to me since his friends got here." I shook my head, confused. "One minute he can't take his eyes off me and the next he can't stand the sight of me."

"Well, clearly he's the stupid one."

I looked down at my tidy outfit. "What's wrong with me that he's so ashamed to be with me?"

"Nothing! You're beautiful, Ev."

I gave a teary chuckle. "Now I know you're full of shit. 'Pretty' I could maybe pull off once every seventy-five years during a Halley's Comet." *Maybe.* "But 'beautiful' is a little hyperbolical, Mel."

"Listen, I'm not here to blow smoke up your ass so believe what you want." She became thoughtful a minute. "I don't pretend to understand any of those weirdos, but I saw how he looked at you tonight." Her shoulder nudged playfully at mine.

"And how was that?"

"Like he was eyeing a juicy prime steak."

I rolled my eyes. "Well, the steak's gone cold."

"Just do me a favor please."

"I'm not gonna ride the mop again, Mel."

"That's a pity," she chuckled. "Because the woman who rode that mop tonight was sexy and confident. I really hope she doesn't let some moody idiot ruin her night. Tristan obviously doesn't have the balls to own up to what's clearly in his eyes."

"I'm starting to think the attraction was all just one-sided."

"Hell no! The sexual tension was like a damn sauna." She fanned herself again. "I nearly had to leave the bar to go lock myself in the storeroom with that damn mop."

"You and me both." My lips twitched.

We emerged from the kitchen a moment later, my gaze pulled helplessly to where Tristan and James were playing pool.

"You have it bad," Mel said with a sympathetic shake of her head. "He must be some kisser."

"Yeah, but I clearly wasn't." *Or his gaze would be wandering to me just as often.*

"Did you slobber your way down his face?"

"No!" I shoved at her playfully.

Our laughter must have grated on Nicole's ears. She started snapping her fingers impatiently for another drink, no doubt deciding we looked like we needed useful occupation.

"I really don't like her."

"Looks like the feeling's mutual." Melissa gave my clenched fist a conciliatory pat. "I'll deal with her."

"Yeah, take one for the team," I whispered, mimicking the sound of a spitting feral cat. "Before I defile her drink with phlegm." I headed off to the bathroom before I gave into the temptation.

By the time I returned to the bar Tristan was gone. His black truck was also conspicuously absent. He'd left without even saying goodbye.

The rest of the night slipped by like a sepia blur. I was impatient to get back to my room because, secretly, I was harboring a small hope that I'd find him waiting for me there. My doorstep, however, was starkly empty under the lonely porch light when I got home. Just my fellow moths were there to welcome me. I checked my phone for the umpteenth time and was bitterly disappointed to see the screen woefully blank of text banners. Finally, I was forced to admit that I'd read far more into that kiss than he had. And that was a bitter pill to swallow.

18

INTO THE WILD

Every side was the wrong side of the bed to get out of after a bitter pill. Staying in said bed with a good book most of the day seemed like the safer option, so that was exactly what I did. Evening arrived all too soon, though, bringing with it a good dose of guilt. I'd hardly fed myself and I was probably incubating bed sores. I'd done nothing productive except stare at my kindle.

The evening deteriorated further when Mom called an hour later to say that the tropical storm that NOAA had been tracking (unbeknownst to me) had intensified into a hurricane overnight, and Juno Beach was now lying right in the middle of the Cone of Probability. The Cone of Death seemed more appropriate in my current mood.

Men were a lot like hurricanes, I decided. They had the power to blow you off your feet, and leave utter devastation in their wake. Maybe it was better to be ignored now rather than later, while he was only under my skin and not settled in my heart. A scab would heal, but a heart could break and leave deep scars. After all, one kiss was hardly the fountainhead of tragic love. What my mom had endured after her divorce—now that was devastation.

I didn't want to think of Tristan, so I imagined my family's last-minute hurricane prepping—hoarding batteries, buying candles, fueling cars, filling tubs, stocking up on gallons of drinking water, and replenishing propane gas. I'd been through all that already: the foreboding anticipation, the deserted streets, and the post-apocalyptic undertones that pervaded every building.

By now the windows would be shuttered and the patio furniture stowed in the lounge. The terrifying solemnity of the approaching storm was probably already lying heavy in the calm, humid air. By tomorrow the hurricane parties would ensue and the suicidal surfers would be riding the warning swells and rip currents. Come hell or (literally) high water, I knew my family would be hunkering down, and I worried for them.

My dark thoughts followed me to the shower like a shadow. The water sluiced at my tired shoulders, kneading as I wiped my eyes. My towel was wrapped like a turban over my hair when I emerged from the steam into my bedroom to see a missed call from Tristan.

I stood glaring down at the screen, my bottom lip gripped between my teeth, hand wavering, contemplating whether or not to return the call. He hadn't left a voicemail or a text. After a moment, I finally pulled my hand safely to my chest, away from the phone. *No.* He'd made it very clear how he felt about me last night.

Just then a text flitted suddenly across the screen, but it was from Alison. "Are you free for a chat?"

Relieved to have a distraction, I replied that I would see her in twenty minutes.

Alaska was a vast state and it occurred to me that I should consider moving on from Thorne Bay. Maybe this chat with Ali ought to conclude with a resignation.

~

Alison watched me expectantly as she rolled her pen between her fingers. "Don't say yes unless you absolutely want to do this."

"That's some favor, Ali," I said, grinning. "Next you'll be asking for my kidneys."

"If you can spare your liver too I'd be grateful." She rifled through her handbag a moment before pulling out a ring of keys. "So you'll do it?"

"Does a bear shit in the woods?"

"Great!" She held one large bronze key out to me from which the keyring dangled. "This one is for the front door. You can take the Yukon for the week, I won't be needing it."

"Better and better!" I took the keys from her.

She was thoughtful a minute. "There isn't much mobile coverage up there, Ev, and your closest neighbor is miles away."

"I know, Ali." I gave a cocky "I got this" wave of my hand, but she could see that I was clearly unperturbed by the warning and keen to house-sit their cabin for a week. For a while now, I'd considered booking a few days in one the Forest Service cabins, like Salmon Lake Cabin. There were a fair few of them scattered around Alaska, surrounded by nothing but hundreds of acres of peaceful rainforest and calming solitude. And here was Alison, offering me a chance to stay in their private cabin (which was likely a little less utilitarian than Salmon Lake Cabin). Practically a paid vacation!

"The cabin's dated, but livable. Get some provisions before you head up there. You can expense it to us, just keep your receipts."

"Other than tidying it up a bit, anything else you need me to do?"

"Dean or Tristan will be doing a last walk around before the closing next month, so just whatever light bulbs need changing please, stuff like that. Basically, make sure it's not infested with squirrels." She winked. "Dean will likely just tear it down, but that's neither here nor there"—one shoulder lifted dispassionately —"there's no reason the ole place shouldn't look presentable."

"Not that I'm complaining or anything, but how come you didn't offer this to Melissa instead?" Melissa had, after all, been here longer.

"I did, but she suggested you needed a change of scenery." She paused knowingly. "Anyway, I really appreciate you doing this."

"Are you kidding me? I should be thanking you." It was exactly what I wanted. I had tons of reading to catch up on, so there was no chance I would get bored. More importantly, I would be avoiding hurricane Tristan *and* doing some much-needed soul-searching. Hopefully, he'd notice me missing from the bar and drink himself into a—

"Text me every day," Alison instructed, disrupting my inclement reveries. "You have your bear spray and a sensible head on your shoulders, so I trust you not to go hiking in the woods by yourself."

"I won't be trudging off to grandma's house, don't worry."

"Speaking of big bad wolves, there are plenty of them up there. Sarah's convinced she's seen some fairly large ones. I asked Dean and Sarah to check in on you."

"Wolves. Got it." Pfft, it was the grizzlies I worried about.

She checked her watch and then urged me to get going at a decent hour. Preferably first thing in the morning. "You don't want to be driving in the dark." Even the large Alaskan critters that roamed along the pavement markings, she warned me, would be harder to see after sunset, especially on the blind curves. Not until it was too late.

I nodded obediently and turned my wrist to check the time. *Yikes!*

After a few more last minute caveats from Ali, I jogged back to my room with every intention of hitting the road within the hour. I couldn't stay one more night in that room, I had cabin fever. Besides, the sun set late in the summer. I could make it. The keys jangled agreeably in my hand, galvanizing my spirits with their metallic chatter.

I burst into my room and began shoving all the essentials into my backpack: undies, toothbrush, journal, condoms... *Wait, what?* Condoms?! "Very funny, Melissa!" I yelled out to the universe.

My room was empty except for me, of course, but I reckoned if I was sarcastic and determined enough, I'd be able to project my displeasure into the ether for her to feel my censure. *Or better yet...* I pulled out my phone to text Melissa. "Just how many condoms have you hidden in my room, you deviant?"

It wasn't long before her answering text whooshed onto my screen. "One for every dirty thought you've ever had over Tristan. THAT MANY!"

Do dirty looks offset the count? I threw my phone into the bag and shoved my woolen feet into rubber boots before finally leaving Bear Lodge. An hour later I was provisioned and fueled. Once the address was punched into the Yukon's navigation system I was on my way. Unfortunately, though, I hadn't factored in delays along the road, namely a flat tire.

"Dammit!" I growled as I pulled over to inspect the front left tire. Throwing out a few more colorful words, I slammed my door and stomped off to grab the jack and lug wrench. Too bad the tire had blown *after* I'd turned off the main highway. Not a single car passed by as I undertook the half-forgotten art of tire-changing. This damsel was on her own. Unless, of course, one factored in the damn mosquitoes. And the gathering clouds. "Great," I muttered, feeling the first of the drops slap my head ominously.

The jack was left abandoned as I escaped into the SUV just

before the deluge hit with full force. The hazards were on and the car was idling comfortingly. My sullen eyes followed the wipers, back and forth, swiping furiously at the sheets of water. I gave a miserable groan and settled back to wait it out. I must have fallen asleep because when I woke up again it was to realize that the rain had finally stopped and my headlamps were on. Dusk had long since settled in. *Shit.*

With my flashlight angled on the running board, I made fast work of swapping the deflated tire for the skinny spare. By the time I finally tightened the last lug, it was completely dark out.

For a brief moment, I thought about turning back to Bear Lodge, but I was already almost at the cabin. No matter how much my nerves protested, it seemed stupid to turn back. Ignoring my better sense, I continued on. A good playlist was what I needed to listen to. Some upbeat rock anthem would steel my nerves. I flipped through my iTunes, eyes darting back and forth between the quiet road and the phone screen.

A violent gasp erupted from my lips as something dark flashed across my headlights. My boot slammed the brakes. The black streak had barely missed the Yukon's monstrous chrome grille. I was white-knuckling the steering wheel as I stared, wide-eyed, into the dark beyond where the creature had disappeared among the trees. It was eerily quiet except for the Yukon's discreet purr. A bear maybe? It had certainly looked big enough.

I checked the rearview mirror where my scorched tread marks had blackened the wet asphalt, but I could see nothing in the red glow of my tail lights. Nothing. Still, my heart hammered with disquiet. With a deep breath, I pulled my foot off the brake, transferring it to the accelerator. The Yukon began inching forward again, but my gaze seemed drawn to where the creature had fled. Finally, I forced them to the road ahead.

The fiery green eye-shine of a large animal appeared unexpectedly in the peripheral of the light beam. My heart stilled instantly. The retinas flashed, eerie and unblinking, through the trees. But the animal vanished just as quickly as it had appeared.

I was pretty sure grizzlies, after reading about them since my encounter, had that exact shade of *tapetum lucidum* that I'd just seen. I depressed the accelerator a little further, eager to get out of there.

The silence in the SUV felt oppressive, adding to that creepy feeling that I was being watched. But I didn't dare try and mess with my iPhone again. It had been thrown into the footwell with my backpack earlier, when I'd hit the brakes, and was now far out of reach. Pulling over was not an option. Whatever was in the woods had looked big enough to bash my window open. Anyway, I told myself sternly, the engine was more than equal to the task of drowning out the sound of my petrified heart. I was not stopping for anything!

The little cabin finally appeared in my headlights like a sleeping troglodyte, the windows dark and the eave frowning low over the door as though the light had angered it. Not even the moon's full glare dared to breach the tree canopy, and all had been painted black before the headlights had obtruded the hush.

I shifted the SUV into park and remained in my seat, hesitating. It occurred to me suddenly that I'd forgotten to ask Alison where the breaker panel was. *Great.* I freed myself from the seatbelt and climbed over the console to reach for the flashlight that had also been hurled into the footwell earlier (my iPhone flashlight had broken ages ago with repetitive dropping).

"Stop being a wuss." I'd hoped the sound of my own voice would steady me, but the words came out like a precarious whisper.

I obediently killed the engine. The front of the house was still basked in light from the Yukon's reassuring glare, but the silence was peculiarly hair-raising. My furtive gaze scoured the heavily wooded perimeter where the darkest of the shadows choked even the light from my steady headlamps. I hooked clammy fingers around the silver handle. The click of the opening door was like a crack of thunder in the stillness of the forest, but I pressed onward.

This is how horror movies start, Ev. "Shut up," I murmured nervously. I was alone in a dark rainforest with nothing more than a measly little torch—just another doomed horror heroine walking toward an abandoned cabin in the woods. My ears strained to hear over the sound of damp leaves beneath my boots.

The snap of a branch froze my blood. My flashlight followed, lightning fast, searching for the lurking culprit. But the trees only facilitated the nocturnal whispers echoing like shadows till I was no longer sure where to look. Another odd sound soon followed the first, this one much closer than before. I yelped and sprinted for the front porch, the torchlight beam jerking erratically. The porch steps I took in one leap, scattering pine needles and leaves as I went. I shoved the torch under my arm and fumbled with the keys, my gaze fixed and frozen over my shoulder. In my desperation, I dropped the keys. Slamming my back against the front door, I aimed the beam at the driveway and slowly knelt down, my movements painstaking. I felt around in the leaves for the errant keys as I probed the dark with my light.

There, to my horror, within the arc of yellow light, I suddenly caught sight of a blinking set of iridescent orbs. And then another set appeared beside its fellow, too high off the ground to be anything but large and predatory. Liquid terror gushed hotly into my gut as my index finger finally brushing cold iron. The rest of my fingers swiftly curled around the keychain. I sprang back up, shoving that large bronze key into the slot so hard I nearly broke the blade. As soon as the lock flipped I yanked the door open and fell inside, slamming the door with a hard kick. I bolted it with numb fingers and collapsed back against the door to sob in relief.

It was a long time later before I managed to calm my ragged

breath. I realized with a sickening feeling that I'd left my backpack and phone in the car. They were both probably still lying in the passenger footwell. But there was no way in hell I was going out there again, not without daylight at my back. Not even for the torch still lying uselessly on the abandoned porch.

19

MAN MEAT

My joints hurt and there was an awful hammering in my skull. I gave a sniff and shivered, convinced that I was getting the flu or something. No, wait, the pounding was at the door! My head jolted up from the linoleum floor. I sat up, disoriented, hissing with discomfort as the blood rushed like steel nails into the cold veins of my dead arm. I'd lain awake till dawn, my teeth chattering with fear, exhaustion, and cold.

I stumbled awkwardly to the front door and checked the peephole. A rangy woman stared back at me with ascetic grey eyes. Her blonde braid—bleached white with age—jostled on her shoulder as she hammered the flat of her palm imperiously on the door.

I snapped the bolt free and unclenched my jaws as I swung the door open. "Can I help you?" Even my voice sounded hoarse and congested.

"Good, you're alive," she said, stomping leaves from her boots before pushing past me into the mudroom, an impatient waft of thyme following her in.

"Last I checked." *Do come in, won't you?*

"Thought the wolves might have dragged your carcass into

the woods." Her tone matched the stoic lines of her face, so I was unsure whether or not she was joking.

Was that what I'd seen last night? Wolves?

"Don't know what Alison was thinking letting a city girl stay up here alone," she continued.

"I'm guessing you're Sarah Dinwiddie," I said, holding a terse hand out to her.

Her grip was leathered and strong. "Alison asked me to check in on you." She raised an admonishing brow. "I drove by last night to make sure the car was in the driveway." Her eyes narrowed skeptically. "People go missing in Alaska all the time, so I hope you'll excuse our concern."

I felt my cheeks burn under her chiding gaze.

"You might want to be a little more conscientious about checking in. Ali is, after all, responsible for you."

Oh shit! "I forgot my phone in the car." The excuse sounded lame even to me. "I got a little spooked last night."

She gave a succinct nod as though unsurprised by the answer. Her brown cotton sleeves were dirt-stained, rolled up above the elbows as though she'd been interrupted from her morning routine (probably milking a moose or something) to babysit me.

She cocked her ear to listen. "It's too quiet in here." Then, testing a light switch, to no avail, she said, "Did you lose power?"

"Not exactly." I avoided her gaze. "Do you happen to know where the fuse box is?"

She gestured to the other door in the mudroom. "In the garage."

I could have face-palmed myself just then. No wonder she was looking at me like I was a naif. The garage was the first place I should've looked. "Right," I muttered, opening the garage door. There was sunlight struggling through a dusty windowpane, and I easily spotted the distinctive metal box on the wall. Once I'd flicked all the fuses on the instantaneous thrum of beautiful electricity coursed through the cabin. The white noise was instantly calming. It had been too quiet up till then, even with Dinwiddie there.

"There's wood in the shed out back." She was back to inspecting me again, a hand perched on each hip. "You should go start a fire, your lips are blue. You do know how to use a wood stove, right?"

"Yes," I lied. I could figure it out, I didn't want her, and therefore Alison, to think it'd been a mistake to send me here.

To distract her, I asked Mrs. Dinwiddie if she was staying for tea.

"Sure," she replied, following me into the living room (where she eyed the wood stove dubiously) and then into the kitchen.

I forced a smile that was probably more of a grimace than anything remotely confident and filled the kettle with water. The stove, however, was not cooperating as I twisted each knob in growing frustration. I felt like crying. "Now what?"

"Out of gas, huh?" Dinwiddie gave a long-suffering sigh. "Should be a spare bottle in the garage." And off she went.

I was seriously questioning my ability to function effectively on my own.

"I'll stop by again this evening," she said later, as she was leaving.

"You don't need—"

"Wanna make sure you've figured out the toilet." Once again, there was no sign she wasn't serious.

I gave her a tight smile.

She scribbled her mobile number onto a scrap of paper from her pocket and placed it in my hand. Then she reminded me again to text Alison. "Which reminds me," she added, trotting down the porch steps, "don't bother trying to text her from here, the cabin's in a dead zone. You'll have to hike up the hill over there—"

pointing to the sloping road from which I'd come "—if you want any signal."

It seemed I just couldn't catch a break. "Wonderful."

The tail lights of Mrs. Dinwiddie's old diesel glowed with censure as she turned a corner. Sighing, I gave a last wave and headed off to find the washroom. My bladder was about to rip a seam. But, of course, there was none to be found inside. I did, however, finally hunt down the outhouse. "What fresh hell is this?!" I glared at the sky and shook my fist. Overcome with desperation, though, I dropped my jeans and heeded nature's call. That done, I hurried to the Yukon to grab my bag. There was no way I was going to brave a shower just yet (not till the water heater had had a chance to thaw the water), and I was too wide awake to bother taking my fluey body to bed. Instead, I busied myself stowing my meager groceries away, and after I'd fortified my blood with hot tea and oatmeal I got back into the car with my wayward phone, resolved to drive myself up 'signal hill' for some dutiful texting. But the starter only sputtered weakly. I'd left the battery on all night!

I slammed my palm on the steering wheel. "You've got to be kidding me!" My eyes prickled with the heat of frustration. Well, I couldn't do much about a dead battery until Mrs. Dinwiddie returned, so I stalked from the SUV. I wiped angrily at my tears, imagining Dinwiddie's silent derision as she jump-started the Yukon for me.

Armed with my phone and bear spray, I hiked purposefully up the hill to the summit, checking constantly for the signal I'd been promised. *Hallelujah!* I had two whole bars by the time I stood panting on the knoll. My phone lit up with a bunch of missed calls and worried texts. Without wasting a precious bar, I made quick work of shooting a conciliatory text off to Alison.

Alison's response arrived instantly. She'd known I'd gotten there safely because Dinwiddie had seen the headlights in my driveway last night. The second half of the message was to remind me to please check in every day and to call her if I needed anything.

My mom, on the other hand, had sent only one text earlier this morning. It was a picture of a rainbow over our weatherbeaten backyard with an inspiring caption: “See, there’s always a rainbow after a hurricane.” It seemed the storm had diverted into the Atlantic overnight, with nothing but a few outer bands to ruffle the trees in the yard.

I grinned, swatting bugs out of my face, absorbed by the image. It took a moment before I finally became aware of distant laughter on the wind. Voices trickled faintly through the trees on my left. Curious, I left the dirt road and picked my way gingerly over the bracken and mud. Over red toadstools that clung hungrily to the damp rot of a nearby fallen log. There was a brisk wind stinging my cheeks, slapping my hair behind me. I inhaled deeply. The woods seemed saturated with dark mystery, ripe with verdure. A murder of crows squawked overhead as they passed, and then an eagle, drawing my gaze up to the treetops only for a moment. I noticed them all distractedly, drawn by the voices; beckoned sweetly by the susurration of a flanking stream leading me deeper into the woods.

What I saw next was certainly not what I’d expected. The source of the laughter turned out to be five naked bodies in varying stages of undress. They noticed me almost immediately, seemingly undaunted by my shocked staring. My first thought was that I had stumbled in on some strange orgy.

“Like what you see?” The voice came gruff and unexpected beside me.

Jolted from my stupor, I turned to see a bare-assed Dean glowering down at me. He’d somehow managed to sneak up soundlessly as I’d stood distracted by three penises and two sets of large breasts.

Before I could stop them, my eyes dropped to the junction of his thighs, popping wider still. *Make that four penises!* Deeply mortified, I abruptly deflected my gaze. "I…I'm sorry!"

"Why are *you* sorry? This is technically not my land…yet."

I didn't know where to look. *Stop thinking about penises!* "Yes. Well"—swallowing loudly—"in that case, I'm not sorry." I peeked back down briefly, just in case he'd magically produced some underwear. Nope. *Penis!* "Uh, aren't you cold?" Shit, now he'd think I was belittling his… "Shouldn't you put some clothes on?" Why did even his penis have to look so damn threatening?

"What for?" That hyena smile appeared again. "You've already taken a good look."

"Yeah, and now I feel like washing my eyes out in holy water."

He gave a genuine bark of laughter. "I don't know whether to be complimented or insulted."

"While you figure that out," I sniffed, turning on my heel, "I'm just gonna head back—oof!" I found my face planted solidly in a very bare and very sinewy chest. "Tristan!" Realizing that each of my palms was pressed firmly to each of his pecs, I snatched my hands back as though he'd scorched them.

Fortunately—or unfortunately, depending on how I chose to look at it—he'd managed to throw some jeans on. But the golden expanse of naked skin above his waistband told me that he'd been just as nude as his comrades only moments ago.

He raised his eyes from my burning face to his brother, the green lit with irritation. The brothers always seemed to communicate without speech.

Unwilling to stick around a moment longer, I mumbled another apology and scrambled away. I was eager to escape the pack of nudists, and Dean's impressive junk, now forever seared into my brain, but even more desperate to avoid Tristan. If I thought for a second I'd seen the last of Tristan, I was very much mistaken. Though he'd let me go initially, I soon heard him giving chase, calling my name. I threw a furtive glance over my shoulder to see that he was plowing after me, barefoot, with frightening agility.

"Will you wait a second?" He grabbed my arm to stop me, his tone exasperated.

I pulled it curtly from his grasp. "Look," I said, holding my palms up to ward him off, "there's no judgment here, okay." *Liar.* "So you're in a penis col—" *Crap!* "I…I mean nudist colony. Whatever." *That's definitely not as creepy as a cult.*

"What?!" he sputtered, two deep clefts forming between his brows. "We're not nudists. Nor am I in a penis colony."

"I'm confused." I pointed back to where we'd just come from. "What was that then?" If he admitted to some kinky cult ritual I was absolutely going to mace him in the face and run!

He followed the direction of my condemning finger with a raised brow. "That's called being one with nature."

"Well, don't let me stop your communion with nature." I promptly turned away, leaving him staring after me.

"Evan—"

"Goodbye, Tristan." I turned back only once, midway down the road, to make sure he wasn't following.

He wasn't. His arms were folded over his chest, still and watchful as his gaze hounded me.

I followed the declivitous dirt track all the way back to the cabin. I reached the front door without further mishap, and without being accosted by anymore flaccid man-meat.

I needed a good shower. All that trouser-less flesh had made me feel icky. Had the world gone mad? Or was I just being a colossal prude?

By the time I finished my shower my stomach reminded me loudly that it was already nearly lunchtime and I'd still not fed it. Being *hangry* and lovesick only made me feel nauseous, ergo I'd take care of the former and, therefore, be better able to deal with the latter. My sandwich-making, however, was shortly interrupted by another knock at my door. This one as polite as the first had been rude. So much for 'hundreds of acres of peaceful rainforest and calming solitude', I thought with a snarl, throwing the door open.

Tristan was standing at the threshold, his hands resting casually in his pockets. When I proceeded to do nothing more than glare at him, he gave a snort and shook his head, saying, "*Deja vu*?"

"Hardly. It's broad daylight *and* it's not raining." So I had no reason to invite him in, unlike the last time he'd come to my door. Nor would I be showering him with French letters. More importantly, he wasn't going to kiss himself out of this explanation.

"So you won't let me in?" He nonchalantly crossed his arms.

"Will you keep your clothes on?"

"Only if you want me to…"

My lip quirked involuntarily. *Damn him.* After a beat, I stepped aside to let him enter. "Be honest, Tristan. Are you guys living in a nudist colony?"

"Getting down to brass tacks, huh?" He rubbed the back of his neck. Then, seeming to come to a decision, he asked me a question instead. "Would you have been as horrified if you'd seen us all skinny dipping in a hot tub?"

I considered his point and shook my head. "No, I guess not. But it's like thirty degrees outside, and you weren't in a frigging hot tub."

"Semantics." He lifted a careless shoulder.

"So you're saying you're not in a nudist colony?"

"Not in a nudist colony and not in a penis colony either."

"So you got drunk and fell out of your clothes?"

"Doesn't everyone once in a while?"

"I wouldn't know." I left him to follow as I headed back down the hallway to the kitchen.

"Pity." He, like Dinwiddie before him, eyed the cold wood stove and shook his head.

"And stop answering my questions with your own questions." *Sneaky bastard.* From the kitchen, I watched him suspiciously as he knelt to inspect the stove. "What're you doing?"

"Making sure you don't catch your death." He disappeared outside, presumably to the shed because he returned with an armload of wood.

Distractedly, I watched Tristan's fire propagate across the logs. I thought about what Melissa had once said about Dinwiddie seeing Dean streaking naked across her yard. "Do you guys do that sort of thing often?" I watched him carefully for his answer. "Run naked across people's yards, I mean."

He sat down on one of the stools at the breakfast bar and gave a curt shrug. "I don't streak across people's yards, Evan."

"Just the woods?"

He nodded.

"No wonder this town think's you're all in a damn cult. Mrs. Dinwiddie probably spread that rumor herself."

He held up his hand with a suspicious frown. "People don't actually believe that shit. It's all just empty talk to amuse one another."

"Don't delude yourself, they one hundred percent *do* think you're in some screwy religious faction." I picked up my unfinished sandwich.

He leaned back with a stony compression of his lips. "Well, that explains why Mrs. D always looks at me like I've eaten her damn poodle."

This time I swallowed my food before speaking. "Did you eat her poodle?" I shot him an arch look.

"Maybe."

"Weirdo."

"What does that make you, Evan?" He arched a dark brow, smirking. "You've willingly allowed a poodle-eating, nudist weirdo into your house."

"You forgot to add werewolf."

"I never forget what I am." His smile turned wolfish as he stood and lazily made his way around the breakfast bar to loom over me. The scent of the forest clung to him.

"Be serious." I tried to move backward, sucking my lower lip into my mouth, but the counter barred my retreat.

"I am very serious about you, Evan. Don't doubt that."

His behavior the night before last suggested otherwise. "Good luck convincing me of that."

"The hungrier the wolf the more tenacious he'll be." His arms moved either side of me to cage me against the wall. "Let me show you."

20

JANE EYRE

I had to tilt my head back to keep eye-contact. My heart gave a traitorous flutter as I tried to stay aloof, but I could already feel myself unraveling beneath his penetrating stare. Beneath that erotic smile. The air lay sultry and thick between us like an amatory vapor. He broke the contact only to lower his eyes to my lips. I felt the press of his stare like a kindling touch. Like a scorching kiss.

"No," I said, my palms returning to his chest. His skin was impossibly warm through his shirt.

"No?"

I'd have sounded more convincing if I wasn't staring at his mouth. "Yes."

"Yes?"

I shut my eyes so that his sexy smile couldn't mess with my fragile equilibrium anymore. "No," I said again. "Don't you have somewhere else to be?" *Like running naked through someone's yard maybe.*

"I'm exactly where I'm meant to be."

I folded my arms. "Remember what you promised that night you kissed me?"

"Yes."

"So what do you want from me?"

"Isn't it obvious?" His eyes seemed to glow with latent heat.

"I *said* stop answering my questions with more questions." I poked a finger at his chest to punctuate the command and shot him a warning look that dared him to ask another one. "And keep your lips to yourself."

He cocked his head playfully. "Why?"

For once his smile had the opposite effect on me. "Because you'll break my heart." My lips gave a devastating tremble. "Because your mood swings are giving me whiplash."

His demeanor hardened instantly. "My mood swings?"

"Hot one moment and then cold the next." There was a sudden burning pressure of tears behind my eyes. "I don't know the rules of whatever game you're playing."

"Evan—"

"Please," I begged, wanting to spill my guts before I thought better of it, "I just want to know one thing: are you ashamed to be with me?"

"What? No!" He dropped his hands and moved away from me, looking poleaxed.

"Then why did you ignore me in the bar?"

Clouds gathered over his eyes and his mouth flattened ruefully. "Maybe some sick part of me wanted you to hate me so that I'd be forced to keep my distance." He gave a terse lift of one shoulder as he glanced around the kitchen. "Clearly, that backfired. I can't seem to stay away."

"You made me feel like I meant nothing to you. I was prepared to be 'just friends' like you said, but then *you* changed the rules with that kiss! I don't know where I stand with you from one second to the next. Do you think I'll make a tit of myself in front of your family? Is that it?"

He shook his head firmly. "You've got it all backward."

My brows rose dubiously as I crossed my arms. "Oh? Surprise me then."

"I worry that *you'll* reject *me* once you get to know me and my family."

"That's ridiculous! You shut me out the minute your brother and friends showed up the other night."

"My family are the ones I don't trust around *you*. They're suspicious of outsiders. I don't want *them* scaring *you* off." He backed away and leaned against the kitchen sink to face me. "But they know how I feel about you, Evan."

"They do?" That surprised me.

He nodded.

"Lucky them because I sure as hell don't know how you feel."

The light from the kitchen window seemed to infuse his eyes with some eerie glow as they fixed themselves to my lips. "It's kinda hard to keep secrets in our family. I tried to deny what I feel around you"—his nose flared as he drew near again—"but every lie has a certain scent."

"Really?" I searched his face.

"Yes, and so does every truth." He dropped his forehead gently to mine. "The truth is I need you. You're in my blood, Evan—I'm addicted to what you make me feel."

"And what is that?"

"Pure animal lust." His voice deepened, and a violent conflagration seemed to roar in his eyes as he held my gaze. "It's all I can do to keep it leashed around you." His breathing intensified. "You're just as dangerous to me as I am to you."

I felt my heart ignite with the primal force of that gaze. My tongue thickened in my mouth. All speech failed me.

Then he shut his eyes a moment, dousing the fire, and gave a shuddering sigh. "But you'd be so much better off without me. I'm no good for you. All I seem to do is hurt and disappoint you every time I try to pull away. Every time I try to do what's right for *you*."

"Stop trying then." My hands were trembling with need. I felt it too—this ferocious desire for him. I was overcome with it. "Let *me* decide what's in my best interest."

"You might regret me later."

"No."

"You sure about that? There might be no going back after today."

Could I give him one last chance? Or would that be fatal? Were my hormones leading me to a dangerous precipice?

"Be sure, Evan." His mouth was hovering just above mine, his eyes burning with the same intensity I felt in my belly. He wanted my final answer. "This time I won't pull away again. You have my word."

"Yes," I whispered, wetting my lips. I wasn't sure what exactly I was agreeing to, the sexual fog had so obliterated my mind. I craved his kisses.

He slanted his warm lips instantly over mine, one hand cradling my head while the other splayed at the small of my back. Sapid heat radiated through my flesh. Each stroke of his tongue charged my flesh with sparking current. Beneath my fingers, his heart echoed deep and resonant. I could feel its rhythm, erotic and obliterating, as it quickened through my body. When he pulled his lips from mine I sagged against him, breathless, my head dropping to his chest.

"What were we talking about again?" My voice was thick with desire.

He guided my chin up with his finger and then ran his thumb over my bottom lip where he'd graze it with his teeth. "Just that you deserve better than me."

"I'm gonna need more convincing of that."

I'd no sooner said the words than he'd fused our lips again, lifting me up and planting me on the edge of the kitchen island to stand between my legs. A sharp yank of his hands behind my knees and my pelvis was flush against his, my legs wrapping instantly around his waist. This kiss was far less bridled. I could feel the pressure of what lay behind his straining zipper. His mouth was ravening and bruising. I felt claimed. My blood spiked as my lips and tongue matched his frenzy.

I groaned into his mouth and he answered with a satisfied growl. Then his jaw, hard and bristled, grazed my neck as he worked his way down my throat. I angled my head back to give him better access, baring my throat to him. My hips moved involuntarily, grinding against his, my shins sliding up of their own volition. Each of my hands seemed to have a mind of its own, one fisting in his dark hair while the other clutched at his shoulder. The harder I clawed at his flesh the more his control seemed to slip. He devoured every inch of my skin with searing lips and raking teeth.

Tristan's hand slid up under my shirt, his fingers gliding up over my ribs like the chords of a guitar, drawing closer and closer to my aching nipple. Suddenly he was there, pulling my bra aside to drag a calloused thumb over my pebbled flesh. He cupped my breast with his hot palm. My chest heaved with soft, exquisite moans. The fire licked and coiled where my pelvis moved against his. Tristan's mouth sought mine again, our breaths mingling. Everywhere he touched I shivered.

Was I really about to make love to a man—this man—right here above the cutlery drawer, amidst the tea stains and bread crumbs? I'd already given myself permission… But there were still things unresolved.

Having sensed my sudden hesitation, Tristan released me. His eyes were a molten topaz as he searched mine.

"Okay," I said raggedly, pushing him away, "I'm convinced." *Almost.* I needed a breather to think.

"Yay, me." He grimaced, adjusting himself as he put some space between us.

I allowed myself to really look at him, searching for flaws. There was a small mole on the side of his nose, but even that was beautiful. Yet the flaws that really mattered were the ones inside. He'd hurt me with his coldness, unintentionally or not. Despite that, there was no question that he already owned me. I was his if he wanted me. But could he truly ever be mine? Why choose me when he could have Nicole? *Because she's a bitch?* Well, that was true enough. The fact remained—he could have anyone he wanted.

His keen eyes had caught the flicker of doubt in my expression. "You're not convinced, are you?" Ostensibly feeling stonewalled by my silence, his brows dropped lower. "You're a suspicious woman, Ev."

As far as his gender was concerned I had every right to be. I wasn't a misandrist, though. Not all men were fucknuts. I just didn't want to be too reckless with my heart. And there was still the question of his secrets. "What are you hiding?" I wanted to ask but didn't. Instead, I said, "I don't get how you think you're no good for me."

He folded his arms over his chest, a taciturn crease at his mouth. "What don't you get exactly?"

"I mean you're *you*—" my hand gestured meaningfully between us "—and I'm me." Surely he understood how incredible that was.

"Well, I'm glad we clarified that," he deadpanned.

"I'm like Jane Eyre and you're…freakishly handsome."

"Well, thanks."

"You can have anyone. What the hell d'you want with me?"

"Who's Jane?"

"What?!" I choked. "Okay, now we definitely can't be friends."

"I don't want to be just friends, Evan." He was looking at me like he wanted to devour me. "I never wanted that; I was lying to myself before." Then his brow furrowed with curiosity. "Seriously, who's Jane?"

Blushing, I explained, "Jane Eyre is a plain-looking victorian woman who falls in love with a man already married to a lunatic."

"Fascinating," he said dryly. "But I still don't see a problem here. You're not plain and I'm not married. Not even to a lunatic."

"Tristan—"

He planted a firm "end of discussion" kiss on my parted lips and then helped me off the counter. "Now that I've brainwashed you with my freakish looks we can go meet the cult leader."

"Huh?"

"Wanna come play in the nudist colony for a bit?"

The penis colony? "Um—"

He threaded our fingers. "I'm asking you, officially, to meet my family, Ev. Whatever it takes to prove to you that I really like you." He pressed his lips to my ear. "Say yes."

A small smile pulled shyly at the corner of my mouth. "Yes."

"And as to 'what I want with you', it's simple: I just want you. I wish you saw yourself as I see you."

"How do you see me?"

"With my eyes." He laughed as I elbowed him. "Come on, beautiful. Let's hit the road, shall we?" The way he was looking at me certainly made me feel beautiful.

"Beautiful?" I wanted to throw confetti and cartwheel across the kitchen.

"And funny and sweet—even when you're pelting condoms at me."

"Ugh, am I never gonna live that down?"

"Nope." Grinning, he pulled me behind him as he strolled from the kitchen.

"Where are you taking me?"

"I told you, to the compound."

"Wait, I gotta grab a jacket." I started for the bedroom, but he caught me around the waist and yanked me back for more steamy lip-locking.

"Those are some sticky lips you have there, Mr. Thorn, I can't seem to get them off my face," I chuckled.

He gave my butt an affectionate slap then grabbed his keys from the counter where he'd left them earlier. "I'll be outside." He doused the fire in the wood stove and then headed for the front door.

"Wait, is it too early in the day for favors?" I asked, suddenly remembering the Yukon's dead battery.

"I don't do sexual favors on Tuesdays."

"Pfft, it's your truck's stamina I'm after not yours. I got distracted last night and left the lights on in the Yukon and drained the battery."

"Distracted? Dare I ask?"

"I thought I saw…" I had no idea what I'd seen actually. "Something was watching me last night. Two things at least. I locked myself in the house and was too much of a wussy to rescue my groceries and backpack till this morning."

"There probably *was* something out there watching you. You're in the boonies now. There are eyes everywhere." He affected a creepy leer, dragging his eyes down the length of me. "God knows I like watching you."

I gave him a leer of my own. "Would you please stop distracting me with your creepy flirting, so I can jump my car."

He snorted. "I'll go jump your car, you go get your jacket."

Once he'd sauntered down the driveway, I shut the door, wrapped my arms around myself and squealed quietly before racing to the room to fix my appearance. My hair was mussed, courtesy of Tristan's fingers, so I brushed it out, swiped some mascara on my lashes, and then headed back into the kitchen with my jacket to grab my phone and purse, chanting my grandfather's mnemonic: *Spectacles, testicles, wallet, and watch.*

I was ready to go, but nervous about meeting his family; nervous and excited about what was happening between Tristan and I. A flush of color spread over my skin as I headed out the door thinking of all the places his hands had gone earlier and the places they had yet to go.

"I found a heartbeat," he said over the growl of his Ford once I'd joined him where he was leaning casually on his brush guard. "But we have to let it charge for a bit." His eyebrows wriggled suggestively. "Now it's just a matter of killing time."

"We can talk politics? Discuss the state of the nation?"

"Nah, I hate small talk." Hooking his fingers at my jean pockets he pulled me against him.

I wrapped my arms around his neck, desire pooling where our bodies touched, and stood on the tips of my toes to meet his lips halfway. Yup, tonight was definitely the night!

21

BOOBS AND BOLOGNESE

The tires chewed at the gravel as Tristan maneuvered his truck off the main road and up along a steep and meandering dirt track. With each stone that disappeared under the tread, I felt my gut tighten anxiously. I caught my knee bouncing and quickly willed it to stop. Tristan's thumbnail was running up and down abstractedly over the stubble beneath his bottom lip.

The wall of western hemlocks stood guard along the road like watchful sentries, their branches arching overhead as we passed beneath. The leaves and needles seemed to draw back like an evergreen curtain till finally, Dean's homestead appeared. It was a massive, vintage-looking log edifice with stone foundations, a wraparound porch, and expansive windows. It stood majestic and shaded at the center of a primeval garden, overrun with shrubs, stout vines, and more towering trees. Some of the branches had stretched themselves guardedly across the second story gables, jealous of the secrets that lay behind the panes.

On either side of the driveway, lining the gravel, the goatsbeard, hydrangeas, and purple fireweed were left to propagate wildly. The effect was of a quiet rampancy—a hostile smile.

"Welcome to the compound," said Tristan, breaking the

silence at last, unaware of how *unwelcome* I already felt. And I wasn't even through the door yet.

"How many people live in Dean's house?" I knew that Tristan didn't. He had his own place a little further up the road, although most of the land that lay between here and there belonged to Dean.

"A few people," he hedged.

"How many is a few?" I looked back up at the sprawling mansion, remarking all the cars and trucks parked haphazardly wherever there was space between the shrubbery.

"Twelve, including Dean." Tristan pulled his truck into a space under a shaggy cedar, alongside a light blue 1957 Chevy half-ton. When he killed the engine, the silence of the woods fell heavily upon us.

"Excluding you, though." I mulled that over.

"Right. I live alone."

I reassessed the 'commune' with leery eyes. Unlike what I'd first imagined, there were no barbed-wire fences between the house and the main road. No guard towers either, only a Trespassers-will-by-mauled-to-death-by-vicious-Alsatians sign posted near the driveway entrance to warn neighbors and lost tourists off. Secretly, I'd half expected to see groups of demure women in identically drab, nineteenth-century-style blue frocks with white bibs and nun-like headdresses. "How come they all live together like this?"

" 'The strength of the pack is the wolf and the strength of the wolf is the pack'."

"It takes more than a Kipling quote to distract me from my questions."

He sighed, leaning back against the headrest. "Not everyone lives in the house all the time. The property is pretty vast and most of the family have their own cabins. James lives in a treehouse near the cove." He watched me from the tail of his eye.

"Think of this as a little town of rogues and misfits that don't fit in anywhere else."

"Do they all work for Thorn Aviation?"

"All of us have a role to play, yes."

"So it's like mutualism? Everyone strengthens the pack somehow?"

"Not mutualism. Family. There's a difference."

Like *The Godfather*. All of them playing their part in the 'family business'. *Holy shit!* What if they were the Alaskan Mafia? A nudist colony of teeth-filing, contact lens-wearing, poodle-eating, bear-whispering, werewolf mafiosi! I almost laughed. My imagination was getting out of control.

"And this house doesn't just belong to Dean, it belongs to the family. And the family is very territorial, so I apologize in advance if they treat you strangely."

"Well, I am a stranger," I murmured, biting my lip as I pulled the door handle.

"It's just that we feel safe to be ourselves here and—"

"Jeez, Tristan, I get it. It's like you're introducing me to your pack of rescued Rottweilers." Was I expected to bend over and let them sniff my business end too?

He chuckled, climbing out. "You're not far off."

Unamused, I followed him to the gabled deck and up the steps to a solid pair of double doors that were marbled red with vivid cedar knots. "We, who are about to die, salute you," I muttered.

Tristan gave a light snort as he opened the door to let me precede him into their lair.

The entry hall was spacious, the light muted by a fixture designed to look like a gas lamp. No glassy-eyed trophies here, I thought with relief. *Yet.* I discarded my boots, following Tristan's silent example, and then trailed after him down the hallway, my socks padding noiselessly across slate stone tiles. I ran my fingers softly over the varnished live edge of a beautiful end-table that had been pushed flush against the timber wall.

Noticing my appreciative touch, Tristan said, "Tim built that. He helped Dean build the house too." He then bade me follow him a little further down the hallway, pausing beside a hardwood wolf stretched across the wall. Its body was easily twice the length of mine. Smiling, a hint of pride in his eyes, he said, "Tim carved it, and painted all the landscapes in the house."

"He probably has people jumping tits over ass for his artwork," I said reverently.

"He's quite the famous artist. He does a lot of commissions for the hotels and airports around Alaska."

I stepped back from the wooden wolf, finally noticing how quiet the house was. "Where is everyone?"

Tristan gave a shrug of his powerful shoulders and continued on down the hallway. "Dunno, probably out running before dinner." He finally halted at a heavy door and gave a terse knock before he pushed the door open, taking my hand to pull me in behind him. The room was empty.

It was a masculine space, serving as both an office and library, with a heavy walnut desk acting cynosure of the room in the absence of its master. On the wall behind that desk was a peculiar mural. The scene was that of a hunting pack of wolves, but that wasn't what made it so odd. In the painted expression of each wolf, there was something almost…human. I couldn't explain it —the effect was so expertly and subtly composed—but it was as though each animal was watching me with a cunning intelligence that was disturbingly unnatural.

"Wait here," said Tristan, unexpectedly releasing my hand and abandoning me in the middle of the room. Abandoning me to the wolves, so to speak.

Before I'd even opened my mouth to protest he was gone and the door shut behind him. I was too nervous to sit still, the dark wolves stared so keenly that I felt my skin crawl. Instead of sitting there like a waiting lamb I beelined it to the bookshelves, soon realizing that most of the titles were unfamiliar. And old. Some weren't even in English. I dragged a curious finger across the leather spines, drawing in the wonderful scent of aged leather and old paper. But it was one spine, a faded cream with green lettering that caught my eye first, urging my fingers to pull it from its perch.

The Werewolf by Montague Summers. I held my breath as I carefully turned the front board, chafed and worn. A first edition! My eyes skimmed across the browned pages, glossing over the introduction and settling on the first chapter—Lycanthropy. I slowed my eyes to take in the old words. With a derisive grunt, I read only a little further and then closed the book soundly, rolling my eyes at the idea of war-wolves, witchcraft, and demons. The next book I removed was a weathered volume I *did* recognize. *Metamorphoses* by Ovid. The part about King Lycaon seemed to be dog-eared and someone had underlined a passage in Latin that I easily parsed only because there was a line by line translation of the poem. My eyes slid across each Latin word before moving to its English counterpart. *Caedis.* Slaughter. *Sanguine.* Blood. I read on: " 'His garments pass away into hairs, his arms into legs. He becomes a wolf…' " Maybe Dean was a fan of dead poets and Greek Mythology?

With an uneasy glance at the door, I set the book back in its slot beside its neighbor, *The Menageries: Quadrupeds*. Most of the books in the collection, I noticed, were, in some way or another, related to werewolfery. There were even a few nineteenth century "Wehr-Wolf" penny dreadfuls hiding in amongst the volumes. At first, I'd been amused by Tristan's innuendos, but I was beginning to feel the first inkling of disquiet. I wanted to believe that Tristan wasn't some sort of idiosyncratic occultist who believed in this shit, but his filed teeth and the lupine influence rife within the house said otherwise. If he was a lunatic then so was Dean.

I gave a little shiver and backed away from the esoteric shelves just as I heard the door opening with a harsh groan. It wasn't Tristan in the room with me now but Nicole. Her expression was as cold as marble.

"H-hi." Well, this was awkward.

"You shouldn't be in here." She was looking through me as though addressing the wall at my back.

"I was told to wait here."

There was a sudden flicker of black in her eyes, something hateful, just before she glanced at the mantle shelf where a clock sat counting the length of the silence that followed. "I'll let Hamish know you'll be joining us for dinner," she finally said in a dead tone. And then she was gone.

My breath expelled with a violent whoosh. I hadn't known I'd been holding it till the moment she left the room. I hadn't realized at first just how much she'd chilled the air when she'd entered. I started when the door was opened almost directly after Nicole had disappeared from it.

Tristan blew in like a storm, Dean at his heels. "What did she say to you?"

I felt myself wither under his glower. "That she'd let Hamish know I was staying for dinner."

He nodded, the clouds dissipating instantly from his face. "Oh."

Unlike his brother, Dean was grinning humorlessly. "He's worried Nicole will eat you." He chuckled at my expression and headed over to sit behind his desk. "How d'you like the old place, Evan?" With a regal flick of his wrist, he motioned me to a leather armchair.

"Very wolfy," I replied, steeling myself to converse with Tristan's formidable brother.

He smirked, following my eyes to the large mural of running wolves behind his desk. "It's in our blood, what can I say."

"I'm just glad there aren't any corpse trophies decorating your walls."

Tristan perched himself on the scroll arm of my chair. "We don't kill for sport. We eat what we kill, and no part of the animal is wasted."

"We were hunting venison this morning when you found us," Dean said.

"Naked?"

"Like our ancestors." He laced his fingers behind his neck and leaned back in his chair, lifting his nose as though to sample the air. "Hope you like venison."

"Oh…um…" I didn't want to insult the guy by refusing his hospitality, but I wasn't in the habit of eating anything that couldn't regrow another limb—or head—never mind a juvenile deer. "I don't, sorry." *Not sorry.*

"Don't you like deer?" Tristan asked.

"I like Bambi just fine. Preferably alive."

"No meat at all?" He seemed bemused.

Dean also looked momentarily poleaxed. "That's okay," he finally said, "we'll get Hamish to throw some salmon on the grill or something."

I groaned inwardly, half amused by their assumption that "no meat" couldn't possibly include fish.

Dean suddenly cocked his head to listen to something. He then looked up at his brother, and by tacit agreement they stood to leave, Tristan taking my hand in his to pull me up from the plush settee. "Dinner's ready," he said.

How could he possibly know that? I looked at the clock. Six o'clock exactly. Maybe they were sticklers for time.

As we neared the dining room, the sound of voices became hushed. The weight of unfamiliar eyes fell heavily on me as I entered the dining room, but at least everyone was fully clothed this time. All the penises were stowed away and there were no large mammaries out to agitate my envy.

"Come sit here, Evan." Nicole patted the seat beside her. "Don't worry, no one's gonna bite you just yet." No smile followed to dull the edge from her odd comment.

"For God's sake." With a dirty look at Nicole, Lydia got up from her chair and took the empty seat beside Nicole. Then, smiling, she said, "Take my seat, Evan. That way you can sit next to Tristan."

"Thank you." Relieved, I followed Tristan to where the two vacant chairs awaited us.

As far as I could tell, no one seemed to find it strange or uncharacteristic that Tristan was glaring balefully at Nicole.

James appeared at the door the next moment. He grinned and grabbed a spare seat from the wall, dragging it over to scoot between Nicole and Lydia. "Hey, spider girl," he said, winking at me.

I grinned back at him, glad to have one more welcoming face at the table.

Dean had taken his seat at the head and Tristan the seat opposite him. I was happy to find a reprieve from all the attention when a short man walked in with the last dish. His features were foxlike but friendly as he greeted me.

"This looks amazing, Hamish," Dean said, reaching for a steak with his fork. "Katie" —he winked at her "my compliments." The others followed suit, diving in with relish.

I discovered that Sandra, the woman beside me, was a lawyer and that Katie (who I'd seen in the woods this morning) and Hamish were the chefs that took care of feeding everyone as well as preparing the picnics that were offered on some of the tour packages.

On the other side of Sandra sat Ben, a shy-looking biologist, and Ed, the accountant, who looked nothing like my idea of a bookish pen-pusher. Like most of the men there, including Tristan, he was almost a seven-footer. His sleek black skin and winsome smile only complimented his striking face. It belonged on the cover of a book, not shoved diligently between its pages. The *man meat* I'd spied this morning had, I realized after being introduced to everyone, belonged to Ben, Ed, and Tim, the *Tlingit* artist. Tim, as it turned out, was short for Timber. He had midnight hair, like Ed, but it was straight as an arrow and lay down his back like a mantle. His skin was a beautiful burnt sienna, stretched across an eagle-like nose, and his eyes were almond brown, seeming to probe every detail around him, as though he saw colors invisible to our naked eyes.

Leanne and Alex were the two IT geniuses (or computer dogsbodies as Alex had put it), and the last person I met was Jack, who worked for the Forest Service in Thorne Bay and looked more like a grizzly than a human. Each person, like Tristan had inferred earlier, really did have an important role here. They had an in-house lawyer, a biologist, a Forest Service officer, a live-in accountant, tech support, chefs, and pilot/mechanics to operate their fleet of aircraft. It was like a well-oiled machine in one neat little family.

I turned to whisper to Tristan, "I thought you said there were twelve people living here?" Excluding Tristan and I, there were thirteen at the dinner table.

"Nicole—" he lifted his lips off his teeth like a snarl "—is only visiting." His demeanor inferred he meant trespassing.

"I'd say she's overstayed it." James nonchalantly reached for another serving of Bambi's seared carcass. He looked up and winked at me, but when he swept an amused gaze around the table it was to see the rest of the family, except Tristan, glaring at him. Especially his sister. He shrugged and stuffed his face unrepentantly.

Before Nicole could add a scathing retort (which she looked about ready to do) Katie turned to me and explained, in a voice that overpowered Nicole's, that the tomatoes in the Bolognese sauce heaped over my plain spaghetti had come from their very own veggie garden. The veal that Dean had 'procured' I didn't touch at all, obviously, but I was no less impressed by their amazing subsistence living.

Tristan's hand slid over my knee, the heat from his skin surprising me. While Tristan and I were stealing hot looks from one another, James began entertaining the table by playing with his dinner rolls.

"Why did you put nipples on the rolls?" he asked Katie. Then he took a lascivious bite.

"It's a brioche," she said, defensively. "They're supposed to be interesting."

He eyeballed the remaining two rolls on his plate. "Great, our first dinner with Evan and you feed her boobs and bolognese."

"Stop playing with your boobs, James." Dean tore a piece of veal off his fork, his cinnamon eyes impassive.

After dinner, Tristan pulled me aside as everyone was clearing the table. "Do you want me to take you home, or are you up for an adventure?"

"An adventure," I answered in a husky voice that didn't sound like it belonged to me.

"Great, you can meet my son."

"Your son?!"

He grinned. "His name's Odin, he's hairy and licks his junk a lot."

"Oh."

"You look surprised." He angled his head askance. "What were you thinking, Spencer?"

I gave an insouciant lift of my shoulder. "Just that I'm glad your idea of adventure doesn't include a Red Room of Pain."

"A what?" He seemed honestly confused.

I waved my hand dismissively. "I'd love to meet your dog."

"And to sweeten the deal, I'll throw in some cheesecake. Sound good?"

"Not as good as boobs and bolognese." Was cheesecake some sort of sophisticated code for *big kid games*?

Tristan didn't seem to notice my flushed skin because he was already making his farewells of back slaps and kisses. I added my diffident goodbyes to his and winced when Nicole pressed her cold cheek to mine. Dean's taciturn cheek received only the briefest and most reserved peck before I backed away. These two, Nicole and Dean, I hadn't quite figured out yet and both of them unsettled me.

"Shall we?" Tristan covered my hand warmly with his, nodding to the front door.

"We shall." *Finally.* The way Nicole had bristled every time Tristan touched or looked at me had left me enervated. I took a deep breath as we strolled back to the truck, my cold fingers threaded tightly into his.

"You did well," he said, remote starting his truck.

"Was it a test?"

"If it was you passed." And then he stopped and drew me closer so that he could press a hot kiss to my lips.

My skin suffused with heat and my stomach cartwheeled as he moved his beautiful lips skillfully over mine, his tongue delving and whetting my nonexistent appetite. The one I hadn't had all night till right now. When he lifted his head his eyes were bright and seemed infused with yellow moonlight.

I shivered in the headlights. "Your eyes change color, did you know that?"

He shrugged and opened the door for me. Once he was in his own seat, he began scrolling through his playlist instead of shifting the gear into drive. I was about to ask what he was doing when Marvin Gaye's *Let's Get It On* began streaming through the speakers.

"Seriously?" I burst into laughter as he finally reversed out the parking spot. Was he joking or was the song a delicious foretaste of what was to come next?

22

GENTLEMAN STRIPPER

A deep, lazy bark greeted us as soon as the front door opened. It was accompanied by a large shadow, tail wagging, that loped toward us. I felt, rather than saw, Tristan leave my side.

"Hey, my boy!" Tristan's dark silhouette hunkered down beside the dog, grabbing him playfully around the neck for a hug. "This is Odin."

"He has a very handsome silhouette." I was wearing a facetious grin, but I knew he couldn't see it in the darkness.

"Sorry." Though I couldn't see his expression, his tone was rueful. "The light switch is just on the wall beside you."

The moonlight through the French doors didn't quite reach the front door, so I walked my fingers blindly along the wall in question.

"A little more to the right," he instructed. "You're getting warmer."

How the hell could he see what my hand was doing? I couldn't even tell where it was, and it was right in front of my face! Finally, my fingers brushed the light panel. "My word, I'll never take my sight for granted again."

Good thing Odin hadn't snuck up on me in my blindness or

I'd have shrieked my head off. I had only a half second warning, from when the bulb was lit, before Odin maneuvered his hulking body directly between my thighs for a doggie back scratch. I obliged him, running my fingers through the coarse grey hair at his flanks. I didn't dare deny the shaggy giant.

"I rescued him when he was a puppy," Tristan said, still kneeling on the floor.

I smiled nervously as the dog lifted beautiful golden eyes to my face, probably deciding whether or not my butt scratches were up to snuff. "He looks like a wolf!"

"That's because he *is* a wolf." Tristan pushed himself off the floor. "I think a hunter must have killed his mother. I gave his brother to my uncle Frank."

Now that Odin had gotten a two for one, he trotted from the room with a hearty sneeze.

"Well, you just got the seal of approval." Tristan leaned down to plant a brief, albeit sweet, kiss on my lips.

"He's a sweet boy. Humans could learn a lot from wolves." Such noble and loyal creatures.

"Yeah, wolves take pleasure in the little things." He laced our fingers and pulled me to the kitchen. "Like butt scratches."

"Who doesn't love a good butt scratch," I agreed.

"Right, and butt sniffing—you can learn so much about a person from butt sniffing."

"I'll take your word for it."

He chuckled as he lifted a wine glass from the cupboard and poured me a generous serving. "Don't worry, I was gonna spare you the details anyway." He winked, placing the glass stem between my waiting fingers.

The chocolaty bouquet pressed upon my tongue like a bold kiss as I took my first sip, holding Tristan's gaze over the rim. "As with most details about your life." I hadn't expected the coldness that seeped into my tone.

Just like that, his humor left him. "I don't want to have any secrets from you, Evan."

"Then don't." I waited a moment, in case he meant to open up a little, to bleed a little, but he watched me quietly as I swirled the wine around my glass. I loved the earthy color of Malbec, like rich warm blood. It was like no other red. I transferred my eyes back to him and gave a resigned shrug. "I guess you'll tell me when you're ready." There was a cautionary voice inside advising me to take it slow with him, that maybe tonight ought not be *the* night for physical intimacy. He was holding back too much, it warned, and, therefore, so should I. But I argued that if perhaps I gave myself to him he'd love me in return; love me enough to expose all of himself.

He turned away and poured himself a bourbon into an enamel camping mug. "Maybe it's *you* that has to be ready to hear what I have to say."

"Do I need to be liquored up first?" I coated my palate with another sip of Malbec.

"Probably." His chuckle held very little humor.

"I'll get right on that. Shall we fill the wait with cheesecake." I was done with talking about this invisible *Sword of Damocles* hanging between us anyway. It would either fall or it wouldn't. I would either survive it or I wouldn't.

"We shall." He pulled two dessert plates from the cupboard.

From the couch, Odin's ears twitched with interest as the fridge door was opened. He peeled one eye open to watch his master pull the cheesecake out. The wolf's legs were spread wide in the air and the family jewels were bared blithely to the world.

Noticing the direction of my gaze, Tristan chuckled. "Yeah, the guy has no shame."

"Can you say you look any classier when you're sleeping?" I absently took the leaden dessert plate and fork from him.

"Wouldn't you like to know."

I did actually.

Tristan winked and excused himself a moment, disappearing from the room, presumably to visit the washroom.

Smiling, I repaired from his kitchen and wandered into the living room. Woodsmoke and cedar incensed the cabin, and I found it reminiscent of Tristan's skin. Wanting to clear my head, I unlocked the sliding door and stepped outside, the brisk air instantly puckering my skin. At the corner of the large deck, I spied a hot tub. There was something darkly inviting about the way his hot tub was guarded by towering woods. Shivers of divine premonition shot up my spine as I approached it.

You know you want to, Evan. Could I? Did I have the guts? *I double dare you.* Without stopping to think too long about what it was I was about to do, I flipped the thick vinyl cover up over the sturdy bracket. Steam wafted up the moment the top was lifted. Hurriedly, I began stripping out of my clothes, shooting furtive glances over my naked shoulders in case I was caught with my knickers, quite literally, around my ankles. I scrambled inelegantly over the side of the square tub and quickly sank into the safety of the roaring bubbles.

I felt so incredibly uninhibited and sensual as the bubbles lapped against my chest. I had never done anything so risqué in my life. Who the hell had I become? The larkspur looming beside the deck seemed to glare with disapproval, their sepals black in the moonlight. *Well, no one asked you.* I stuck my tongue out at it.

As the seconds slowed, the wait became increasingly suspenseful. I sat there agonizing over my spontaneity, second-guessing my daring. I glanced down at myself, trying to see through the foam—the way a certain pair of probing, aqueous eyes might soon see me—and felt my pulse spike because, although the bubbles obscured most of my body, very little was actually left to the imagination. The lights beneath the water shifted from dreamy blue to dark purple before silhouetting my body in an erotic red glow.

I looked up at the milky starscape and took a deep breath of the steam roiling off the surface in hot wreaths. A movement back on earth, however, drew my gaze. Tristan had slipped through the sliding doors as soundlessly as a jungle cat. He approached the tub slowly, his eyes primal as they transfixed me.

My belly tightened. "Say something, you're making me nervous." So much for playing the cool seductress.

"Give me a second," he murmured, setting his mug of bourbon on the side of the tub, "it's not every day I find a nudist in my yard."

I giggled self-consciously and splashed a bit of water at him before sinking lower into the hot bubbles.

Gaze lingering, Tristan reached behind his head to pull his shirt off in that sexy and deliberate way that men do, the plains of his abs inviting me to follow each muscle flex greedily. Once his shirt was discarded he held up a finger to pause the show and then disappeared back inside for a hot minute to fetch us each two fluffy towels. Those he hung on the towel rack, beside the hot tub, and then made short work of unzipping his jeans. He pushed them off with not a single sign of reserve. When he'd stepped out of them, he stood in nothing more than his navy boxer briefs, allowing me to enjoy the view for a few precious seconds before he hooked his thumb at the waistband where that gorgeous pelvic 'V' (the arrow to heaven) disappeared from view. My eyes lingered reverentially over every male contour, across the smooth expanse of golden skin that had been poured over the strong sinews of his six-foot-something frame. Tristan was more quarter-back than linebacker or, in rugby terms, more scrum-half than prop. He angled his head wickedly, warning me that he was about to continue with the show. I gave a small nod and began chewing nervously at my thumbnail as he slowly pushed the band further down.

I gaped. I blushed through the haze of sultry steam. I couldn't look away. He'd as good as dared me to watch and I was too curious to deny myself. It wasn't like I hadn't seen male parts before. In fact, I'd been inundated with penises recently—literally been given the willies this morning—and I had to admit they were all extremely unattractive-looking organs. But when one was looking at a certain appendage belonging to a certain demigod of a man, all thoughts were obliterated. There was room only to marvel.

This work of beauty belonged in the Sistine Chapel. But would it even fit on that glorious ceiling? I gulped. It was definitely in proportion to the rest of him and did nothing to assuage the butterflies from my stomach. He, of course, appeared to be enjoying my discomfit, and my inspection, and took his sweet time climbing into the jacuzzi. Even when that beast had finally been banished to the depths of the bubbling tub, I still continued to fidget because I knew that it was *there*...nearby. Its mere presence threatened. He, however, nonchalantly kept to his side of the tub.

"Oh crap," he said unexpectedly, his mouth awakening into a mischievous curl. "I forgot the cheesecake."

"Wait!" I squeezed my eyes shut and threw my hands up to stop him, my heart wholly unprepared for another show. "I wasn't gonna eat it anyway." And I wasn't talking about his *man meat* either.

"Aha! So the cheesecake was just a ploy to seduce me?"

"Pfft, it's not like I had to try very hard. You kinky bastards seem all too eager to drop your pants in the woods."

"Says the voyeur," he quipped.

"What? No way, I'm the unsuspecting victim here. Your brother practically shoved his bits in my face before I knew what was happening. And I heard he ran starkers through Mrs. Dinwiddie's yard recently too." As for *my* lady bits, they'd only yawned at the sight of the other meats. Not now, though. Tristan's nakedness was a whole other animal.

"Maybe if we flash her enough she'll move to Australia." He began to get up.

"*I'm* about to move to Australia!" I averted my gaze again. "Sit down before you scare the wildlife."

"Evan…I *am* the wildlife," he chuckled, but complied and sat back down. "The gentlemanly thing to do is not to argue with a lady, I guess."

"So you're a gentleman stripper, huh?"

"I admit that this was not my first live show. I wish the audience had been a little more vocal with the encouragements tonight."

"I gotta tell ya, I feel cheated. Where was the music?" *Pony,* by Ginuwine, would have been the perfect musical complement. "And where was the sparkly thong?"

"You didn't hear the music? I definitely heard the chorus of angels when I saw you out here…"

I rolled my eyes. "So about that cheesecake—I have a confession."

With one raised brow, he took a sip of bourbon.

Who drinks bourbon from a mug anyway?

"What about my cheesecake?"

"I don't eat the stuff. I don't eat cheese anything."

"Seriously?"

"Yeah, no cow pus of *any* kind."

"Cow pus?!" He looked about ready to spew his mouthful of bourbon. "What about fish then, you heathen?"

"Negative. I told you, no meat at all."

"Eggs?"

"You mean chicken abortions?" I shook my head. "No."

"It's a sad day when a woman gives up hotdogs."

"Gross, nothing but lips and sphincters."

He swiftly brought his hands to his ears. "Sacrilege!" When he saw that I was laughing too much to speak he uncovered them again. "Keep your blasphemies to yourself, woman."

"Yeah, yeah." The water had worked my blood into a fever and beads of sweat were rolling down my temples. Sitting next to a naked Tristan hadn't helped. It was time to get out. But how to accomplish that without flashing the merchandise?

"Getting too hot?" Tristan guessed my plight immediately and, without imparting any wisecracks, hauled himself out of the water. My eyes flew instantly to his rosy backside as he grabbed a towel to wrap around his lean waist. As soon as he'd done that he took the other one and held it out for me. "I'll close my eyes," he promised, smirking.

Did I want him to? I ran my teeth nervously over my lips and stood up out of the water before he had a chance to make good on his chivalrous promise. It was a tacit invitation for him to keep watching. I didn't need to look down to know my nipples had hardened under his stare. The rills streamed down over my flushed skin. No sexy black dress from a half-forgotten fantasy could've ever made me feel one tenth of the power that I felt right then and there in my own naked flesh, under those glowing green eyes. I had no idea what had gotten into me tonight, but I felt beautiful and delicious and alluring. It was liberating. The effect I was having on him was evidenced by the straining of his towel below the waist.

His eyes were glutting themselves on every inch of me as I moved to the edge with dilatory care, stepping over the side and onto the top step so that we were eye level. He wrapped the towel snugly around my shoulders, his Adam's apple shifting as he swallowed. Then he set to work replacing the cover over the hot tub before following me inside.

"Should I take you home?" He shut us in from the cold and leaned back against the double doors. Something primordial shifted in his gaze like a sudden yellow bolt across the night sky.

The stirring in my core seemed to mirror the heat in those otherworldly eyes. This had been the steamiest, literally the steamiest, night of my life and he had barely touched me, yet my loins were pyretic. "Do you want me to go home?" I whispered, becoming shy again.

"I *want* you to tell me what *you* want." He gestured at the bulge in his towel. "It's pretty clear what I'm feeling, but you're the one who needs to be sure what you want."

I swallowed, hard, and the sound of it seemed to echo through the house. "I *want* to spend the night here. With you."

As soon as I'd spoken those words, he growled with relief. He pulled my body flush against his and leaned down to claim my mouth. I kissed him back with an abandon that rivaled his. My towel dropped absently to the floor when he lifted me up to straddle his waist, his arms like steel bands locking me tightly against him. "Are you sure?" he asked against my lips some moments later.

Every inch of my skin was flushed with desire. "Yes. I want you, Tristan."

23

THE SLEEPOVER

"G'night, Odie," Tristan said, switching the light off. The wolf lifted his head briefly from his paws to watch as we passed him by.

My towel was back in place, as was Tristan's, and my hand was trembling feverishly in his as he lead me upstairs. Our fingers were twined in a steamy foretaste of what was to come. At the door he halted and waited, with an almost predatory stillness, watching with hooded eyes as I preceded him into his room. At his bedside I bit my lip, feeling both excited and anxious, my eyes floating abstractedly over the sheets. Without turning around, I knew that Tristan was right behind me. He always moved so silently. He wasn't touching me yet, but I could feel his body heat radiating like a wood stove. His room was steeped in his spicy scent.

Strong hands suddenly appeared at my belly, fisting in my towel as he pressed hot lips to my neck. I dropped my head back against him, face angled away, my throat vulnerable against his mouth. My arm I lifted around to clutch desperately at his sinewy nape. He dragged his lips and teeth hungrily over the sensitive skin beneath my ear. Then, with a palm at my jaw, he angled my face around to take my mouth again, the steely length of him pressing insistently at my backside as we kissed. He inched me around to face him, never once relinquishing my mouth, so that our bodies were perfectly molded. He did nothing more than brush his lips gently over mine as he held me close. For a long while, that was all he did, worshipping me with kisses and soothing my temples softly with the pads of his thumbs.

My fingers were far less patient. They tightened in his hair as his tongue began to play along the contours of my lips, cajoling me to open wider, his kisses deepening. Desire rolled between us in shuddering, salty waves. Tristan pulled me closer, held me tighter, taking full advantage of my mouth as he walked me backward till the bed nudged beguilingly at my thighs. Only my towel stood as the flimsy barrier between us. His was long since discarded.

And then we were on his bed, the sheets cool against my burning skin. Tristan's kisses wandered lower, his chin sweeping down along the column of my throat until he reached the confluence of my neck and shoulder. There he stayed a while, leaning over me on one elbow as the other hand raked up over my bare ribs before tugging the cotton aside and tossing the towel away. My breath hitched as his palm cupped my breast. He halted a moment, lifting his head to look at me. The colors in his eyes were muted by the low light from the hallway, a shame since they were always changing. The green always so bright and intense whether infused with a wrathful yellow or lustful gold.

His gaze dropped to my breasts, and his hand soon followed with assiduous caresses. Then came his mouth, his tongue swirling alternately over one nipple before paying equal deference to the other. Every nerve in my body seemed concentrated in that small sensitive region, firing like static beneath his breath, and hardening like marble against his lips. He explored every inch of my terrain, every peak and valley, with worshipful passion. I was drunk with erotic languor—the smell, touch, and taste of him coupled with the Malbec coursing hotly through my veins was deliciously overwhelming. As his talented mouth delved across the topography of my chest, his hand progressed southward, investigating all that lay below the equator. As he continued shifting further down along my torso, his belly gliding torturously over my straining flesh, my breathing grew more ragged. My eyes were sealed shut and my fingers were digging into the pillow behind my head as his chest forced my thighs still wider apart.

"Look at me, Evan," he said, his words no more than a husky growl.

I instantly complied, mesmerized by his raw voice. He'd scooted off the bed and was kneeling on the floor. He pulled me swiftly to the edge and positioned my legs over his wide shoulders, his hands clamped firmly around my thighs to lock me in place. I resisted the urge to close my legs and cover my breasts. I couldn't have even if I'd wanted to. His eyes were drifting over me with such need that I found myself hypnotized by him. I watched his nose flare ravenously as he dipped his head. My eyes rolled back and my body jolted with the stunning contact.

I could barely think. His tongue on me and the grazing of his stubbled jaw on the insides of my thighs, against the vibrant pulse of my inner flesh, was maddening. The pressure spiked, the tension became agonizing. My fingernails were gouging at the mattress beneath me. Finally, every cell in my body discharged blindingly against his mouth. Shockwave after shockwave rolled from my epicenter out toward my heavy, palsied limbs. But Tristan continued unremittingly even as my body shuddered with exquisite aftershocks and my legs tried to close themselves. My eyes were heavy and clouded when he lifted his head, a fervid look in his eyes.

When he stood and moved away, I thought it was to let me recover, but he moved no further than his bedside table. A short moment later he was back again, leaning over me with a very decided look.

"Again?!" I asked, my voice hoarse and my heart still wheezing with effort. Could I possibly come so soon after?

Tristan seemed taken aback, his expression priceless, but he quickly recovered himself. "We've only just started, Evan."

I grinned shyly, my lips feeling divinely bruised.

"Remember this?" He opened his palm to reveal the little square wrapper he'd just retrieved from his bedside table. "Some sexy voyeur left it in the backseat of my truck." It was the condom I'd thrown at him. Our French letter.

I watched, absorbed, as he tore the condom packet open with sharp white teeth and then fitted the latex over himself.

In one fell swoop, he monopolized my lips again and scattered my thoughts to the four winds. My knees parted in welcome. *This* kiss was different. This kiss was the prelude to the grand finale. The first round had been a total seduction of my body; now he meant to consume me completely. With the vestigial ripples of my orgasm still churning my blood, I ran my palms eagerly over his flanks to feel the hard sinews rolling and bunching beneath his smooth and heated skin as he moved over me.

This stage of our lovemaking was far headier, far more intense. This was by far the most powerful kiss we'd ever shared. He was no longer gentle. Control had become tenuous. I didn't care, his passion only fueled mine. His feverish attentions both ignited and saturated me. I was mindless now and barely registered the hard length that pressed between us, questing lower. The tip of it became an insistent, painful pressure at my core. Almost unbearable. Although I had expected it to hurt, I couldn't help stiffening, and that only made it more uncomfortable. Tristan, of course, was so in tune with everything my body did that he paused, having barely made any headway at all. He gentled his kissing again, his tongue coaxing me to relax.

Relax? With a hot naked man between my thighs? Yet, under Tristan's soft kisses, I did exactly that. My body gradually loosened around him, drawing him in by a fraction of an inch. If he was at all frustrated by the delay, or by the added workload, he didn't show it. In fact, he seemed eager to pleasure me as completely as he had done before. This relaxed me still further.

My breasts were lavished with more kisses, this region evidently his favorite bailiwick, as he gained yet another fraction inside of me. My chest, my heart, was being inundated with so much pleasure that it nearly eclipsed the pain. I was panting not from the two hundred and fifty pounds of male brawn between my legs but from the aching thrill. Without warning, there was a sudden sharp sting as Tristan shoved past that final barrier. My gasp he quickly swallowed with another deep kiss. He now filled me completely.

"Better to just rip the band-aid off," he murmured against my lips, muscles straining as he held himself still. "Tell me when to move, okay?"

"Uh-huh." When the dull throb finally subsided a little, I gave a small nod for him to continue.

There was obviously no need to tell him twice. Before I'd even completed the gesture he was moving inside me, cautiously at first, gauging my reaction. Though the first few thrusts were uncomfortable, eventually that sweet tension coiled at my center again. It wasn't the divine coalescing of before, but that was because of the sharp ache that still lingered no matter how careful he tried to be.

Tristan's cheek was pressed against mine as his breathing escalated. I met him thrust for thrust and matched my body's pace to his as my periphery blurred and limbs tightened again. He was right against my focal point, his body stirring to life another climax.

I squeezed my eyes shut the better to follow the threads of sensation with my mind, pulling myself up along the steep slope toward that invisible summit. And then, abruptly, I tensed through the upsurge, my body convulsing as I let go of the cables that had anchored me.

It was obliterating and stunning—that power behind the nothing. I drifted, floating weightlessly before I sank back down to earth like a feather, only half conscious of Tristan's own release from somewhere overhead.

We lay there a long moment, conjoined, our breathing unsteady, my limbs like butter. All too soon he lifted his weight from me and my skin puckered from the loss of his warmth. I cracked an eye open to admire that powerful frame that had so satisfied me. After placing a kiss above my damp brow he left my side and made his way quietly to the bathroom.

I should go shower. The thought was only a halfhearted one. I was too drowsy to move more than a finger, my lids shuttering over my eyes in protest. I yawned, stretching my tired limbs and arching my back like a cat before turning onto my side. The night rushed in suddenly from the open windows as Tristan flicked the hallway light off. Soon after, the mattress dipped behind me as he climbed back into bed. A steely arm snaked around me, pulling me back against his chest. My lips curled in utter contentment as he kissed my shoulder. Thereafter, I sank into the deepest sleep of my life, lulled by the nocturnal sounds of the forest.

But I woke up with a startled gasp, jolting upright, the sheets pooling in my lap.

"What is it?" came Tristan's sleepy, sexy murmur at my ear as he sat up behind me.

"Just a dream," I whispered, relieved. *No, a nightmare.* I pressed my hands to my chest, willing my heart to calm itself, but the shadows in the room seemed to yawn threateningly around me, stalking me like the thing in my nightmare. The monster that had killed me. Devoured me.

Without saying a word in reply, Tristan pulled me onto his lap to straddle him. I sighed into his mouth, instantly aroused and distracted, as his fingers glided from my breasts down to the tense chords between my thighs, working their magic over my still very tender flesh. The dregs of death and dismemberment, the terrifying flash of fangs and blood that had ripped me from my sleep, fell by the wayside as my heart switched tempo. Still, it lurked like a banished remnant at the fringe of consciousness. I moaned pleasurably, lifting myself up to guide him inside. As the moon peered between the curtains, my mind unraveled and my body came apart around him.

There was a beautiful frailty about that moment—losing myself in his arms while darkness lingered at the fringe of wakefulness. As I drifted back to sleep, I let Tristan's arms anchor me safely to the reality of this moment. To the here and now. Because he was real and the nightmare wasn't. There was no such thing as werewolves.

24

MR. HYDE

Sunlight streamed in through the open curtains and bathed the room in muted shades of amber. Even the dust motes looked like specks of gold floating overhead. I stretched, my muscles feeling gloriously tender, and turned on my side with a yawn, only to discover that I was being watched.

Those gold-flecked eyes above me were already roving, clearly enjoying the view. Tristan's head was propped up on his hand, the better to see me with, and his other hand lay splayed between us, fingers inches from my breasts. It was *very* distracting.

"Morning, beautiful."

"G'morning." I blinked shyly.

"Sleep well?"

I nodded, yawning again. "You?"

"I had the best sleep of my life despite your snoring."

"What?!" I instantly shoved my hand over my mouth in horror.

"Yeah, it was brutal."

"Ugh!" Before turning away and shoving my face into the

pillow, I caught sight of his lips twitch mischievously. "You'd snore too if you were getting the flu."

"Is that what it is." He leaned over to nuzzle my neck and then began laying silky kisses over my back. "I don't get the flu. I've got a freakishly strong immune system."

I lifted my face from the pillow to watch him over my shoulder. "How nice for you." Actually, it was more than likely just allergies. Apart from the stuffy nose, I'd never felt better.

"I brought you breakfast in bed," he said between kisses, easily disarming my shyness with that heart-stopping dimple in his left cheek.

"You did?" My face lit up at such a thoughtful and adorable gesture. This guy was way too good to be true. "What are we having?" I looked around, expecting to see a platter of fruit and a vase of orchids next to a steaming cup of coffee. Perhaps even a red ballgown and a limo waiting outside to take me to the opera on a private jet… Good grief, I needed desperately to stop watching Richard Gere movies.

Tristan opened his left hand to reveal a pitiful-looking, little dandelion. "I only have cow pus in the fridge, so I foraged around in the woods for this tasty morsel. You're welcome." The look on my face sent him into hysterics.

"You're sweet, but I can't possibly eat all of that."

He tucked the dandelion flower behind my ear. "So I think I've probably forfeited my man-card, but I raided all my cupboards, read all the labels of anything that looked suspiciously like rabbit food," he admitted, screwing his nose up, "and it turns out that your breakfast menu for this morning includes apples, oatmeal, peanut butter, and blueberry bagels. Take your pick."

"Coffee and oatmeal sounds pretty amazing," I said. A dollop of peanut butter in my porridge to make it creamy was usually what I ate every morning anyway. He had everything I needed, I thought hungrily, my eyes stealing over his body as he rolled out of bed.

Moments later the shower spurted to life, sibilating temptingly, like a mating call I was powerless to resist. When I slipped into the bathroom, Tristan was already under the spray, the shape of his large frame alluringly blurred behind the frosted glass. He'd dropped his head forward beneath the showerhead, his hands spread on the tiled wall as though anticipating a good frisking. The idea had merit, I decided boldly. Without further ado, I climbed in behind him. The muscles along his back rippled expectantly as I reached past him to take the soap from its niche in the wall. I lathered the bar between my hands and spread them over the taut muscles I'd been feasting my eyes on seconds ago. Over his shoulders I slid my hands, along the vast expanse of smooth skin, massaging my fingers over his ribs and down his long spine. When I moved my hands to his hips I began to grow more daring, digging my fingers abruptly into the spot I assumed all people were most ticklish. But, I realized with mild disappointment, he barely reacted.

With a lazy smile thrown over his shoulder, he shook his head. "Nice try."

"How can you not be ticklish there?" I tried again, but all he did was shrug. "I swear, you're not even human."

He shot me a penetrative look and then turned the rest of his body around to face me. "Werewolves aren't ticklish."

Ignoring the remark, I ran my fingers across his pectoral plains and the sexy ridges of his abdomen. But I didn't dare go any lower. Not yet.

"My turn," he murmured, reaching for the soap.

I held my breath as strong fingers played across my shoulders and down over my breasts, his palms gliding leisurely over the peaks that seemed to reach out for him, begging for his touch. I thought he would delay his visit there a while, but he continued lower and spread his hands over my ribs and then my belly, drawing circles over my skin with an artist's touch. His eyes absorbed everything his hands did, and I was studying his movements just as avidly. It was like he was memorizing my highlands and lowlands, mapping them out in his head as though he never wanted to forget me. Watching his eyes slaking themselves on my body was almost as erotic as the touch of his fingertips and calloused palms. We were like the water—rushing heat and billowing steam. I was inundated by him, my senses reeling, and drunk on what he made me feel. In the reflection of my lover's gaze, I felt like the most stunning creature in the world. I closed my eyes, breath shuddering out as his hands slipped lower, neglecting no part of me. Then he turned me around and began washing my back as assiduously as he'd done to my front. When he'd finally finished, his hands left my hips and dropped to my cheeks, grabbing them possessively as he nipped my shoulder. I giggled and swatted his hands away from my backside. So instead he moved them up along my spine to the middle of my back. There he began writing something across my skin in suds and water, but I couldn't parse his cursive, so, instead, I closed my eyes and enjoyed his touch.

When he dropped his hand I turned around and stood up on the tips of my toes to lock my hands around his head, pulling his lips down to mine. He was only too happy to oblige me, our tongues clashing fiercely, thirstily. And then he lifted me up onto him, my legs locking him in place as he pushed my heated skin to the cold wall, filling me completely. Now our bodies were as fused together as our mouths.

We strained together under the spray, our thrusting tongues emulating what our slick bodies were doing. My fingernails were hooked into his back and shoulders, marking him now as I did last night. I held on for dear life, that euphoric pulse point between my legs swelling with liquid heat. There was an unbearable gathering that both promised and denied my ecstasy. Finally, under the roar of the water, I imploded around him, my whole body jolting with the force of my climax. It was so powerful and all-consuming that I barely noticed his own release. I kissed his neck and rested my head on his shoulder, my hair soaked and lying in messy ropes down his back as he held me tight.

He set me on my feet and then stepped out of the shower to grab a fresh towel, which he used to bundle me up before grabbing one for himself. We dried off, laughing and kissing like maniacs, and then he pulled himself away to head over to the sink to shave. As I brushed my wet hair out with my fingers he watched me in the mirror, pulling the razor down his lathered cheeks and throat. Now that I was feeling more confident in my own skin I threw the towel off and sashayed to the bed to retrieve yesterday's clothes.

Tristan, meanwhile, had paused to fix me with a sexy glare. "You're brave."

Grinning, I searched for my bra. I was sore now and there was no way I could survive another round with him. My nether parts trembled at the thought. I sat down on the edge of the bed, distracted from my underwear hunting, to admire his profile as he brushed his teeth. I was still naked, though, and so leaned back on my elbows to cross and uncross my legs, *a la* Sharon Stone in *Basic Instinct,* to which he responded by shooting me another provocative glare. "I'll behave," I said, giggling. "But your self-control really isn't my problem. I *want* you to release the Kraken!"

He choked on his toothpaste and quickly spat it out so that he could unleash another glare on me. "I swear I'm gonna have to make sure I have no dangerous objects in my mouth whenever you're in the room."

"That sounds like a challenge, Mr. Thorn." Sniggering to myself, I pulled my jeans on sans my underwear. I had never gone commando before and I couldn't say that I relished the idea. My jeans were of the tight and skinny variety, so I was instantly self-conscious of flashing a bit of the ole camel's toe. Or was it Moose-knuckle now that I was in Moose country? *No, only men can do the Moose-knuckle thing.* I'd probably have to google the difference later, I thought, checking my crotch with a satisfied nod. *No camel here.*

Once Tristan had vacated the room, I finished dressing and then answered nature's call. After that, I finger-brushed my teeth and then headed downstairs to satisfy an appetite of a more prosaic nature.

Later, on the drive back to the cabin, Tristan became strangely taciturn, dampening the post-coital bliss I'd been enjoying. But even over breakfast he'd seemed distracted. I knew he had some flying to do today after he dropped me off. Was it something work-related that worried him? Or was it me?

"Are you okay?" I asked. "Have I done something wrong?"

Instead of answering my questions, he said, "We need to talk." The four dreaded words that spelled imminent doom to any fledgling relationship.

My face blanched. Had he used me? Had I completely misread his character? My expression had been broadcasting all the doubt that was suddenly churning inside me, evidently, because Tristan, with a grim frown, suddenly pulled the truck off to the side of the road and turned to me.

"If you're thinking what I think you're thinking, Evan, then you don't know me at all."

"Yeah, I'm starting to realize that," I said, voice stiff and cold. God, my mood had plummeted quickly. "Was this a one night stand?"

He gave a frustrated sigh and clenched his eyes momentarily. "I've tried to be honest with you without scaring you away. I wanted to move slowly. You were completely unexpected. I swear to you, I did try to stay away, but obviously I have very little self-control where you're concerned." He dropped his head back and closed his eyes, pained. It had all rushed out of him in an incoherent mess that I was struggling to follow. "I've abused your trust, Evan."

What did that even mean? "What? No, I wanted—"

"I wanted it too, but I should've been honest with you first. I'm a coward. I wanted to pretend to be normal for a while."

"Honest about what?" What the hell was going on? "Tell me."

"I will, but not here like this." His eyes softened. "I want to tell you everything…tonight."

My shoulders relaxed somewhat, he didn't look like a man about to break a woman's heart. "Should I be scared?"

"It's a pretty huge deal, my secret. One that might make you run for the hills and never look back again. I wouldn't blame you if you did." The thought of me running for the hills seemed like anathema to him, so I was further mollified. Definitely not the look of a man about to break a heart.

"Do you have herpes?" I was digging in the weeds here, my filter evidently failing again. Though, really, it would serve me right for being so cavalier in the shower earlier. "AIDS?"

"Neither! Jeez, Ev." The abject horror plastered on his face was telling enough.

"You're in the Alaskan mafia?"

"I'm not in the goddamn mafia." He gave a frustrated growl and shifted the King Ranch into gear.

"So it's not a family secret then?"

This question seemed to give him pause. "It is."

"Does Dean know the secret?"

"It's a condition that affects him too, so yes."

"So it *is* a disease!"

"In a way, it is something incurable, but I don't view it as a disease, no."

Who else knew about this *condition* of his? "Tell me this: does Nicole know your big, dark secret?"

He grimaced. "Yes." The silence after that little confession was horribly stilted.

I looked away, the landscape blurring past my window as the truck ate up the dirt road. "Tristan, if you're still together with her then—"

"We're not together!" Then less vehemently, "We never were."

Maybe that was why she couldn't stand me? Because he'd chosen me over her. "Now I'm dying to know what this damn secret is."

"Tonight. I promise I'll show you then."

Show? "Show me what? I've seen all of you—" my eyes settled pointedly at his crotch "—so there's nothing else to show."

"There's a *whole* helluva lot more to show." He appeared grim.

So much for misplaced humor. "Is it Mr. Hyde?" I asked as we pulled up alongside the Yukon. I'd only met Jekyll, but now and then I'd glimpsed a Hyde.

Without answering he climbed out of the truck, presumably to open my door like he always did, but I forestalled him by jumping down myself before he'd even passed the brush guard.

"I'll see you tonight," I muttered. When he made no move to leave me, I looked up to see him scanning the edge of the surrounding woods. "You'll be late for work, you should probably go."

"My flights can wait," he said, pulling his gaze away from the trees, "I want to make sure you're safe."

"Okay, grandma, I'll go lock myself in the cabin if it'll make you feel better."

He grunted and gently twisted my ponytail around his finger before laying it over my shoulder. "Don't open the door to anyone." The warning was soft yet firm, like the kiss that punctuated it. Then his eyes shifted back to the woods again, hesitating. His nostrils flared as the wind picked up.

"Why are you so jumpy?"

"Do you smell…?" He took another deep noseful of air.

"Smell what?" Was there another damn bear in the woods?!

His brows drew together. "Gasoline."

I tried to sample the air like he was doing, but my nose, I was quickly reminded, had stopped working properly. *Damn allergies!*

"Maybe Dinwiddie's fixing to burn her refuse." He stroked his jaw, still peering into the shadows.

"I don't smell anything." I studied him dubiously. "Dinwiddie lives like ten miles away. How would you know what she's—?"

"Tonight, Evan," he promised. "I'll explain everything tonight."

"Tonight," I echoed, backing up to the house. "Fine."

Once the black truck disappeared from the driveway, I headed up to the cabin. I was dog tired and determined to take a nap. I'd slept well, even after the nightmare, but it had been all too short. That nap, however, was not destined for me. I'd just entered the bedroom when a knock sounded at the door.

With a foul curse, I turned back around to head to the foyer, in no mood to deal with Dinwiddie. *Enough with the bulldog mouth, Evan, she's probably just checking in on you.* The voice of reason had a good point, so I pasted a resigned smile on and opened the door.

"Hello, Evan." It was Nicole. "Can I come in?"

25

THE VOICE OF RAGE AND RUIN

There was something inhuman and chilling about Nicole's smile as she stood on the porch waiting for me to invite her in. Then her mouth suddenly fell as she wrinkled her nose. The cold spectral blue of her eyes raised my hackles.

I would have thought it was my scent that offended her, but I'd just showered earlier, so it certainly wasn't my body odor. "Tristan isn't here, Nicole." She couldn't possibly have come here to see me since I knew she hated my living guts.

"Perfect," she said through gritted teeth, forcing her smile back into place. "Well, can I come in?"

"Will you be nice?" I wanted to ask. I didn't though. Instead, I moved back to let her in, watching her from under pinched brows. Watching her as I would a circling shark. I hated the inkling of foreboding that struck my gut with primeval force as she prowled in past me. I'd made a mistake to let her in, I knew that somehow, but this was Tristan's friend (or whatever) and I couldn't very well kick her out now.

"Tea?" I asked.

She nodded, studying me as though she couldn't quite make sense of me.

Once in the kitchen, I began busying my trembling hands with the cups and the tea bags. I noticed out of the corner of my eye that Nicole was hovering near the entrance—blocking my escape route. *God Almighty, Evan! You're being ridiculous, she's only a silly tart with a mean stare.* A silly tart who was also tall and wiry enough to take me down, I suspected.

"I hear hurricanes a-blowing...I hear the voice of rage and ruin." Creedence Clearwater Revival crooned on as I glanced surreptitiously over my shoulder at Nicole, keeping her always within sight. I noticed her nostrils still flaring in that morbid way. It irritated and unnerved me. Where in the hell had I put my phone? Not that there was any signal to be had.

"You slept with him," she blurted.

I was so shocked by her bluntness that I nearly dropped the kettle on my foot. "That's…really none of your business, Nic—"

"Did he tell you?" she asked, a hint of pain behind her glare.

"Tell me what?"

My confusion was answer enough and seemed to satisfy her. "Thought not."

She was obviously referring to the big secret he was yet to share. "If all you came here to do is gloat and stir shit then you can turn around and—" *fuck off* "—leave."

"Don't you want to know his secret? I could tell you if you like."

"I think that's Tristan's privilege, not yours," I said, steeling myself for a possible bitchslap—even smiling she looked unhinged enough for violence. "And I think it's time you go."

She took a seat on the stool at the breakfast bar as if I hadn't just rescinded my invitation. "We got off on the wrong foot."

"I suspect you only have two wrong feet, Nicole."

There was a momentary flicker of something vicious in her gaze, but she blinked it away and pasted a toothy smile back on her face. "I've been a bitch, I know"—she sighed and dropped her head into her hands—"but can you blame me?"

Uh, yeah.

"The man I've known all my life—the man I was supposed to marry—is sleeping with another woman."

"Excuse me?!" Blood welled in my mouth from where I bit my tongue. "You were engaged to Tristan?"

"He didn't tell you?" She bristled.

With a headache beginning to stab at my skull, I pushed my hands to the countertop to steady myself while I assimilated her words. "You're lying." I set the kettle on the burner. She would get no tea, but I certainly needed something warm to fortify my nervous stomach.

"You and I both know you don't really believe that."

Didn't I? She did seem extremely sure of herself, I thought desolately. I hated the fact that she knew him better than I apparently did. That she knew his big *secretum secretorum* and I didn't. "Is this his big secret?"

"Partly. He has a dual persona, you know?"

"What I *know* is that you're full of shit."

Animus glared coldly from her eyes. "It's not just him—we're all *bicorporal*."

Of two bodies? Was this chick on some freaky magic mushroom high. "Who's *we* exactly?" I asked, glancing at the knife drawer.

"All the families."

Families? "What, like the *Cosa Nostra*?" I scoffed. Tristan had already denied that.

Her eyes slitted thoughtfully. "Yeah, like the mafia. Our families are also based on a 'boss' system, but instead of the Bratva you have the Southeast Regional Pack; instead of the Yakuza you have the Yukon Territory; and instead of the Cosa Nostra you have the Athabaskan Region, where I'm from. The last two are the largest and strongest syndicates in North America."

So they *were* mafiosi! "Which one…which does Tristan belong to?" I asked in a whisper, my head reeling.

"That's complicated, I'm not completely sure anymore." She lifted one shoulder irritably. "He's a bit of wild card lately which is why his father wanted us united. Anyway, his brother is the president of the SRP. The Southeast Regional Pack," she clarified, noticing my confusion at hearing the acronym. "Thorne Bay—" spreading her arms meaningfully "—is all part of Dean's territory."

"And you're from…?"

"The Athabaskan Region, like I said. Aidan's pack." She said this with overt relish as though I was supposed to know who this Aidan guy was. "Aidan's pack is the most powerful in Alaska, that's why Dean and Max were looking forward to the match between Tristan and I—for the alliance it would secure with the Athabaskans. Max Thorn is head of the largest pack in Canada." Her teeth gleamed threateningly as she smiled. "The Yukon Godfather, if you will. And when Tristan finally sorts his shit out and goes home, he'll be the Yukon heir." One eye gave a sudden minacious twitch as she considered me. "But your presence here has thrown a spanner in the works. And Max is furious."

The godfather was enraged at me? I felt my stomach curdle at the thought. *Lies.* It all sounded too far-fetched. I had to keep in mind that Nicole was here to scare me, not to enlighten. I'd never heard of any Alaskan mafia, and I certainly didn't think they'd refer to themselves as "packs" if indeed they even did exist. More importantly, I hadn't thrown any spanners anywhere! Tristan had made the first move, not the other way around. All I wanted now was for Nicole to get the hell out of the cabin, out of my head, and to take her crazy elsewhere. Far far away. "Why are you telling me all this anyway?"

She said nothing, only shot me a predatory wink that implied she was having fun at my expanse.

"I want you to go." I was bracing myself for some violent outburst, but she surprised me by pushing herself carelessly from the stool.

"I didn't even get any tea," she pouted. She was halfway out the kitchen when she turned around unexpectedly. "Mind if I use your washroom first? I've got a long drive ahead of me." Her tone was almost affable all of a sudden.

Her mood swings, I was coming to realize, were even freakier than Tristan's. "Outside," I said, for once relieved to have an outhouse. *Better yet go pee in the woods!*

"I'll let myself out then." She backed out of the room with a strange look on her face. Once she was out of the room I expelled the cold air from my lungs, feeling inordinately relieved to have her out of the kitchen. The kettle began to whistle its shrill warning from the stove, distracting me a moment. *Ah, there's my phone!* It was on the shelf above the stove. After I'd pocketed it and pulled the kettle from the blue flames, I hurried to the mudroom to lock the front door. It snicked soundly, bolstering me with relief. Back at the kitchen I facepalmed myself for being so single-minded that I'd left the gas on. I flicked the knob off and peered out the kitchen window at the outhouse. I waited long minutes for Nicole to emerge, but she never did. Maybe she'd left already? No, her black SUV was still in the driveway. Finally, I grew anxious when she still hadn't appeared after twenty minutes had come and gone. Either she'd fallen down the loo (wishful thinking) or she'd decided to jog home. *Yeah right.* Had I heard the front door open and close, signaling her departure from the cabin? I couldn't remember. Maybe the screaming kettle had drowned the sound of the closing door? Then why was I feeling uneasy?

"Nicole?" I called out, moving down the hall to check the two bedrooms. They were empty.

The whole house, in fact, seemed heavy with silence despite the music drifting faintly from the kitchen. But I didn't *feel* alone. Nicole was a grown-ass woman and as much as she disturbed me I didn't for a minute think her the type to play hide and seek. Then again, she had just been spewing nonsense about heirs and mafiosi in the kitchen earlier, so clearly she was unpredictable.

As I passed from my room back into the hallway I was stopped in my tracks by a sudden shuffling that emanated faintly from down in the basement. "Please be a rat," I whispered, a fatal tremor seizing my hand as I reached out for the basement doorknob. The metal was like ice beneath my fingers.

"I hope you are quite prepared to die..." God, had I put that song on repeat or something?

I flicked the useless switch at the top of the stairs, cursing myself because I hadn't yet had time to change any light bulbs. I tried to see into the darkness that lay waiting at the bottom of the stairs. *Don't go down there,* came that familiar, cautious voice which I'd ignored when I'd let Nicole into the cabin. *Call Tristan.* But, despite my determination to ignore her, Nicole's lies had left chinks in the trust I'd had in Tristan. It was now tenuous at best.

I pulled my phone out, briefly noting that there was—surprise, surprise—zero signal, so I couldn't call even if I wanted to. Then I tried to use the backlight of the screen to illuminate the black stairwell, but it only produced a pitiful glow.

"Nicole!" I shouted down the stairs. "If you're down there please answer." Nothing. "This isn't funny..." *You crazy bitch.*

Again there came no answer. There was only that crawling at my nape again as though an evil eye had slid over me. The hairs leapt up from my skin, alert with dread. Well, I'd definitely heard something down there, but if it was just the sound of a bunch of humping rats then I seriously didn't need to investigate that badly.

However, I wouldn't be able to sleep in the house unless I satisfied my fear with an investigative look around. Resigned, I lowered one foot to the first step and held my phone out like a ward against the evil darkness. I could only just make out what I assumed was the halfway mark. Carefully, I descended a few more steps. And then I froze, a cold terror slicing instantly through my gut.

There was something moving in the shadows below. My heart ground abruptly to a halt and my limbs palsied as I glared into the shifting darkness. Or was it my imagination? *Fuck this!* This was how horror movies started. Obeying my fear, at last, I began to back away slowly up the steps, looking briefly over my shoulder at the door to see how much further I still had to go. But when I dropped my gaze back into the murky stairwell an involuntary shriek was ripped from my throat.

A large black toothsome face reared up from the darkness. With a feral growl of snapping teeth, it lunged up at me. Reflexively, I kicked out and felt my heel connect the thing's throat as I stumbled backward, jarring my elbows. Screaming, I scrambled up the remaining steps, my phone now surrendered to the stairwell. Pure adrenalin surged into my blood as I clawed my way through the doorway. I bolted down the passageway, too horrified to look back in case the monster was at my heels.

I was no longer a thinking creature at this point, and later I would have almost no recollection of this moment except for long teeth and ghostly blue eyes. Everything blurred past me—the brown walls, the scuffed floor, and the dying fire in the wood stove. I had suddenly become a frightened animal, trusting my body's primordial instinct to flee without question. There was only a sharp awareness of terror and snarling. My hands lunged at the front door. I tried to yank it from the wall, but it was locked. "Heeelp!" I shrieked. "Tristan!" But the rest of my screams were snuffed by a violent blow from behind. It sent me hurtling face first into the locked door.

My nightmare had caught up with me. Its fangs thrust deep into my shoulder. The sound of ripping flesh and snapping bones drowned out my hysteria. I was going to die here, mauled to death by a rabid bear. That was my last cogent thought before I slipped into oblivion.

26

RED DEVIL

I was pulled gradually from that bloodless oblivion by the steady rhythm of a car engine, the blind agony of torn flesh throbbing mercilessly at my shoulder. Was that John Fogerty singing about "trouble on the way"? My lips were parched, and my throat made no sound as I tried to discharge the searing pain with a scream, but it came out as a gurgling whimper. My chords were as damaged as my shoulder felt.

My body was heavy, my muscles atrophied. I couldn't force even my eyelids to move. There was only the fire at my shoulder, the roar of an engine, and wetness at my cheek. Suddenly, I remembered the thing in the basement. I'd been attacked! Was I even alive? Flashbacks of stark blue eyes against stygian fur and bloodied fangs and whiskers induced a violent trembling in my broken bones. I'd been mauled by Gmork from *The Neverending Story!* For a blissful moment I told myself that I'd only had another nightmare, this wasn't real, but the merciless pain was quick to disabuse me of that.

I couldn't bear the dark anymore, I forced my eyes open into slits. Through the blur of tears and pain, I could make out very little detail except that dusk had fallen outside. Why was I outside? All I could see were shadows and the vague shapes of black trees speeding past the window. I willed my eyes to focus and blinked rapidly, panicked, until finally my vision cleared enough for me to confirm that I was spread across the back seat of an unfamiliar car, my cheek plastered against the leather seat by tears and cold sweat. And blood. The car reeked of awful coppery bloodshed. At the wheel was a dark shadow with muted blonde hair. An angel? The ruts in the road pummeled the tires, but I saw her clearly through the pain. Nicole.

I must have said her name, must have groaned because she suddenly whipped her head around to me. Then to the road again; then back at me, her eyes twitchy with panic. Even through the tears and darkness, I recognized what was still afflicting me—horror. Had she also been attacked by that thing in the basement? I wanted to reach out a hand and thank her for saving me. But how had she done it? I gritted my teeth as another pothole slammed my brain against my skull. It didn't matter *how*, I thought tiredly, I was alive and that was all I cared about now. What exactly she'd saved me *from* I didn't know. It was nothing I had the energy or courage to contemplate right now. I was safe. As long as that monster was far far away, I didn't care what the hell it was.

With a grateful sigh, I succumbed to the darkness again, sure that she would get me to the hospital before I bled out completely.

"There's a bad moon on the rise..." If I'd had the strength I'd have begged Nicole to turn the radio off. God, why did that song make me want to wretch?

~

"Are you sure?" said a man, his voice steely and authoritative as it cut through my coma.

"I'm positive!" Nicole's voice I recognized instantly, her usual cold lilt replaced by something desperate. "I saw him myself."

"That's unlike him."

"Well, he's been pretty unpredictable lately! I mean who abandons a presidency to follow his rogue brother?! C'mon, the guy's clearly got a few screws loose."

Then a harried sigh. "Speaking of which, we should call Max. This should be his problem, not ours."

The voices were muffled, then clear, then muted again. I drifted back and forth between awareness and a numbing abyss. The audible grinding of my own bones as I twitched involuntarily yanked me back to awareness. My blood was saturated with chills, yet I couldn't move to curl into a ball and conserve heat; I was paralyzed.

"How long has she been out?" asked the man, sounding gruff. It was him, I presumed, that was dabbing at my shoulder with something that felt ice cold and stung like a bitch. The doctor maybe?

"Since we left Thorne Bay," Nicole answered him. "More or less."

Moments later I felt the tug of a needle at my ragged flesh as the doctor began to stitch the wound.

"Does it always smell like that?" Nicole again. There was a sweet-smelling rot permeating the room. A festering sort of odor that sickened me.

"How should I know?" he answered tersely. "Never seen anything like this before. But I know a kill bite when I see one…"

I felt my body twitch again as I struggled to open my eyes.

"Give her a shot of Fentanyl," he commanded, still plying his needle, "she's waking up."

Hot strong fingers obediently gripped my arm and then a dull sting at my forearm followed shortly thereafter. My eyes had just begun to flutter open, the beam of antiseptic light stabbing through the fog. Almost immediately, I felt the drug shoot warmly to my brain till, finally, it numbed my thoughts with welcome darkness. The two shadows above me were snuffed out in an instant.

Time passed by in dull beats of my torpid heart. Awareness seeped into my brain miasmically, and by degrees. Once again there were voices murmuring above me, but this time the pain in my shoulder was only a vague ache.

"Why didn't you take her to Dean? Why bring her here?" said a stern female voice I didn't recognize.

"I panicked!" Nicole again.

"Clearly," said the male doctor from before.

"Dean or Max should be dealing with this." The woman's voice was low and stentorian. "This is dangerous."

"How dare you judge me! You don't know what it's like to be in love. You're cold and—"

"Enough," the woman growled. "Tell me *calmly*"—she seemed to stress the word through gritted teeth—"what happened yesterday. Take your time."

Nicole was sniffling pathetically. "I headed to Evan's place yesterday morning to warn her off, but she's obsessed with Tristan, so it was pointless to stay longer. Can't fix stupid. Anyway, I left and got halfway down the road before I realized I'd forgotten my phone. When I got back to the cabin I heard her screaming inside. When I found them, Tristan had her by the shoulder. He was shaking her violently."

"So you brained him and then took off with Evan?" The stranger's voice sounded dubious.

"Yes! God, why are you putting me on trial?" There was brief, heavy silence.

"No one's putting you on trial, calm down." The other woman's voice was calming enough to relax my own breathing. "But something doesn't smell right."

"And it ain't the wound, Nicole," The doctor said scathingly.

"I know I should have gone to Dean, but he'd have only protected Tristan."

"That would have been far more preferable." The mystery woman sounded irate now. "Now we're involved in something that never should have been our mess to deal with."

"I *want* an unbiased judgement!"

A tired sigh followed from the opposite side of my head. "At the risk of marriage?"

"Do you think," Nicole continued, seething, "I'd marry into a pack like that?"

"Yes, that was the idea. You volunteered, remember? You wanted him."

"*Now* I want Tristan to pay! He should be punished."

"The girl needs to be dealt with," said the man, swiftly interrupting Nicole's diatribe as though he'd had enough of her.

I felt all gazes resting on my paralyzed body and I struggled aimlessly to open my eyes or move a finger, but nothing happened.

"Yes," the woman said, something of weariness in her tone. "I know." Whatever was said after that, I was unaware of it because either they moved off to whisper in a corridor somewhere or I'd fallen unconscious again.

When the anesthesia finally wore off, and I was able to crack my eyes open, I felt as though I'd been left to rot in a desert—my mouth felt as though I'd swallowed half the Saharan sand and my skin felt desiccated and itchy. I lifted my head gingerly from the pillow, my muscles groaning with desuetude. I sat up weakly and dragged my struggling gaze to the only source of light in the room.

There was no window, only a faint yellow glow creeping into the darkness through the small square pane of smudged glass in the door. By this feeble light, I studied my surroundings. The space was sterile-looking and, as far as I could see, devoid of any furniture except for the spartan iron bed beneath me. No other beds; no other patients.

An IV needle was embedded in my arm, but I was clearly *not* in a hospital as I'd first assumed. It was more like a cell. But something *had* attacked me, I remembered that much, and I'd heard my own bones splinter between its maw. Where was I if not in a hospital? I lifted a leery hand to my bandaged shoulder, the whole area feeling stiff and numb beneath the gauze.

Something wasn't right—the prickling along my spine told me that much, as did the fear twisting in my gut. *Get out of there!* I wasn't about to ignore my fear again.

Spurred into action, I ripped the needle from my arm and leapt from the bed, but as soon as I'd taken one step toward the door, the deafening white noise reared up from my periphery to swallow my vision. With a panicked whimper, I gripped the bed to steady myself and ride out the waves of blindness that swept in to knock me off my feet. Finally, it ebbed away.

"You should get back into bed," said a quiet voice from the corner of the room.

A scream froze instantly in my chest as I whipped my head around to the darkened corner of the room I'd so readily dismissed in my first scan. There, cloaked in shadows, stood an almost invisible figure leaning against the wall. Then, suddenly, the light burst into the room as she—the woman with the deep calm voice— flicked the switch.

I gave a hiss as the light burned my sight. Once my eyes adjusted, I gaped warily at her. The woman had, meanwhile, pushed herself off the wall and approached me.

"Who are you?" I asked. This was no doctor in a lab coat but a woman clad in jeans and a dark green blouse, her body athletic and her posture like steel.

"My questions first," she said, guiding me forcibly into the bed.

I flinched as she reached for my neck, but all she did was peel the gauze away from my shoulder in such a way as to deny me a glimpse. Her dark brows met over solemn green eyes and a sharp stern nose as she inspected the wound, looking far from pleased.

"How bad is it?" I whispered, terrified that I had contracted rabies or something.

Schooling her features, and they were *very* attractive features, I noticed abstractedly, she concealed the wound again and fixed a militant gaze to me. "It's bad."

"Are y-you a doctor? Can I call my mom?"

"No and no," she replied abruptly, folding her arms.

I shook my head, my eyes brimming with dismay. "I need to—"

"Your needs—" her voice was hard and her gaze indifferent "—are the very least of my concerns just now. Tell me what happened to you two days ago."

"Two days ago?!" Had it been that long?

"What happened," she asked again, ignoring my shock.

"I…I was attacked."

"Yes," she said, winging an elegant brow, "I see that."

I swallowed nervously. She was even scarier than Nicole. Even Nicole displayed emotion sometimes, whether her eyes were spitting venom or her teeth were bared in some parody of a smile. This woman's silence, however, was icy and grim like an iceberg in the night—you knew there was danger, but it was cold, silent, and hidden beneath a terrible calm.

Ostensibly done with waiting for me to volunteer information, she closed her eyes briefly, a hint of impatience stealing into the calm. Finally, she prompted me with another question. "Did you see what attacked you?"

"I can't be sure. A bear I think?" A bear that had looked

nothing like a bear. "Or a wolf maybe?" But that wasn't right either. "I didn't get a decent look."

"Well, what *did* you see?"

I closed my eyes and tried to force myself back to the cabin, tried to relive my nightmare. "Black!" My eyes popped open as I shuddered. "It had black fur."

"What else?"

"Blue eyes. It had bright blue eyes, like a ghost's."

This finally seemed to penetrate that cool facade of hers. "Blue?" She leaned back, her eyes narrowing to steely points.

"Yes." I'd never forget those eyes glowing from the black beyond.

"Not green?"

"No, they were ice blue. Almost white. I'm pos—"

"Be very sure, Evan."

So she knew my name. I wasn't sure I was comforted by that. "I'm sure."

"Any distinguishing markings?" Her eyes scared me with their desperate intensity. "Think."

"I-I…" I closed my eyes and the monster reared up from the hinterland of my mind. "White tips on the ears." My body convulsed with repulsion, begging me to suppress it all forever.

Instead of being relieved by the information, her mouth compressed dourly as she searched my eyes. Finally, she nodded, looking away.

Now it was time for me to get answers. "Who are you? And where am I? When can I go home?"

"In what order shall I answer those questions, or would you like to try again? One at a time."

"Where am I?"

"Red Devil."

Where the hell was that? My mom would be going crazy with worry. "Where's my phone?"

"That I don't know." She gave an inscrutable shrug.

"When can I go home?" Jeez, was she even human? "I want to go home."

"You can't," she said, her eyes flickering down to my bandaged shoulder. "There are complications to consider now."

"What complications?"

Instead of answering, though, she gestured to the far side of the wall where a bleak-looking stainless steel toilet had been fixed. Beside it was a small basin, and above that was a mirror. "See for yourself."

Wasting no time, but careful of getting up too fast, I carefully made my way over to the mirror and made quick work of lifting the bandages away. It was disgusting. I gasped, too horrified to speak. Or breathe.

The skin was a mangled chaos of black and green, mottled around the angry-looking puncture wounds. Frankenstein-looking. There was a strong-smelling discharge around the sutures, and even my bones looked misaligned underneath the hot mess. But none of this horrified me as much as the dark veins under my flesh, furcating from the bite marks in all directions like minacious black branches.

I backed away, eyes starting from my head. "What's happening to me? Am I gonna die?" I whirled around on her, noticing with dread that my horror meant nothing to her. "Who are you people?!" I screamed, finally realizing that I was in deep shit. And utterly alone.

"We're Athabaskans," came the deadly calm answer, as if that meant anything to me.

It didn't. Tears streamed relentlessly down my face as I sank down against the wall beside the toilet, my knees pressed to my chest. "Tell me your name."

"Aidan," she replied. "Nicole's sister."

Aidan? Where had I heard—?

"Aidan's pack is the most powerful in Alaska," Nicole had said.

"And you're in my territory," she went on. "Welcome to Red Devil."

And my hell, I would soon find out, was only just beginning.

27

DELIRIUM

The fever took me that same night. Or was it daytime? I had no windows and no reliable concept of time. Whether from exhaustion or trauma, I'd become severely ill. That was all I knew. My flesh burned and raged without reprieve, and my bones ached as I tossed and shivered on my sweat-soaked sheets, clawing at my skin, my own blood seeming to excoriate my veins like blades. The walls themselves seemed to skulk closer, threateningly, as though to devour me. The darkness shifted and coalesced into monstrous shapes and nightmares as I screamed and tried to escape them; tried to run from the fierce blue eyes. But I always faltered, always fell under the heavy weight of deadly claws and teeth. Those were the times my shoulder ached the most.

I was in my death throes and that was all I perceived through the fog of an excruciating pyrexia. Sometimes I'd see shadowy faces above me, indistinct mouths moving wordlessly as I moaned and writhed. Hands moved to restrain me—the monster pinning me to the floor as it ripped mercilessly at my shoulder, its midnight fur invisible in the darkness of my cell. Other times its grim blue eyes became suddenly pale green and flecked with gold —Tristan's familiar gaze, solemn and keen, from atop a protracted black muzzle. His whiskers were bloodied, and he was begging me not to hate him.

Delirium consumed and ravaged my mind. I called for my mother. I called for Tristan. But it was always the nightmarish thing that answered me from the bottom of the basement stairs; from the hinterland of my battered mind. "You're dying," it taunted. "I've killed you."

"No!" I shrieked.

"Run." Its eyes glowed a murderous inhuman blue as it licked its lips. "Run away."

I obeyed Death's warning, tripping up the stairs away from the yawning darkness that hunted me. Then, suddenly, there were hands on my brow and voices murmuring from afar. Blurry faces hovering again. *Help me!* Another sting in my arm and they faded as I drifted helplessly to the bottom of the basement where the thing waited to gorge itself on my tired flesh.

A cold wet cloth was suddenly pressed to my brow. I twitched. I moaned. I begged for water. I felt the saliva fill my mouth like bile; felt the tears spill helplessly over my cheeks. Water instantly materialized at my lips to quench the fire there. I drank it thirstily. It felt cool and refreshing. Was I in the shower now? Who was washing me with careful strokes? "Tristan?" I croaked, my words lost in moans and tears. "Is that you?" Why did he smell so different? Like citrus and cloves. "Where have you been?" More tears stung my eyes, the rills burning over my furrowed temples.

"Shhh," he murmured, "save your strength."

I sobbed, turning toward the voice. "I called out for you, but you never came!"

We were in his shower again, his soapy fingers swirling over my wet back. But when I turned around to face him he was gone. In his place, the black thing sat panting ravenously, its eyes a luminesce, eerie citrine. A monstrous canine leer framed long white fangs.

I ran from it. I was naked and running, my skin turning black with coarse fur, my own fangs pushing past my bleeding gums. My throat was raw from screaming, but the nightmare always found me; it always caught me in its snapping jaws. Each time I felt the sharp press of teeth, the darkness swallowed me.

Then, suddenly, I was awake again. This time I knew I was awake, and alive, the bed felt solid beneath me. There was no vicious voice in my ear daring me to run. I was in the same spartan room as before, but I felt different, as though I was wearing someone else's skin. This body felt nothing like mine—my brain felt swollen, my tongue was sandpaper, my skin felt too tight, and even my teeth throbbed in my gums.

The bite! I groaned as I lifted a shaky hand to my numb shoulder. That was why I'd been dead to the world up till now—rabies! I'd been attacked by some freakish black wolf thing. I'd been infected.

"Run, I'm coming for you." The echo from my nightmare had me jolting up from the pillow with a yelp, my weight on my elbows.

I couldn't be sure anymore what was real or what I'd dreamt, but I *was* sure I hadn't imagined the monster in the basement. I knew I hadn't imagined the bite. Or the sickness that followed. But had I conjured the cruel black veins spread ominously over my flesh? Had my mind evoked that strange conversation with Aidan? Was Aidan even real? My life had become a phantasmagorical slideshow of bizarre and frightening things. My world had spun completely off its axis.

Groaning, I pushed myself up to sitting and then gasped when the sheet slipped down to reveal my pale naked breasts. At the very same moment, the door flew open. I shrieked and lifted the sheet right up to my chin.

A tall man entered as casually as if, by all rights, he slept here and I was the intruder. “Have a good nap?” he asked, looking anything but solicitous.

I glowered balefully at the man. “Don’t you knock?”

“I knocked the first few times, but you were comatose.” He came over to my bedside with a stethoscope, paying my glares no mind as he pressed the cold metal diaphragm to my back. Then he did the same to my front, smirking when I gripped the sheet harder around my chest. A sportive black curl drifted across his forehead as he studied my face.

I was studying his just as intently. I found myself slightly distracted by his mismatched eyes—one grey and one a golden brown. I was relieved when he finally moved away, my sigh far more telling than I’d intended.

He gave a sardonic grunt. “Relax, you’ve got nothing I haven’t already seen before.”

“You haven’t seen *my* parts though.”

“Haven’t I?” His lips curled like a jackal.

“You’re disgusting.”

“God, you humans and your precious modesty.” He sounded bored. “Even if I was into mongrels, which I’m not, you're a little too lippy and scrawny for my taste.”

“Mongrel?” I blasted him with an affronted scowl. *Scrawny?* I knew I wasn’t beautiful, not like Aidan or Nicole, but mongrel-like? What a bastard this guy was. “And what do you mean ‘you humans’? Are you an alien then?”

“Oh, I’m otherworldly all right.” He leaned a hip against the end of my sad little bed. “Technically so are you…as of today.” He dragged his gaze critically over my body as though he couldn’t quite believe what he was seeing. “And how the hell you managed to survive…”

“The rabies.” I gave a shuddering nod, probing at my bandaged shoulder again. That accounted for the fever and delirium, as well as the muscle spasms and paralysis. Hadn't Owen made some comment or another about the area being overrun with wolves? Or had that been Dinwiddie? Either way, I'd been attacked by something rabid. "But I'm okay now?" My tone was more hopeful than certain.

He grunted and shook his head. "Not even close."

I licked my lips, unnerved by his attitude. "It's f-fatal, right?" Once the virus was established there was no cure; no treatment. I'd learned that when our neighbor's dog had been bitten by a rabid raccoon.

"Usually."

I felt lightheaded just thinking of how close I'd come to death. "I'm stronger than I look, I guess."

Another disparaging sweep of his eyes.

"Even for a *human*," I added scathingly.

"Well, check again—" he lowered his eyes pointedly to my bandage "—coz you ain't even that anymore. And you're not out of the woods just yet, Lippy."

Climbing gingerly from the bed, I stepped cautiously around him and headed to the mirror to remove the gauze, looking over my shoulder, aware suddenly of a strange sense of *deja vu*. I knew that most of the damage was close to my spine and that I'd need a mirror to inspect it properly. When I peeled the layers away, I drew in an abrupt breath that hissed past my teeth as I stared, stunned.

The wound had healed almost completely. There were only a few pink marks to attest to the fact that I'd ever been attacked at all, and there was no sign of the black veins and bruising I'd noticed before. Part of the nightmare, maybe? An agonizing and stuttering breath rent my lungs as it rushed from my lips. "H-how long h-have I been out?" Months? Years? The scars were pale and silvery smooth where there should have been stitches and scabs; these scars looked months old already.

He came to stand beside me, peering thoughtfully down at the healed marks. "It's been five days since you spoke to Aidan."

"Impossible!"

He gave a mirthless chuckle. "Oh, Lippy, you've barely even had a taste of the impossible."

I backed away from him, his words feeling heavy and foreboding. "My name's Evan, not Lippy. And you are…?"

"Augustus," he answered, pulling his phone out of his pocket to scroll through his contacts.

That was a mouthful. I listened as a disembodied voice answered his call. Augustus immediately reported my condition to the stranger, his eyes affixed to mine.

"Yeah, no side effects. Completely conscious. Uh-huh. Rabies." He rolled his eyes and gave a few nods, as though the other interlocutor could see him. Then he hung up. "Get dressed." The last was addressed to me with a finger pointed at my soiled and discarded clothes lying beside the bed. "Aidan wants to have a little chat before the council meets."

I glared at the blood-spattered shirt and ruined jeans. "I can't wear those, that's biohazard now!"

He shrugged. "I figured it was a wasted effort to wash them."

"Hygiene is a wasted effort?!" This guy was something else.

"You weren't supposed to survive." The sides of his eyes tightened with something between regret and confusion. "We hadn't expected you to." He gave a tight shrug. "Why wash a dead woman's clothes?" With that, he turned on his heel and left me standing there as though I'd been punched in the gut (except no punch would have winded me more than his words had). "Get dressed, I'll wait outside."

The door slammed shut, the noise precipitating me to scramble into my dirty clothes, my shirt still torn and stiff with blood. Furious tears spilled from my eyes as I marched to the door to confront my ill-mannered jailor. I yanked it open to see him leaning casually against the wall opposite my door. "Where's Nicole?" I growled. I didn't particularly miss the woman, but hers was the only familiar face I knew and I wanted even that small comfort—seeing someone I recognized from my old life. The life that seemed so surreal now.

Augustus, however, ignored my question and pushed himself off the wall, gesturing for me to follow him into the dimly lit corridor.

Maybe this *was* some sort of old hospital, I thought as we passed by a deserted transport stretcher, my rubber boots padding noiselessly along the vinyl flooring. His footsteps, though, produced a hollow and unwelcome echo. The light was impersonal, and so was the peeling grey paint on the walls and the brown leak stains on the ceiling. Everything smacked of desuetude and abandonment, like a post-apocalyptic ward. He lead me through one set of swinging doors and into an empty, featureless laboratory, then into another antiseptic corridor with more empty stretchers, the blue leather stained and rotting.

"Where are we?" I asked. "What is this place?"

"The clinic," he replied dispassionately, glancing over his shoulder to catch my dubious look. "It's usually empty, we don't get sick very often." He left it at that.

"Are you a doctor?" I recognized his voice, and my mind, for some reason, had identified him as such.

"No."

I glared at his back, resenting his curt answers. "I need to call my mother." She was probably already in Alaska searching for me, beside herself with worry. Alison, Owen, and Melissa likely were as well. Maybe even Tristan? Bitterness and longing instantly filled my chest as I thought of him and what Nicole had said that morning she'd knocked on my door; that morning that already felt like a lifetime ago. "Everyone will be looking for me by now."

"No one's looking for you, Lippy."

"But Tristan—"

He halted suddenly and whipped around to pierce me with a harrowing glare. "You have no fucking idea how much shit you're in right now, do you? Forget Tristan. Forget your old life!" Gone was the smirk and irritating aloofness, and in its place was a thunderous incredulity, his grey eye stormy and the brown one molten. "Anyway, he's apparently the reason you're in this godforsaken mess!" And then he was marching off again, seemingly unconcerned whether I followed or not.

"Tell me what's going on. Please!"

"It would have been better for you if you *had* died." This he muttered as he turned a corner, but I heard him loud and clear.

For the second time today, he'd wounded me, his words cutting like a sharp lash. The bastard hadn't even brought me food or water either. The latter of those needs, however, I was able to quench at a drinking fountain that, thankfully, still worked (if a bit feebly) despite its obvious lack of maintenance. Once I'd siphoned off as much water as the fountain would surrender, I hurried off again to catch up to Augustus.

Like a dark angel, his movements fluid and his figure imposing, he shoved a pair of large double doors aside, the light rushing in like a celestial halo to blind me as I squinted in his wake. An angel or a demon? *Worse!* He'd proved himself to be nothing more than a devil in disguise. Maybe this shitty town really was full of devils.

Once my eyesight had adjusted to the daylight I noticed him waiting impatiently by a black Land Rover. Black—the color of his heart, if he even had one. A short while later we were speeding along a deserted country road. The houses that were visible from the road were sparse and unassuming. The silence that pervaded was almost suffocating. Fortunately, it was disrupted a moment later when Augustus' phone rang over the hands-free system.

He hit a button and uttered a curt, "What is it Shenton?"

"Aidan called for a conclave?" a male voice said excitedly. "And Nicole's back in town? What's this all about, boss?"

"Can't talk now," was all Augustus replied before hanging up, eyes darting accusingly to me.

"Did he just call you boss?" I asked nervously.

"I'm Aidan's lieutenant." After that explanation—which was hardly much of an explanation at all—we lapsed into an uncomfortable silence again.

It was getting darker now, the sun sinking lower and the shadows lengthening as we passed a dilapidated sign that read "Red Devil Ranch. Private Property. Do Not Enter." Shortly afterward, the *lieutenant* steered the SUV over a ramshackle old bridge that protested loudly beneath the tires and then continued along a narrow road, the woodland becoming denser as it strangled the dirt track. Finally the headlights cut through the twilight and landed on an unremarkable rectangular building. Unremarkable except for the large pair of oaken double doors with a wolf's head guarding each side, and an iron ring latched between each set of serrated jaws. It all looked sinister enough to deter even the most indefatigable trespassers. The building itself was cloaked in shadows, situated in a small clearing over which the backwoods encroached with subtle menace.

Just as Augustus shifted the Landie into park, the double doors swung open and Aidan strode out confidently, her expression as remote as I remembered it. The last of the natural light lit the chestnut in her hair as she jogged down the stairs toward us in a scarlet shirt. There was the red devil herself.

"What is this place?" I asked him, my eyes still fixed to Aidan.

He killed the engine and turned to me. "This is where the pack council gathers for conclaves."

"Conclaves?"

"Pack business," he said, getting out.

When I hopped out of the SUV, Aidan took one look at my shirt and shot Augustus a withering glare. "Really, Gus? You could've at least given her a clean shirt?"

"Hell, I thought I was heading to the clinic to find a corpse." With a last meaningful look at Aidan, he then shot into the woods at a brisk jog.

"Where's he going?" I wanted to know, purposefully disregarding that last shitty remark of his.

"I'll show you," she said, also heading into the forest after him, but at an unhurried pace. "follow me."

"Do I have a choice?" The woods seemed to be glaring darkly at me.

Without glancing around, "You want answers, don't you?"

"Yes," I said to her back. Yet what if there were more of those monsters in there? If there were, I really didn't want to be here alone in the gloaming. After an indecisive minute, in which I chewed my bottom lip and scanned the shadows for movements, I shoved away from the SUV and sprinted after her. I was tired, dirty, starving, miserable, and scared as hell, but if she had answers then into the woods I'd go. What other choice did I have? I was in the middle of nowhere and the only shelter in sight was some creepy old building that looked about as welcoming as the woods I was entering.

When I slipped past the thickets, Aidan was waiting for me with a preternatural stillness, her striking green eyes unblinking as she watched me scurrying toward her. I faltered suddenly, my eyes wavering over an odd shape in the damp earth—a frightening imprint. My nails dug into my palms as I recognized the large simian contours, so bear-like and unnatural. I'd seen a print like that before.

"I don't have all night." Though she hadn't raised it, her voice was crisp and clear, drawing me instantly from my morbid abstraction.

I dragged my eyes away from the sinister footprint and, with a shuddering sigh, I moved to where Aidan stood statue-like.

"So you think some rabid dog bit you?" she asked with sudden glaring irony. It seemed we were down to brass tacks. After I'd given a wary shrug she continued on, "You think the worst is behind you and that now you get to go home and pretend this was all some inconvenient little nightmare?"

"Yes."

"Wrong." Her face clouded as she set her teeth. "You were bitten, Evan. Your life as you knew it is over. The Evan you were no longer exists."

Suddenly the fever was back and I felt my brow break out in a cold foreshadowing sweat, my hands trembling as she began to circle me. "What bit me?" But I was almost too frightened to know.

One side of her upper lip peeled away abruptly to reveal long, supernatural canines. "Did Tristan never tell you what he is?"

Horror-struck by her fearsome teeth, I stumbled backward. "My God!"

She cut off my retreat with superhuman speed, the green of her eyes almost fluorescent beneath the darkening sky. "What *we* are?"

I was catapulted straightaway to Dean's library, my fingers skimming over yellowed pages; over one unbelievable word. *Werewolf.* My mind screamed what I wouldn't dare say out loud. *Werewolf.* All of Tristan's allusions and hints sprang to the fore, taunting me with what had always been right in front of me: the way he'd scared that bear off; his uncanny hearing; the rumors;

him naked in the woods; that animalistic undercurrent that had always thrilled and intimidated me. *Werewolf.* “Impossible!”

She finally sealed her lips again. “Werewolves, Evan. That’s what we are; that’s what your boyfriend is. And the thing about werewolf venom is that if it doesn’t kill you, it claims you; it changes you.”

I’d been bitten by a werewolf?! My hand flew to my shoulder. I wanted to call her a liar, but deep down I knew she was dead serious. Even on some unfathomable primal level, my gut recognized the truth in her eyes. The awful truth flashed before me the way her fangs had just done. Undeniable and dreadful. “Am I…?” I couldn’t even finish the question, I was that terrified.

“Yes,” she answered anyway, understanding my horror perfectly. To emphasize the point, her lip curled back again to reveal her pretercanine teeth. “You’re a werewolf now. But less than that—you’re a mongrel.”

28

CONCLAVE

"Do you know what we do to mongrels?" Aidan's eyes were a dark hunter green in the lengthening shadows. "We kill them." There was no satisfaction in her expression. In fact, there was nothing there at all, just a clinical stare that chilled my blood. "We don't suffer them to live."

"I don't believe in werewolves!" My own conviction, however, tasted false even to me. "You're lying."

She gave me an obliging shrug and shifted her gaze past my shoulder. "If it's proof you're after, I can certainly indulge you this once." She was staring purposefully into the darkness behind me, daring me to turn around and see for myself what had transfixed her gaze.

I could feel the tension prickle and coil around me, feel the sudden blast of a cold gaze at my back—probing insidiously along my spine.

Aidan, however, seemed impervious to the strange hush in the forest. Something, or someone, had materialized behind me. I didn't need her to say it out loud, I could *feel* it. A sharp imminence crackled along the air. With a choking scream lodged in my throat, I turned around to face the devil I knew was waiting behind me.

A stunning and debilitating fear held me rooted as I confronted the thing from my nightmare. It was impossibly large; larger than I remembered—tall and almost sapient but for the fur and canine physiognomy. Its coat was thick and black, its muzzle slightly ajar to reveal a hint of gleaming fangs. Wolflike but not. Simian but not. A *Canis Lupus-Bigfootimus* hybrid!

It made no move toward me, only watched with dual-colored eyes: an eerie glowing heterochromia. One orb radiated with silver and the other glowed a deep amber brown.

I processed it all through some mental rigor mortis. A primal immobility held me still. I was lucid enough to know it would only give chase if I ran.

"Look at his eyes." Aidan's voice cut through my terror.

The blood rushed instantly from my head as I recognized those strange eyes, so unlike the pale ghostly blue of the one that had attacked me. Its ears were longer and devoid of white grizzled tips. This was not the creature that had bitten me. "Augustus?" I whispered, fearful and still not quite convinced. But it *was* him. The scent of cloves and citrus clung to his pelt.

The bipedal wolf gave an imperceptible nod of its head and raised its strange, humanoid eyes to its mistress. A question in its canny gaze.

"Do you want to see him shift back? Will that convince you?" Aidan asked behind me.

I gave a fervid shake of my head, stepping as far back as I dared without looking like I was ready to bolt. I squeezed my eyes shut, trying to regain my lost equilibrium. This was too much all at once.

The rustle of leaves beneath heavy, retreating footfalls evoked a flinch; I was almost certain it might bite me yet. But nothing happened. When I opened my eyes the creature was gone, a swaying branch the only sign that it had ever been there at all. "Is that…?" I licked my lips. "Will I look like that?"

"No," she said. "You'll look a lot less majestic when you first change. A mongrel even less so than a pure-born."

That thing was majestic?! I nearly burst into maniacal laughter. Nearly. Instead I felt the hot sting of tears threaten my splintered composure. "You said mongrels…aren't suffered to live." Trembling, I turned to face her again. "Are you going to kill me now?" Why hadn't she just killed me already? Why the show of proof? Why waste her time on explanations? Why had any of this been done to me at all? I was a good person. I recycled and everything. I never hurt anything except mosquitoes.

Heedless of my churning thoughts, her facade cracked only slightly as she heaved a weary sigh. "You somehow survived the venom." She seemed frustrated by this. "I don't know how—" But she stopped herself and narrowed her eyes at me as something monumental seemed to occur to her. "Tristan," she snorted. "Of course. You're mated, aren't you?" This appeared to make sense only to her.

Was that werewolf for, 'Did you have sexual relations?' "That's none of your—"

"Werewolf venom needs to be injected straight into the bloodstream to take effect; near the heart." She seemed to be talking to herself now, her eyes momentarily unfocused. "Your jugular vein was pierced, and the venom injected straight to your heart. Had you been bitten anywhere else you'd have died. If your neck had been snapped, you'd have died."

"Tristan was never violent! He never—"

"This is just a theory," she went on, disregarding my interruption again, "but by mating, right before he bit you, you'd have had trace venom in your blood. The wolf gift. A sort of temporary inoculation." This appeared to satisfy her. "That's why you survived." I was subjected to another of her derisive looks, up and down, as though she couldn't believe that I *had* survived at all.

Wolf gift? I liked the sound of that better than the term mating. He'd used a condom, though. *But not in the shower.* "So, indirectly, Tristan saved my life."

Her lips compressed distastefully. "You wouldn't have *needed* saving if he hadn't tried to kill you in the first place."

"No! Tristan would never hurt me," I said with a steadfast lift of my chin.

"He lied about what he is. Maybe you don't know him nearly as well as you think you do."

"He didn't bite me!" I gritted my teeth as a dawning and instantaneous clarity lifted the fog from my eyes. "Nicole did!" I knew that now, the links in this fucked up series of events were starting to connect themselves. My brain had been reeling under the colossal weight of all that had happened and all the implications I was yet to understand. I was drinking from a firehose, but suddenly it was all clear. "Your sister bit me!"

"Tristan—"

"Tristan doesn't have cold blue eyes! I recognized Augustus"—pointing to where her crazy-eyed henchman had disappeared moments ago—"and I now recognize your sister for what she is: a crazy, murderous bitch that nearly killed me!"

"He slept with you first and then, before the venom could leave your blood, bit you exactly where he knew you'd have the best chance of survival."

"You weren't in the cabin. That monster tried to maul my head off!" I could still see those familiar crazy eyes whenever I shut my own.

"Then why did Nicole bring you here? Why not finish you off and bury you in the woods for the maggots? She saved you by bringing you here to—"

"I don't fucking know what goes on in that deranged head of hers. I don't speak crazy."

"Enough," Aidan seethed. "Your clothes reek of Tristan even now. Moreover, in this pack, my sister's word will always stand unalloyed against a mongrel's."

So much for justice. "Then ask Tristan. Ask Dean. They're not Mongrels." Or so Nicole had implied that day in the cabin. She'd made it sound like Tristan was an aristocrat or something—some or other werewolf royalty.

"This matter is now an Athabaskan one. Dean won't interfere unless I invite him here."

I snapped my jaws shut, cowed by her furious glare. Then, in a calmer tone, I said, "Believe whatever you want, but you don't need to kill me if there's reasonable doubt."

"There's every reason to kill you," she countered. "You don't even know yet what it means to be a mongrel. You're an unknown danger. You'll be unpredictable." Her eyes flickered back to the woods behind me. When she spoke again, it wasn't to me. "You took long enough."

I whipped my head around to see Augustus loping toward us.

He winked at me as he zipped up his jeans. "Lippy here is a little naked-shy. Thought I'd better cover up first, didn't wanna scare her."

I snorted incredulously. What freaky twilight zone had I stumbled upon? So it was okay to scare me with a giant werewolf but spare my fragile sensibilities the sight of a penis? "I already saw you naked," I reminded him, feeling my hackles rise.

"Well, it don't count when all this length—" he grabbed his crotch suggestively "—is hidden behind all that fur." He gave another wink. "Trust me, you'd have fainted for sure if you'd seen it."

"Are you done?" Aidan checked her watch impatiently.

The smirk slid instantly from Augustus' face and my anger

subsided behind the fear again. She had that kind of power over both of us. The irrefutable power of an alpha. She considered me narrowly. "You say Nicole bit you. Even if that's true then you're still my problem to deal with because the wolf that bit you belongs to my pack; and, therefore, I decide your fate. Not Dean. And certainly not Tristan."

I took a shallow gulp of air. "What have you decided?"

"I'll let the pack determine whether or not you live or die." She then glanced back over my head at Augustus. "Let's get this over with."

"Wait!" I cried, edging away. There had to be a better way. Her tone and the way she'd glanced down at me had been extremely ominous. Dreadfully final. Maybe it wasn't too late to run away. Without a second thought, I bolted.

One minute I was hell-bent for leather and the next thing I knew, Augustus, with his quicksilver reflexes, had grabbed a fistful of my shirt and yanked me back, restraining me, kicking and screaming, against his granite torso before I'd even worked up a good flight.

"The meeting will go one of two ways," Aidan said to him, as though I hadn't just tried to escape, speaking calmly over my vociferous struggles. "Whatever happens, you know what to do." I noticed the silent, arcane message that passed between them.

I had just braced myself to bolt again, or bite, my fingers already stiffening into claws, but suddenly the fire was snuffed from my breast and my jaw slackened with fascination. I blinked in confusion, letting my captors' words drift meaninglessly into one ear and out of the other. My gaze widened mesmerically. Even though dusk had fallen swiftly and the stars were already visible, my eyes were adapting strangely. Nightfall had obscured nature's colors, like it always did, but for the first time ever, my eyes cut through the gloom with startling clarity. Everything was weirdly enhanced. The shadows were strangely iridescent. A whole other spectrum was unfurling around me. Air whooshed out from my lungs as I realized that I could see perfectly in the dark!

There was a muted sort of glow infusing every detail of the forest, a thermal pulse radiating even from the trees themselves, as though they were alive. Hundreds of varicolored life forces surrounded us from all the creatures I had now become aware of. Nightjars, toads, owls, foxes, and deer! Even the insects were emitting a visual scent.

The smells that greeted me were more piquant, richer, and the night sounds sharper. A rodent shuffled through the dead leaves on my right. A beetle gnawed through the damp wood of a moldering log nearby, and something with scales was burrowing beneath the soft earth beneath my feet. I could even hear the grinding of wheels along a distant dirt track, the low mechanical hum of pistons, the growl of a far-off motorcycle. But we were so deep in the woods that I instantly questioned what my ears were revealing. Besides the animals, there was no one else out here but us three.

My own blood began to fill my ears as I gaped at my hands, noticing every pore and each fine crease around my knuckles, every follicle, as I held them up in front of me. *Amazing!* I'd been so caught up in my supernatural sensory wonderment that for a fateful instant I'd let these burgeoning gifts overshadow my dire predicament. And the two scary creatures beside me.

The gag that was suddenly shoved into my mouth quickly dispelled my awe. My hands were instantly yanked away from my mouth, where they'd flown to dislodge the obstruction, and then restrained behind my back. Then I was swiftly lifted up over Augustus' shoulder, like a shrieking bag of garbage, and carried off to the meeting hall for my supposed sentencing. Presumably toward my otherworldly jurors.

When we cleared the tree line I was immediately confronted

with the source of the sounds I'd heard earlier—almost every available space around the meeting hall was occupied with trucks, motorcycles, and cars, and from within the building itself, I could hear the excited and variegated murmuring of voices.

I struggled like a panicked worm, my hair flying into my wet eyes. Finally, with an irritable grunt, he swung me down and for a brief moment, it seemed as though I'd won my freedom from him. But I was wrong. He took my shoulders in his large fists and gave me a shake until my teeth rattled. Aidan passed us by without a word, clearly unconcerned for my fury or safety. When she'd disappeared through the swinging doors, the voices becoming sharper for a moment until the doors closed again, I met his stormy bi-colored eyes with a terrified glare of my own.

"There's no conceivable way you'd ever outrun me, girl. I'll snatch you bald-headed, so don't piss me off trying. Now, do you wanna be carried in there over my shoulder, hogtied, or do you wanna walk in with what little dignity you got left? Either way, you're going in." He waited till I'd given him a curt nod.

I'd bloody well walk in under my own steam.

"Good, our world ain't for chickens. We eat chickens. So harden up and pay attention otherwise you ain't gonna survive past your first change." He was speaking so low that I strained my ears to listen, blinking mutinously.

As far as pep talks went, that was one of the worst I'd ever heard, but by now the fight had gone swiftly out of me, my limbs trembling. My shoulders slumped under the weight of my impending doom. "I'm not a chicken," I tried to say, but my words came out muffled as I chewed on my gag.

He understood me though. "Maybe not, but you got yourself some henhouse ways."

With a look and a gesture, I pleaded for him to untie me.

"Here's something for nothing, Lippy—" he pulled at the knot he'd tied at my wrists "—we don't respect the weak and you look like you wouldn't bite a biscuit. So fix your face." Then he straightened. "No more theatrics, got that? No one's gonna have any patience with your screaming, bitching, or crying."

I gave a stiff nod as I pulled the gag out with numb fingers.

"You ain't got no say here. You're just a mutt, as far as they're concerned, and if you open your trap again, or get your tail up even once, you'll be gagged quicker than a sneeze through a screen door, understand?"

I nodded again, looking up at the imposing doors. My energies would be better served paying attention and figuring out how to escape.

"Glad we understand each other." He gestured for me to precede him. "In you go, they're waiting on you."

I'd already guessed that much from the very conspicuous hush that had settled around us. Steeling myself, I went in.

29

LUPUM CAEDES

Execrating eyes stabbed at my flesh when I entered. I could feel the hostile pressure of them as I fixed a wide-eyed gaze at the scuffed wooden flooring, relying solely on what I noticed from my periphery. Even the silence was glaring and hollow as I followed the alpha and her lieutenant past the many nameless faces toward what appeared to be a dais of sorts. There stood Nicole, front and center, with *preterlupine* stillness, eyes cutting palpably across my downturned face. She moved aside for her sister and Augustus, but my shoulder was none too gently bumped by hers as I passed.

What pernicious whispers there had been abruptly ended as Aidan climbed the single step and turned to face them all, addressing her pack of stony-faced monsters with lethal coolness and formidable self-possession.

I shifted uncomfortably on my feet as she explained why she'd summoned them here; and the problem I now posed them. Despite what I'd seen so far, I was still of two minds about this impossible fantasy I'd become a part of, still half-convinced I'd soon wake up back home in Jupiter (the town, not the planet, although waking up on another planet seemed infinitely more plausible than the existence of werewolves in the universe) and realize, with exquisite relief, that my biggest problem was nothing more sinister than that I'd just spilled tea over Andy's crotch again. But no, here I was in Red Devil surrounded by supernaturals and enclosed by smells and sounds that overwhelmed and suffocated me.

The musky and unfamiliar redolence of each stranger elicited an overwhelming urge to run. Each individual scent was unmistakably and subtly different from another. And there were many of them. They bombarded me. It was too much. Too intense all of a sudden, their cunning whispers like a thousand blades of grass raking my eardrums. It was by pure force of will that I stood frozen in place.

Up till now, I'd allowed most of the conversation to fade into incomprehensibility as though all of this meant nothing to me and *had* nothing to do with me. I was, after all, only a cockroach under the floorboard and they were only discussing some flea-bitten stray. Not me. Seeing as the largest werewolf in the room was standing directly beside me, I couldn't very well ignore the stentorian voice of the mighty Augustus himself when he finally added to the discourse, abruptly dispelling my sensory overload.

She's hardly a threat." He gestured down at me with a nod. "Half-starved maybe. How can we damn her without first waiting to see—"

"They all turn rabid!" Nicole interpolated. "She'll be no different."

"The bite affects everyone differently. We should wait."

"Wait for what? For her to kill someone?"

I could feel my dark warden bristling at Nicole's tone, the wrath rolling off him so much so that it hit me in tangible waves. Why was he playing devil's advocate on my behalf? Did he see right through her like I did? "Let Dean or Max decide," he said. "If Tristan bit her—"

"If? I'm telling you he bit her!"

"Nicole." At Aidan's warning tone, temperate though it was, all became silent again. "I don't know how conclaves were conducted in Dean's house, but here, in mine, you'll maintain a respectful tone and leash your tongue. You haven't been gone that long."

I relished Nicole's chagrin and peeked up to meet her withering and overpowering stare. Instantly, I dropped mine to the floor again, despising myself for my cowardice.

"*If* Tristan bit her," Augustus said again, "then she should be theirs to destroy and Tristan their problem to deal with."

The discussions had recommenced, but I'd stopped listening. I became temporarily lightheaded. I couldn't remember my last meal. Water and air would only sustain me so long. Only Augustus' firm hold on my arm kept me steady enough that no one, except him, noticed my momentary faintness. But he, thankfully, gave nothing away, barely even glanced at me. I wasn't worth a glance after all. No one would bother to look a mouse in the eyes, what was the point of that? No one wanted to 'humanize' what they meant to destroy. I was just a slaughterhouse cow to them.

"Unfortunately for you," came the echo of Dean's long ago caveat, *"you've already established your rank in the pack."*

Eyes up, Evan! From beneath the harsh spotlight of this pseudo courtroom, encircled by my would-be adjudicators, I finally lifted my eyes off the floor for the last time and met each werewolf glare with a defiance I didn't quite feel yet. But I would fake it till I did. I would *not* be intimidated anymore, I decided. My timidness had gotten me nowhere! Easier said than done though. Defiance was hard to pull off, especially in the face of one particularly feral-looking man who licked his chops vulgarly at me, dissecting me openly.

Okay, clearly I *would* be intimidated. In spite of my natural inclination to balk and tuck tail, however, as I'd just done with

Nicole (which was why she'd thought me easy prey), I summoned my meager pluck and held the man's predatory gaze. What did I have to lose now? I was dead anyway. The best defense against predation was, after all, *not* to act like prey. To bare my own fangs and claws, latent though they were. By degrees, strangely enough, he began to lose the look of virulence and instead began to appear nonplussed. Then the incredible happened: he averted his eyes.

Now I was the one to become bemused! Had I just…? Could I really establish my dominance over someone with just a look alone? Maybe there was some unforeseen and unfathomable power that coalesced in the heart of the damned who had nothing more to lose. A reckless and unfettered power that was gathering in my belly. With awful lucidity, it hit me: all my life I'd been silently shrinking, always eager to be invisible and passive, without ever truly understanding or appreciating the fundamental laws of body language. Maybe that's why Andy had never really noticed me as anything more than a little love-struck puppy to be humored and amused by.

Here, amidst these unsympathetic strangers—in the most unlikely place in the world to find my strength or determine my newborn puissance—I was suddenly hit by the epiphany that I was the only one thus far who'd never believed in myself. Who'd never believed in my own worth. Well, I resolved angrily, if I wanted to run with the big dogs—and survive—I'd need to stop pissing like a puppy!

In consideration of that, I dragged a far more confident gaze around to study the hall and its unnatural occupants. The place was something between an old barn and an abandoned church with it's naked, dust-ridden beams, cloudy windows, and spartan box pews. It was at the serried pews that I glared. This was more so to test a burgeoning theory than to antagonize any of the wolves. I was by no means suicidal. Knowing I was going to die didn't mean I was going to facilitate that eventuality. I was testing myself. And them.

One by one, I gauged those closest to the front, refusing to shrink from them, pitting my own steely glare against theirs. Though not every eye inevitably shied away, I was surprised by how many *did* yield to mine. It was empowering and compelling. Finally, though, I came full circle, my scowl colliding with Nicole's. Hers was considerably blacker than anything I was capable of summoning.

Here was my worst aggressor. She'd already determined her superiority above mine from past encounters, and in this strange and incestuous hierarchy, I was definitely her inferior. Or so she thought. No matter how much I hated her for what she'd done to me, no matter how much I wanted to rip at her flesh with my aching teeth, it took every ounce of self-possession to hold myself steady and ignore the perspiration at my temples. This time I wouldn't back down. Couldn't. The more I held her glower, returning it full force in fact, the more her color darkened. An impasse. Her hate practically frothed and gathered at her mouth, but I glared on, unbridled. *I am your equal!*

She got the message loud and clear, and she made no secret of how much she hated not being able to leap at my throat, I could see it in the slaughterous set of her features. Her raised hackles. The expectant hush. The room seemed to tremble with the tension that roiled between us.

Suddenly, Augustus moved to stand between us, like a concrete wall, and, with a severe look (as if to say, "Pay attention!"), he neutralized (or neutered) the threatening tension. I blinked the strange fixation away.

"We need to put her down before the transition." Nicole's venomous words flew at me. "Why are we even discussing this? Of course she's a threat. When have mongrels ever not been?"

"A threat we can contain," Augustus seethed.

"The law speaks for itself!" came a booming voice from the back. "Why should we make any exceptions. Who the hell is she to us?"

My eyes raked the crowd, settling on a barrel-chested figure leaning against the far wall. If anyone looked werewolfish he did, with his wild beard, fierce mien, and rangy arms.

"Nothing, as a matter of fact," Aidan replied coolly, "but the same can't be said for Tristan. And I've yet to determine if the repercussions are worth our interference."

"Ain't he the one that bit her?"

"That's a lie—" The rest of my objection was rudely forestalled by Augustus' iron fingers clamping down almost to my bones. I gave a grunt of pain.

"Interrupt again and you'll only make matters worse for yourself." His words were dangerously low.

"Tristan's offense is a matter for his alpha," Aidan replied to the man at the back.

"For the sake of equity, shouldn't the Council of Alpha's be involved, considering who he is?" A different voice had now joined the debate—a woman's, clear and without heat. If there was any sympathy to be had here, limited though it was, her expression was the only one that held any for me.

"Sylvie's right," Nicole said unexpectedly. "His father and brother won't act objectively. Give him to the council and let them mete out his punishment."

"Hmm, yes." Aidan sent her sister a quelling look. "Blood is thicker than water. It seems there's nothing we won't do for family." Next she turned to consider me. "But we're here to decide Evan's fate, not Tristan's."

"You think the Southeast will pose a threat if she's harmed?" said the lycanthropic giant I'd locked eyes with earlier.

"I do, Heath."

As in Heathcliff? He certainly fit the bill—swarthy and menacing.

"Well," said Heath, "he shouldn't have broken pack law."

"No," Aidan agreed, "yet the point is still that the girl *was* bitten. Let's not lose sight of why we're here tonight."

So far, I understood enough from this evening's debate to know that The Bite was hugely taboo, the crime in and of itself as heinous as the stigma of being bitten.

"It's not worth the risk to make exceptions for her just because of *who* bit her," Heath went on gruffly. "Rules are rules."

"Agreed, but what's the rush in euthanizing her—" Aidan spared Nicole a keen look "—before we know for certain if she's rabid or not."

"Because I wouldn't put it past Tristan to sneak over here and steal her away." Nicole again. "He'd never kill her, foaming at the mouth or not, and then we'd all be guilty of negating our duty to prevent her attacking the public and putting us all at risk. Every single pack, not just ours, would be at risk. Heaths right, it's not worth it."

"Neither is a pack war worth one mutt's death," Augustus rejoined, ignoring the blatant looks of dubiety.

"Tristan's ole man wouldn't let it come to that," Nicole said confidently. "Nor would Dean."

"You sure about that?" Sylvie asked, her gaze stoic.

"Once we put the girl down, Tristan will see reason."

"Clearly he's proven he has none." This from Heath, punctuated with a disgusted snort.

One after the other, opinions were weighed, and all the while Aidan watched on like a preeminent goddess. By now I'd had enough, my spleen rupturing with pent-up frustration. "You're all wrong about him! Mongrel or not, I'm standing right here! Don't talk about me as if I'm dead already!"

"You're as good as!" Nicole spat. Then she turned to face her pack-mates. "I propose we make an example of the mutt and teach Tristan a well-deserved lesson." She waited a beat and the tension increased. "I invoke *Lupum Caedes*."

The audible gasps and ensuing, heavy silence was evidence enough that I was *not* going to like whatever *that* entailed. Didn't *caedis* mean slaughter?

"That's archaic!" Augustus thundered, whipping his head around to Aidan who was silently studying her sister's self-satisfied smirk. "You can't seriously be considering that, Aidan? It's crazy!"

"What's *Lupum Caedes*?" I shifted my gaze between the alpha and her lunatic sister warily. But everyone ignored me, my trembling voice lost amidst the crescent murmuring.

At last, Aidan raised her hand for silence, took a deep breath, and allowed her gaze to drift across the animated faces. Finally, it settled over mine, seemingly unaffected by my silent pleading. "It is unorthodox," she said, turning a reflective gleam over her pack.

"Defunct, you mean," Augustus growled.

"Yes. As your alpha, I advise against it. However, this is not a dictatorship, so I am willing to put it to a vote." Then she lifted her chin an imperceptible degree. "You've all heard our sister's testimony as evidenced by the girl before you."

I shook my head, aghast. "What evidence?! The only one guilty of anything is Nicole." I ripped my arm from Augustus' restraining grip and threw a damning finger at Nicole. "She bit me!" But my accusation had about as much effect as a toddler throwing a toy from its cot.

Nicole folded her arms smugly. "I told you she'd say anything to protect him. For all we know she probably asked him to bite her. They're both sick."

"Liar! The thing that bit me had blue—"

"Why would I condemn my own fiancé?" she snarled. "No,

you're both getting exactly what you deserve." Then she swiftly turned to Aidan again. "Just muzzle the damn mutt."

Aidan spared her sister a quelling look. "I'll muzzle you both if you're not careful."

"I say we allow the Council of Alphas to deal with Tristan and his little pet," said Augustus, moving to block my view of Nicole again. "We should never have been involved in the first place." There were a few nods of agreement, but not nearly as many as I'd have liked.

I kept shooting the door desperate looks as though expecting Tristan to fly into the room at any second. I blamed Nicole for planting that hope when she'd inferred that he might try to 'sneak' in and 'steal' me away. Rescue me. Why hadn't he come yet? Why was I alone in all this? Was I delusional or had he bitten me after all? I rubbed my aching shoulder. A kernel of doubt had already been sown (Nicole's fault), despite the blue eyes still haunting me, and I hated myself for feeling confused and desperate. My emotions were running amok inside me. *No!* I couldn't doubt Tristan now. Hope was all that was keeping me sane.

"Fine, let them deal with Tristan then," Nicole was saying. "But she—" she stepped around Augustus to scowl at me "—has to die. The transition will probably kill her anyway, why not put the runt down before her first cycle. *That's* humane, isn't it?"

"I'm not convinced she will die," Augustus argued. By now their argument had come full circle again. "If she does turn rabid, let Tristan put her down. It serves him right."

I balled my fists.

"A vote then," Nicole said, glancing at Aidan. At her sister's stoic nod she went on. "Who here wants a little bloodsport? Why shouldn't we be the ones to see justice served? The Yukon alpha will more than likely thank us for disposing of the mutt quietly and quickly. He'll be grateful to us for not dragging his son before the council." There were cheers of agreement all around.

But when Aidan spoke the clamor stilled instantly. "So what you're proposing is this: her death to satisfy Tristan's violation? To punish him. And the bloodsport to satisfy your bloodlust for Tristan's hide?"

With increasing horror I noticed that the pack was in agreement, the latter part especially having cinched their approval—I would die and all would go back to how it had been before I'd had the audacity to get myself bitten. My life as forfeit for Tristan's offense.

Nicole smirked, satisfied with my imminent death sentence. "Yes. We'll have our *Lupum Caedes* and in return, we'll give Maxwell Thorn the satisfaction of sweeping his son's little scandal under the rug. No one's gonna start a war over some little mongrel, not when there's no body left to war over. Max will control Tristan."

No body? What the hell were they going to do to me?

"Next time Tristan will think better of screwing a—" She faltered a moment. "Of screwing with nature."

"Are you people nuts?!" To Nicole, specifically, I said, "Tristan will rip you apart when he finds out what you've done!"

The pack, however, jeered and muttered excitedly.

"So this is your final judgment?" Aidan asked the assembly. In response, she received a hearty roar of affirmation. "All in favor of *Lupum Caedes* show a raise of hands?" Only Aidan, Augustus, and a handful of others, Sylvie included, kept their claws at their sides. Aidan gave a curt nod. "It's decided then."

I stood frozen on the makeshift dais, the wolves chattering animatedly as they stood and filed out after Nicole. Aidan was the last to leave, her face grim as she gave Augustus a pointed look from the door. After a moment she too was gone and all was silent except for the insects and night murmurings. Only Augustus and I remained in the old building now.

I raised my face to his and saw that he was watching me pityingly. "What is *Lupum Caedes*?"

"A very old rite saved only for the very worst offenders."

"They're going to…will I be…?"

"Slaughtered." He nodded.

"Well, thanks for sugar-coating it." I sounded strangely anesthetized despite the tremor in my voice. "When?"

"The new moon. *Lupum Caedes* is always on a new moon."

I glanced out the smokey window to see the waning yellow crescent glowing in the black sky behind the jagged tree line. *Not long then.* A fatal lump pulsed thickly in my chest. It was so painful, and my throat so parched, that I could barely swallow the tears that I'd licked from my parched lips. "He'll come for me." But, like the moon, even my conviction was waning. "Earlier, Nicole said—"

"No, he won't." His words were rueful. "You're in Red Devil now. None but the pack know where our conclaves take place. Or where we keep our convicted. But more than that, you're in the territory of one of the strongest packs in North America. No one —not even the Yukon heir—would dare trespass on another alpha's territory. Especially not Aidan's. Not without an army at his back."

30

NEW MOON

The hours passed, so did the days and nights (which I measured by the arrival of each of my meals), but there was no lupine army come to rescue me. Tristan never came. The new moon, however, arrived with lethal swiftness. The darkness outside was so absolute that I could feel the weight of it even through my concrete hell. My time was up.

It was ironic how time raced or slowed in excruciating defiance of the heart's most desperate wish. I'd dared to blink and now it was time to die.

After the conclave I'd been returned to the austere, windowless cell I'd first woken up in, then fed and watered like an unloved pet. Kept healthy for the slaughter. I shivered at the thought, revulsed enough to want to heave my dinner. But I kept it down and conserved my strength despite the terror—I had no intention of dying meekly; no intention of allowing them to cannibalize me. If that's what they even meant to do. Did wolves eat their own kind in nature? No, I didn't think so. But humans did. It seemed that werewolves possessed the worst traits of both species.

Tristan didn't seem like a monster though. But where was he?

The sound of the lock turning in my cell had me swiping at my tears. I sprang off my stained mattress as the door swung open.

It was Augustus. "Evening, Lippy." He cocked his head and scrutinized the long white tunic I was wearing. Then, with a shake of his head and a snort, he said, "You look like a sacrificial lamb."

"Isn't that the point?" I sniffed miserably.

"Hmph." He shrugged his large shoulders. "Let's go. It's time."

"Where's Eliza?" I hadn't seen Augustus since the night of the conclave when he'd brought me back here to my cell. My dedicated warden the past few days had been a girl named Eliza, the daughter of Sylvie, with the kind eyes. She'd brought each of my meals, her eyes as sympathetic as I remembered her mother's being, and had talked to me a little, up till I'd brained her with my bowl, when her back had been turned, and bolted from the room. Unfortunately, I'd only pissed her off instead of felling her as I'd intended. She'd been a helluva lot stronger than she'd looked and she'd promptly wrangled me back into the cell, kicking and screaming. From that day onward I'd been treated to nothing but sullen glares and silence.

"Eliza's with the rest of the pack. Waiting."

Did he have to make it sound so ominous? My shoulders slumped and I followed him obediently from the hospital cell. There was no chance I'd overpower him, so I decided to play meek and bide my time for now. *Time. Ha!* It had clearly proven it wasn't on my side. "So what exactly is gonna happen tonight?" I needed to prepare myself.

"Aidan will cite the rules of the rite. After that…" He shrugged.

I gritted my teeth when he said nothing more. "After that?"

"Probably best you know as little as possible." He sounded grim.

Great. Back through the labyrinthine clinic I followed him, the stench of neglect stronger now that my senses were feral. It felt as haunted as before, and I was now just another of its derelict ghosts. Already, I felt as dead and gloomy as the drab grey walls. At the deserted 'reception' area I caught a glimpse of movement in the glass, the dimly lit hallway reflecting back at me in the dusty silence. At first, I thought I really was seeing a pale-faced ghost, but almost instantly I recognized the lonely creature for who she was. Me.

The tunic was an overly dramatic and macabre touch, though unintentional on Eliza's part. She'd merely donated an old nightshift for me to sleep in. After I'd attacked her, she'd not been in much of a charitable frame of mind, so I hadn't dared to ask her for something more practical to die in. I looked like a hollow-eyed phantom, my dark hair stark against the white linen. White had never been my color, and tonight was no exception. Augustus was right, I really did look sacrificial. At least I'd not be dying a virgin. Sort of tragically poetic that I'd been given the *wolf gift* on a full moon but would die on the new.

The sound of my companion's impatient throat-clearing obtruded upon my morbid revery. Squaring my shoulders, I turned from the dead girl in the glass and proceeded after him again.

"Not since we settled in these lands has *Lupum Caedes* been invoked. Not for over a hundred years." Aidan stood on one side of me as she addressed her people, and Augustus somberly occupied the other. No escape.

I had been brought to a different location tonight. Although it looked no more distinct than the previous woodland, I could sense that we were miles away from the council hall. Here, the air smelled almost like pastureland (a farmstead nearby, maybe?), despite the thick forest enclosing us. Close by, I could hear the muffled burbling of a small brook. We'd hiked a good distance up the hillside to get to this small clearing and, had I not been forever *changed,* I wouldn't have been able to see my hand in front of my eyes—it was that dark. But I was changed, or at least my senses were. By the faint light of the Milky Way, and my keen nocturnal vision, I could see clearly the faces of each and every monster assembled around me. Even the black face of the moon glared down at us, leaving a void where it obscured the starlight.

"But tonight," Aidan continued with a flinty look, "you've chosen to resurrect a practice that our ancestors abolished for good reason." She expelled a heavy sigh. "I am mother and sister and daughter to you all. As such it is my sacred duty to serve, nurture, and protect you. To guide you. That being said, let me caution you all one last time before we begin." She had their complete and undivided attention, even I was fascinated by her eloquence. "We are no longer the wolves that our forefathers were—we haven't their prejudices and cruelties. Nor their bloodlust. We are finally at peace with the other packs, and we live only to uphold the laws that ensure our success and survival. Take a moment to consider carefully what we are about to condone. Do you still demand your wolf hunt?"

I dared to hope, my eyes searching the shadowed faces.

Then the voice I hated above anything suddenly piped up from the ranks. "What you say is all true, sister. Likewise, there hasn't been a case of biting in recent years, but what is that—" Nicole pointed at the bite mark on my shoulder "—if not cruelty?"

"Glad you can admit that, you crazy bitch." The rage filled my belly. Every ravenous eye instantly snapped toward me, including the hypocrite's—my nemesis.

"There you go again, Lippy," Augustus said with a surly grunt, "making it worse for yourself."

"An act of violence," Nicole went on, disregarding my

outburst, "such as this is, deserves a violent resolution. *Lupum Caedes* will serve as a means to discourage others from attempting further violations against pack law so that every pack will know that there are consequences to every breach of nature. Because we Athabaskans will not stand by and overlook them, no matter the prestige of the bloodline. Better that we put the mutt down tonight."

Aidan folded her arms and scanned the mood of her pack briefly. As did I. Though their alpha had momentarily cast some doubt over them, Nicole had now stemmed that doubt completely; moreover, incited them. They wanted blood. My blood. They were not only punishing Tristan but exterminating an aberration. Me. They, therefore, thought themselves to be shifting the natural balance back to its rightful equilibrium. Or so Eliza had briefly explained before I'd attacked her.

"I hope, Nicole," said Aidan, "that you never have such a convincing prosecutor in the event you ever disturb the laws of nature."

Nicole flushed and stood back.

"Very well," Aidan went on, briefly looking up to the barren night sky, "let's begin. The rules are as follows—Evan will be given a thirty-minute advantage whilst your three chosen runners shift skins. On my signal, and not before, they will give chase. The rest of us will spectate at a distance. The hunt will ensue till one of three things occurs: moonset, a kill, or the mutt reaches the perimeter. Any questions?"

"The perimeter?" I glanced at Augustus, the rest of the pack talking amongst themselves. "Wait, there's a chance I'll—?"

"Ha!" Nicole gave a derisive hoot. "You seriously are delusional."

I ignored her and fixed a pleading gaze to Augustus. "There's a chance though, right?" So I *would* be given a fighting chance!

Thirty minutes was more than enough of a running start. Here was my chance to fight for my life then.

After a pause, the beta (was that the right term for a lieutenant?) shrugged. "Sure, there's always a possibility." Yet he looked far from convinced of that.

"But you don't think so, do you? Not really." My heart was hammering wildly against my sternum.

Another shrug.

I wasn't satisfied with that. "Has any…mutt—" how I hated that word "—survived before?"

"No. Never."

"What happens when they catch me?" I asked in a whisper, watching as a man and a woman stepped forward to begin undressing. Two of the runners had already been selected. One more to go.

"I don't need to tell you that, Lippy."

True, he didn't. I knew what would happen. It wasn't called the *wolf slaughter* for nothing.

"If I get away do I get to live?"

"Yes. Till the day you kill someone, which is also likely… considering what you'll become. We, as a species, are great advocates for corporal punishment. Manslaughter is punishable by death."

"Who will you choose as your third?" Aidan's voice rang out over the assembled wolves, effectively ending my Q and A with her lieutenant.

"Me." Nicole was glaring spitefully at me as she eagerly volunteered herself.

"No." Everyone seemed stunned at Aidan's stern and instant refusal. "You're far too involved already."

"But—"

"I said no, sister."

"I'll do it." When Augustus proclaimed himself as the third—

amidst general nods of approval—I felt my last ounce of hope wither and die.

Whether or not it was some weird case of Stockholm Syndrome, I'd begun to feel a fraternal affinity toward the beta despite his occasional cutting remarks. Which is why I burst into tears as he distanced himself from me and began stripping his clothes off his powerful frame. Nicole was right, I'd been delusional to think I could outpace even one werewolf, never mind three, but not at my most delusional would I ever think myself capable of escaping the monster I knew Augustus would soon become. I'd seen his other *skin* once before. I had no chance.

"Come with me, Evan." Aidan had come up beside me and was gesturing me to the makeshift starting line, a fallen tree at the edge of the clearing. At least she'd called me by my name and not 'mutt'. I was suffering enough degradation as it was. "Head south," she said, gesturing into the woods ahead. "There's a narrow road that separates our land from a neighboring farm. Once you're on the bitumen, you're safe." With an imperceptible turn of her head, she cast a forbidding look at her sister. "At that point, no one can touch you." Then after a pause, she said, "You're no longer my problem once you cross the road."

I knew now why she'd kept her sister to heel instead of allowing Nicole to run. Nicole couldn't be trusted to stop short of the road if I made it safely across. That one wanted me destroyed. Did that mean Aidan believed me? She seemed too astute not to. I decided to confront her. "You know Tristan didn't bite me, don't you? I *know* you know."

She made no answer except to say, "You run in five minutes, I suggest you save your breath. You'll need it."

I wiped my clammy palms on the white linen, feeling the mossy earth beneath the pads of my feet as I anxiously shifted my weight from one leg to the other. In the hush of the forest came the sound of pained grunting behind me. It instantly precipitated my gaze over my shoulder to discover the cause.

A naked Augustus, however, was not what triggered a bloodless yelp from my throat. It was his bones—his spine, his ribs, his jaws—protracting unnaturally under his flesh, flexing and swelling like some bizarre series of contortions. His forehead was pressed to the earth, his skin drenched with perspiration, and his sharp fingernails were gouging at the ground as he panted, small grunts of exertion issuing through his clenched teeth. My knees threatened to buckle beneath me.

Beside him, the arms of the unfamiliar female were bulging rhythmically, and every time her muscles jerked it seemed to thrust coarse, dark hairs out of each follicle till finally she was completely covered in fur. By this time, each of the runners was sporting pelts in varying shades of black—the female had a unique ridge of grey along her spine, and the unknown male had a white streak up his nose. His chest had begun expanding impossibly, and his legs seemed to thicken and shorten into stocky limbs. Their haunches, all three of them, had become markedly more compact than their forelegs. Or were forelegs still considered arms? All three now had stubby, bristling tails that had sprouted grotesquely from their sloping spines. Augustus' tail was longer, the tip streaked with grey. It was the only part of his pelt not completely black.

The Augustus that had been shuddering and convulsing moments ago, whose bones had been snapping and muscles palpitating, was no more. In his place there now stood a sort of heavyset, ape-like wolf with a blunt muzzle and elongated ears that sat lower on the head than a wolf's would have. The creature's heavyset shoulders were easily as high as a grizzly's and it's skull just as broad, but there the similarities ended.

Its back had a considerable downward slope to it, the withers far higher than the hindquarters, and its neck was thick and short in accordance with its torso. There was an undeniable glint of intelligence in all three sets of eyes that pinned me keenly. But mine were fused to the heterochromatic glare of the largest wolf. The last time I'd seen the dark side of him, Augustus had been standing on his hind legs, but tonight he remained on all fours, the way a grizzly might…if it was of a mind to chase its prey. Grizzlies ran best on four legs, not two. I was the only two-legged of the runners tonight. And those blunt, non-retractable claws that jutted out of their fierce-looking paws seemed all too eager to eat up the space between us.

"Now, Evan. Run." Aidan's soft command drew my eyes away from the three waiting predators. "Your thirty minute head-start begins now."

"Wha—?"

"I said run!"

She didn't need to tell me a third time! I ran.

31

HYSTERIA

Terror shot straight to my marrow. My bones felt brittle, like ice, and unbearably heavy as I forced one clumsy foot in front of the other. I pulled myself through the trees like a thing possessed. Possessed and consumed by ravening horror. Past blurring streaks of malefic shadows, I ran for my life. The monstrous trees watched coldly as I fled, stretching their sharp fingers out to gouge at my face and tear at my dress. They whispered low, lifting their roots out of the ground to trip my feet. I fell and I stumbled and I sprinted and whimpered in terror, sure I could feel hot fetid canine breath on my shoulders; sure I could hear the excited grunts of wolves at my back, snapping violently at my heels.

Again, I fell, my ankle buckling over a pine cone. I lay, winded, on my back with a frozen stare cast at the starscape above me. Except for my painfully heaving chest and the pestilent needles and rocks stabbing at my back, I felt dead already. Dead and alone. A chill brushed across my skin as I struggled back onto my trembling legs. I gave a wince as my ankle protested—the same ankle I'd sprained not so long ago when Tristan had startled me. When he'd carried me up that hill. Rescued me. But where was he now?

Disregarding the jarring pain, I let the ankle bear my weight as I fled again, adrenaline-fueled, praying that I was still heading southward toward the safety of the road. Just to be sure, though, I skidded to a halt and glared furtively through the canopy to search the night sky for the Big Dipper or Polaris. Anything that would help me navigate. There it was, the North Star, so much higher in the sky than I was used to seeing down in Florida. With the constellation for guidance, I readjusted my bearing, tearing southward through the thickets and midnight boles.

How long had I been running? How much longer before they gave chase? Even as the last question materialized in my shattered psyche, I heard the signal I'd been dreading. A long, ominous howl rent the hush. A dooming knell. Panic surged viscous and frigid through my veins before pooling in my gut. Then came the answering calls, excited and frenzied—a baleful chorus of awful wolf-song.

It had begun. My half hour was up. Now I was no better than a frightened ungulate, heart stampeding wildly. And wasn't that the point? Didn't my terror add to the piquancy of my blood?

I hadn't thought I could run any faster, not with my throbbing ankle and tears flooding my eyes, but I did. I hurtled headlong through the trees, allowing my nose to guide me through the night. I even deluded myself I could smell the bitumen I was so desperate to cross. I tripped. Fell. Clawed my way back to my bruised feet and ran again. Once more I stumbled. An anguished and frustrated sob tore from my throat as I scrambled back up.

Calm down! From somewhere deep within I heard my mother's voice, steady and sharp as a lash. *Think.* Or was it my own voice snapping the whelming hysteria out of my terror-soaked mind. Panic, I knew, was as deadly as a werewolf. *Get up. Quickly now!*

Obeying instantly, I grabbed a sharp-looking rock from nearby and, despite the added weight, pressed on. The weight was almost negligible anyway, but it made all the difference—it anchored me to the earth and to sanity. I felt a little more in control with a missile in my hand.

My heart stammered suddenly as another terrible howl reached me. *Too close!* They were closing in with supernatural speed. I had only two legs to carry me, they had four.

Pricking my ears over the din of my pounding feet, I thought I detected something to my left. Maybe I'd seen a dark shadow flash past me. Maybe my mind was so overactive and I was seeing and hearing danger all around me. How did natural wolves hunt? My eyes darted left again, straining into the darkness. Was I being herded like a caribou? Would I be eaten alive?

Once more I searched the moving shadows, cocking my ears to catch every sound. But when I bent my eyes forward again it was too late. I screamed as a massive ten-foot shadow suddenly reared up on hind legs, rampant as a bear, my momentum carrying me straight into its solid chest. I convulsed and struggled like a dying fish, shrieking madly. It held fast.

Yet nothing was happening, I quickly realized. No fangs were poised at my neck to snap my spine. My eyes flew up to see large, bi-colored eyes glaring down at me. One brown. One grey. Both eerily bright. It released me almost instantly, stood aside, and then gave me a peremptory shove in the direction I'd already been headed.

I tottered backward, confused. "I don't under—?"

It gave a bestial snap of its long teeth and uttered an impatient growl. Incentive enough for me to run again, which I did immediately. I yelped when I felt the thing—Augustus—poke its muzzle between my legs. A yelp that swiftly transmuted from horror to abject surprise as he wedged his large head forcibly between my thighs and gave an almighty flick of his head so that I was thrown up like a ragdoll into the air. My chords froze mid-scream and then the air rushed out of my chest in a jolting whoosh as I landed on his broad withers, my fingers fisting swiftly into his mane. He began to increase his pace then. When he was sure I was as good as locked in place, thighs clenched at his wide ribs, he began to sprint in earnest. He streaked through the trees at a speed that left me dizzy. So I shut my eyes tightly and relied on my remaining senses to supplement my vision.

I felt the werewolf's muscles bunch and stretch under me, the pads of his feet almost soundless over the fallen leaves and bracken. The salt of my tears, I tasted on my lips. Sampled the cedar and pine on the wind cutting over my face. I could smell his fur, the musky warmth of it. Also, I could smell the farm up ahead—the distant herbaceous stench of newly plowed earth and ripe hay bales.

It was all I could do to keep myself from digging my heels deeper into his flanks to urge him faster. But he was no horse, and I wasn't brave enough to antagonize him, still unsure whether or not I was being rescued or lulled into a false hope. With every southward mile he gained, however, my courage swelled.

Unexpectedly, he halted and turned around to lift his nose in the air. He waited a few precious seconds that attenuated my nerves to breaking, his ears pricking and head cocking in all directions. What were we waiting for? My legs jiggled nervously as dread returned. I imagined the rest of the pack, those other two large runners specifically, hot on Augustus' stumpy tail. In an instant he was off again, finally, zigzagging through the trees like a black bullet and I like a wide-eyed monkey clinging to his back. A few more miles later, he stopped again, but this time he shrugged me right off his back, catching me roughly with a long-fingered paw right before I nearly split my skull on the ground. I pushed myself up to standing—although he was on all fours he still towered over me—and looked askance at him. With an incisive glare, he nudged me to continue on and then he glanced over his shoulder. For a hair-raising instant, he was motionless before he fixed his pointed stare back to me again. "Go!" he seemed to say. Then he bolted off.

I backed away and watched as his hulking shape disappeared into the underbrush back where we'd just come from as if he meant to retrace his tracks and mislead the other runners somehow. Or at least I *hoped* that to be the intention. His deep howl echoed through the woods a short while later, further west, even as I was sprinting over roots and ducking under insidious branches. Again there came the answering calls of his brethren. Far too close for comfort. But Augustus had given me another fighting chance and I was *not* going to waste it. Not even for the burning in my lungs would I slow down.

Except, suddenly, the choice was taken from me. There was a werewolf blocking my way. And this was *not* Augustus! The glacial eyes appeared out of nowhere, glowing blue with fevered animus. Even in the pitch black, I recognized those white-tipped grizzled ears—like demon's horns! Without a moment's thought, my adrenaline shot my arm into action. The stone I'd been carrying till now flew from my fingers, as though from a sling, and nailed Nicole directly between her creepy eyes before she even knew what hit her. I felt only a brief moment's satisfaction before she charged at me, teeth bared and snarling viciously.

With no more stones to protect me, I threw my arms up to brace for attack. It was queer the way my brain was able to spike into hyperdrive; queer the way that even the blurring speed of a raging *werebitch* could be slowed mid-lunge. It was almost as though I was watching my last moments in extraneous slow motion. Just an observer of my own violent end.

But she never reached me. Before my death cry left my lips,

she was intercepted. Another set of jaws flashed suddenly out of the dense night. They clamped themselves murderously around her jugular. Time swiftly fell back into blurring motion as I watched, paralyzed.

The black beast shook her throat with brutal force, snarling malevolently as she tore at its stygian pelt. Two werewolves were now seemingly locked in mortal combat. Up till then, I'd stood palsied, but I did finally scream when a pair of large hands closed over my shoulders without warning. In that fleeting moment, two things happened: I turned to discover Dean, of all people, standing beside me. Simultaneously, the fighting ceased. The larger werewolf's head jerked around to me the instant I screamed, which allowed Nicole the upper paw. Those claws descended with stunning vengeance, and before her opponent could rally himself, she seized its neck like a striking viper, eliciting a furious roar from the bigger wolf. The newcomer swiftly set its own fangs at her shoulder, ripping with almighty fury.

I was quickly shoved aside as Dean loped toward the pair. He wasn't the only one. Augustus had arrived as well, his weight barreling straight into the antagonists like a mad boar, tusks gleaming. For a split second there was confusion and the combatants disengaged, but Nicole—having noticed her pack-mate's arrival—quickly rallied and lunged again. Augustus, however, leapt at her back and pinned her down with his greater bulk. Dean, meanwhile, had taken the other wolf in a savage head-lock. The wolf seemed torn between wanting to attack Nicole and wanting to heed the commands of the large man battling to restrain it. Awe-struck, I watched Dean and my monstrous savior finally back away. The brute's sable mane was almost erect at its neck, it was that charged with violence.

"Hold her down, Gus!" Dean commanded through clenched teeth, glaring at the wolf thrashing beneath Augustus.

The Athabaskan male spared a terse grunt as he held a very

irate Nicole to the ground, her body bucking and her cries enraged.

At last, Dean released his hold on the massive werewolf. I almost expected the thing to tackle Nicole again, but, though its body appeared tensed to pounce, it remained eerily still as it impaled her with bloodshot eyes.

"Don't do it, Tristan," Dean warned, grabbing me by the wrist to pull me away.

Tristan?! I gasped.

The sound I'd made was evidently enough to snap Tristan from his bloodlust. He blinked those topaz-green eyes at me, that lethal yellow dimming somewhat from his glare, as I was dragged away in Dean's wake. We stared at one another like strangers, me gaping over my shoulder at him. We *were* strangers. I was truly seeing him for the very first time. The real Tristan. Yet I was now just as much a stranger to myself as he was—I shouldn't have been able to see anything at all in that moonless, midnight back-woods. Not without the aid of whatever rabid thing was mutating my blood.

With a clearing shake of his large black head, Tristan made to follow us, his ears flattening over his skull as he turned to glare one last time over his own shoulder at Augustus and Nicole. After that, I was then the recipient of that uncanny stare. Unblinking. Fierce. Yet tender. I turned away, preferring instead to stare at Dean's granite back. It was a safer point on which to focus. Suddenly, it dawned on me that we were crossing a road. *The* road. I'd made it. I'd survived!

I could hardly believe it at all. In fact, my movements were catatonic as I continued on. Still alive, though, existentially speaking. Like a fragile bird, Dean lifted me up into the back seat of his Land Rover, neither of us saying a word. Neither of us commented on the frustrated howling of the two runners prowling at the edge of the road. Tristan was, for the moment, standing beside the SUV, guarding me, sharp ears pricked forward as he glared into the shadows. His sinews were taut and his neck bristled with unconcealed warning.

Every time I looked at him, I felt another fissure split my chest. I hid my eyes behind my sandpaper lids and dropped my head back against the leather headrest, desperate for the oblivion of sleep. Desperate for a time that didn't include werewolf bites or *Lupum Caedes*.

I must have dozed off a few minutes at least, the echo of wolf grunts and menacing growls notwithstanding, because suddenly I felt myself being pulled against warm solid skin, my cheek guided instantly to a broad chest sticky with blood. Strong fingers kneaded at my scalp and neck as the Landy roared to life and lurched onto the road.

Still, I kept my eyes shuttered. I wasn't ready to see what I knew was in Tristan's eyes—that same feral chartreuse I'd seen when he'd faced the grizzly. God knew the clues had all been there! If only I'd put all the pieces together: the werewolf jokes; the "bear-whispering" and that growl he'd loosed at the brownie; the way he'd healed so quickly; the weird rumors; the penises in the forest; those unnatural footprints outside my door. Wasn't hindsight a bitch.

With a gentle touch of two fingers beneath my chin, he lifted my face to his. I could feel him watching doggedly. Probing. Silently urging me to look at him. Then I felt my tattered sleeve being tugged away from my injured shoulder. Investigative fingers brushed across my scars, the fury radiating off him. There was a savage rumbling in his chest as, presumably, he studied the damage. At last, I opened my eyes to meet his.

The dam ruptured. Agonizing sobs overwhelmed me. He tightened his arms around me and nuzzled my neck. Physiologically and mentally, I'd been stretched beyond all limits and, finally, *finally,* I'd cracked wide open. It wasn't even Tristan's rage that had set me off, nor the guilt he wore like a cilice. It certainly wasn't the painfully tender kisses he pressed to my brow. No, it was the brief flash of disgust I'd caught in his glare. I was a mutt after all. And rabid now too.

32

THE HALF-CASTE HEIR

The distant hollow pounding, I quickly realized as I pried one groggy lid from the other, was not, in fact, the interminable throb of an impending migraine but the bite of iron splitting logs just outside my window. At intervals, it stopped and then started again and I found myself picturing the prosaic scene, of whoever was so diligently chopping wood, as I stared at the ceiling of my unfamiliar room. The pause between each downward ax stroke seemed somehow infused with a strangely lamentable hush. The gloomy thwacks fell in rhythm with my own misery.

My phone had been returned to me yesterday morning when we'd finally arrived at Dean's homestead. Tristan had discovered it in the basement right after he'd found my dried bloodstains at the front door, the same fateful night he'd promised to tell me *everything*. Nicole's scent, I'd been told, had cohered like a cloying stench to every wall, leaving Tristan in no doubt as to who'd attacked me. But there'd been no stench of death. That, more than anything, had kept him searching. And hoping.

Lydia, as it turned out, had been replying to all of my text messages so that my absence had gone largely unnoticed. Although I could tell that my mom wasn't quite fooled because she was threatening to fly up and drag me home if I didn't soon answer her calls. I never went a single day without hearing her voice, and it had been over a week since I'd spoken to her! Whenever she'd tried to call me (while I was fighting for my life), Lydia had promptly replied by text, blaming the godawful reception.

"Chill, Mom, I'm fine." I shook my head as I reread the text. Lydia didn't sound anything like me, even via the relative safety of a text. I supposed that flying beavers all day was hard enough work without trying to impersonate someone she'd only met a handful of times. Lydia hadn't even acknowledged my mom's cute Chris Hemsworth banter—no wonder Mom was suspicious that I'd "hied off to Nome and had my brain scrambled by aliens". The story that my friends and family had been fed, so I'd been informed, was that I'd gotten the flu and was staying with Dean's family while I recovered. Alison and Mel had tried to come to see me but been turned away because I was too "contagious".

Yesterday I'd stared at my phone a whole hour before I'd finally dredged up the courage to call my mom, and then I'd lied through my throbbing teeth about how "fine" I was doing. I'd even managed not to bawl like a kitten. But when she'd insisted on flying up, I'd shut her down like a cold bitch and said I wasn't a baby anymore, that I could take care of myself. This Evan, this saturnine imposter, was unrecognizable to me, and to my poor mother most of all. It was heartbreaking lying to her, and I'd undertaken damage control with a clinical detachment that scared me. At least Mom had had some of her worry assuaged by hearing my voice, though that was cold comfort to me.

When the woodcutter commenced his melancholic hacking again, after another of those long pauses, it snapped me from my gloomy woolgathering. Further distraction came shortly afterward in the form of a knock at the door.

Lydia emerged with a supper tray, her large whiskey eyes

creased with a smile as she shut the door behind her. "Oh good, you're awake."

With a voice that felt like coarse grit, I asked how long I'd been asleep this time. It seemed to me that since being bitten I was more often comatose than awake, unsure of what was real and what I'd imagined.

"You've been asleep most of the day, understandably," she answered, depositing my dinner on the walnut dresser. "Should I get Tristan to—"

"No." I'd spoken almost inaudibly, but the word rang out like the lash of a whip. I'd refused to see him all of yesterday too after I'd cloistered myself up here. I didn't want to see anyone, but I especially didn't want to see him. My reasons were many, but the foremost among them was the thought that I couldn't stand to see *that* look on his face again. I couldn't stand to feel that niggling sting of blame for a man I loved and revered above any other. "I don't want to see anyone." The wood-chopping halted, and we both sat in silence a moment, Lydia inclining her head knowingly.

When the ax fell with splintering force again, she came to sit beside me on the bed, deftly inspecting my scars without flinching. She was clearly not as disgusted by mongrels as some folks were. Or perhaps she hid her aversion better than most. "Gus did a good job stitching you up."

"Are you one of those flying doctors?"

She chuckled. "Not yet. Dean and I do the best we can, but the pack definitely needs a physician."

Small talk had never been something I was good at, and right now I was feeling anything but chatty. "What's gonna happen to me? Will I die?"

She dropped her hands into her lap. "I don't know, each case is different, I'm told. The bite is something we're raised to fear and avoid at all costs. It's supposed to be punishable by death, so you can imagine how many cases I've come across in my lifetime."

"What's the average lifetime of a mutt? I mean one that survives the first change."

"Same as the rest of us." She gave a hesitant smile. "Most wolves, if they don't fight amongst themselves, can live at least thrice as long as humans."

"How old are you?" I asked, intrigued despite my dolor.

"Old enough." She gave a little wink. "My brother and I are the oldest in Dean's pack actually."

I looked her up and down. She and James couldn't be more than thirty, I decided. But did that mean I had to multiply that number by three to determine their real age?

"How old is Tristan?"

"You should ask him that."

"Am I the first mutt you've ever known?"

A shadow fell over her face. "No."

"When was the last time a—?"

"Dean's mother." Lydia's words fell like an ax across my question. She shook her head, ostensibly regretting her long tongue. "But that's a complicated story."

"Dean's mother was human?! Who…who bit her?"

Lydia glanced surreptitiously at the door and gnawed her lips uncertainly. Then, as if coming to a decision, she said, "Dean did."

"Holy shit!"

"Yup." She fixed me with a level stare. "Dean went through his change at an uncommon age. He's…sort of unique. Usually, males start shifting at about age twelve, right around puberty, but he was only nine when he shifted the first time. Just nine years old when he realized what he was."

"So his mother didn't know what he was? What Max Thorn really was?"

"No. Max was already married to Tristan's mother, Elaine, when Linda fell pregnant with Dean. It's almost unheard of—half-caste kids hardly ever make it through the first trimester. But somehow Linda carried full term and bore Max a healthy son. A boy that, to some, was considered no better than a mutt."

"Omigod!"

"Yeah, being a half-caste is only slightly better than being a mongrel. Max had cut himself off from them for years, with regular reports from Max's uncle, Frank, hoping that Dean would never shift. Half-castes, if they survive, rarely shift. Max hoped Dean would just end up being like his mother. He didn't though. And everyone, including Max, was unprepared for what happened afterward." Lydia stared broodily at the floor as though she'd witnessed a lot of it herself. Maybe she had. "Linda thought her son was dying when he shifted the first time. They were camping, just the two of them, and 'uncle Frank', up at Whale Pass. When she realized what Dean was, she knew she couldn't take him to the hospital or go to the authorities, not without risking her son being studied in a lab like a freak. Not that Frank Thorn would have allowed a doctor anywhere near the boy. Max was forced to take her son from her and installed him in the pack to be raised by his wife alongside his younger son. As you can imagine, Dean was never really accepted, not by anyone except his brother. He neither belonged with humans, nor with wolves. The Yukon pack, as with most of the oldest packs, consists of a bunch of parochial purists, so he never stood a chance. They decided unanimously that the right of primogeniture belonged to Tristan even though Dean was technically Max's firstborn." She shifted her gaze to me. "You have to understand, he had no one. Not even his mother. Tristan was just a young kid then, what could he do for his brother?" She released a grave sigh. "So a lonely kid ran away to find his mother and bit the only person who loved him, hoping that she'd change too. By that time, he'd learnt enough to know that a werewolf could be created if bitten. After all, he'd been labelled a mutt himself. That's the long and short of it, he was too young to understand that he had killed her with that bite."

"What happened to Linda?"

"She lasted longer than most would have, probably because she shared some DNA with her son."

"The first change?" Was that what killed her? I almost didn't want to know.

"No, she didn't survive the fever." Lydia stood from the bed, preparing to leave me. "But you have, so there's every hope you'll also survive your first change."

"But I might turn…rabid."

"Then we'll keep you in a cage every full moon, but if you think Tristan will allow anyone to hurt you then—"

"I don't need his pity or for him to stay with me out of guilt!"

She seemed momentarily taken aback by my bitterness. "You have no idea, do you?"

"About what?"

"It wasn't pity that had him tearing Nicole's room apart. It wasn't pity that nearly caused him to come to blows with his brother when he wouldn't calm down. And it certainly wasn't pity that made him almost unrecognizable to us. The Athabaskans own thousands of acres of land! He had no idea where Nicole took you, but he left to look for you anyway. I'd bet my canines he wasn't human even once during the whole time he was out there on his own. He never stopped looking; and I know he hardly slept. He was already in Red Devil when he finally checked in with his brother. But Dean wouldn't tell him where and when to find you, not till the last minute. Aidan had made him promise to keep Tristan 'to heel' till Gus brought you to them. She was protecting her sister as much as you." She eyed me pointedly. "Evan, Tristan even asked his father for help, that should tell you how desperate he was to find you."

"I bet I can guess what answer his father gave." I wasn't up to speed on the werewolf politics, but I'd bet my humanity that Max had said hell no. It was in his best interest to see me dead rather than pollute his legacy with my 'muttiness'.

"Yeah, well, Dean and Tristan have enough powerful friends without needing to rely on their father's help."

"Why is Dean helping me at all?" I gripped my pounding head and leaned back against my pillows, wincing.

"He's not helping you, he's supporting his brother. He loves Tristan."

"They don't exactly act loving."

"Well, it isn't natural for a wolf that's as dominant as its brother to heel and obey. Tristan tries his best to be what he isn't, but he's had to move into his own place for the sake of making this dynamic work effectively."

"But Dean disapproves of me."

"It's more that Dean lives with the fact that he killed his own mother. A fact his father never lets him forget. Interspecies mating is dangerous, Evan. Dean wanted to protect his brother from that." She offered a sympathetic smile. "But he knows it was the right thing to do, helping Tristan find you. Tristan feels responsible for what Nicole did to you, and, as alpha, that responsibility now lies with Dean too." Then she shrugged. "Anyway, from a political standpoint, it's in the best interest of Dean's pack to ally themselves with the Yukon heir. The future alpha of *the* strongest pack in North America."

So I *had* been 'dating' royalty. "Why wasn't Dean put down like the Athabaskans tried to do to me? For biting his mother."

"His youth saved him. Not to mention being the son of Maxwell Thorn, even an unloved one, comes with certain benefits. He would have been the heir presumptive if something had ever happened to Tristan. But after biting Linda, it was decided he'd be stripped of all those rights. Disowned. In case you're unfamiliar with the term, that's what it means to be rogue: a nobody without a family. Some of us choose to leave our packs and some of us have no choice. He was sent away to live here, motherless, under the stern eye of Frank Thorn. Old Frank's only job was to stay vigilant and make sure Dean didn't screw up again. One more false move and they'd have killed him."

"Frank Thorn?" I tapped my bottom lip. "Why does that name sound familiar?"

"Thorne Bay's an old logging town that took its name from Frank Manley Thorn in the eighties—it was his family that settled here first. Their name was misspelled on a map once, and it's never been rectified." She lifted one shoulder nonchalantly. "Frank pretended to be a proponent of logging when in actual fact he was working to minimize the destruction of his woodland home. His father was originally Manley Thorstensen back when they moved down from the Yukon during the Klondike Gold Rush. Truth is, there were werewolves here even before Manley came. There were indigenous wolves among the *Tlingit* and *Haida* tribes long before our ancestors came here from Greenland and Iceland.

"What ever happened to Frank?"

"We have long lifespans, Evan, and we age differently. There's only so long a werewolf can live in a human community without the general public becoming suspicious of us. By being reclusive we can prolong that time by a few years, but eventually we have to leave. That's why a lot of us live in pack townships, away from humans where we can live our entire lives in one place. Like the wolves of Red Devil.

"Anyway, Frank moved back to Canada after Dean was fully grown. By then, Tristan had moved down here to join his brother, and Thorn Aviation was already a fledgling company. Dean's not feral, he never required a watchdog for very long, and Max knows that. Everything you see here is what he created from nothing—a pack of unwanted misfits like him, and a thriving business he and his brother conceived with a small investment he got from Frank. In the end, I think uncle Frank, as gruff as he can be, grew a little fond of Dean."

"So why did Tristan leave his pack?"

"He's always loved his brother. Though they take the piss out of each other more often than not, don't let it fool you, those two are inseparable. He came here to join Dean because he doesn't believe that he should be the heir apparent to the Yukon Territory. He believes that's Dean's right, but Dean doesn't want it either, so Max is shit out of heirs." Lydia moved silently to the door, but before withdrawing from the room she had one final thing to say. "Tristan's loyal to a fault. And when he loves someone, it's forever, never out of pity or guilt. When a werewolf picks a mate, that's forever too. He's picked you, Evan, anyone can see that. You smelled of him from the first day, we all noticed it."

"What?"

"When I first met you in Thorne Bay Market you reeked of werewolf musk."

Eww.

"Almost from your first night in Thorne Bay, he was playing guard dog around Bear Lodge."

Those strange prints I'd found outside my apartment finally made sense now!

"His brother gave him so much hell for that." She gave an amused little grunt. "It doesn't mean much to you because you weren't born into this life and you don't appreciate what it is to be one of us. Not yet. But that's something special—finding your mate. We're not all so fortunate." A low cloud swept into her gaze just then. "Anyway, it's why Nicole probably hated you the first moment she clapped eyes on you. She'd have smelled him on you too; she'd have understood what it meant. He'd never shown any interest in her. He chose you."

When I only continued to stare desolately at the ceiling, Lydia slipped from the room with a heavy sigh. The door closed softly behind her as my tears rushed pitifully over my cold cheeks. Finally, with a frustrated growl, I rolled out of bed. "How much goddamn wood needs to be chopped?" I muttered, padding over to the window to investigate that incessant dull thudding.

However, there was no one at the chopping block when I reached the windowsill, just the abandoned ax still embedded in the scarred stump, seemingly waiting for its master's return. I didn't have to wait long. A dark-haired giant soon materialized out of the adjacent woodshed. Tristan. He stalked from the outbuilding, his golden skin smeared with dirt and sweat, oblivious to the cold fog that clung to the ground, a grim set to his jaw as he ripped the blade free of the stump. As I watched, eyes avidly devouring his features, he positioned a new victim on the block and began splitting logs with gusto. When his pile was gone, he left his post for the woodshed again, but this time he paused at the door he'd left ajar, staring fixedly into the shed with unseeing eyes. He gave no warning before he suddenly threw his fist into the sturdy door with enough fury to splinter iron. The force of the blow snapped it from it's hinges and rent it in two so that it lay against the frame, doubled over and useless. No easy feat since it was rather a new shed and a very solid hardwood door. Not something a human could have done with such ease. My shock must have been palpable, must have touched him somehow, because he whipped his head around and caught me staring from the window.

Without thinking, I instantly ducked to the side and sank down the wall like a coward. Why was I so afraid of that penetrative gaze? The starkness of his eyes had struck me even from this distance—they were glowing amber with lupine wrath. After a silence the ax began to fall again, each blow somehow like a death knell, more brutal than the last.

A knock fell against my door for the second time today, but I was too lost in thought to answer. When Dean entered, I felt like upbraiding him, but what right did I have? This was his home, and I was under his roof. What was more, even if he'd caught me in my birthday suit it wouldn't have impressed him in the least. I'd already learned that werewolves were about as bothered by nakedness (seemingly delicate human sensibilities) as *normal* wolves were.

He strode in and joined me where I sat below the window, his eyes narrowing thoughtfully as he gazed out to see who it was I was so obviously hiding from. His scowl grew foul as he shook his head, presumably noticing the damage to his shed. He turned away with a muttered oath and then paused to consider the untouched food on the tray nearby. "You haven't eaten since you got here," he said, schooling his features. "To survive the change you need to fuel your body."

"I'm not hungry."

"That's beside the point."

"No, that's exactly the point! I'm gonna die anyway."

"Perfect, that'll make my life a lot easier."

I set my teeth and glared at him.

"Question is," he went on, "do you really want to make it that easy for Nicole? Dying without a fight, I mean. Maybe you'd consider living just to spite her." He allowed the silence to rest heavily on my shoulders. "Think about your mother if not yourself." Coming from him, the words seemed far more poignant.

My mouth twisted with resentment and guilt, but he merely met my glare with his usual apathy. Finally, I stood and headed over to the dresser to grab my food tray. "You're as cold as Aidan."

"Kind of ungrateful of you to say so considering she saved your life."

"Augustus saved my life, not—"

"And who gave him his instructions? Who invited Tristan and I onto her land and told us where to wait for you?"

I set my teeth and dropped my head. He was right and I was too exhausted to fight with him.

"Maybe she's not the monster you take her for." His jaw clenched. "It might very well be Tristan's fault that you're in this mess, indirectly, but it's also because of *who* he is that you're still alive."

Which begged the question: what would they have told my family if I'd been killed? *No body, no crime.* I'd have likely been immortalized in some dusty Alaskan cold case file, but that would've been about the extent of it, no doubt. And when my mother eventually passed on, in the far distant future, any memory of me would have died with her.

"Stop sulking up here," Dean continued, unaware of my contemplations. "What's done is done, no use crying about it anymore. You've got a rough time ahead of you, girl. You need Tristan." His face hardened as he turned back to face me. "Otherwise you're alone. Trust me, that's the last thing you want. A wolf can't survive without a pack at his back."

I tried not to cry as he left the window with a disapproving look at me. He and Aidan seemed cut from the same cloth. Even their scowls looked identically fierce.

At the door, he gestured down to the pilot bread and smoked salmon dip still untouched on my tray. "Eat your veggies, girl. You're gonna need it." After that grand pep talk, he strode from the room, leaving me once again cocooned in heavy silence. Even the somber thuds of Tristan's ax had stopped. I was alone. Again.

33

THE SILENCE AND THE AFTERLIFE

A crack of thunder ripped me from my pillow. It resounded in my skull with splintering force. I screamed, the blinding hot panic slicing sharply through my brain. Another horrific crack cleaved my bones, and I knew then that it wasn't a storm raging outside but one fulminating within. Again, I shrieked, terror-stricken by my body's sudden brutal self-destruction.

Too immersed in the assault, I didn't hear the door fly open, nearly shattering against the wall, or Tristan calling my name. Not at first. But I did finally become aware, once the pain ebbed briefly, that I was being dragged against steely warmth, arms enfolding me so that the left side of my body was pressed securely to hard flesh, my head tucked under Tristan's chin as he held me close.

"I'm here, Ev. Breathe for me," he said, his voice steady in the darkness as the lightning returned, ripping through me again and again.

"Tristan!" I gasped. "I'm d-dying!"

"Breathe. You're not dying."

My chest heaved as I struggled to fill it with air, my ribs like lethal claws clamping and puncturing the life from my lungs. I whimpered and nodded as Tristan whispered soothingly, exhorting me to focus on my breathing. He stroked my hair, making no sound of protest when my nails suddenly impaled his arms during the peak of the whelming agony. Unrelentingly, the torment continued. Tristan stayed with me long after the worst of the convulsions had passed, till dawn broke with its roseate light through my window.

Still drenched in sweat from the long night, my hair matted to my face and my insides battered, I stayed in his arms, clutching at him whenever he made to slip away. Eventually, though, he disconnected my clammy fingers and left to get me some water. My tongue was swollen with thirst or I'd not have let him go at all. He climbed back into bed with me moments later and, after I'd downed a gallon of water, he wrapped himself protectively around me again, my cheek to his chest. We lay there quietly as my breathing returned to normal. His fingers brushed the snarls from my hair while I listened to the slow and comforting beats of his heart. When I opened my eyes and lifted my face to meet his gaze, he brought his lips gently to mine, holding them pressed there a long moment so that we could breathe one another in.

"See," he whispered, leaning just a fraction of an inch away, "you're not dying. Sometimes pain is there to remind us how alive we are."

"Will it happen again?" I croaked.

Tristan threaded our fingers together and kissed my knuckles. "Yes," he said somberly. "Your body's trying to do in a matter of weeks what mine took years to accomplish. It's kind of like a growth spurt."

"So what you're saying is that I get to go through puberty twice." I winced as I readjusted myself to lie on my back, my bones and muscles protesting loudly. "Lucky me."

He gave my hand a squeeze. "You won't be alone. Not ever

again, I promise you that." There was something of rage at the edge of his vow.

"Tell me what happens after. If I survive the change."

"When—" his tone was brusque "—you get through this, it'll take years before you can shift at will." The mattress shifted as he also turned onto his back. "You'll be like an adolescent at first, running—that's what we call shifting—will be instinctive and inevitable, it'll be forced on you."

"Every full moon." That much I knew. I turned my head to the side, tracing his profile in the grey light.

"The older we get the better we are at controlling the change. When we're young and hormonal everything's haywire, so the only time juvies run at all is during syzygy. Our cycles peak at the full moon." He folded his hands over his torso and turned his head so that I was now locked in his shadowy gaze. "It's half physics, which I won't go into now, and half PFM."

"PFM?"

"Pure Fucking Magic."

I released a wearied sigh. "Well, I'm not in the mood for physics anyway."

We lay on our backs staring at each other as the silence stretched, my eyes becoming leaden.

Finally, Tristan broke it, his words heavy with the livid regret still left unuttered between us. "I'm so sorry, Evan. I had no idea Nicole was psychotic. This is my fault, I should have tried harder to stay away from you."

And if he had? Would I still be living my dishwater life, seeing the world in achromatic shades? That seemed somehow more tragic to me—existing so blandly—than the possibility of dying in less than two weeks. If I'd been given the choice, if I'd proceeded knowingly, would I still have abandoned the safety of mundanity and risked the heady thrill of paranormality? I had no answer for myself, least of all for Tristan. At first, all I offered him was enervated silence, then, after a while, I said, "At least now I know your big secret."

He nodded slowly, becoming taciturn himself.

"Would you have told me that night?"

"I would have tried to tell you, yes. I had planned to."

I wondered briefly how he might have expounded the impossible—what the world still naively considered impossible. I hated to think that I'd have thought he was crazy and then bolted. If he'd shifted, and *showed* me as he'd promised to do, would I have tried to brain him with a frying pan? Would I have been too terrified to stay? Too incredulous to listen? Too horrified to love him? I honestly didn't have the answers.

Tristan's features hardened as he noted every expressive thought and every uncertain crease flickering across my face. "You would have run," he decided finally.

"What about being engaged to Nicole?" I asked through the bitter lump lodged in my throat. "Would you have started with that confession?"

I could almost hear his teeth grinding together like iron. "I was *never* engaged to her. Part of the reason my father never forbade me joining Dean's pack was that he considered it temporary, and because I promised him I'd spend some time with Nicole if she came down to Thorne Bay. I let him think I'd consider marriage because I wanted to get away, but I never actually agreed to it. She was always a spoiled brat even as a kid. I had no intention of taking her on. Whatever delusions Max and Nicole developed along the way were strictly their own fantasies, not mine. Their disappointment is their problem, not mine."

But, consequently, it had been made my problem too. "Well, it's all pointless now—we'll never know one way or the other how I would've reacted if you'd told me. Nicole stole that moment from us." I should have told that mangy bitch to go pee in the woods when I'd had the chance. "And now it's gone forever."

"I wonder—" his eyes darkened to a piercing, lustrous amber "—if that's the only thing gone forever?"

The shadows of death weighed on my tongue and kept it frozen. Something needed to be said, but I was blank and too scared to feel anything. In the aftermath of pain there was only this cold listlessness in my chest, my heart suddenly thick with lidocaine. I had become strangely vacuous. Even his pained looks couldn't touch me.

Tristan closed his eyes resignedly, and when he opened them again they were remote. He rolled away and abruptly left the bed, his abandoned pillow seemingly indented with the heavy silence he'd left behind. At the door, he hesitated, as though he might say something else, but, evidently, he thought better of it and, instead, promptly withdrew from the room.

The instant I was alone with myself, the numbness evaporated and the chill crept in. My chest was suddenly desolate with loneliness. It wasn't the physical agony of before—not like my werewolf puberty—it was the sharp torment of a fragmenting heart. Although the tears surged from my eyes in torrents, I made no sound. I couldn't risk Tristan coming back, I wanted no one near me. No one, especially not him, to see what a freak I was becoming. It was one thing to be a werewolf, but I was becoming another thing entirely—a disgusting rabid mongrel incapable of control. Something to be reviled. Something to be put down if she snapped.

By the time the sun crested the horizon, however, I'd fallen into a fitful sleep, never realizing that the torture last night was nothing to what lay in store for me in the days to follow. After that night, the 'growing pains' came often and swiftly. At first, they plagued me only during the night, and every time I screamed Tristan came. He never spoke a single word except to whisper distractions, and he never left me to endure those miserable spasms and convulsions alone, no matter how much I pushed him away. The lulls in these nightly attacks, however, became steadily shorter and the agony only more intense. Finally, I was forcibly secured to the bed because I'd begun to gouge at my skin like a deranged thing. A violent desperation was now driving me beyond all rationale, and the need to scratch the itch burning inside my marrow was too much to bear.

As bestial as I probably looked, Tristan, who now never left my side, looked not much better. When I wasn't writhing and shrieking wildly, I was sobbing or being force-fed to keep up my strength. I hated everyone and everything and I just wanted it all to end! I wanted the seductive oblivion of death. Whenever the pain abated enough for me to speak, I begged Tristan to make it stop. To kill me. But I always got the same answer, the same gesture—he'd rake his hands through his hair and shake his head miserably, his eyes bleak as he begged me to stop asking.

Each time he denied me, I growled and flung execrations till the stabbing fits began again, my rage transmuting instantly to agony once more. This suffering was nothing like the fever that had afflicted me in Red Devil. I hadn't wanted to die in Red Devil. Now I longed for death. The delirium before the new moon, just after I'd been bitten, had been like an analgesic fog. Now, however, I was aware of nothing but the searing of my blood through my veins, the agonizing distortion of my bones, and debilitating nausea.

Three days before the full moon, I could keep nothing down, not even water, so they hooked me up to an IV. It was now unrelenting, the torture, and my throat was so ragged that even my screaming was silent. The entire house seemed suffocated by a miasmic death pall, the silence crypt-like. My survival was no longer expected, I knew this. They thought I couldn't hear them whispering downstairs, or they didn't care, but I could hear *every-*

thing. I heard exactly what they planned to tell my mother, listened as they discussed what to do with my body. Burned and buried in an unmarked grave—not far off what I myself had imagined they'd do.

"I can hear you!" I wailed. "Kill me, please!" Why were they waiting? I was ready now. I welcomed death. My dignity was long since gone already.

"No one's going to kill you," came Tristan's voice in my ear, anguished. "You've survived this long, you'll survive tomorrow too."

And then tomorrow came. Finally. With it came the awful crescendo of bones and cartilage snapping and grinding—muscles tearing and tendons severing like frayed catgut. An antiphony of agony. My heart thundered like a jungle drum all throughout the onslaught.

"Dean!" From far away, Tristan's subaqueous voice filtered through my fitful grunting. "Dean!" he called again. "It's happening!"

Running feet. Doors slamming. Fingers yanking the bindings from my chafed wrists and ankles. The IV needle sliding from my vein like the sting of a wasp. I was blind to it all, my eyes hurt too much to open. Even my hearing was somewhat distorted. But I could feel. Everything hurt. Everything was broken. I'd forgotten what it was like to be devoid of pain. Then I gave a weak moan as I was lifted and cradled against an unfamiliar chest. This chest smelled like a lesser breed of pine and cedarwood.

"Remember your promise." Dean's voice cut through the fogginess of my brain. "Get out of the way, we both know you won't do it if she turns rabid."

Do it? Do what? After that, I heard nothing more, just my heart slamming against my fractured ribs. Suddenly, my brain exploded with a terrifying rending sound. My muscles came apart around my joints, my bones liquified. A deafening roar pierced the silence and I wasn't sure if it was the sound of my dying heart or a Mack truck plowing through my skull. I was blinded and couldn't see, though I was sure my eyes were wide open. Hours passed, or merely seconds, I couldn't tell, but it seemed like I was aware of nothing else but the sickening sounds of my body, the burning itch along my flesh, and the ever-present throes of death. And then, blessedly, there was one last almighty crack. My spine jolted with the force. Then nothing.

Strangely, there was no tunnel of light as I died, just the feeling of floating away on ripples. As though washed ashore, I became aware that I was lying on something soft and fragrant. Everything was dark and tasted of verdure. For the first time in what seemed an eternity, my heart slowed and the world was hushed. The pain had finally ebbed.

Was I dreaming? Or was I now truly dead? Pain couldn't follow a soul into death, so I had to be dead. And if I was dead, then this was one murky afterlife—light and shadow blurred around me as my eyes adjusted. From overhead, there was an intense and soothing light that washed over me and swept the vestigial memory of pain from my tired body. This then was the divine tunnel of light.

I lifted my head heavenward and drank in that silver light, breathed in the sylvan quality of the air, dug long nails into the cool earth, and savored the redolence of shuffling leaves. The perfume of the night was like a heady drug, calming my blood. I stretched out my bruised muscles and gave a shake of my body, luxuriating in my hair as it rippled around me like a silky black cloak. Then I pressed my nose eagerly to the ground, frisking and snorting like a child before bounding away, feeling freer now than I ever had in my life. Cool wind whisked and eddied past my face as I raced through the towering, woodland giants.

Whether or not I was in limbo or just dreaming didn't matter.

The thrill of this newfound freedom and my affinity with the night was

surreal and addictive. I embraced it like I would my mother and sucked in the deepest breath I'd ever taken, pulling its essence into every cell before I lifted my face back to that heavy orb above and called out long and loud.

It was a cry of liberation, my pain now finally gone. I hailed the freedom of this strange half-existence thrust upon me. But the tail end of that howl suddenly took on a lugubrious tone. In death, I'd found relief, but I was far from happy. I mourned the short life of Evan Spencer. The pathos in my lupine moan was for the girl I'd been, and for the beautiful mother that had loved her so well. And for Tristan too.

In life, I had loved him keenly and I loved him even from the afterlife. But I had never gotten to tell him so. That was my eternal regret.

34

BLOOD

The deeper I plunged into the woods the more primal I became till finally I had shed my past life entirely, discarded it in the dead leaves underfoot as I ran beneath the stars. My mind was full to bursting with all the elemental rhapsodies of the forest. I could hear each shuffle of an insect's wing and every sigh of a sleeping bird in its nest. The tang of the moss, the pine, and the frightened spoor of smaller creatures all called to me. My woodland paradise was saturated with life, and all of it was piquant. The wind itself seemed to be gathering up the variegated scents just for me, casting it into my face like a loving zephyr before stroking my whiskers back and tugging playfully at my lolling tongue.

That luminous eye followed me over the canopy as I loped through the trees. It caressed my back with argent beams that pulsed and rippled through my blood, my exhilarated heart, in turn, synchronizing with its heady cadence. My otherworldly mother. I answered her with another howl, but this time there was none of the melancholy of before. In fact, there must have been something terrible in my song because the next instant a flash of a shadow leapt into the air and fled through the trees up ahead.

I'd barely seen the creature, but I identified it immediately by smell alone. A startled leveret hared off madly into the underbrush in the hopes of escaping me. My reaction was immediate. Instinct-driven, I gave chase, my nostrils fluttering to draw in the nectarous spice of its terror as I fixed my eyes to my zigzagging prey.

I was like a bolt shot from a crossbow, anticipating its moves, and delighting in its errors. I was far larger and so much faster. I drew up alongside, close enough to strike, shooting a great big paw out to trip the young hare. And it did so beautifully, somersaulting through the air and kicking in vociferous panic. The scream of my prey I hardly heard, but it lasted only as long as it took my jaws to clamp around its small head with abrupt and lethal precision.

Once the hare was silent, once its heart ceased its trembling, I hunkered down and tore into my prize with satisfied gusto, relishing the savory warmth of the kill as it spurted, hot and salty, into the back of my throat.

Suddenly, the wind shifted, warning me that I was by no means the largest beast in my Elysian woods. I paused my gnawing and lifted my head up from the carcass, ears cocking warily. Even my forest stilled so that I could listen. No longer enamored with my kill, I stood and backed away from it, eyes peeling back the shadows for a glimpse of what I sensed but couldn't see. Before long, a large shadow ambled forward, the moonlight finally unveiling the monster I'd perceived. Thankfully, he kept himself well out of my personal boundary, instead settling onto his haunches in a manner that evinced only calm and respectful inquisitiveness.

I, however, was threatened despite his clement behavior, my tail—short though it was—tucking instantly. He was far larger than me and his eyes (a gilded, radiant green) studied me with a grave intensity I didn't like. Yet he seemed so familiar to me somehow, his scent almost tempting me forward. It was that familiarity that held me still, and hesitant, although I was barely aware that my ears had flattened against my head and my nose was rucked so that my lips were pulled back from my teeth.

"Stay back," I growled, trying to make myself seem bigger. My hackles rose in protest when he neither dropped his eyes nor backed away.

In fact, he pushed himself back onto all fours so that his large head and stubby tail were held high. The fur around his sable mane was fluffed confidently, his ears were cocked forward and his mouth appeared relaxed. An unthreatening stance, yet clearly expressing his dominance. I could sense his mounting excitement as he studied me. In response, I closed my mouth and backed away.

Without warning, I sprinted off as the rabbit had done only moments before, eager to put some distance between me and my unwelcome visitor. The male, however, shot forward and bounded after me, keeping pace no matter how fast I hurtled into the forest. After a while, he seemed to grow uneasy, his censure palpable. He gave a warning bark. Then he growled impatiently when I ignored every attempt he made to corral me in a different direction. I dodged and sidestepped him time and time again. Though he easily could have overpowered me, his size and speed far superior to mine, he never once touched me. Instead, he fell back a pace and gave me some distance, whimpering in frustration.

A black, acrid whiff stung my nostrils well before the pads of my feet suddenly hit the unnatural winding causeway that cut rudely through my forest like black ice. Skidding to a halt on the unfamiliar surface, I allowed myself a moment to inspect this strange and foul-smelling earth, half-way conscious of a queer and distant mechanical growl that was steadily growing in amplitude. A beam of blinding light appeared abruptly over the rise. It sliced harshly through my vision so that I snapped my eyes closed and gave a startled yelp. The monstrous growl was now ear-splitting and foreign, and I felt the light spill over me like a violating touch. However, before I thought to head back where I came from I was knocked to the wayside by the giant wolf I'd momentarily disregarded.

He hauled me down the embankment and then, body tensed and vigilant, listened for the growling thing to pass us by. I heard the thing slow briefly, but, eventually, it moved on until the harsh sound of it was only a receding purr in the night. Meanwhile, I was struggling beneath the giant's heavy paws, becoming ever more panicked the longer he held me down. Finally, I lashed out with fangs and claws, clamping a mouthful of his flesh and fur, desperate to dislodge him, almost convinced he'd reciprocate in turn.

But he didn't. Even so, he refused to let me go and the more he held firm the more violent I became. I had no idea how long I struggled, or what damage I was inflicting. I only snapped and snarled and bucked and ripped at him, but nothing I did gained my release. So, finally, I quietened down, exhausted.

Enervated now, I was aware that even the moonbeams were seeping out of my veins. There came a strange popping and rippling of my body that was only somewhat uncomfortable, as though I was stretching overexerted muscles. My spine gave two more audible cracks and then all was still as I lay panting, naked, wet, and sticky. I was too tired to peel my lids back.

When I woke up, the ground was frost-covered and dawn was filtering through the icy fog. I was alive! I sat up, oblivious to the cold and feeling strangely revived. Until I saw my hands. They were awash in crimson. Looking down at my nakedness, I discovered that my abdomen and breasts were just as thickly coated in blood. Then I pressed my hands to my face to inspect with fingertips what I already felt was daubed on my face. More blood, dried and flaking and tight across my chin and cheeks.

I vaguely remembered the hare. *I killed it!* Shame washed

over me as I buried my face in my bloodied hands. Instantly, I froze. Yes, there was the unmistakable tang of a leporid on my flesh, but only a trace. Pulling my hands away, my nostrils flaring bemusedly, I tried to make sense of the predominant scent coating my fingers. Unmistakably canine!

Confused, I turned my head to inspect the clearing, finally glancing over my shoulder. There was Tristan, as naked as me, lying deathly still, his flesh tinged with blue, and as bloodied as I was.

I screamed his name and thrashed my way over to him, my fingers trembling in horror as I discovered all the gaping wounds in his arms, face, and torso. Fierce bite marks riddled his beautiful skin. Near hysterical now, I didn't notice that the forest had grown silent around me. My sobbing grew louder as I gently tapped Tristan's cheeks and begged him to wake up. I then bent my head to his chest and listened for a heartbeat. It was faint and so weak that I felt my terror mount instead of subside. Even his usually golden skin was pallid in the grey light.

The sudden low grunt behind me so startled me that I gave a shriek and snapped my head around to see a massive grizzly already on its hind legs, clearly angered by my screaming. Clearly furious at finding me so close to its lair.

I stumbled backward and fell right over Tristan's prone form as the bear inched vengefully closer. However much I wanted to run away, I couldn't leave Tristan here for the grizzly to maul. Desperately, I grabbed a stone and stood to my full height (which was nowhere near as intimidating as the bear's). Without hesitation, I stood my ground protectively enough that the bear paused, confused. I focused my glare at it and waited, my body as still as the mist.

Unexpectedly, I heard a strange rumble emanating from deep in my chest. It clearly surprised her. Hell, it surprised me as well! But not enough that I released her eyes. I kept mine fixed to hers and watched as she wavered, uncertain now how to proceed. Well, I could certainly help her decide. My missile embedded itself in the bark of the tree beside her like a bullet that only just missed her head. The wood splintered loudly. The bear gave a start and swiveled intelligent eyes to the damage I'd done to the tree. Then it glanced back at me, wary.

In the meantime, I'd already gathered two more stones, making no secret of the weapons in my hands and of the mayhem I was capable of. The bear, having noticed the stones, took a step backward, and when I gave another growl of animus, it backed up even further away. Then disappeared altogether.

I stood like that, tensed in my aggression, for long moments. My ears were trained for the slightest sound, but the grizzly never returned. What did finally snap me from my silent guardianship was the sudden spray of leaves behind me as two men came sprinting down from the road. Dean and Tim. Now that I was no longer alone, I was once again overwhelmed by tears and horror for Tristan. My dismay only escalated when I noticed Dean's face turn white at seeing his brother's torn body.

"Tristan!" He bent over his brother and examined his wounds.

Tim, meanwhile, pulled his phone out and began muttering coordinates into the receiver.

"What happened?" Dean demanded of me, eyes accusing as he stripped his shirt off to daub at the blood still seeping from Tristan's chest.

"I don't know!" I sobbed. "I woke up and found him like that." I still wasn't even sure what was happening to me, or what I recalled of last night, never mind what I'd done to Tristan. I had thought I'd been dreaming. Vague flashbacks of the night were all I had—the rabbit and then the giant who'd chased me through the woods. Most of the night was a phantasmagorical blur.

The sun was clear of the horizon by the time I heard wheels screech to a halt on the road, a door slamming urgently moments later. Shivering bemusedly, I watched as Lydia appeared beside Tristan. He was swiftly field-dressed and then Tim and Lydia carefully carried him up to the car. I watched the whole scene as one removed and unwelcome. Like a convict. Like a mutt. I felt dirty, naked, guilty, and miserable. Before long, it was just Dean and I alone in the woods, the pressure of his sharp gaze almost unbearable. When the sound of Lydia's car speeding along the road could no longer be heard, I finally glanced up at him. Unlike me, he was fully clothed (minus the shirt he'd used to soak up some of Tristan's blood earlier).

His gaze was almost calculating. "Are you hurt?"

I must have looked like a naked Carrie White on prom night. "No," I answered, my voice like gravel from all the weeping.

He nodded. "C'mon, let's get you back to the house."

I averted my gaze, diffidently covering my breasts with one arm as I dropped my hand to cover the lower half of my nakedness. "Umm…"

Dean gave an impatient snort, bent down to retrieve his soiled shirt from the ground and then threw it at me. The one stained with Tristan's blood. "You're only naked if you think you're naked," he said disgustedly. Then he marched off to the road, knowing that I'd follow meekly behind him.

After I'd scrambled into the sticky, oversized shirt I set off after him, purposefully avoiding the large blood puddle in the leaves where Tristan had only just been lying.

How had I done that to Tristan? More importantly, why had he let me?

35

DEEP SCARS

My palms itched. I dug my nails into them as I stood outside of Tristan's room, uncertain of whether or not I should go in. Whether or not I'd even be welcome. Dean's cold glare still disturbed me even now, though it had been hours since we'd returned from the forest.

Despite having effaced Tristan's cold blood from my lips and nails, I still felt tainted. Unclean and unworthy. I called my mom after my shower, thinking it would make me feel better, but it hadn't. I had, however, promised Mom that I'd come home soon, and though I wasn't sure I'd be permitted to leave yet, I knew I had to try. Somehow. Especially after that stilted meal I'd just shared with Dean's pack—no one had said a word at the dinner table except Lydia and James, but even their efforts had been awkward. Though, if I was being honest, I hadn't exactly tried to make conversation either.

I licked my blood from my wrist, where I'd been scratching all the while I'd stood staring at Tristan's door, and then finally lifted my hand to the bronze knob to twist it open. As soon as I stepped into the room, Dean stood from the chair at Tristan's bedside.

“What are you doing here? You need rest.” His eyes dropped briefly to Tristan. “And so does he.” What he’d actually meant to say was, “What the fuck are you doing here?” But thankfully his lips refrained from uttering what was clearly expressed in the harsh slash of his brows across fierce bourbon eyes.

“I wanted to see how—”

“He’s fine.”

No thanks to you. There was no need to say aloud the words I felt like a stab from his eyes.

“You should go now, Evan.”

I felt myself bristle under my own heavy guilt. “No. Not till I see for myself that he’s okay.”

The tick at Dean’s jaw warned me not to push my luck, but I squelched the momentary upsurge of fear. The thing about it was, I hated myself enough that anything he did to me, whatever physical pain he was capable of inflicting, I felt I deserved anyway.

Sensing my determination, Dean took only a slight step back from the bed, eyes narrowing forbiddingly. I took immediate advantage of his tight-lipped consent, grudging though it was, and moved past him to lean over Tristan. His pallor was a little less bloodless and his breathing seemed even, but I still felt the horror of what I’d done rush over me like acid. I was a monster! Every deep wound still weeping into his bandages had been inflicted by my nails and my fangs. Every ugly yellowing bruise and laceration on his face was of my doing.

Hot tears instantly welled and burned my eyes before coursing down my face into my lips. I pressed my mouth to his—a kiss heavy with shame and regret—and tasted the salt of my tears on his skin. His lips were warm, almost feverish. For a split second, I thought I felt them move beneath mine. I pulled away. Though they were now glistening with my tears, his lips remained deathly still and his beautiful, azure eyes prevailed behind closed lids.

“Okay, enough. Time to go,” Dean said gruffly.

"Why don't *you* just go?" I rejoined, sobbing.

"Evan—" the sound of my name spoken low, like a warning, agitated the hairs on my nape "—I said get out."

"No!"

Dean's nostrils flared irritably. "You're not human anymore, remember whose pack you belong to now and in whose house you're living. My mercy stretches only so far."

"I never chose this! I never chose you to be my alpha! And you can't make me—"

"But I can!" His teeth gnashed audibly. "I can easily make you do whatever I want."

"Stop," came the groggy command from the bed, instantly wrenching Dean and I from our challenging glares.

"Tristan!" I flew into his arms and nuzzled his neck. "I'm so sorry!"

"Shh, it's not your fault." He stroked the back of my head.

"Of course it's her fault," Dean snapped under his breath. "Or did you do this to yourself?" He gestured to Tristan's bandages.

"Dean…" Tristan's warning tone was as dark as his brother's had been.

"You're avoiding the elephant in the room, brother. Your little girlfriend is rabid."

Tristan pushed himself up onto his elbows to glare at Dean. "She's not. I watched her all night. She's the furthest thing from rabid."

"Then how the hell did you end up nearly neutered, you idiot?"

"I cornered her and restrained her when a truck nearly hit her."

"Great!" Dean snarled. "As if she couldn't be more of a liability, now she's already brought attention to herself!"

By now I was trembling, the tears falling uncontrollably as I listened to myself described as no better than a mindless pest.

Tristan, seeing this, seemed to get some of his color back, his face becoming red with anger. "I made sure she wasn't seen," he shot back, voice brusque. "And anything she did to me was done in self-defense."

Dean grunted and stalked to the door. He'd obviously had enough of us both. "We'll talk later." Before leaving, he fixed one last sharp glare at me. "Understand something, Evan" — he waited a beat so that I felt the full force of his glower — "if you stay here, you're part of the pack. *My* pack. And you *do not* get to disobey direct orders again." Here he transferred his eyes to his brother. "No exceptions." Then he was gone, leaving Tristan and I alone. Finally.

"He's more like my father than he'd care to admit," Tristan snorted, his tone weary.

"I'm not rabid?" I asked hopefully, almost too scared to believe it. "Are you sure?"

Tristan lifted a surprisingly strong hand to my face to brush the tear-soaked hair from my cheeks. "You're not rabid." He gave me a reassuring smile. "I swear, I'll never keep anything from you again. I'll never lie. You're not rabid."

"Then how did I…? Why…? How could you let me…?" I took his hand in mine and kissed his palm, drawing his keen eyes to the scratches at my wrists and palms.

His brows drew together as he brushed his thumbs over my self-inflicted scratches. "You were terrified, and you didn't recognize me. When I threw you from the road, I gave you no warning. Everything you did was in self-defense. You thought you were being attacked."

"But I should have known you and—"

"The memory of your attack, by something that looked just like me—" he was talking about Nicole "—is still too fresh. You panicked, and you haven't yet learned to correlate instinct and rationale. You're still developing."

"Why did you let me hurt you?" I sounded angry, but I was horrified at myself.

He gave a tired shrug and leaned back, pulling me with him. "Because I would rather gnaw off my own paws than hurt you. Because, honestly, I feel responsible for everything that's happened to you. My injuries were deserved."

"Bullshit!" I lifted my head from his chest and glared at him. "Nicole did this, not you."

He ran the pad of his thumb under my jaw. "Because of me. I couldn't stay away from you." He searched my eyes. "Although I bet now you wish I had."

This was a question I'd already pondered, and I gave him an honest answer. "I don't know, Tristan."

"Well, like you said before, it's pointless now—Nicole gave you no choice. You're one of us."

"I'm not, though, am I? I'm a mutt," I finished vehemently. Disgusted, I averted my eyes.

"No! You're exactly like me." His fingers tightened on my chin perceptibly, turning my face till I brought my eyes back to his. "Do you know what the difference is between a werewolf born and one bitten?"

I actually didn't, not really. I didn't even know what I looked like when I was changed. I shook my head.

"Nothing." His eyes held mine steadily. "You look like a juvie now, but you won't forever."

"Huh?" Aidan had failed to mention that.

"All of us, when we first change, look no more sinister than a natural wolf. Mother nature's way to protect us, I guess. We're unbridled and don't have the discipline of the mature wolves, so if we're ever spotted by outsiders, all they see is a large black wolf with a cropped tail."

I listened intently, drinking from the firehose as though my life depended on it. Maybe it did.

"That's what you look like, Ev—just a wolf. Not hideous, and not like an aberration." He brushed his fingers gently over my sternum. "You have an adorable little patch of white on your chest, did you notice?"

"I can't remember much of anything, Tristan."

He gave a sad smile. "It's your wolf's badge of purity." He dropped his hand. "As we get older, we begin to look different. The oldest amongst us—like every elder in the Council of Alphas—looks nothing like a wolf. Most of them have silver-lined backs and walk easily on hind legs. They're something between a gorilla, a bear, and a wolf if I was to describe one. My father is one of the largest 'grey backs' around."

I remembered Aidan calling the pure-blooded majestic-looking and that mongrels were anything but. "Aidan told me I'd never look majestic."

"In her defense, wolves bitten are few and far between, they don't tend to survive. The ones that do pull through look like juveniles for a lot longer. But, Evan, there's no difference now, biologically, between you and me."

"Then why were you so disgusted by me back in Red Devil? When you saw my scars. When you realized what I'd become." That look of his in Dean's Land Rover, the night of *Lupum Caedes*, I would never forget.

He seemed affronted suddenly. "I was never disgusted by you! I never could be." He sat up again and, despite that he was weak from his wounds, pulled me into a fierce hug. "If you ever saw disgust then it was all for myself. And for Nicole." Her name was like a curse between us, it held so much rancor. "You're the innocent in all of this. Only the words mutt and mongrel are disgusting to me. How is a mutt any less of a dog for not being a thoroughbred?"

"Then why does Dean hate me?"

"He doesn't hate you. He despises all the old buried feelings this has all forced him to confront again."

I opened my mouth to argue, but then snapped it shut just as quickly. *His mother!* Of course. "Because of what happened to…"

"Linda." Tristan nodded. "He has deep scars, Evan, so have a little patience with my brother."

"Not if he keeps ordering me around, Tristan." I was no one's dog to be commanded. I had left Florida to escape my grandfather's autocracy and the feelings of inadequacy. I'd be damned if I'd let Dean or Nicole or anyone else make me feel unworthy again. I was deprecating enough to myself as it was.

"Being in a pack is a completely different dynamic, I get it. You'll figure it out, I promise. But listening and respecting your alpha is for the good of the whole pack's survival."

"Dean isn't my commander."

"No, technically Aidan is since Nicole bit you." This clearly infuriated him as much as it did me.

"I say differently." No one owned me. No one had the right to dictate my future.

"Evan, you can't survive in this world without a pack," he warned. "We're not necessarily a democratic species, so—"

"But you do! You survive just fine without a pack."

He seemed taken aback a moment, bemused. "I…"

"Aren't you the stereotypical lone wolf? Where's your pack, Tristan? Is it your father's or is it your brother's?"

There was a long silence in which he seemed not to know how to respond. Then, finally, he answered, "Dean's pack is where I belong."

"No!" I left the bed and headed to the window. "You're as displaced as I am and you know it."

He said nothing, so I turned around to study him. He, in turn, was scrutinizing me just as closely.

"You're an alpha," I continued. "I sensed it even as a human

—you aren't a follower. And I refuse to belong with any alpha but you. I don't *trust* anyone else."

This surprised him, his eyes flared briefly. "I have no pack of my own. My brother is my—"

"Stop lying to yourself!" We glared at each other. After a silence, I went on, "Why the hell are you denying your birthright? Your father is—"

"You—" he gritted his teeth "—of all people should understand how I feel about my father."

I swallowed. He was right, I wanted nothing to do with mine, so I couldn't expect any different from him.

Tristan rubbed at his temples and closed his eyes, sighing heavily into the hush. "My father really loved Linda." He looked up at me. "*She* was his life-mate, not my mother." There was a deep pathos in his expression as he stared past me, gaze faraway as it drifted into the past. "But he let the pack elders convince him she wasn't worthy. Just a human. So he married Elaine instead—my mother. She was the eldest daughter of the Blackfoot alpha. Through her, my father's pack grew more powerful, their allies stretching the length of Canada. It was a political match. Their marriage was—is—an unhappy one.

"When Dean came to live with us, my mother resented him. To placate my mother and the elders, Max insisted I be the Yukon heir. Dean never knew a moment of kindness or compassion from the instant he came to our pack. And then, desperate for any form of love, he ran away and bit his own mother."

"I know," I said, shoulders dropping wearily. "I've heard the story."

"I'm nothing like Max," Tristan said, shaking the past from his eyes. "*He* arranged the alliance with Nicole, not me. I needed time to think about it all, time to forge my own alliances if need be. So I left. But he won't accept that I've severed myself from his pack. I can't go back, Ev. His price is too high…"

"Marry Nicole." I nodded my horrified understanding, stepping away from the window to join him on the bed again. He winced only slightly as I curled onto his lap like a kitten. Trailing a finger along his bandaged arm, I asked, "I thought you'd heal faster." I remembered the wounds in his palm that day the bear had appeared at the helipad. I recalled how quickly the skin had fused together, so swiftly that I'd questioned what I'd seen. Even the wounds from his fight with Nicole had mostly healed by the next day.

"Werewolf bites take a while to heal," he explained. "Those from an adolescent take even longer—juvie venom is the worst."

I lifted my face to his and raked my eyes over the scratches at his cheeks, neck, and jawline. "When will you be better?"

"Soon," he promised.

My hand came to rest over the bandage at his forearm. "Have I scarred you forever?"

"No." One corner of his mouth lifted roguishly. "You've marked me forever." He pulled my hands to his lips for a kiss then placed them on his heart. "And I'll wear those marks proudly." Tristan lowered his head to kiss me softly, his lips lightly skimming across mine and then across my jaw to my ear. "I nearly made the same mistake my father did. I nearly let you go."

His words had sent a shiver through my body that surged into my heart and made it tremble excitedly. What was he saying? Was I his life-mate? "You nearly let me go because I was only human?"

"No, because you don't deserve this life. It can be a cruel and unforgiving one. Being a werewolf isn't for snowflakes."

Yeah, I'd definitely had my fair share of that cruelty already. I turned my head slightly so that our lips were aligned again and then I fused our mouths hungrily, eager for him to touch me like he had the last morning I'd been human. Eager to forget the werewolf politics and my abysmally fragile future.

At first, Tristan seemed just as eager as I was, his hands slowly edging up my shirt and along my bare ribs. When his thumb brushed the underside of my breast I felt my whole body jolt with the power of my reaction to him, but he instantly dropped his hands and gently pushed me away from him. "Will you stay here, Ev? With me?" The amber flecks in his green eyes seemed to pulse keenly. "With Dean's pack?"

Instantly, my libido ebbed. As of this morning, I'd promised my mom I'd come home. But nowhere felt like home now, least of all this pack. I was now as directionless as I'd been when I left Florida. The scant few times I'd felt anchored was in Tristan's arms, but he seemed as unsure of his place in the world as I was, despite his reluctance to admit as much. Finally, I shook my head. "I have to go home. I have to see my mother."

"No, it's too dangerous. You still can't fully control—"

"So I'm a prisoner here?" For the second time in an hour, I felt my hackles rise.

"Don't put words in my mouth." His eyes darkened to yellow. "Public transport is too dangerous while you're still this unstable. You're better off waiting a few months."

Unstable?! "No! If I'm not a prisoner here, and Dean's not gonna kill me, then I'm going. He's not my keeper, nor is Aidan." I met his glare with my own. "By your own admission, you're not my alpha. I'm leaving. I belong at home." The last part wasn't necessarily true because I belonged nowhere, but I needed to see my mother and I needed to clear my head for just a few days; I needed to escape this new *status quo* that had been forced on me.

"So this is goodbye, is that it?" His lips compressed almost bitterly.

"Yes, this is goodbye," I answered through that insidious lump wedged in my throat. *For now.*

"Will you come back?" He shifted his eyes to the window, becoming distant.

"I don't know. Maybe."

Those eerie green eyes instantly fixed to mine again, leaden with disappointment and disapprobation. I waited for him to argue or plead or convince me to stay, but he only sat there contemplatively, his gaze watchful and piercing. When, after long moments, he still hadn't spoken I finally got up and headed to the door.

When my hand fastened around the knob, however, he finally broke that awful silence. "Tomorrow, Evan. I'll take you to Ketchikan tomorrow."

Swallowing the hard lump down, I gave a curt nod. "Tomorrow." Then I left him, closing the door softly behind me.

36

GOODBYE

How different everything was now. How changed I was. The Evan that had left Ketchikan all those months ago, laughing and blushing like a maniac, had undergone chrysalis and emerged as something else entirely. Something worse than a moth.

I'd still never gotten my Sex on the Beach, and by the look of the broody lines marring Tristan's brow this morning (not to mention the scabs and bruises) I likely never would. Unlike my initial flight to Thorne Bay, my return to Ketchikan was stilted by noisy silence, the radio chatter and the steady whine of the turbine did nothing to drown out the unbearable taciturnity that stretched between the occupants in the cabin.

Tristan and his brother were sitting up front. I was in the aft port side seat behind Tristan, shooting despondent glances at the back of his head. The whales throwing spume and saltwater into the air, over Clarence Strait, briefly distracted me and I found myself smiling for the first time that morning. Dean banked the helicopter gently left and brought us around for a steep approach over the runway (which, oddly, appeared situated higher than the tower). In diametric opposition to my gloomy spirits the sun was out for once. I would miss the beauty of this verdant wilderness, and the freshness of the air. I would miss Melissa, Alison, and even Owen's unfiltered jokes. Most of all, I would desperately miss Tristan.

Once the helicopter was parked, and the blades had come to a halt, we were hastily deposited at the terminal entrance by the guy that had marshaled us into our parking spot. Even the poor marshaler had sensed the tension and had made no effort to hide his relief as he sped away from us.

Dean shook his head, none too pleased, for maybe the fiftieth time since he'd been told of my plans. "You shouldn't be traveling on public transport," he muttered as we passed through the sliding glass doors. "All we need is for you to lose your temper or something."

The woman at the front desk, who'd blanched to see his scowl, stammered a greeting. Taciturn, Dean continuing past her toward my departure terminal.

"Maybe *you* should control *your* temper," I retorted. For my cheek, I received a black look from Dean and an amused snort from Tristan. Well, if Dean murdered me before I boarded my flight, at least I'd gotten some reaction out of Tristan today. That was almost worth courting death.

Dean leveled a particularly grave look at his brother. "This is a bad idea."

"She's not our prisoner, Dean." Pale eyes raked over me momentarily. "I can't force her to stay."

"I can."

"Drop it."

The alpha's scowl settled over me. "Nothing good is gonna come of you running away, Evan."

"Oh, you're talking to me now?" It had rankled when he'd talked about me, over me, as though I'd been invisible up till now.

"Stay."

I resented the command. "I'm not your dog, Dean."

He halted suddenly, turning on me. "You're gonna get yourself in trouble. Take it from me, there are no second chances. Not in our world. Not for rogues, and especially not for rogue mutts."

"I just want to see my mother."

"So you'll be back before your cycle peaks?" He asked dubiously.

"I didn't say that..."

"You're gonna get yourself killed." The corner of his upper lip lifted off his canines in disgust. "Or worse, kill someone else."

"Put a cork in it, Dean." Tristan glared pointedly at his brother. "Just let her go."

Whatever the meaning behind those brief silent looks, it must have mollified Dean somewhat because he gave a clipped nod and took up his marching again. He seemed to have timed my arrival perfectly, for the sake of his own impatience, no doubt, because the moment we reached my gate my zone number was already being called out and most of the passengers had disappeared onto the airstairs. There was literally no time for any drawn-out goodbyes. Not that Dean expected or wanted one for himself.

"Keep your shit together, girl. Call us if you need anything." With that said, Dean gave me an awkward pat on the shoulder and then told Tristan he'd wait back at the helicopter.

Now that I was alone with Tristan, and under a time crunch, I had no idea what to say. I shifted from one foot to the other, biting my lip nervously as he handed me my backpack.

My Alaskan departure had been such a rushed and impromptu decision that I'd not even returned to Bear Lodge for the rest of my stuff. I'd made some lame excuse to Alison and Melissa, something about my grandfather being admitted to hospital (which he shortly would be doing, but I'd omitted the part about it being for non-life-threatening hip surgery) and that I needed to rush home. Melissa had promised to pack my stuff up for me and send it down to Palm Beach if I decided not to come back.

As if reading my mind, Tristan caught my chin and lifted it gently so that I had no choice but to meet his heated regard. "I'm giving you time, Ev. This isn't goodbye," he said quietly. "You need us. You need a pack."

"Right now all I *need* is to be with people that love me." I'd been treated like nothing but a second-class citizen since I'd been infected. Beseechingly, I stared up at him, hoping for him to give me a reason to stay.

"Last call for Alaskan Airways flight sixty to Seattle," came the stern voice of the attendant at the departure gate.

I tore my gaze from Tristan's to see a woman eyeballing me severely from the ticket scanner. Everyone else had already filed onto the plane. Except for me.

Pushing myself onto the tips of my toes I hurriedly pressed my cold lips to Tristan's, willing the tears away. "Bye," I whispered, as his arms tightened around me. Then I pushed away from him and, swinging my bag up onto my shoulder, beelined it for the gate. As with my mother all those months ago, I couldn't look back. But I felt him watching me.

Almost as soon as I'd stowed my bag under the seat in front of me, and strapped myself in, we were underway, taxiing out to the runway. I barely heard the safety brief and watched with glazed and unseeing eyes as the flight attendants went through their rehearsed little spiel about lifejackets and oxygen masks.

Snuffling, I pulled my phone out and opened the last photo I'd taken: it was a selfie captured the last morning I'd been human. I'd snapped it right after Tristan and I had eaten breakfast. I'd plagued him for one (he hated selfies) because my mom had been pestering me to do it—eager for a glimpse of the man she'd heard so much about. I was glad now that she had. It was the only photo

I had of Tristan without his flight helmet on, let alone of he and I together. God, he was so beautiful. So attentive, and kind, and genuine. Yet unable or unwilling to tell me he loved me. Maybe he didn't? I'd felt loved, though, ever since he'd kissed me in the kitchen. Was it really so important to hear it if I felt it?

As the Boeing 737 hurtled into the sky, I realized that I'd left my heart back on the ground. With Tristan.

"You two are a beautiful couple," said the nosy old lady beside me.

I turned to see her peering over at my picture. Embarrassed to have been caught crying over a benign little photo of a happy couple I hardly recognized anymore, I turned the phone off, finally, and shoved it back into my pocket. "Thanks," I murmured, annoyed at her intrusiveness.

"Don't worry, dear. I saw the way he looked at you at the gate. You'll see him again." Though she'd posed it as a statement, there was a questioning lift to her wrinkled brow, as though she wanted me to confirm this for her.

"Maybe." If I had learned one thing these last few weeks it was that life was anything but certain.

"Maybe?" Her smile fell. "Well, that's a shame if you don't." She pushed her spectacles higher up her nose and then settled back against the seat with her book. "I'm sure you both know what you're doing."

I turned my head to the window, lifting my shoulders absently. *Glad someone's sure.* I definitely wasn't.

~

"Hope you got your things together. Hope you are quite prepared to die."

Mom maneuvered the black Pathfinder into the only available

parking spot beside a sleek white Mercedes, Creedence Clearwater Revival filling the unnatural silence between us. Poor Mom, she didn't know what to make of me anymore. I'd been home almost three weeks already and she was still walking on eggshells around me, averse to saying the wrong thing in case I burst into tears or snapped at her. I'd done both the former and the latter almost every day since coming home. My mood swings were out of control, and they only got worse the more the moon filled up each night.

"Looks like we're in for nasty weather. One eye is taken for an eye."

She slipped the gear into park but left the car idling in the hospital parking lot as she turned to consider me thoughtfully.

"Well don't go around tonight, well it's bound to take your life. There's a bad moon on the rise."

I reached forward abruptly and jammed my finger into the power button, instantly cutting Fogerty off mid-chorus. "I hate that song."

She seemed startled by my sudden churlish reaction to poor John, who'd always been one of her favorites. "But you've always liked Creedence—"

"Not anymore." It reminded me of Nicole for some reason.

"Ev" — she bit the corner of her mouth — "you seem so… different." And she clearly didn't appreciate the changes.

Nor did I. "You have no idea," I replied, opening the car door (and effectively obviating the heart to heart she was trying to instigate), finding the interior unbearably stifling despite that the humidity was all outside.

"Are you sure you don't want to talk about—"

"Maybe later, Mom." I was getting good at brushing her off. Maybe I'd been infected with some of Nicole's shitty attitude too? I shuddered. *Perish the thought.*

I never imagined that I'd crave the distraction of my grandfather's irascibility at the dinner table, but I had. Since he'd been in the hospital, I'd had to constantly fend off my mother's discerning comments and level looks. My grandmother, bless her, was as oblivious as ever and never gave me a moment's unease. The woman was a saint to have tolerated my grandfather all these years. Either that or she just had ridiculously low standards.

I hurried through the automatic doors, knowing Gramps would monopolize the conversation with his complaints, and thereby distract my mother. I tensed as soon as the blast of air-conditioning hit my face. The antiseptic smell was too reminiscent of that awful dilapidated asylum in Red Devil. The smell of Pine-sol, as opposed to pine trees, was giving me the mouth sweats. As we entered the hospital room where my grandfather was convalescing, I tried to breathe through my mouth to keep from vomiting, but I could taste the air.

"Hi, Gramps." I leaned down to kiss his wizened cheek, catching a faint whiff of mothballs.

"You're late," he said to Mom.

We'd visited him every day that he'd been hospitalized, and every day he'd griped about our lateness no matter what time we came. As per usual, neither Mom nor I offered an excuse. None would have satisfied him anyway. My grandmother only smiled congenially as I moved to kiss her hello.

The nurse, meanwhile, had stepped in and was attending one of the other bedridden occupants. I caught my grandfather glaring suspiciously at her. Then he gave her a few testy replies when she stopped by to check on him as well. She was, surprisingly, unconcerned by his curtness. Ostensibly, she was as used to his brand of charisma as I was.

Before she'd even moved out of earshot, he turned to me and, in a loud whisper, said, "That nurse is a lesbian."

"Dad!" Mom muttered sternly, grimacing. "That's really none

of your business."

I rolled my eyes and shot the nurse an apologetic smile. She, however, appeared mildly amused and left the room with the same air of brisk capability that she'd entered with.

"So she's a lesbian because she doesn't take your shit?" I snorted.

He shifted his rheumy eyes from the door, where the nurse had disappeared, and beheld me with the same narrowed suspicion. "You're different," he said bluntly. "Don't tell me you're a lesbian too?"

God, he was an intolerant bastard. I looked pointedly at my mother, holding my hand out for the car keys. "No, I'm a werewolf."

Ignoring my retort completely, he watched as Mom dropped the keys in my waiting hand. "You're leaving?"

"She managed to pick up a few shifts at The Turtle," Mom answered him. "Just like old times."

That sounded depressing. I'd been moldering in my room (just like old times) ever since I got back from Thorne Bay. Finally, unable to stand the silence a second longer (unwilling to spend another tormenting moment staring hopefully at my phone, waiting for Tristan to call), I'd called in at the cafe to see if they needed any help. Luckily, it being the start of snowbird season and all, they'd jumped at the chance to have me back again, however temporarily.

Gramps shook his head smugly. "Guess nothing's changed after all." He sat back against his pillows, my gran rushing over to fluff them dutifully for him. It had been a premeditated cut, implying that I was reverting back to my past useless ways. Retrograding to the lost and pathetic little Evan of before. "You're still the same."

"I wish," I answered. Not even five minutes into my visit and I'd already had enough of him. I was ready to bug out, despite that I'd be early for my shift. "Later, Mom. Gran." With the keys jangling in my fist, I made quick my escape, knowing Mom would grab a ride home with my gran. As guilty as I felt about leaving my mom to listen to my grandfather's complaints about the other patients in the room all being "commies", I was far too relieved to be on my own again to give it more than a passing thought.

But when I was alone with myself, and no longer distracted by my family's idiosyncrasies, my mind would invariably fill with Tristan's face. Missing him had become a dull ache that never went away.

Gramps was wrong, I was nothing like the self-conscious wallflower that had left Florida earlier this year. His barbs didn't bother me anymore. I wasn't scared of his stupid prognostications about my downward spiraling future. Not even my mother's worried looks made me feel like a failure. And if I was feeling empty just now, it was only because my heart was back in Thorne Bay. It seemed that the "space" Tristan had promised to give me had only confirmed that much.

I might not belong to any pack, but, during my brief human happiness with Tristan, my soul had been at peace. I'd felt wonderful. I'd felt capable of anything. I'd entrusted a man with my heart and my body, and I'd felt loved. I'd even loved myself for a time. I wanted all of that again. Wasn't that what a life-mate was? Someone who made you peaceful, and made you want to strive to be a better person. Someone in whose company you felt capable of conquering all your darkness. Tristan was my home. So why the hell had I left him? And why the hell hadn't I heard from him? It hurt that he hadn't texted or called me even once since I'd kissed him goodbye.

Once free of the hospital stench, I paused in the parking lot as a shiver of premonition brushed my nape. Searching the sea of cars proved futile. Nothing looked out of place and no one appeared to be staring at me, but the uncanny sensation of being watched persisted. *Weird.* Maybe because I was disconnected from a pack, and completely without protection, my inner wolf was on some sort of high alert. Shrugging, I opened the car door and disregarded the crazy *wolf-spidey* senses.

37

BAD MOON RISING

Storm clouds had long since blotted out the sun. Evening had crept over the buildings like a thief, unnoticed and insidious. With a garbage bag in each hand, I shouldered my way out the back door of the cafe.

The black scud swept intermittently across the moon, promising rain soon, and the wind whipped plaintively at the fronds of the tall palms looming over me. God, why did it reek of gasoline out here? That was the problem with my nose, every astringent smell seemed to stab my brain.

I glared up at the ominous harbinger of my wolf curse as I swung the black bags into the dumpster, letting the lid fall back with a slam that only exacerbated the migraine edging in behind my eyes. Was it even a migraine? Or something more foreboding. Maybe I could shove tampons in my nostrils. Maybe that would keep the stench of the world out of my head.

My muscles gave an unexpected jerk. It felt as though an army of scarab beetles was crawling beneath my skin. I dragged my nails over my nape in dread and then turned away to hurry back into the restaurant, giving my back to the still waxing moon;

it was already full of presage. Tomorrow. I would need to drive out to the Everglades tomorrow night.

Time had flown, just as the dead leaves were flying aimlessly around the nearly empty parking lot. It was unseasonably cold tonight. My flesh, however, was feverish and itchy, perspiration beading incessantly on my brow despite the wind.

I closed the door behind me and leaned back against it, relieved to have escaped that heavy glow of imminence I was already growing to hate. But Mrs. Goldstein's sudden squeal of laughter tore across my eardrums. With a painful flinch, I cut my eyes balefully across her features as she cooed and laughed at the fat poodle beside her—the "emotional support dog"—gobbling scraps from her fingers.

"That's enough now, Felicity," she informed the dog adoringly. Felicity instantly protested with a sharp little bark that had me grinding my aching teeth together. "No, baby. No more." A second high-pitched bark of objection and Mrs. Goldstein relented with another amused squeal, her fingers bearing the remains of her dinner from the plate to the spoiled dog already lunging at the old lady's fingers.

Catching my black look, yet seemingly immune (or oblivious) to my disgust, Mrs. Goldstein gestured for me to bring the check over. This I would gladly do. It was in her best interest that she and her "service dog" leave the cafe before *I* started barking at her too (or worse).

As soon as I reached her table I nearly gagged as her hideous perfume billowed into my nostrils with cloying floral profusion. I swallowed down the sudden nausea convulsing my stomach. My susceptibility to strong scents and noises had intensified during this last gibbous quarter—if someone's laughter was too loud, or, heaven forbid, a man's aftershave was too strong, I'd find myself having to run to the restroom to purge my stomach at the least provocation. Tonight had been the worst, and taking the garbage out earlier had nearly done me in altogether. The dumpster itself had smelled like month old dirty diapers or something equally rancid.

Felicity's low growling caught me off guard as I returned for Mrs. Goldstein's credit card. The poodle's grey muzzle was pulled back threateningly from her yellowed teeth as she glared her suspicion at me. I glared back.

Somewhere in my periphery, I watched the old lady castigate her poodle, her smudged lipstick moving slowly in tandem with her pursed little mouth, her voice indistinct and her words unintelligible. Blood rushed into my ears with dull echoing throbs as I fixed my eyes to the dog, my canines descending painfully from my gums. My mouth filled with coppery saliva as the dog's growling suddenly progressed into panicked barking.

"Evan!" Mrs. Goldstein's voice finally yanked me from my strange and dangerous fixation.

I swallowed the bloodlust and transferred my gaze to her. She'd likely said my name more than once, by the look of frustration about her.

"Hmm?" I mumbled, making sure to cover my mouth with my hand.

"Did you step on her tail?" She was petting fretfully at her still growling dog. "You must have, she's not usually like this."

I narrowed my eyes at Felicity, trying to steady my breathing. Meanwhile, the old woman's prating filled my ears like an incoherent rush of water.

"You should take better care…bleeding…Did you know?"

"Pardon?" I mumbled around a mouthful of teeth.

She gestured to my mouth with a disproving tut-tut. "You should get that gingivitis checked out, dear." She then favored me with a proud little grin. "My nephew's a dentist, you know."

I grunted noncommittally, wiping roughly at my lips. The metallic tang of blood washed over my tongue. My teeth probably looked horrifying, but, thankfully, I'd had enough forethought to keep them hidden. A little blood was nothing to a glimpse of the canines I could feel nudging behind my lips. She'd have had a coronary had I bared my wolfish smile at her dog.

"You don't look at all well." Mrs. Goldstein was now looking me over skeptically, shrewd little eyes focused on my sweaty brow. "Are you ill?" With a displeased crease between her bespectacled brows, she glanced at her empty dinner plate, ostensibly inspecting it for viruses.

I rolled my eyes.

She and Felicity, meanwhile, were exchanging worried glances. "I hope it's not Zika."

"Why, are you pregnant?" I said under my breath, leaving to run her card. I returned a moment later with her receipt, still shaking my head at her ignorance.

She held out a cautious hand and I obligingly returned her card to her, watching as she wiped it off with some disinfectant gel she'd scrounged from her bottomless handbag. Afterward, she dug around a moment more and lifted out some cash which she placed on the table (along with her nephew's business card) before ushering a vociferous Felicity, still clearly excited by my wolfy pheromones, out the door.

"Bye, Mrs. Goldstein," I said irritably, counting the measly tip she'd left. A mere ten percent, if that. *Whatever.* I had bigger problems now than Zika and shitty tips. Namely that I'd nearly just become a poodle-eater. Which was what I'd, not too many moons ago, accused my boyfriend of being.

"What does that make you, Evan? You've willingly allowed a poodle-eating, nudist weirdo into your house."

God, I missed Tristan. Maybe he was right. Maybe I couldn't do this *werewolfing* thing on my own. I'd nearly just let my lunacy take me down a dark path. Right in front of Mrs. Goldstein! What was I thinking?! I needed to get the hell out of here. I needed help.

The bell chimed over the cafe door to alert me to late dinner arrivals.

Irritably, I turned to the group of men that had shuffled in from the cold, collars pulled up against the stormy wind that had blown them in. "We're closing for the—"

"Hi, Evan." Andy flashed me one of those charming smiles of his.

"Hi." I'd forgotten how unnaturally white his teeth were. Forgotten how pretty he was. Like Surfer Ken pretty.

"Heard you were back."

"Yeah, for a little while." Had I really been so besotted with him earlier this year? His features were arranged neatly enough, but I found his face too tame. Almost effeminate when compared to Tristan's rugged beauty. I nearly laughed when he shot me what he probably thought was a sexy wink as he followed his friends to their usual table.

"Waters for everyone?" I asked, depositing four menus on the table.

"Iced tea for me please"—one of Andy's friends dragged his eyes over my breasts as he read my name tag—"Evan." The other three, Andy included, ordered the same.

I checked the clock on the wall longingly. It was usually dead in the evenings, so tonight it was just me and the sous chef, Mario, holding down the fort. Technically, it was just me since Mario was in the storeroom arguing with his girlfriend on his phone, ignorant to the fact that I could hear every single nasty word she was screeching into his ear. Compliments of the freaky werewolf hearing I now possessed, I could hear everybody's private conversations. I still cringed to think about how many of *my* private conversations Tristan had overheard. Poor me. Poor Mario. I shook my head as I poured the iced teas into four tall glasses, absently listening to Mario's useless placations to the yelling voice. But my ears soon pricked toward the table behind me instead. Toward the conversation that I was now the subject of.

"She looks hotter than I remember. Reckon she got a boob job or something?"

"Bet you she spills the iced tea on your crotch again." This was followed by snickering. "Remember the last time she was here?"

My hands stilled as I frowned.

"I think she wants you, Andy. That girl falls apart every time you smile at her."

"Oh yeah. She wants the D for sure," Andy drawled.

I felt myself bristle. *What a piece of shit.*

"So you in?"

"Not yet. But soon." Andy again.

"Are you *in* on the bet, fucker." The guy with the stupid haircut that looked like a cow had licked it askew was shaking his head, tickled by Andy's crude joke. "Got a twenty here says she spills it on your dick again."

"Spills what exactly?" came the suggestive retort. The group erupted instantly into obnoxious laughter. "Are we talking iced tea or…?"

"Oh, I think she'd rather *you* do the spilling…"

Ugh. I'd had enough listening to those jerks talk about me like that. I marched over, teeth set irritably. Once I'd placed the teas down, none too gently, I asked if I could get them something to eat.

Two of them coughed into their fists while Andy and the cow loogie hairdo guy beside him snickered suddenly, tickled by the unintentional innuendo I'd presumably dropped.

Jeez, how old are you knuckleheads? Twelve? How the hell

had I not seen through Andy before now? Had he always been this conceited, childish pretty boy?

"Yeah, Evan" —with another stupid wink— "we are kinda hungry…"

"For what exactly?" I shot a glare at his friend who was snorting into his iced tea. My scowl quickly shut him up.

"What would you recommend tonight?" Andy asked. It was beyond ridiculous because he knew the menu as well as I did, being as he'd practically grown up in this cafe.

"The crab cakes," I answered with a shrug, checking my watch. The crab cakes were old and smelled funny.

"Crabs it is!" Andy's friend nudged him pointedly.

I rolled my eyes. "Clever."

"Cut it out, Jimmy." The guy on the opposite side of the table smiled apologetically at me. "We'll just have a plate of fries for the table, thanks, Evan. We know it's closing time."

I nodded and left them to give Mario the order. But just because I'd disappeared into the kitchen didn't mean I couldn't hear them carrying on as before. Even Mario shot me a few odd glances as I continued bristling at all the lewd jokes that were being uttered at my expense. All the stupid innuendoes that would never reach Mario's ears (even if he hadn't just had his hearing blistered by his girlfriend's screeching).

"Shit, when did she get so feisty?"

"Actually," I heard Jimmy say, "on second thought, I bet my left nut she turns you down."

"No way, she's had a thing for me from day one. That girl can't control her hands every time I'm near. I have tea-stained shorts to prove it."

"Bro, did you not just see how she looked at you. Her hands aren't getting anywhere near your junk any time soon. Her knee maybe…"

"Classic hard to get tactics, believe me."

"I dunno," Jimmy went on, "she looks like a little ball-buster."

"I'm always up for the challenge."

"Do women never say no to you, man?"

"Nope. Bet her mother wouldn't turn me down either."

More laughter.

What a slimy turd.

"What're the stakes?"

"If she turns me down I'll pour tea down my own goddamn shorts."

"Deal!"

The table became conspicuously quiet as they watched me approach empty-handed, their stupid fries forgotten in the kitchen. I leaned over the table to pin Andy with a feral smile. "How about I save you the trouble, Andy…" With that, I lifted his glass and promptly emptied the iced tea onto his crotch.

"What the fuck?" he sputtered angrily, wiping at his jeans.

"My answer is no, by the way." I yanked my apron off and threw it on the table.

"No what?" he muttered.

"I'm saying no. There. Now you've heard a woman turn you down for the first time." Then I slammed the measly tip I'd gotten from Mrs. Goldstein down on the table in front of him. "Here, go buy yourself some class, asshole." That said, I stormed off, passing a bemused Mario who was holding a steaming plate of fries.

"How the hell did she hear us?" I heard Jimmy whisper as the door slammed behind me.

But I never heard Andy's response, nor did I make it to the car. I was filled with so much rage as I stalked across the parking lot that I could feel my veins swelling at my temples. Felt my eyes kindle with heat even as they were pelted by the rain. I cried out as the wolf roared for release beneath my skin just as a clap of thunder struck the ocean nearby. Suddenly I was on my hands and knees, my nails digging into the asphalt as my bones began to give way.

Not now! Too soon! It wasn't supposed to happen till the full moon. *Not till tomorrow!*

Terrified, I tried to let out a human scream, but the night and the thunder swallowed my agony and all that escaped my lips were small grunts. It was too late. I was changing. Just before I blacked out, though, I heard a woman's voice in my ear. Felt cool fingers clasp my wet face.

"Evan," she said.

Who was she? Her scent was so familiar, but I couldn't see, my eyes were clamped shut. The world, all the sounds and sights, were already dissolving around me, giving way to the pain. The next instant the darkness consumed me.

38

MANSLAUGHTER

It wasn't the rush of waves across the sand that startled me awake but the sudden harsh cry of a seagull. At first, I merely lay there, disoriented, annoyed at myself for falling asleep in the sun again, like I used to do when I was younger. My grandad would probably tell me that I deserved the sunburn already inflaming my skin. Smug old grouch.

Wait! My eyes swiftly popped open to confirm what my other senses had already revealed. What was I doing on the beach? The question formed in my head even as my blood curdled. Dreadful realization struck like lightning, and last night's events swiftly careened into focus. The last thing I recalled was being doubled over in the parking lot. The debilitating muscle ache was easily explained—the result of my early transmutation. The stickiness on my skin, however, was not. Flinching at the sunlight that bore down on me with glaring ferocity, like some sharp celestial judgement, I rolled onto my naked stomach and pushed myself onto all fours before sitting back onto my haunches. I was covered in sand. And blood.

Morbidly, I lifted my fingers to my nose and took a delicate whiff. Human. I blanched and searched the beach with terrified eyes. All was quiet this time of the morning. Evidently, I was on some secluded beach. Somehow, I'd made it to Blowing Rocks Preserve during the night and had, during moonset, passed out amidst the grassy dunes. Thankfully, though, there was no mauled and limbless body nearby. Then where had the blood come from? What the hell had I done?! Bile shot up hot and acrid into my mouth as I tried to recall more of the night. What if there was more than one death on my hands?

Overwhelmed with disgust and dread, I buried my bloodied head in my hands, raking my sandy nails over my cheeks in hysteria. I was a monstrous cannibal! I'd killed someone! There was too much blood on my hands, and my belly was distended with last night's bloody feast.

I remembered the voice in the parking lot, a worried female voice that had seemed incredibly familiar to me, but I'd been so far gone by then that I couldn't, even now, recall the woman's identity. Only that she had sounded concerned. A friend maybe? Was it my mother?! Had I, in my lunacy, killed her? The thought sent terror shooting through my gut.

After a quick search of my hiding spot, I was forced to accept the fact that I was naked and alone. There was no phone and no crime scene hereabouts either. Whatever I'd done, I'd likely done it in the parking lot outside the cafe. *Fuck!*

Desperate to get home, I scrambled through the Burma reed, eyes flitting furtively along the empty shoreline. Once I was sure there was no one around, I darted into the water and washed the blood off, distraught and trembling, until I'd nearly scraped the skin from my bones with abrasive handfuls of sand. After a while, once I'd snuck away from the water, I managed to pilfer an abandoned towel on someone's lawn chair. Thievery was, after all, just a lesser offense to add to my growing list of heinous crimes. Like possible matricide. By the time I'd run home in my 'borrowed' towel (the long walk of shame to trump all walks of shame) the sun had already been up three hours. Whatever odd looks I'd attracted from joggers and fisherman along the way, I barely noticed, my eyes had been too dimmed with tears. Barely sensate at the time, it was only much later that I thought to question how my mother's borrowed car had returned itself to the driveway.

It was with tears of relief that I heard Mom singing in the shower. I slipped in through my bedroom window and I bolted to my bed, messed the covers up, and then escaped to the bathroom to shower. But no amount of soap and water would ever wash the sins from my soul. Not even acid could strip that from me. The water was scalding as it sluiced over me, but I didn't care. I burned with guilt already. When I emerged from the bathroom, in a cloud of steam, Mom was just opening her door, still clad in her pajamas. Briskly I readjusted the towel up to cover the scars that might be peeking over my shoulder. T-shirts with higher necklines had been a must since coming home even though the scars were silvery and faint.

"Morning, Ev." Her eyes shifted from me to my room and the rumpled bed visible from the hallway. "Late night? I didn't even hear you come in."

"Yeah," I croaked.

"Coffee?"

"Please." I had no appetite, even for coffee, but she knew I never turned coffee down in the morning. *Act natural.* Now I knew exactly how a criminal might feel—the need for normalcy and routine to throw the dogs off the scent, so to speak, was paramount. My sanity was crumbling and this small bubble of surreality (in which I was an innocent human just going about my day) was all I had to cling to. I needed every bit of normality I could grasp at the minute before my bubble burst its mayhem over me forever.

Mom kissed my cheek, nodded, and headed downstairs. "On it."

Once in my room again, I began shaking. But panic hadn't saved me back in Red Devil, and it wouldn't save me now, so I swiped the tears off my chin and got dressed. Prosaic routine was what I needed to calm me. My clothes were hanging off me these days, I'd lost too much weight lately. Dean had warned me to keep my strength up. The stress and lack of appetite might have contributed to my loss of control last night. Had I heeded his warning—stayed in Thorne Bay and fed myself properly—I might not now be in this horrifying predicament. Might not now be a murdering bitch. Literally.

"You're gonna get yourself killed. Or worse, kill someone else." How his words haunted me now.

I pulled a chunky sweater over my shirt, the better to cover my weight loss from my perceptive mother, and then went down to join her at the breakfast table. I made a point of eating two full bowls of oatmeal, even though my stomach was still unnaturally full from…whatever (whoever) I'd eaten.

"Wow, someone worked up an appetite in the night," said Mom, heading over to the TV to grab the remote.

So much for acting normal, Evan.

"Active dreams?"

"I guess." Yawning, I rubbed at my temples. My periphery flashed and I stilled with horror as rain and sand cut across my eyes and thunder roared brightly overhead. A sudden full-blooded swell of excitement flitted across my memory as arteries burst between my teeth and something large struggled in my jaws. Nothing I remembered came in any rational order.

"Holy shit!" Mom gasped.

My head spun around to where she stood in front of the TV watching the news. "What is it?" I asked, my stomach dropping out from under me. Mom never swore!

"There's been an attack"—her mouth was solemn and drawn as she turned around to face me—"at the cafe."

"What?!"

Mom turned the volume up as I joined her.

The newscaster's voice was like a discordant buzzing as I stared with horror at the screen. The cafe parking lot was cordoned off with yellow tape, police cars and news vans blocking the activity from view.

"And to think," Mom whispered, shuddering, "you were there only a few hours ago!" She pulled me against her suddenly. "That could have been you, baby!" She hugged me tightly while I stood peering, still paralyzed, over her heaving shoulder.

"Florida Fish And Wildlife are investigating the animal attack," the reporter was saying, almost relishing the drama, "but residents are advised to keep vigilant until the animal has been seized. Authorities all agree, from the bite marks sustained by the victim, that the animal responsible is likely a bear, but FWC has not yet confirmed that."

"A bear?!" Mom turned back to the TV. "This far east?" She shook her head, nonplussed.

"Did they…?" The saliva had dried from my mouth. I tried again. "Did they say…was it a fatal attack?"

Even as I posed my stuttered question, prerecorded footage appeared onscreen as if to taunt me with the critical answer—the coroner's van leaving the scene earlier. That could mean only one thing…

"Yes," mom affirmed unnecessarily. "A man. Found dead."

I barely heard her, because suddenly I was staring at Mario's pallid face, his voice shaking as he faced the cameras.

"I got here early this morning," he was saying gravely, "around five thirty." He dragged his trembling hands through his hair. "And there was Andy—" his eyes shifted to the side, ostensibly to where he could still see the body in his mind's eye "—lying over there." He covered his face with his hands, overcome with emotion. "I can't believe it, man. He was alive only a few hours ago, you know?" He lifted teary eyes to the reporter. "Last night he told me to head home. That he would shut the place up since we were short-staffed. He knew I'd be opening this morning." He began sobbing. "If only I'd stayed…" He was clearly too distraught to continue talking.

It didn't matter, I'd heard and seen enough. My heart was battering like a suffocated fish against my breast as I sank to the floor. "Oh my God!" I whispered disbelievingly. "Andy." I'd killed Andy!

"His poor mother." Mom paced the carpet, distraught. Unexpectedly, she collapsed against me, sobbing again, carrying on about how it could have been me in that parking lot.

If only I *had* died in Red Devil. Then Andy would still be alive. He was a jerk, sure, but death was hardly retributive justice. Had my rage really been that intensely focused that I'd premeditated my ambush? That I'd purposefully waited in the shadows for his friends, and Mario, to leave Andy to his undeserved doom? Evidently, I was two very different creatures—one of which was a cold-blooded, psychotic killer.

It took almost the entire day to convince Mom to stop hovering over me. I needed space to think and agonize in private. Only after she'd made me promise not to leave the house, Mom finally left to take my grandmother to the hospital. There'd been complications with Gramps' hip and he was still convalescing his curmudgeony ass in that room of "commies". Anyway, Mom was taking the "animal attack" seriously, and taking no chances with my life. Little did she know that the monster she feared was right under her nose. Tonight was a full moon, but there was no way I was going to stay in the house and endanger my beautiful mother. I knew where she kept her pistol. If I started to change, or felt the first pressure of that sinister migraine, I'd gladly shove that gun barrel into my mouth. End it all tonight. Just not where Mom would find me. I'd do it in the swamp and let the gators have my sorry carcass.

Where was my phone? Where were my clothes and purse? What if the police had found all my stuff at the scene? I'd be implicated somehow, I just knew it!

Call Tristan! The voice of logic was unequivocal and firm. Insistent. It was with a surprisingly steady hand that I grabbed my mother's cell phone (she'd left it at home for me since I'd lost mine) and dialed the number I knew off by heart. He'd know what to do. But, of course, there was no answer. Straight to voicemail.

"No!" I threw the phone at the couch and slipped to the floor in a panicked and dejected heap, my knuckles white as I gripped my knees. "Fuck!" Why was this happening to me?!

Being bitten, and the awful aftermath of that attack, had been literally the darkest and lowest point of my life. Or so I'd thought then. I was willing to reassess that because I now knew better. There was nothing in this life worse than knowing I was responsible for stealing an innocent life. Nothing worse than robbing someone's son or daughter from them. Those tears that fell in that moment, there on my mother's spaghetti-stained living room carpet, were the most pitiful I'd ever shed. The most guilt-ridden and miserable. And I was completely alone. Yet again. Always alone.

About an hour later I woke with a start, hearing Mom's Nissan pull into the driveway. Hurriedly I rubbed the traces of dried tears from my eyes and headed to the front door to meet her. I'd been so caught up in my own misery (and rightly so) that I'd not stopped to consider what she was going through. She knew something was up with me—something deadly serious that I was being uncharacteristically taciturn about—and probably kept imagining my mangled body in that parking lot. I, however, couldn't even begin to imagine the worry of a mother. I'd have to do better by her, I decided. Then I'd somehow figure out what I was going to do to save myself. Because if she lost me…! God, I couldn't let that happen. I *would* live, if only just for her. I'd stolen Andy from his parents, but I wouldn't rob Mom of her only child.

Just on the other side of the door, I heard her, an uncharacteristically high pitch to her voice as she chatted in the driveway to my gran.

Feeling a little more comforted by my newfound determination, I pulled the door open, never in a million years expecting to see my wayward boyfriend on the other side. Yet there Tristan stood like a guardian angel at my threshold. I gaped at him as fierce emotion swept through my body in trembling waves of shock and immobilizing relief.

He and Mom were standing on the porch, Mom's key poised at the door. "Look who I found in our driveway!" she said brightly, her anxious smile notwithstanding.

"I came here straight from the airport," he said, thumb gesturing to the black rental on the curb.

It was all I could do not to pounce on him like a starved kitten, but I was very aware of Mom's probing eyes and I suddenly had no idea how to act. I sensed the same churning emotion in Tristan. After a tense pause, and without warning, he pulled me into a fierce hug (disregarding my mother's keen regard) and pressed an unyielding kiss to the side of my head. "I tried to call you last night," he murmured in my ear. "And again this morning." He leaned away and fixed me with a dark look. "Does no one answer their fu—" he threw a sidelong look at my mother and hastily aborted that particular expletive "—their phones anymore?"

My sentiments exactly!

"I'll just give you two a minute," said Mom, brushing past us with a mischievous curl of her lips, dragging my clueless grandmother in behind her.

"It was nice meeting you both, Mrs. Spencer." Tristan's brow unfurled a small degree as he glanced first at my mother and then, with a civil nod, at my gran. "Ma'am."

"You too, Tristan. And please call me Aloma." Mom paused under the lintel a moment, her bottom lip caught between her teeth. "Are you staying for dinner?" she inquired with a wink at me.

Tristan, in turn, looked to me for an answer, his head cocking adorably to the side. Well, as adorable as a stormy werewolf could look. Although I'd never been happier to see him, it was disconcerting the way his black brows sat severely over his eyes.

Did he know about Andy? Did he hate me as much as I already hated myself? Just like that, the fleeting moment of relief and solace I'd found in his arms (thinking I was now saved and could possibly allow myself a moment's peace and happiness) disappeared with a splash of proverbial ice water. These extreme ups and downs of werewolf emotions would be the death of me.

Mom cleared her throat expectantly.

"Evan?" Tristan prompted me. "Am I staying for dinner?"

"Yes." I turned to look over my shoulder at my mom's knowing grin. "Yes, he's staying." *Forever.* I needed him. I was never leaving his side again.

Once Mom had closed the door behind her (both to keep the air-conditioning in and to give us some privacy) Tristan instantly stole my breath with a kiss so passionate that it momentarily stilled my heart and muted my brain. His one hand was splayed on the side of my jaw as his teeth grazed my lower lip. The other hand was pressed firmly to my back. "You haven't been eating properly," he said, his tone gruff. "I can feel your bones sticking out."

Was that what had put the frown on his brow? "I'm sorry." He had no idea just how sorry I was.

"I should have come sooner," he murmured against the corner of my mouth. "I've missed you."

I breathed his woodsy scent deep into my lungs to steady myself. "I tried to call you!" I dropped my forehead on his chest.

"When did you call?" He lifted my face, studying my features gravely. The bruises and scratches had healed completely from his face except for one almost imperceptible scar below his chin.

I knew now that he'd probably been in the air when I'd called earlier. Feeling self-conscious, I only shrugged.

"I've been waiting for you to call me for weeks," he said pointedly. "Trust me, I'd have known if you'd tried. Remember, *you* wanted space. Not me."

I shook my head. This was all beside the point. "Tristan I…I need to tell you something." My throat thickened with misery.

"You're worried about tonight. I know." He kissed my temple. "Don't be, I won't let anything—"

"No!" I ripped my chin from his fingers. "You don't get it." With a furtive look at the door, I lowered my voice so that only he could hear me. "It happened already."

Tristan stilled, eyes narrowing. "What?"

"Yeah. Last night." My words were almost inaudible, my voice quavering.

"Fuck." Jaw clenching, he dragged a frustrated hand roughly down his face before scrutinizing me again. "Did anything—"

"I killed someone." Abruptly, I threw myself against his chest, my words muffled against his shirtfront so I wouldn't have to see his disgust. Beneath my fingers, his muscles were tensed with shock. "I killed Andy!"

39

HARVEST MOON

"Evan." Tristan's hands gently, yet firmly, pushed me back so that he could search my face. "Are you sure?"

Hiccuping miserably, I nodded. "I was furious at him. I remember leaving the cafe. My blood was boiling. Literally. And then"—with effort, I swallowed the rising panic back down—"I changed. It wasn't supposed to happen so soon!"

"Do you remember the attack?"

"No. Should I?"

His palms moved to knead roughly at his eyes. "Sometimes. You become more aware as you mature. I just thought maybe you'd recall something."

"I woke up covered in blood. A lot of blood, Tristan."

The skin at his eyes tightened frighteningly. He swiped at his phone screen and then lifted it to his ear, hand grasping anxiously at the back of his head. However, there was no answer. "Fuck," he muttered. "Does no one answer their fucking phones?" He then began texting hurriedly.

The gravity in his tone, and the fucks that had ensued, horrified me as not even his blackest rage would have. "I thought I only had to worry about changing on the full moon. Why—"

"You'll be volatile for some years, Ev." He looked up from his phone, a broody set to his jaw. "Add stress or temper to the mix and you'd easily undergo an early change if the moon's full enough. It won't take much to set you off…" Not once had he said I told you so, though it was implied in the silence that followed. He'd warned me more than once not to leave Thorne Bay. So had his brother.

Who the hell was he texting? I peeked at the screen. Alex? "What now?"

"Hell if I know." But he bent his eyes to his phone again and began scrolling the favorites list. "You need to tell your mom you want to head back to Alaska. Tonight."

"What? No! My Mom—"

"Evan." His expression turned thunderous. "We are in a whole hell of a lot of shit, don't you get that? You can't stay here! We're *both* leaving. Now. Non-negotiable."

He'd never spoken to me this way. At first, I was too shocked to move, too taken aback by his fulminating glare and harsh tone.

"Am I or am I not your alpha?" he asked with deceptive quietude.

A thrill of alarm and adrenaline-soaked lust swelled suddenly in my core. I'd never seen this side of him. Or if I had, that glint of warning, of wrathful heat, had never been directed at me. Not until now.

The acquiescence in my gaze was answer enough. He gave a curt nod and then pressed his phone expectantly to his ear, the ringing sounding discordant somehow. A motorcycle sped by and a dog barked nearby, but I stood impotently beneath that intense chartreuse glare, deaf to all else but him. "Dean," said Tristan when his brother answered, "we have a problem."

"No, *you* have a fucking problem," came Dean's deep familiar timbre. "I told you—"

"So you've heard?"

"Everyone's fucking heard! The Council's on the rampage."

Tristan's mouth tightened grimly. "How'd they find out? It only just happened."

"Doesn't matter." There was something of both dread and sympathy in Dean's voice that further sickened me. "You need to get both your asses back here. Now."

"Already got Alex booking our tickets." With an impatient jerk of his head, Tristan gestured for me to get packing.

Normally, I'd have gotten my dander up at his uncharacteristic peremptory tone, but these were extenuating circumstances. His wolf was very near the surface, and I took the warning instantly to heart, nodding acquiescently. There was time enough later, if I survived, to bark back at him.

At least I'd not been forsaken. The second most awful feeling in the world (after manslaughter) was oppressive, maddening solitude. I'd been surrounded with familial love all month and had never felt more alone. My dark secret isolated me completely. But now Tristan was here!

I left Tristan on my porch, brainstorming with Dean, as I slipped indoors, still unsure of what exactly I was going to say to Mom. Explaining my sudden departure to an already fretful and histrionic mother was going to be extremely awkward. I'd need a good bullshit story, and the only one I believed she'd accept was one in which I professed desperate and irrational love. *That* she *would* understand perfectly—she'd fallen victim to it enough times herself. I'd explain that I'd been acting so out of character because of how much I'd been missing Tristan (true enough). And here he was, finally, demanding that I return with him (no lie there either). I'd just tell her I was terrified of the monstrous bear on the loose and that Tristan was taking me away till the 'animal' was caught. We'd leave tonight. She'd find it odd and rash, but incredibly romantic.

A beautifully fabricated bit of bullshit, I thought with a satisfied nod, sprinting upstairs.

"I don't know where the hell she is!" Tristan's growled response was too low for human ears, but I caught his words easily enough despite the ambient noise of the street. "She's not answering her phone…" His conversation receded as he stalked off to pace in my driveway.

Briefly, I wondered who they were referring to, but as I hesitated outside my mother's bedroom door, my thoughts were instantly refocused on my looming deception. The sooner this was done the sooner I would be on a plane back to Thorne Bay where I couldn't hurt anyone else.

"Did you hate him?"

"Huh?" I'd been staring out the window, distracted by somber thoughts and passing shadows. Tearing my eyes away from the black woods towering over the lonely road, I peered around to study Tristan's obscured profile.

"Did you hate Andy?" he asked again.

"No!" Aghast, I glared back out the window. We'd spoken very little since leaving West Palm Beach, each of us lost in our own gloomy thoughts. Now that we were minutes away from pulling into Dean's driveway, the tension inflamed.

I could feel Tristan's eyes probe me in the darkness. "So why did you kill him?"

"I don't know!" My eyes heated with fresh tears. "I was hoping you could tell me that." Then again, I wasn't sure I was ready to hear him say he'd been mistaken and that I actually *was* rabid.

"Did you want to hurt him?"

"I don't know. Maybe." I shook my head, confused. "I overheard him say some hurtful things." The answer to his first question, though, was unequivocally no. I hadn't wanted Andy dead, not even in a blind rage. "But I didn't hate him, Tristan, and I didn't want him dead. No life is mine to take. Clearly, though, I can't control the mutt inside me."

After a thoughtful silence, Tristan said, "So you think your wolf is a disparate entity? Your own Mr. Hyde?"

It wasn't lost on me that this was a comparison I'd used before. "Yes, she is." She was a stranger that terrified me as no other could.

"No, Evan. It's nothing like split personalities. You never disappear, you just become more primal. That's essentially you in there underneath the fur. Your skin changes, not you."

"Then why did I kill Andy?" I sobbed. We were going around in circles here. "You said I'm not rabid!"

"You're not." He gave a dreary shrug. "The only thing that makes sense is that you must have hated him. Your wolf is just a magnification of all your most powerful and primitive emotions, but she'd never act against your basic nature or contrary to your desires. She *is* you."

"Then clearly my wiring's all fucked up!" I lifted my hands up as though I could still see them imbrued with blood. "I killed an innocent man. That makes me a rabid mutt!"

Abruptly, he pulled his truck over to the edge of the road. "Evan, look at me."

When I'd finally fastened my watery gaze to him, he pulled my hands to his mouth and kissed my knuckles tenderly. The red haze dissipated from my gaze.

"The only fucked up thing here is what Nicole did to you," he said. "But not for a single moment have I questioned who you are. You've always been honest, and quirky, and beautiful, and kind. That was all I saw in the eyes of the beautiful wolf you became that night you first changed. You were in there. I know you're not rabid."

"You don't think I'm damaged?" I asked in a small voice. "Promise?"

"Never have I ever. And I have *never* met someone like you." Citrine flared in his eyes, warm and sincere, as he leaned closer. "I love you, Evan. To me, there is no woman more perfect than you."

"What?" *This* I had not expected. That such a simple and heartfelt confession was powerful enough to strip me bare, and touch my soul, was staggering.

"I love you." He kissed me then, lips in fierce espousal of his claim. A kiss that left no doubt of his feelings. After a hot minute, he pulled away. His breathing was as ragged as mine. "Even if we have to run away and live like strays, I won't let the Council hurt you. You're mine. And I was yours the moment you spewed granola at me." Playful, yet no less genuine, he kissed me again.

Unable to help the giddiness that burbled from my lips, I laughed. "You love me?" I ran my tongue tentatively over my lips, wanting to savor his revelation as much as his beautiful kiss.

"I do." He smiled gently.

I tried not to feel unworthy or afraid. "I love you too, Tristan." Even so, I felt my brow pucker with dread.

"What is it?" His expression quickly mirrored mine.

"Nothing sane attacks what it loves, Tristan." I'd almost done to him what I'd succeeded in doing to Andy. "What's wrong with me?"

"You've never hurt me." Tristan kissed my brow and then tucked my head under his chin. "Not on purpose."

Confused, I blinked up at him, tracing my finger over that scar at his jaw. A testament to the violence I was capable of. "You're sure of that?"

"Self-preservation—you thought I was attacking *you.* Maybe

you didn't at first recognize my musk. Maybe the forest reeked of the others and it all overpowered your keener senses and threw you into confusion. I dunno." He gave a wry sigh. "Evan, the first change is the most traumatic. None more so than yours. Your instinct was to fight and get away, but I knocked you from the road and held you down. Of course you attacked me, any threatened wolf would have." His thumb brushed the corner of my mouth. "But you also saved me from that grizzly. You made that bear your bitch."

Well, I'd been mostly human then. "I didn't know you were conscious for that?"

He shrugged. "Only just."

I was still so deeply reviled at myself despite that he adamantly downplayed my assault. "I wish I was conscious of what happened with Andy." Or maybe (like when I'd attacked Tristan) it was better that I didn't retain any egregious full moon memories.

"Me too." Suddenly Tristan was reaching for his phone again, but this time the line went straight to an automated voicemail. He growled in frustration.

"Who do you keep trying to call?" I'd meant to ask him this earlier.

"Lydia."

"Why?"

"Because she was told to watch over you until you—"

"What?!" I'd been inundated with so many odd sensations since my first change that I'd completely disregarded the feelings of being watched as nothing but wolfy paranoia—a result of cutting myself off from the pack. "You had me spied on?"

"No, I had you protected; I promised you you'd never be alone again. You needed space from us, I get that, but until you can control the change I had to placate the others somehow. Dean wouldn't have let you go otherwise."

I was trying not to get my knickers in a knot, but I couldn't help feeling affronted that he'd arranged to have me followed without even warning me. "The others?"

"The Council Of Alphas."

That sounded pretty official. I clamped my bottom lip thoughtfully between my teeth. "Oh." *Still...*

"I couldn't watch you myself since I knew it was me you wanted space from, so I sent Lydia. I know you like and trust her more than the others." With one more last disgusted look at his phone, Tristan chucked it in the center console, a gruff sigh issuing into the darkness as he leaned back against his headrest. In the gloaming, his pensive gaze suddenly took on an eerie incandescence as it settled on me. "How do you feel right now?"

Confused, I lifted a shoulder diffidently. *Well, considering I'm a mutt with anger issues...* "Fine, I guess."

"No pains?" he asked pointedly. "No weird sensations?"

My eyes shifted past him to the bloated moon mounting the jagged horizon. The last time I'd looked up at a full moon it had been with canine eyes. Beautiful as it was, the moon filled me with dread and humility. Though there was no sharp, foreboding migraine gathering in my skull, I still perceived a deep hum of power radiating straight to my bones. "I feel...I feel strange." Brooding, I looked back at him. "But there's no pain."

Tristan's mouth quirked in that boyish way that always left my heart stuttering. It was kind of an inappropriate time to be amused, what with the Council of Alphas' wrath hanging over me like the Sword of Damocles. There had, however, been nothing blithe about his brief half-smile. There had been something almost wistful in that left dimple. Something sad. "We have tonight, Evan. Come morning, everything will change, and not necessarily for the better." He leaned in closer so that his breath fell like silk against my lips. "Wanna steal a moment in time for ourselves?"

"What do you mean?"

"Pretend we're the only people in the world and that tomorrow will never intrude."

I nodded slowly, completely seduced by the moonbeams filling the hush, and utterly lost in the amber flecks pulsing amidst the lambent green of my lover's otherworldly eyes.

"Wanna try and change on your own?"

It took me a moment to comprehend his meaning, but when I did I leaned back, wary. "Shift? Like now?"

"Like right now," he said, taking a teasing nip at my bottom lip.

"I thought you said it would take me years before I could shift at will?"

"This cycle's different—you've already peaked." He paused to search for a better explanation. "You've vented the steam and now there's no more pressure; but the moon's still full, so it should happen easily enough if you try. The real challenge is learning to shift out of cycle. *That's* what takes a while to master."

"It hurts, though." That was an understatement.

"The first time always does. It's awful for everyone, and its worse for those like you."

I twisted my hair nervously around my finger. What he was suggesting was surely tantamount to asking a woman to go through childbirth again hours after she'd already pushed triplets out. Without an epidural! Madness.

"It won't hurt if you don't fight it. Try, Evan." He gently kissed the base of my neck near where I knew the silver scars of the bite were just barely visible. The same scars I'd taken pains to hide from my mother. "Please. For me."

"I don't know how. I hate myself, Tristan. I hate what I've done. I'm a monster!"

"Stop it." His voice lowered with unsuppressed anger. "You're innocent until proven guilty. Flip the switch, Evan. You have to conceptualize the world through a new paradigm. Like a Gestalt shift—change your perception. Tonight. Right now."

"I don't know if I can." I was trembling.

"Then let me have your guilt." The yellow in his eyes flickered in the dark. "Let me worry about tomorrow. Learn to let go, or it'll drive you mad. Compartmentalize. Flip the switch," he said again. "Right now. For tonight at least let's be the Tristan and Evan of old."

Though my gut clenched fearfully, I finally relented and gave him an uncertain nod. I had to trust that he knew what he was asking me to do. God knew I wanted to shift my perception—I hated hating myself even more than I hated what I'd done to Andy. "Okay. I'll try."

No sooner had I uttered my assent than Tristan shifted the truck into gear, the tires protesting as he sped back onto the road. There was a determined edge of excitement in his mien. The miles we ate up stretched quietly as I glared with distrust at the moon. Unexpectedly, Tristan veered onto an overgrown track that might once have been a dirt road or a hidden driveway, the trees serried and darker here. The adumbrative foliage brushed ardently at the passing truck like eager black tongues drawing us into the otherworld. He parked his truck deep in the woods, the stillness of the witching hour creeping in as he killed the engine and opened his door.

"How do I…?" The theory of *werewolfing* was simple enough, but now that it was time for me to actually shift on my own, I was lost as to how I might flick the physical switch. The mental shift I was still working on.

Understanding my plight, Tristan ran a confident finger down the buttons of my shirtfront. "Start by undressing, beautiful."

I looked pointedly at the woods around us and then narrowed my eyes at him. "Is this some kind of freaky werewolf porno?"

He winked and pulled his shirt off. "It could be…"

Since we were, after all, stealing time and reality couldn't obtrude here in our stolen midnight bubble, I gave a loud wolf whistle (like the Evan of yore would have done) and feasted my gaze on his powerful sinews, forcing the weight of my woes to the outback of my troubled psyche.

Now completely naked, Tristan fixed wolfen eyes to me and waited. "Your turn."

When my clothes had been piled atop his, I shrugged self-consciously and averted my face back to the moon. "Now what?"

"Now," he said, moving to run his fingers softly over my midriff and up my sternum to my neck, "you welcome it in."

Something intoxicating and electrifying gathered and thrummed in the air between us. Whatever primitive emanation it was that murmured into me, whether from the moon or the heat of the werewolf beside me, it stirred a dark fever in my blood.

"You've resisted it till now." His silken tone only kindled my desire all the more. His nose flared, drawing my scent in, as preternatural eyes bored into mine, his chest rising and falling with increasing rapidity. An unrestrained passion billowed—the desperate want of flesh (my flesh) and the need to answer the moon's call. "You've hated and distrusted it."

"Yes." It was more a groan than a simple word. Already my voice was guttural like his.

"But not tonight." Tristan backed away from me suddenly, the cold biting where his spicy warmth had disappeared. "No more fighting it. Now you draw it in. Embrace it." And then he was running into the woods with one last challenging smirk over his shoulder. "Unless you'd rather wait here…like prey?"

"What?" The wilderness had already swallowed him up, and only the trees caught my glare. "Tristan!"

I was uncertain whether or not he was giving me privacy to change or if he was unwilling to shift in front of me just yet, worried that I'd been conditioned to fear the sight since *Lupum*

Caedes. Either way, he'd be back in one form or another and I didn't want to remain here naked and meek. I was sick to death of feeling uprooted. With a bolstering shake of my head, climbing down from the truck, I took a deep breath. Then I lifted my face to the moonlight peering through the canopy.

"Okay then"—gesturing the moon over with a dubious crook of my fingers—"come at me, bro."

At first, nothing happened, and the gooseflesh rippling over my skin was nothing more than the brush of the falling temperature, a sensual, momentary night whisper. But at length, I felt an answering pulse beat surging from my core. I let it coalesce and expand, ignoring the panic that threatened to do the same. This time, the pain came in pleasurable and undulating spells as I let it perfuse my body. For a brief moment, I was compelled to fight it, an unconscious impulse, and the pain spiked sharply and instantly—a slap to curb my remonstrance. I took another deep, calming gulp of air and opened myself up to it again, drawing in that argent power nudging at my periphery, pulling firmly at my bones and plucking at my muscles with invisible fingers.

The sounds of the insects and the night birds magnified so that every voice became distinct and multifaceted. The verdurous colors of the forest rushed over me and swelled into me as I gasped with the fullness of it. I felt my skin erupt with hair. Felt my teeth protract from my gums with numbing, copper-soaked jolts. My jaws shifted and lengthened to make room for the growing fangs and my nails became black as they jutted into the earth. Then, with an almighty popping and rippling, my chest burst with a euphoric animalistic cry before, finally, I collapsed to the ground in a sated mass of fangs and fur.

Tonight's transformation had been nothing like my last. My eyes dropped to the fierce-looking black paws beneath me, so much larger than a wolf's. I turned my head around to my powerful flanks and obsidian pelt, mesmerized by the changes wrought by the harvest moon, and amused by the little patch of white over my heart. More than anything, I was elated and relieved to be myself. Perhaps not physiologically but certainly cognitively. Without the trauma of fighting the change, there had been no blackout. In fact, there had been considerably less pain, likely due to the analgesic hormones that had flooded my blood right before I'd started shifting.

For the first time since Nicole stole my humanity, I felt a newborn flicker of unadulterated excitement and confidence, as of a young wolf set free from her cage. My self-loathing and fear had impounded her for so long now, murderer that I was. I acknowledged the insidious sting of guilt with a whine. After all, I didn't deserve to feel happy. But I'd promised to let go, so I surrendered all those useless trammels to the night, giving in to the frisking spirit of my primal self, trusting her. She wanted to be free if only just for one night. Unfettered, I hurtled into the hemlock woodland to find my mate.

I could smell him and I knew he sensed me too. That earthy lupine musk was beckoning me into his lair. I could feel him waiting for me.

40

LOVE AND DEATH

Tristan had made it easy for me to find him. I heard him before I saw him. He was twisting playfully on his back like a great black grizzled shepherd, grunting in pleasure as I loped onto the scene. Having noticed me, he stilled his supine back-scratching and grinned that wolfish, upside-down grin, tongue lolling out between long white fangs. Infused with moonlight, his eyes appeared more yellow than cerulean green. Wolf yellow—a dead giveaway that he was either furious or lustful. Tonight my bet was on the latter. Though the creature before me looked nothing like Tristan, the spice of its scent was unmistakably his.

The fur around his muzzle was far darker than the rest of his head and his gleaming black mane was shot through with chestnut and sable. The fur directly over his spine was a little longer than the rest of his torso and matched his mane except that it was brindled with inky streaks. But the browns gradually faded over his flanks so that the majority of his coat was as stygian as the night that cloaked us.

Edging closer, I sampled that fascinating musk that was no longer diluted by distance. It was divinely masculine. Tristan gave a waggish grunt as he rolled onto his belly to watch me. He was so much like a bear in proportions, from that stumpy tail to those massive shoulders. All except his head. *That* was far more canine in physiognomy. Not for a moment could he be mistaken for one or the other, at least not in good daylight. To look at him was to know you were seeing something impossible. The paws were too simian, as was the intelligence burning in his otherworldly eyes. Whether or not one was familiar with the word, you couldn't help but know, deep down in your bones, that you were looking at a werewolf. And this werewolf was studying me just as avidly as I examined him. There was a patient curiosity in his body language that beguiled me into playfulness.

I closed the distance and pushed my muzzle into his shaggy neck before running my head along his shoulders, down his ribs and over his flanks like a large cat. He, in turn, began to do the same to me. Unlike me, I knew that Tristan would be just as comfortable standing on hind legs, but he remained on all fours like a lovable shepherd, relishing my affection.

Unexpectedly, I felt his teeth graze mischievously over my ear and then my foreleg, tugging and nipping until I reciprocated in turn. Soon we were scuffling and wrestling on the damp earth like children, each vying for the upper hand. Finding myself continuously outmaneuvered by Tristan's colossal bulk (in spite of it really), I took the first opportunity to bolt away. He, of course, bounded after me with long, eager strides. I was convinced, though, that my speed (seeing as I was so much rangier) would be far superior to his and that I would easily outpace him in a race. However, I soon discovered that Tristan's muscles had been honed for speed for far longer than mine had and he expertly cut me off, as though I was some yearling doe, swiping me off balance. We tumbled headlong down a small hill into a bank of dead leaves, yipping heartily as we continued to play.

Never had I ever felt so alive and free. No shadow of looming tragedy could touch me here in this magical dell. No judgment could penetrate the thick canopies shielding our lively antics. The moon, at least for tonight, cloistered and possessed us. We were just two souls discovering one heart's twin in the other, familiarizing ourselves with all the beautiful scents and textures of the other's body.

We hunted. We rested curled up tight against each other so that we appeared as one creature. But we were too unruly to remain still for long, so we resumed our playing again till the small hours of the morning. By now, there were amorous undertones to our capering that waxed even as the moon dropped below the trees. The bites became more sensual and the nuzzling more heated. My blood burned for him as intensely in this body as it did in my lesser, naked flesh.

Tristan pinioned me to the forest floor with weighty forepaws, licking the side of my face as I squirmed provocatively. From my throat erupted dulcet canine purrs that were instantly matched by his deeper, male resonance. I closed my eyes and felt my body writhe and undulate as our heavy panting muffled the romance of the night and the crickets still playing their dark violins. My muscles shivered and trembled underneath him as he ran a long, red tongue over my belly, the hair there rapidly falling away beneath the hot strokes.

Then I was naked again, the night air rushing against me where, moments before, there had been a thick coarse pelt. When I opened my eyes, it was a human-looking Tristan that loomed over me, grinning wickedly. Human-looking except for his long teeth and burning eyes. His canines had not yet lost their predatory edges, and nor had they retracted out of view. Far from being disturbed by the sight, I felt my womb clench with excitement. My need for him was a powerful impulse that blotted out all my former, human timidity. Grabbing him firmly behind his neck, I pulled him down flush against my breasts and delved his mouth with hungry strokes. This seemed to precipitate Tristan into a lustful frenzy. His kisses became almost painful, gloriously so, as he devoured me. I knew that, had I been less than superhuman, I'd have been black and blue by morning. This new body welcomed the violence and fervency of our lovemaking. It craved the feral edge of each hungry, bruising kiss he bestowed.

Iron fingers thrust their way along my ribs and anchored themselves to my hips as he roughly nudged my thighs apart. I growled, pleasure-soaked, as he dragged his canines over my jaw and closed them over my neck. Not hard enough to break the skin, though, only to mark me with shameless passion. Lost in my own delirium, I clawed at his back and bit at his own neck, bent on tasting every inch of him too. When the faint hint of copper infused my mouth I realized, belatedly, that my teeth and claws, like Tristan's, were also still preternaturally sharp. I gentled my biting after that, but only marginally.

Surprising him suddenly, I pushed Tristan to the side and onto his back so that I could climb on top of him. From this vantage point, I felt sensuous. Inordinate feminine power seemed to hum in my breast as he gazed up at me with molten eyes. I tossed my head back as he pressed a hot palm to each tender breast, his kneading no longer as rough as before. The way he drank me in, thumbing my peaked nipples, gaze awed and primed with unrestrained lust, only served to heighten my own ravening appetite. It was the work of a second to lift myself up and onto his steely length. Then, with exquisite and deliberate languor, I sank down onto him. His breath hissed out, torrid with the effort of holding himself still, his fingers gouging deeper into my hips, though his claws were retracted. I could feel his sinews bunching with latent, savage energy. I moved with long strokes up and down his iron body, grinding with a slowness that was in desperate contrast to the heady ferocity that had gripped us before.

Finally, having withstood it as long as he was able, Tristan assumed the lead, infusing our lovemaking with bestial passion. It was all I could do to hold on as he bucked fiercely beneath me. Soon I was matching his rhythm, riding his untamed wolf up a jagged incline as the pressure built and vibrated between us. It was a fierce mating. Teeth and claws were once more employed to rake and taste.

That glorious knot between my thighs began to tighten and pulse as I moved against him. It became so overwhelming that I cried out, giving voice to the release that radiated from our joined bodies. My body was seized with a blinding palsy so vibrant and all-consuming that once the violent climax ebbed from my core, leaving me shaken and raw, I nearly fainted. Tristan, having already undergone his own debilitating release, caught me to him as he sat up.

We sat like that for ages, my legs clamped tightly around his lean waist as he held me close. We were so deeply connected that any words spoken just then would have felt profane. The silence was profound and resonant—a pause in time. No two beings could've been any closer and yet I'd have pulled him nearer, and deeper, if I could have. I'd have fused my soul to his. Maybe I just had.

"I love you," he said into the stillness, voice still gruff and primal.

I tightened my arms around him, feeling overmastered by the intensity of what I felt for him. Love seemed too tame a word for what connected us. I could define it only as pure and transcendent —I'd give my life for him without a moment's hesitation.

We dozed after that, waking every now and then to slake our hunger again and again. By dawn, I was finally, utterly, beauteously depleted. Neither the rocks poking my shoulder or the twigs spearing my flanks could induce me to move away from Tristan's side. My head was nestled peacefully at his shoulder, my arm was thrown over his abdomen, and our legs were locked in a lover's knot. The indigo sky was already quickening with lilac.

As before, nothing worried me here, cocooned as I was by Tristan's protective warmth. Not even the possibility of puppies.

I almost giggled at the thought. I'd asked him about *that* after another bout of exuberant lovemaking. We'd been at it enough times to repopulate the earth ten times over with were-kids. But he'd laughed, unconcerned, and assured me matter-of-factly that I wasn't ovulating. That awkward conversation still replaying in my head, I drifted into a deep sleep as the birds began to rouse themselves from their aerial beds.

"Evan." Tristan's fingers, though gentle, were insistent as he tightened them on my hip. "Evan," he said again, this time a little louder, adding a small shake for good measure.

I muttered incoherently and lifted one heavy eyelid. When his face swam into focus, I became instantly alert, disturbed by the wary tightness around his eyes. He wasn't looking at me but past my shoulder. "What time is it?" I pushed myself upright.

But before Tristan could answer, I became aware of an unfamiliar scent obtruding our privacy. At the very same moment, a stranger cleared his throat. My head nearly flew off my shoulders, I turned it so quickly, recoiling at the sight of not one but *two* men in our midst: Dean and a stern-looking stranger.

It was the latter's cold voice that answered me instead. "Time, Miss Spencer, to get up."

My hands, by this time, had already flown up to shield my chest from his frigid gaze, but the man was far more interested in blasting Tristan with uncanny cyan eyes than noticing my meager breasts. A cyanide gaze, I thought morbidly.

"You've both wasted enough of my time." That said, he gave us his broad back and stalked past Dean who had, all the while, been leaning impassively against a tree.

"You could've warned us," Tristan grumbled at his brother, helping me up before distractedly pulling leaves out of my hair.

Dean shrugged inscrutably. "Yeah"—with a roll of his eyes —"because Max definitely would've listened if I'd told him to stay put while I sniffed your ass out."

"Wait!" My face blanched as I looked back and forth between the brothers, my nakedness forgotten. "*That* was your dad?" Awkward!

"No," said Dean. "That's Tristan's dad. I don't have one." Then, like his estranged father before him, he marched off too, leaving us to make our way back to the truck and into our clothes.

I for one was burning with mortification, but Tristan's mood seemed to vacillate between brooding reticence and tangible unease, though I couldn't tell if the unease was because of his father's displeasure (somehow I doubted this) or because he sensed something awful brewing in our immediate future. At any rate, we reached Dean's house all too soon, the grounds were packed with unfamiliar cars. The place was evidently overrun with wolves, and that did *not* bode well for me. Once the engine had been silenced, neither one of us appeared in any rush to meet the inevitable.

"Dean looks a lot like Max," I said into the quiet.

"Don't tell him that."

Tristan likely resembled his mother in all but the eyes. Those he definitely shared with his father. But Max's were a more glacial shade, whereas Tristan's greens and blues were flecked with golden warmth. In fact, I could still feel Max's glare cutting over me like honed, dry ice. Shivering, I reached for Tristan's hand.

He lifted my fingers to his lips. "We better get this over with."

"Or we could just run away?" I suggested hopefully.

Just then, as if my whispered words had been heard, the door flew open and Max prowled out onto the front porch. “Well?” he asked pointedly, voice stentorian and curt.

He’d definitely been listening out for Tristan’s truck, I decided. Thick, corded arms were folded thunderously over his chest as he waited. The guy was even tetchier than my grandad.

My stomach quickly filled with dread. Max was an imposing man of an indeterminate age, though the hint of grey at his temples and the deep furrows at his brow were attestation enough of his seniority. Of his primacy. Not for the first time, I wondered about Tristan’s age.

Not wanting to appear meek, I tried to emulate Tristan’s steely calm. Saying nothing, he gave my hand a squeeze. His other hand was poised to open the door, but Dean’s sudden emergence onto the porch forestalled him. The expression Dean wore had stilled my hand too. I’d never seen him like this. Cedar eyes stared starkly at us, haggard and bleak as Death itself.

“Something’s wrong,” Tristan whispered, frowning, his hand tightening on mine before he released me altogether and threw open his door. It certainly seemed as though something had happened in the space it had taken us to dress ourselves and drive to the house.

Side by side, we proceeded to the waiting alphas, Tristan’s quiet gravitas anything but submissive or fearful. My heart, however, thundered with dread. I ascended the steps and met Max’s brittle gaze and then Dean’s red eyes with affected steadiness.

Without preamble, though, Max immediately shattered my poise into a million tiny pieces. “Lydia’s dead,” he said grimly. Seeing that both Tristan and I had been dealt a crippling blow to the gut, he gestured us inside with a peremptory nod. “Step inside, Miss Spencer. You and I have a lot to talk about.”

41

AIRWOLF

A lusty fire snapped and roiled along the red cedar logs glowing in the grate, but Dean's library was eerily cold and stifling this morning. This was still far preferable to—far warmer than—the frigid atmosphere in the living room. Of all the baleful glares that had left their kerfs across my burning face (and there had been many, most of whom had been direful Yukon strangers), James' had penetrated deepest. I felt his condemning eyes the keenest—I had, after all, killed his twin. With her death on my hands, I'd forever lost what tentative esteem I'd had in Dean's pack. If Dean himself had not been standing behind James, his heavy paw on the man's shoulder, I was sure James would have flown at me with claws and fangs. His body had trembled with violence as I passed them by.

The cold, quiet click of the library door shutting behind me, therefore, had been oddly welcome. Only for a very brief moment, though. The glares of the wolves in the mural, on the wall behind Dean's desk, quickly took up where the others' had left off, leering knowingly at me. Hatefully.

God, these people were not, and had never been, subtle at all. The place was rife with wolfy paraphernalia. It shouldn't have taken a bite to force me to see what had always been glaring right under my nose. That surely said something about human cynicism and happy ignorance. No one believed in much of anything anymore, let alone Sasquatch and werewolves. Things that were different and inexplicable were resolutely disregarded. Squelched. The world was full of happy idiots. But I was no longer ignorant of the paranormal. There were indeed monsters in the world and I had proven myself the worst of them.

"Your presence, Tristan, isn't required here." Max had been surveying the grounds outside the library window with a critical eye. Now that captious gaze was pinned to me as he seated himself at Dean's heavy walnut desk.

"Noted," Tristan drawled, clearly having no intention of leaving me.

His father's stern brow fell lower still. "Am I to understand you feel somehow responsible for the girl?"

"You are to understand that exactly."

Dean and I were the only two who had yet to speak, my eyes volleying back and forth between the frosty interlocutors. Other than a brief flash of irritation, when his father had seated himself at his desk, Dean, for his part, had remained silently cold and inscrutable.

"You'd better not be implying—" through gritted fangs "—what I think you're implying, son." The guy could barely pass for human.

"With respect, *sir,* there's no implication. It's done. We're mated."

That sounded so official. Was it like marriage? Lydia had hinted as much. I mean, I knew we'd mated biblically, but I had a feeling that, in the language of werewolves, *being* mated (and everything it entailed) meant so much more than just the physical aspect. Yet Tristan had stated this in such a contumelious way that

I was hardly flattered by the declaration. I would make sure Tristan explained this to me later.

Max, meanwhile, instead of erupting into a rage and forbidding the match, shifted that icy glare to me. "I see."

I felt my heart shrink. If ever there was a reason and a way to find me guilty and have me "put down", Max had clearly just "seen" it during his uncanny examination of me. Through one exterminating look alone, he made absolutely no secret of the fact that he found me unworthy of his son.

"Ironic," he went on with a low grunt, scrutinizing both sons. "One son aimed too high and the other too low."

This remark, though casually dropped (or so it seemed), appeared to have dealt the wounds it had been marked to hit. Even the stony-faced Dean flinched. For the first time since I'd known him, his face burned with shame, but he set his teeth and said nothing. I understood the reference as it pertained to Tristan (given I was a lowly mutt), but who had Dean aimed "too high" for?

Tristan's teeth ground together furiously. "Only you would value power over love."

"And duty," his father snapped. "Where do you place your duty, son?"

"First and foremost, I have a duty to the woman I love. Unlike my father."

"An alpha," Max gritted out, "does not have the luxury of acting like a love-struck puppy. He has responsibilities—"

"To his family first!"

"The pack *is* the family!" Max roared, coming out of his chair like a raging bear.

"But the support and love of a life-mate makes an alpha great." Tristan and his father now stood nose to nose, ice seething against fire, their teeth bared in mirrored snarls of warning. Had I really likened Tristan's eyes to his father's? I was so wrong—Max's were far bluer. Far colder.

I scurried out of the way to stand beside Dean who, I knew, would be a handy shield in a werewolf brawl.

"Enough!" Dean bellowed, coming to stand between his brother and father. "Both of you sit the fuck down or get out of my house."

Without taking his eyes off his youngest, Max closed his lips over his long teeth and folded his arms across his chest. A muscle jumped menacingly at Tristan's jaw, but he backed away and lowered himself into the chair I'd vacated. With forced calm, he gestured me over. Warily, I moved past Max (forcing iron into my spine) and took the armchair beside Tristan's. His hand instantly locked over mine, his steady warmth effacing the clamminess from my palms.

"You're an idealist, Tristan. Always have been," Max growled.

"No, I just don't feed into that Aryan bullshit you do."

Max bristled, eyes falling against our linked fingers like a guillotine. From there, they traveled to my face, condemning me for being ignoble and impure.

"When I'm alpha, I won't surround myself with myopic old councilmen," Tristan went on, finally calmer. "I won't make the same mistake you made."

"No, you've already made bigger ones of your own. Even love—" his nose corrugated with disgust "—has its limits, boy."

Into this tense little scene, a stranger entered the library unannounced. He smiled an affable greeting at each of us (as though the tension wasn't a thick miasma). The grim countenances that answered him did nothing to dim those startling azure eyes. They were clear and untroubled, and stark against the cropped espresso curls framing his face. "Didn't miss anything, did I?" he said to no one in particular, shutting the door softly behind him.

"We were just getting started," Max replied, gesturing the handsome stranger into one of the armchairs.

"Good to see you, Josh," Tristan said, his face finally relinquishing its hostility. "How've you been?"

"Good, buddy," Josh replied in a mild southern drawl. He was shorter than the rest of us, but his powerful presence and easy confidence dominated the room completely. Once he was seated, his demeanor sobered a little. "Wish we were meeting under different circumstances, though."

Tristan's lips compressed as he nodded ruefully. He then introduced me to Josh and explained that when a wolf was to be cross-examined by the Council of Alphas (which, I learned, comprised of all the alphas of one particular state—mine being Alaska), a mediator from another pack, more specifically from a different state, always had to be present during each hearing so as to keep the proceedings neutrally objective.

"Is this m-my hearing?" I whispered. Suddenly, the guillotine blade was looming closer.

"An informal meeting," Max answered before promptly turning to Josh. "Have you had a chance to examine the evidence yet?"

"Nah, won't see it till Red Devil tomorrow. It's all been very hush-hush."

"What evidence?" Tristan asked suspiciously.

"Y'all know about as much as I do. All I know is that there were certain personal effects retrieved at the scene and overnighted to the Athabaskans. Clothes and suchlike, I understand."

"Retrieved by who?"

"Dunno."

My face blanched as I turned to Tristan. He considered me warily but addressed Josh and his father. "How're we supposed to plan a defense if we don't even know—"

"The truth, son." Max's interjection was sharp and almost smug. "Looks like the truth will have to set her free." Then he shrugged. "Or not."

Or set Tristan free from me, I thought darkly. The guy hadn't even tried for subtlety. I knew exactly what he hoped the outcome of my second farcical trial would be.

"How do we know the Athabaskans haven't tampered with this *evidence*?"

"Why would anyone tamper with it?" Max's curt, derisive snort visibly enraged his son, but thankfully Tristan bit his tongue. "Now," Max continued, focusing his attention back to me, "tell me what happened, and don't leave anything out."

Needless to say, my statement of the facts as I knew them filled no more than the space of a minute. And that with me stuttering and stumbling over my words. I knew nothing more than that I'd woken up covered in blood. With a full belly. An altogether damning account, and by the end of it, when I left Dean's office, I felt like a dead girl walking.

"I'm glad it's Josh mediating." Tristan kissed the side of my head as we headed up to the room I'd occupied when I was 'sick'. "He'll keep things honest."

"How do you know him?"

"Our mothers are close friends, so we saw a lot of each other growing up. He's salt of the earth, you'll see."

I nodded distractedly, my mind in ruinous turmoil. Josh could be as uncorrupted as Gandhi himself, but that didn't mean I'd survive another *Lupum Caedes*. The packs were already biased against me, and there was no way I was coming out of this alive.

Tristan halted me at the top of the stairs and pulled me in for one of his fierce kisses. "Remember what I said last night, Evan?" He pulled me just far enough away, murmuring softly so that only I could hear him. "You're mine…" There was a meaningful glint of steel in his gaze, urging me to remember the rest. *Even if we have to run away and live like strays, I won't let the Council hurt you. You're mine.*

I remembered those words vividly. He'd said them right after he'd told me he loved me. I wanted so badly to believe in them like I believed in his love for me, but I felt a heavy doom building overhead even as I gave a tiny jerk of my head to evince that I understood him. "And you're mine."

I allowed his vow to soothe me as much as it could, hoping it would sustain me through the litigative nights and days ahead. We were heading to Red Devil first thing in the morning. Once there, my fate would be in the hands of those that were already prejudiced against mutts. Moreover, there was one powerful alpha in particular (arguably *the* most powerful alpha) who would likely do whatever he could to ensure his son was never paired off with a mutt.

Even if I'd wanted to run away, I'd have never made it down the wooded driveway. Dean's house had been invaded by a werewolf army. The Yukon army—all of them as grim-faced as Max himself. There was no use in bothering. Instead, I masked my fear as best I could and was thankful that the only other occupant in the car during that short drive to the Thorn Aviation hangar, besides Tristan, was the ever impenetrable Dean.

Oddly, I was starting to find some comfort in his broody stoicism. There seemed to be very little any of us wanted to say, so we mostly kept our thoughts to ourselves. Every so often, I'd look back with a shudder, disquieted by the werewolf convoy conducting us north toward Coffman Cove as dawn burst over the trees.

I was, at first, surprised to see an unfamiliar helicopter in a dreadful camo paint scheme on the pad when we arrived, but there was no need of an explanation as to whose it was. Soon after Dean's Defender pulled up to the hangar, I watched Max, Josh, and eight other men pile into what was obviously Max's helicopter.

"A Bell 222," Dean supplied, catching my open-mouthed stare as he and Tristan preflighted.

The 222 only had two blades, though, but they were far broader than the 407's slender blades. Flying directly to Red Devil, though far more convenient, meant my doom was that much closer. I'd been pretty much comatose when I'd been rescued from Red Devil, so I had no idea how I'd made it to Dean's pack house. Well, I was about to find out how these wolves got around. Supposedly, we were about to do that fateful trip in reverse.

The 222's thundering engines were started shortly after Max climbed in. It shook the trees as its wheels left the pad, and then circled us like a beady hawk till our skids did the same. A literal *Airwolf.* I'd have laughed at the analogy if I wasn't so frightened. But this was no fictional television series and Max was no romantic, cello-playing Stringfellow Hawk.

The rest of Max's werewolf motorcade was still packed around the pad as we soared northward. Just my luck, the skies were brilliant blue and devoid of any foul weather. I wanted so badly to call up a fog bank so that we'd be forced to delay the inevitable, but my calls were ignored and the helicopters pressed on, unimpeded, toward Red Devil.

It was the last place on earth I wanted to be. I wasn't the only one. Dean seemed to grow more agitated the closer we drew. It wasn't very often that he gave anything away. It was very imperceptible at first, but, even from where he sat mostly out of sight in the back seat, it was palpable. By the time we'd refueled for the second leg, his jaws were clenched and his hands were constantly raking through the shaggy sunlit locks falling past his shoulders. I'd peeked back at him enough times to notice.

What's up his butt? I was the one about to die, not him.

All too soon, we were touching down in Sleetmute where the fleet of dark Athabaskan SUVs was parked, waiting for us. Evidently, I was to be conveyed to Red Devil by the werewolf secret service. My stomach dropped as Augustus emerged lazily from his black Land Rover. He and Dean seemed to have the same bad taste in cars, though I had to admit a Defender was far more respectable than a Range Rover.

"If shit hits the fan," Dean said, "you know where my loyalty lies."

The brothers exchanged a curt and significant look before Dean pulled his headset off. Leaving us alone in the 407, he headed off to Augustus, each man clasping the other's forearm in a perfunctory greeting.

Knowing full well that no one—not even a werewolf—could hear us over the sound of the turbines (both helicopters were still cooling down at idle) I whispered into my mic, "Why would he help me? I killed Lydia."

"You don't know that for sure."

"Tristan…" We both knew what everyone thought.

He sighed into his mic. "He's my brother, he loves me. And I love you."

I wished it was as uncomplicated as he'd made it sound. "He's helping me because I'm your mate?"

He gave a succinct nod. The gravitas in my tone had not escaped him.

"What does that mean exactly? Are we married or something?"

"Something like that."

My eyes narrowed. "Just like that? Why wasn't I consulted?"

His sigh was half growl. "It isn't some tenuous human rite—

there's no flimsy document to be signed. No rings to be placed on or pulled off at whim." He placed his hand on my thigh. "It's out of our control, Evan. It's something our wolves decide."

"Ha! So my inner mutt *is* a 'disparate entity'?"

"No." He rolled his eyes. "When I refer to your wolf I mean your baser self—the part of you that doesn't need definitions or titles. The part of you that obeys instinct. It just is. You can fight it, but then you'd end up going against your own nature. You'd end up like my father."

Heaven forbid. I watched as Tristan began flicking avionics switches off. "Was Lydia Dean's mate?" Dean always seemed so distant and untouchable. I wondered suddenly if he'd ever even been in love. Loved anyone enough to overlook the killer inside. The way Tristan loved me.

"No." His mouth compressed introspectively. "He's only ever loved two women." He snapped the throttle closed, watching the trucks grimly. He pulled the rotor brake and the blades finally came to rest like a giant X over the fuselage.

"His mother?" I asked, pulling my headset off. To this, I received the single nod I'd anticipated, but no further expounding was offered. "Tristan, who was the other?" I grabbed his bicep as he pulled his headset off and reached for his door handle. I needed any and every diversion I could get. Those black trucks were glinting ominously at me in the late afternoon sun. They were waiting and I was stalling.

Tristan's gaze was fixed to where his brother stood with the others, hand poised on the door. We watched as Dean and Augustus were joined by Max, Josh, and the other Yukon wolves. Shortly thereafter, the Athabaskan alpha emerged from her car. She stood assertive amongst those male giants, so striking that I found myself awed by her—an Amazonian Cleopatra. Whatever puissance shrouded her, it was infinitely more than just the potency of a woman's power over man. It was a masculine power, dominant and estimable. The animus of an alpha female.

"One son aimed too high and the other too low."

"Oh." The answer was right there before my eyes! "Dean loves Aidan!

"Yeah," was all Tristan said before he too joined the group.

42

THE COUNCIL OF ALPHAS

As dusk rushed into the woods, so too came the ground fog. The glow from the headlights seemed to diffuse into the swelling, turbid mass, lending a sinister shade of sepia to Red Devil's stark landscape. It was *Black* Devil if anything. Winter must have killed off some of the trees earlier this year, I thought. They'd been struck bare by the arctic rage. The ones that weren't fixed in the dark like blackened skeletons were no less horrifying. Their shaggy needles seemed to move in the frozen mist, waving me to my doom. Ushering me into the lap of the wolves of the Underworld.

In a stupor, I barely felt the pressure of strong fingers calming my jerking knee. The ominous terrain blurred steadily outside the window. My fingers were leaden and cold-soaked, like the world outside. Not even Tristan's warmth, as he slipped his fingers between mine, penetrated my dread enough to thaw me.

The darkness only curdled my blood further, so I tore my eyes away from the window and latched them instead to the back of Aidan's dark head. And then to Dean, who was in the passenger seat beside her.

The painful tension roiled palpably between the two alphas up front, icier than the viscid dread that saturated my blood. If not for my numbing terror, I'd have wondered about their past. And there was, without a doubt, a *lot* of history between them. The sour stench of my fear, however, completely overmastered their tragic silence and any trivial curiosity I might have felt otherwise.

Suddenly, Aidan's SUV began to slow as she turned around a sharp bend. My heart leapt into a funereal series of sharp knells as that awful meeting hall, and those eerie double doors, appeared through the gloaming. As before, the space surrounding the looming building was packed with vehicles. Only this time there were easily triple the number that had been present at my first 'trial', the thirst for my blood that much keener.

The rest of the Athabaskan convoy filed in behind us like a fleet of black hearses. My legs were stiff as I left the vehicle. Max marched past like a grave-faced undertaker, pausing only briefly to hurry us along with an arbitrary jerk of his head, eyes a frosty blue in the twilight. Swallowing the upsurging bile back down, I dragged my feet along like deadweights.

A raw and suffocating restiveness filled the room. There were no whispers this time. Not even an awkward cough, only bleak and wordless enmity and the unbearable magnitude of hostile eyes transpiercing. My numbness, though, never wavered. It shrouded me from a hundred glares like a wall of ice fog. Unlike last time I was here, tonight there were some among the packs that had come in their wolf skins. Tristan had said that some of the elders were more comfortable as wolves than humans.

The silent snarling and restless movements ceased instantly when Aidan moved to occupy the center of the hall. There was no blunt report from a gavel to silence the room. None was needed. She commanded absolute attention without a single quirk of her features, or gesture of those long elegant fingers. Not a single word had fallen from her lips, yet all ears were pricked intently, eager to hear what she would say. They loved and respected her, it was clear. I envied her that unchallenged loyalty.

"Firstly," she said, at last, turning to face Dean, "I want to extend our deepest condolences to Dean and the rest of the South-east Regional Pack." She held his gaze a moment. "Lydia was a good and honest woman. She'll be missed by us all."

I could feel the icy press of accusation against my face as Aidan took another moment to eulogize Lydia. Her body, so I'd been told, had been sent to her estranged parents. I hadn't known that she and James had once been part of Max's pack. It was all I could do to straighten my spine a little more and keep my eyes forward and clear of stormwater. I was seated on a lonely chair facing Aidan and the Council of Alphas—Max, Josh, Dean, and four other stern faces I'd never seen before. They were all relatively young, powerful and masculine. Aidan had since introduced each alpha, but I'd already forgotten the names of the faces I didn't know. What did their names matter—I was just a mutt to them and they were just my nameless executioners. They all sat behind a long rectangular trestle table, only one chair remained unoccupied: Aidan's.

Her Athabaskans (Nicole included), had arranged themselves in a sort of crescent shape at my back, the group tapering toward the bench of glowering alphas. Tristan stood at my periphery, directly opposite Nicole, and his quiet rage fulminated like a blaze, staving off a little of the bite of cold surrounding me.

I became aware that Aidan was no longer talking and shifted my eyes to see her running her gaze over her congregation. I felt my blood chill as she finally fixed her gaze to me.

"An irremediable wrong has been perpetrated. The willful disregard of life is unforgivable, the loss unnatural and immutable. Only death can balance the scales of nature." Her jaw tightened. "A life for a life—that's the law of the pack."

Tristan's growl rumbled through the rafters. "And what about a life stolen?" The words seemed to hiss through his canines, his scowl peeling the flesh from Nicole's bones.

For just a moment, her eyes widened fearfully and she shrank back from him. I could almost hear my cold sweat falling from my brow, the stillness was so horribly acute. I should have been consumed with hate for her. Tristan seethed with it, enough for the both of us, unwilling to temper or hide it. I was inundated only with unalloyed terror, there was no space for anything else.

It was Max that answered him. "We're not here to weigh in on *how* she became a mutt, only her crimes." He held up a hand to his son when Tristan opened his mouth to fire off a retort. "Go on, Aidan."

"Tonight," Aidan went on, "we settle things once and for all." She aimed a hard, cursory look at Tristan and then transferred it to the assembly at my back. "Tonight we abnegate one of our own"—she turned to me again, a pathos tightening her mouth—"and the cost of blood will be great. Blood I myself will shed." Her fists clenched at her side as a moody excitement reverberated through her pack. But when she continued the room fell silent again. "Let's begin." She nodded to Augustus, who instantly withdrew from the room, and then she took her place at the judge's bench with the other alphas.

Before long, her second-in-command returned, a clear plastic bag in hand, and deposited what looked like "evidence" on the bench for the alphas to inspect.

My gut twisted as Max pulled out a blood-soaked shirt. *My* blood-soaked shirt. But *not* my blood. My missing phone and purse were there too.

Max took a delicate whiff of the stain and then passed it to Dean. "Is it…?"

"Lydia's." Dean nodded stiffly, pushing the shirt away.

A vicious murmuring suddenly swelled up behind me.

"You're sure," Josh asked, stern-faced.

Dean nodded again. "I'm sure."

An uprush of disgust and horror threatened to choke me. I'd killed her!

With an impatient snarl, Tristan loped over and snatched the shirt for his own scrutiny. Jaws clenched, he breathed in deeply and then carefully tasted the fibers. Finally, he lifted his nose from it, a dour pleat in his brow.

"Are you satisfied?" Max asked coldly.

Ignoring his father, Tristan brusquely handed the shirt back to Josh. "Tell me what else you smell."

After a diligent sniff, Josh lifted his gaze back to Tristan. "Gasoline."

"Uh-huh." Green eyes narrowed keenly.

"Irrelevant," Max drawled, watching as Dean also took a whiff. "The shirt was found in a parking lot. Gas—" with a supercilious snort "—is a logical concomitant of parking lots considering leaky *cars* are generally found in them." He waved his hand dismissively. "Let's proceed, shall we."

Tristan set his teeth and after a tense pause, in which the whole room seemed to hold its breath, he moved to stand at my side, an expression of confidence sublimating his cold rage.

"Now for the witness account," said Aidan.

Witness?! My gasp was swallowed by the shocked silence pervading the hall. Clearly, no one had expected this except, of course, Aidan herself. Even Max and Tristan were stunned by the development.

Augustus, meanwhile, had moved to stand beside the bench so that he was both facing the alphas and addressing the spectators. Here, evidently, was the eyewitness to all my crimes.

“You’re the eyewitness?” Tristan’s fists were balled. “Why weren’t we informed of this before?”

“I’m really more of an earwitness,” Augustus replied. “And we’re in the business of uncovering the truth, not warning the accused.” This was followed by a tense silence in which one feral glare pinned the other.

“For God’s sake, man, get on with it.” Josh pinched the bridge of his nose before dragging his hand impatiently down over his mouth. “Some of us are tired and jet-lagged.”

“Why were you there that night?” Max asked Augustus.

“Aidan had reservations—” his eyes flickered briefly to me “—about the girl’s ability to control herself. Clearly, she was right to doubt.”

The crowd instantly rumbled their scathing agreement.

From the tail of my eye, I noticed Nicole studying Augustus with a curious frown. She then exchanged a quick glance with her sister, but both women’s looks were so guarded that I could make no sense of either one. When she turned to catch me staring, Nicole parted her lips smugly and shot me a cold-blooded wink.

I wanted to vomit.

“Wherever she went, I followed her,” Augustus said. “I didn’t know till later that Lydia had been sent to Florida for the same purpose.”

There’d been those brief moments, like in the parking lot at the hospital, when I’d thought I was being watched. Now it all made sense because they *had* been watching me! “You could have stopped me” —coming out of my chair, shaking with violence — “you useless bastard!” He should’ve saved Lydia from me!

“Control yourself, Miss Spencer!” Max thundered. He then shot Tristan a pointed look as if to say, “Keep your mutt on a leash!”

But his son had not yet unfastened that murderous glare from

Augustus yet. Through clenched teeth, he said, "It sure as hell sounds like you could've prevented two deaths that night."

"If you'll both shut up a minute I'll explain." Augustus, unlike the rest, appeared both bored with my outburst and unaffected by Tristan's threatening glares. Only when I'd planted myself back in my seat, still trembling with anguish, did he continue. "That night, at the cafe, I observed her through the window. It was starting to rain and the wind was picking up. Pretty miserable night," he muttered irritably, "to be out babysitting, but Aidan didn't trust anyone else to watch the mutt."

"Careful…" Tristan growled.

He shrugged, unapologetic. "For a moment there, I thought she was gonna tear into that old lady's poodle right there in front of everyone. Damn thing wouldn't stop growling." The hush was charged as everyone waited for him to go on. "But she seemed to snap out of it. The old bag and her suicidal runt finally left and I got back to cursing the storm. That is until Lippy here lost her cool a second time and got into an altercation with the victim, Alex."

"Andy," I corrected him quietly.

"Yeah, Andy, the pretty boy."

"What altercation?" Josh asked.

"She overheard them talking shit." He gave another infuriating shrug. "Just your stereotypical college brats running their damn mouths. They didn't mean nothin' by it, and they never meant for her to hear them." His teeth gnashed as he shook his head at me. "You should've controlled your temper, girl."

I wish I had.

"What happened next?" Josh again.

"Like I said, there was an altercation. She made it clear that she'd heard them." Outraged whispers crescendoed as he paused. "No human *should* have heard them."

I flinched.

"Then she threw a fit and stormed out."

"There's your motive," Nicole muttered scathingly.

"Shut up." For all his tone was low, Tristan had never sounded so savage, or homicidal. I almost feared for Nicole. Almost. "I'm this close—" he pressed his thumb and forefinger tightly together "—to going rabid on you."

"I was livid," Augustus proceeded, undaunted by the interruptions, "and wanted to run after her, maybe slap some sense into the girl, but by then I realized I had company."

"Lydia." This from Dean.

"Yeah, she'd been watching from the other side of the building and as soon as Evan took off she followed, bolting over to my side." He shook his head ruefully. "We never even sensed each other."

The rain! Though it couldn't completely thwart a werewolf's nose, it did, however, confuse and dampen scents into olfactory chaos. It was why I loved the rain so much, it offered a little reprieve.

Augustus scratched his chin. "She was fit to be tied, that she-wolf. Railed at me for sticking my nose where it didn't belong. And there I was, riled at being discovered. I'd been told to remain invisible." For the first time, his face softened with remorse. "Then we heard Evan scream. Just once. Heard it through the thunder. That was the last time I saw Lydia alive. She warned me to get lost, then she hurried away. Figured I'd let her think I'd slunk away like a good dog. I waited at that window, biding my time. Suited me just fine since I needed to be sure Andy and his boyfriends hadn't worked themselves into a suspicion over Evan's mutant hearing."

"Were you satisfied they hadn't?" Josh asked.

"Yeah, those chumps had nothing on the brain but sex."

"Wait, so you didn't run after Lydia and Evan?" Tristan cocked his head suspiciously. "You didn't see Lydia die?"

"Like I said, I kept an eye on Andy. He promised the cook he'd close up since Lippy here had left in a huff."

"No one heard any screams?" This from Max.

"Nah, the storm was wailing something fierce by that time, so Andy and the others stayed put. No one heard a thing. The storm seemed to distract them from Evan's tantrum too, so I decided to go check up on Lydia's progress. I was upwind, but I figured the rain would help a little to confuse my scent." His mouth fell at the corners. "Turns out I had bigger problems."

"She was already dead?" Dean's face was drawn and his voice gruff with suppressed emotion.

"Yes."

Once again, I felt every eye flaying the flesh from my back.

"She'd gone to help Evan and it got her killed."

43

LAW OF THE JUNGLE

Throughout Augustus' testimony, Aidan had barely blinked her flinty eyes. She sat there as formidable as a marble Lion Dog guarding her Forbidden City.

Augustus gave a tired sigh and explained that Lydia's jugular had been torn from her throat. Her eyes, he recalled, had been wide and glassy, empty of every last drop of life. He appeared grave as he pictured her for us—her gaze frozen as the rain spilled over bloodless cheeks like cold tears.

Disturbed by this vivid imagery of Lydia's crying corpse, I felt the tears course hotly down my face into my trembling mouth.

"She was so much stronger than Evan," he said, "and could've easily overpowered her. Why hadn't she?" He shook his head, incredulous.

"I told her to protect Evan with her life." Dean's eyes were clouded over as he watched his younger brother. Although there were no recriminations in the look, there was regret. She'd followed her alpha's directions down to the last fatal blow it seemed.

After a protracted silence, Augustus spoke again. "Lydia's body was lying beside Evan's car, near the cypress trees out back, but there was no sign of Evan except her clothes lying torn and discarded next to Lydia. I made sure no one could see the body from the cafe or the road—not that anyone was out in that wet hell—and then I bolted after Evan."

"You didn't at least try to hide the body properly?" This from one of the nameless alpha's. Maybe his name was Bob? I knew a Bob back in South Africa who, like this alpha, had wild hair and an unkempt beard that was probably harboring a colony of feral chipmunks.

"Couldn't have a deranged wolf running rampant in Juno Beach, now could I?" Then he swatted the air dismissively. "Like I said, I was the only asshole out in that godforsaken weather. The rain was coming down in sheets and the wind was howling from every which way. It was a cluster fuck, man."

"Obviously, you didn't find her." Bob's beard rustled ominously as he spoke.

"Her scent was wet and weak, but I eventually tracked it to the beach and found what was left of her trail disappearing in the surf. She was headed north along the shoreline. I did catch a brief glimpse of a large black mutt streaking off in the distance, but by the second time the lightning lit the beach she was gone. And, like you said, I'd left the body in the parking lot way too long already. So I abandoned the chase and headed back for Lydia."

"And the evidence," Max added, giving my soiled shirt a scornful prod.

"Yeah..." Augustus let the word drag. "The evidence. About that." He approached the bench to bend his wily eyes over the crimson stain.

The blood still smelled so fresh—even from where I sat, it choked me with the stench of roaring accusation.

"When I first found Lydia's body," Augustus said, "I don't remember seeing any blood on Evan's shirt. When I doubled back, though, it was soaked in blood."

"Well, a severed jugular would naturally cause a sizable bloodstream to—"

"I know that," he interrupted Bob. "But Lydia's blood was being washed downhill into the storm drain. Evan's shirt had been lying, unstained, upslope of the body." He shifted his mismatched eyes to Aidan. "Tell me how that makes any damn sense."

Every gaze, including mine, followed his as though all the answers lay with the taciturn young matriarch, which maybe they did, but her eyes remained illegible and steely green.

"Doesn't take a wolf to know that that shit just don't smell right."

"What—" Max's voice was thick with ire "—are you getting at?"

"Simply this: the way I see it, there's reasonable doubt as to Evan being Lydia's killer—inadvertent or not."

The whole room shared my stunned and silent shock.

"Evan must have circled around." Max was emphatic about my guilt, the bastard.

"With respect, sir, that's impossible."

I sat up straighter in my seat, as alert as Tristan was beside me.

"Her tracks showed her heading north along the shoreline. I told you, I saw her for myself. I know a mutt when I see one. There's no plausible way she could've covered the distance back to the parking lot in the time it took me to backtrack."

"Notwithstanding the fact," said Tristan with some heat, "that you've all accused her time and again of being rabid." He was glaring at Augustus as he said the last. "And, therefore, incapable of premeditated murder."

"Down boy," Augustus said coolly.

A combative spark flared between the two males. I'd never known Tristan to allow anyone to rile him up the way Augustus was doing. Well, except Nicole. Sometimes Dean. It was frightening. I was saved the trouble of defusing his anger when Josh gave an impatient sigh.

"Hold up." He dragged a frustrated paw down his face before leaning back in his chair to fix Augustus with a long look. "What about Andy? We have two slayings to account for."

"Well, this is where the rabbit hole really gets dark and twisted. While I'd been on my goose chase, Andy's friends, the cook included, had made a run for it. The rain was nowhere near letting up, so I guess they wised up and bolted. There were only two cars left in the lot when I got back—Andy's and Evan's. The building was shut up and the lights were all out. I didn't see or smell his body at first because I was hell-bent on getting Lydia into the trunk of Evan's car. She'd all but bled out, but I laid her on my jacket and dumped Evan's bloody clothes on a rubber floor liner. Then I finally smelled it. He was lying beside his car. Poor bastard had been attacked from behind and disemboweled. There was nothing I could do. The boy was dead, I checked. Wasn't gonna waste time with him, since I still had to figure out what to do with Lydia"—he began enumerating his chores on his fingers for us—"then take Evan's car back to her mother's. Plus, I still had to head back out to look for my stray mutt."

"You're absolutely sure it wasn't Evan?" Josh asked carefully.

"Brother, I'm not sure of anything, but you tell me how a scrawny mutt magically doubled back and beat me to the carpark, disembowel the kid, and then transferred the shirt downstream of Lydia's blood. All without me catching wind of it." He gave an incredulous snort. "I only had a small distance to cover"—his eyes narrowed—"and I didn't waste any time."

"Who then?" Dean's voice had become menacing. He was looking directly at Nicole.

"What the hell is going on here?!" Max looked thunderous.

The same question was etched in the rest of the alphas' faces, except Aidan's, and they were glancing at one another with growing outrage. Furious whispers crescendoed from all corners of the hall. My heart raced maniacally, my thoughts were thrown into chaos.

At last, Aidan stood from her seat, her face grim as she faced me. "I understand you were covered in blood when you woke up on the beach."

"I was."

"Human?"

"Yes," I confessed.

"There! She admits it!" Nicole hissed.

"Say one more word," Tristan growled with a black look. "I dare you."

Aidan shot her sister a severe look and then went on with her interrogation of me. "Whose blood?"

"Andy's, I think." Revulsion settled heavily in my gut. "I-I think I ate him." I remembered waking up feeling as though I'd consumed a horse. The thought of any carcass rotting in my belly had always disturbed me, but knowing I'd eaten Andy…! Well, that was inconceivable.

"That's impossible, Lippy," Augustus said matter-of-factly. "I examined the body. All organs and limbs were accounted for." He folded his arms, smirking. "Hate to break it to ya, but you're no cannibal."

Confused, I shook my head.

"You ate a loggerhead. I found it next morning—looked like a shark had been at it. Reeked of mutt though." His teeth were long and sharp as he sneered at Tristan who was bristling, the word having stuck in my mate's craw yet again. "Jus' sayin'."

"Wish you wouldn't," Tristan snarled.

"Wait!" I gasped, "I wouldn't have had either Lydia's or Andy's blood on me. I couldn't have!" My eyes narrowed. "I was running in the surf." Bits and pieces were slowing becoming coherent—like a lost dream coalescing into something tangible.

"And it was raining so hard." I remembered my teeth sinking into the leathery shell. The flesh had been tough and the turtle had tossed its limbs out desperately. I remembered it struggling. "I didn't kill Andy!" I came out of my chair with the force of my epiphany. "It wasn't me!"

"But you just told us you woke up coated in his blood," Max argued, ignoring the bit about my saltwater bath.

I gritted my teeth, frustrated, willing myself to remember more.

"What else do you remember, Evan?" Aidan's body was tense with expectation. "A smell maybe? Something other than blood."

Where was she trying to lead me? I could feel it on the tip of my—holy shit! Incredulously, I turned to face Tristan. "Petrol. I smelled petrol. Faint, but it was definitely there."

Aidan sank back down into her chair, her eyes closing briefly. Sadly. There was no need to silence the room—everyone was already struck dumb with confusion. "You're free to go," she said, gesturing me from the hot seat.

Feeling as though I'd just been pardoned from death row, I allowed Tristan to pull me away. I could hardly believe it.

Max followed my progress with a lowered brow.

"Let's not waste any more time," said Aidan, turning to her sister. "Take a seat, Nicole."

Amidst the sudden deafening uproar, Nicole stood paralyzed. "What?"

Aidan said nothing, merely nodded peremptorily at the chair I'd vacated, her impatience sublimating that impenetrable poignancy.

Poleaxed, her sister slowly made her way to the center of the room. "I-I don't understand."

"You will," Augustus answered coldly.

All this time, I'd mistaken that coldness in Augustus for flippancy, but as I watched him scowl at his pack mate it dawned on me that he was livid. He had taken pains to hide it till now. I glanced up at Tristan, a little disturbed to see a look of bloodlust filling his eyes. They were eerily fixed to Nicole.

The mist of confusion had slowly lifted from my mind by now. In a bizarre and unexpected twist of events, I'd been absolved of all guilt. Nicole's innocence, however, was now evidently in question. I searched her face for clues, summoning the vengeful hate I knew I ought to feel for her—the same malice that had driven her to bite me. The same spite that had craved such a hideous death for me. But as I took in her gaping mouth, inhaling her dawning horror, as she silently begged her sister with watery eyes, I felt my own thirst for blood subside. There had been enough blood spilt already. Mine; Lydia's; and Andy's. But her fate was out of my hands, she'd brought this on herself.

"You told me yesterday," Aidan said without preamble, "that you'd spilled gas on yourself filling up your car."

"I did! I swear—"

"Where were you the last few weeks?"

"I sure as hell wasn't in Florida if that's what you're implying."

"Stop lying to me!" Aidan had finally lost her patience. "You've always been a good liar. Even I have trouble smelling them out, but I expect that's because you almost believe them yourself." When she'd regained her composure, she addressed the alphas. "Gasoline, as we all know, is a very effective scent-inhibitor. It confuses the senses. Coupled with the rain and the wind that night, Nicole was presented the perfect chance to frame an easy target."

"No! It wasn't me. I was staying up north with—"

"I checked your credit card, Nicole." Aidan promptly pulled a sheet of paper (a bank statement by the look of it) from her back pocket and handed it to Max. "I know exactly where you were staying."

"Juno Beach?" Max's mouth fell at the corners as he skimmed his eyes over the page. The evidence was, in turn, passed to the rest of the alphas, Dean included.

That this was Nicole's own sister signing her death warrant appalled me a little. These people—wolves—were so cold-blooded in their meting out of justice. Not even the blood of sisterhood seemed to sway Aidan.

But, I conceded, this was the Law of the jungle… *'And the wolf that may keep it shall prosper. But the wolf that shall break it must die'.* Aidan was an alpha, she didn't have the luxury of sentiment. Not even toward her own toxic sister.

"W-why are y-you doing this?!" Stark betrayal spilled wetly from Nicole's eyes as she glowered at her sister. "I love you! I love my pack!"

"No, you love only yourself," Aidan sighed tiredly. "You were spoiled and indulged by Father. I hoped you'd grow out of it, but you only became more selfish and cruel. I protected you once…"

When she'd bitten me, I thought darkly.

"Only because Evan survived." Aidan paused to collect her tattered thoughts (at least I thought they were tattered. She was too stoic to tell for sure). "I thought to validate your statement—" Aidan's voice dropped to a whisper "—by testing the fur and blood I found under Evan's fingernails when you brought her to us after she was bitten. I don't need to tell you what I discovered, sister. You lied to us then too."

"Aidie, please…" Nicole was hoarse with terror. The cloying scent of it permeated the hall, exciting the wolves to a low murmur.

"I won't protect you again. I can't." Her breath hitched with anguish. "You have blood on your hands, Nicky."

"She—" pointing at me "—woke up with blood on *her* hands!"

"Blood," Augustus seethed, "That *you* planted while she lay comatose on the beach. Bit of a rookie error to plant your victim's blood on a mutt that's already gone swimming."

"I hate you!" She howled shrilly. She was looking wildly at me and then Augustus. "Stop treating me like a mutt! I'm the daughter of Forest Rex!"

"And you've tainted that good name!" Aidan slammed her hand down on the table for emphasis. "He'd be ashamed of you now. Don't be a coward, for God's sake. Tell the truth."

Nicole finally shifted her crazy eyes to me. "You stole him. You were supposed to die! You're just a mutt." Then, shaking her head desperately, she turned to Tristan. "Why?" Her tears spilled down from her trembling chin into her lap. "I don't understand why you chose her."

"Because," I answered for him (and for myself), "I don't bite." From the corner of my eye, I caught the inconspicuous twitch of Tristan's lips. I knew he loved me for far more reasons than merely *that*, but, besides Tristan and I, it was no one's business why he'd chosen me over her. "You're just filled with hate and entitlement. That makes you the mutt, not me." I had done nothing but act with integrity. All I was guilty of was loving a werewolf.

"And if being a pureblood," said Dean, "means being like you —" glancing very briefly at his father "—then I'd sure as hell rather be a damn mongrel."

With that, Nicole sprang at me like a spitting cat, screeching with vengeance. But she was forcibly restrained by Augustus who received a few good blows and scratches.

"Down, kitty." Despite his words, Augustus was anything but amused.

I dragged my gaze from them to see Dean watching me. It was a very brief and inconspicuous movement—had I blinked, I'd have missed it—but I caught the subtle quirk at the corner of his mouth. The secret smile that was so like Tristan's. It was the first time he'd ever genuinely smiled at me, though, granted, it was tinged a little blue.

"Dean," said Aidan. The way she'd said his name, her voice like a hollow whisper, instantly commanded his attention. "Since it's your pack that has suffered the loss of Lydia, and born the injustice done to Evan, you must decide how we Athabaskans may requite ourselves."

"That's simple," Tristan said before his brother could answer. He stalked past Nicole, ignoring her frightened whimper, and stood directly before his father and the pantheon of grim-looking alphas. "I demand *Lupum Caedes*!"

44

LITTLE RED

"So do vampires exist?" My eyes were closed and my head was resting back against the side of the hot tub.

"Don't be ridiculous. There's no such thing as vampires."

I chuckled at Tristan's tone, peeling my eyes open for the sole purpose of rolling them at him. "Says the werewolf." After that, we lapsed into companionable silence.

The moon was suspended high over the trees, engorged and silent. An inviolate hush filled our forest. There was only the vapor drifting off the water, and the soft flutter of snow flurries kissing my shuttered eyelids. Tristan had turned the pumps off in the hot tub so that we could lose our thoughts in the gentle silence of a winter night festooned with ice lusters. Our wolf tracks had long since vanished beneath a fresh blanket of snow.

What a difference these last few months had made—running was something I no longer feared but craved and relished. Admittedly, though, I'd been repulsed by the idea of being nominated a runner in Nicole's *Lupum Caedes*. No matter how much I hated what Nicole did to me, I couldn't bring myself to be part of the triad of bloodthirsty hell hounds hunting our own kind, galvanized by the sweet tang of terror. I wouldn't have done it, not for anything. After all, I'd been on the wrong end of that disgusting custom once before. I was done with violence. Nicole had forfeited her right to live, I couldn't very well dispute that—I was no bleeding heart. She'd coldly stolen not one but three lives (though I couldn't very well regret my lot now that I'd so fully embraced it) and, as Tristan had explained it to me, once a wolf went off the rails, as she'd done, there was no conceivable way that she'd be suffered to live. All our lives hung in the balance. It was our inviolable covenant with nature, a means to protect ourselves from the destructive laws of man. We were a secretive breed and any threat to the pack was to be swiftly expunged. In short, human sentiment and bureaucracy had no place within pack law.

Still, I had no taste for Nicole's bloody 'expunging'. It was bad enough my she-wolf was controlling the local rabbit population with ravenous dedication. Fortunately, I was saved from that morally impossible dilemma. A week before (what was supposed to be) Nicole's last night on earth she'd thwarted her sentence and taken her own life. Maybe I should have felt something—rage or sorrow—but I'd felt nothing. How she'd done it hadn't been divulged. The Athabaskans had remained very reticent on the exact details of her death. In the end, I believed, she'd abhorred the thought of dying like a disgraced mutt. She hadn't been able to stomach the idea of the very death she'd intended for me.

"Alcoholic beverage for your thoughts?" Tristan playfully flicked some water at me, startling my eyes open.

I knew he hated talking about what had happened to me. As far as he was concerned, we'd talked it to death and it was time to move forward. I supposed I agreed. Not wanting to ruin our peaceful interlude, therefore, I decided against broaching the subject of Nicole's death. "Yes, I was just thinking that you still owe me a Sex on the Beach."

"That's not true." He smirked over the rim of his camping

mug as he sipped his bourbon. "Or does last night mean nothing to you?"

I hid my own smirk behind my fingers, acknowledging his point with a reminiscent sigh. We had indeed spent a glorious interlude on the beach last night.

He pulled his hand from the water to stroke Odin's brow as the dog raised adoring eyes to his alpha. The wolf usually joined us at the hot tub most evenings, resting his head on the edge so as to be near his pack.

I turned to look at the green shale beach, listening as the humpbacks sang their midnight lullabies. "How old are you exactly, Mr. Thorn?" I couldn't believe I'd not asked this till now.

"In doggie years?"

I pursed my lips. "Just use the Gregorian calendar, wiseass."

"I was born July seventh."

"Of what year?"

"By human standards I'd be considered about twenty-eight."

I folded my arms and considered him with a determined lift of one brow. "What year were you born, Tristan?"

The corner of his lip twitched. "The same year the Hubble Telescope was launched."

"Oh." He really *was* only twenty-eight. Well, that was anticlimactic. "I thought you were a lot older."

"Excuse you." With a sharp flick, he sent a hot tub tidal wave at my face. "I have fewer wrinkles than you."

I laughed. "Relax, old man, I thought werewolves age differently." Though he looked his age, I'd anticipated him being much older.

"We *do* age differently, but it's hard to quantify. An adolescent werewolf ages a lot faster—on par with humans actually—but as we mature, senescence slows down drastically."

"How drastically?"

"By now, I'm aging about three times slower than the average human." He leaned over to close my gaping jaw with a gentle nudge of his index finger. "My dad's seventy—still a spring chicken."

"Seventy!" If I hadn't known better I'd have guessed Max's age to be around forty-five at most.

"Yup, you're going to be stuck with me for a very long time."

"Vampires are still way cooler—they're immortal."

"Yeah," he said blandly, "but they sparkle like fairies."

"Not Lestat."

"You do realize that if you have sex with a vampire it's basically necrophilia—that's if they can even get it up."

"Tristan—"

"I mean they're stiffs but not in the sense that—"

"Okay, Tristan." The sternness I'd been valiantly trying to affect evaporated in one fell fit of giggling. "I repent, just stop already." The comfortable silence that followed Tristan's smug grin lasted only as long as it took for me to recall that I still had more questions. "You still haven't filled me in on Aidan and Dean's story." I was a sucker for a tragic romance.

"That's because I don't poke my nose where it doesn't belong. Well, except in the case of beautiful South African dart-throwers." He sighed when I only drummed my fingers impatiently. "It's a long story, Ev."

"A sad one too, I bet?"

"Uh-huh."

"There's still time for a happy ending though." I was more hopeful than determined that there should be.

"Hmm." He left the opposite side of the tub, the water sloshing excitedly, and angled himself next to me, pulling my legs over his lap so that my calves were resting on his hip and thigh. "The only happy ending I care about is ours…" There was a very provocative twinkle in his eyes.

I lifted my face to his, my fingers gliding gently over his jaw.

"I love you, Tristan. Best damn decision I ever made was letting go of that dart." And following my heart. "Sometimes I can't believe you're mine."

"It's my life's privilege to belong to you, my beautiful woman." His eyes glowed tenderly. "And I'll love you forever."

"You better live at least that long," I said firmly.

He leaned in for a heated kiss, stealing my breath. His hand descended leisurely down my naked chest, then over my ribs before finally settling on my hip to pull me tight against him. "What time are Melissa and Matt getting here?" He asked, his breathing ragged and hungry.

"There's no time for *that*," I said, snickering.

"There's always time for *that*."

"Well, I don't know"—poking him in his ribs with a teasing finger—"I still have to slip into my creepy cult uniform or they'll never believe I've joined your freaky secret society. Gotta make it all look legit."

"Yes, please don't ruin my reputation with your sneaky normalcy. Poor Dinwiddie would have a stroke."

"Only if you eat her poodles." Actually, she was more likely to have pet raccoons than froufrou dogs.

Smirking, he pulled away, shaking his head at me. "Seriously, Evan Spencer, never change."

"That's out of my control," I said, looking up at the full moon. "I kinda don't have a choice in the matter." *Yet.*

"It'll get easier."

It already had.

He ran his knuckles lovingly down my sternum before resting a splayed hand over my heart. "You're still you. *She*—" tapping a finger where the patch of white fur ought to have been "—is still you."

"My she-wolf?"

"Yeah."

"I know." I smiled up at him. "Funny, the moment I accepted her she stopped fighting me. I felt so mindless before. So terrified. Now everything has changed. It's like there's this constant vibration of power in my belly." It was humbling and exhilarating to feel her life-force beat in sync with mine as though we were finally one and not two spirits.

"Because you've evolved. You're freer now than you've ever been. By accepting her, you've accepted yourself. All that time you wasted thinking you were unhinged it was only your mind trying to let go of all that was dragging it down. You've always been powerful, Evan. You've always been a wolf. It's a shame that most people ignore what connects them to nature." He transferred his eyes to the watchful moon. "That's another reason why we live out here, far removed from the superficial and deafening stampede of humanity. The urban decay, the destructive greed that's slowly choking them, and eroding whatever small piece of unspoiled earth we own." His tone lowered bitterly. "Sometimes I hate them."

"No, you don't." I placed a hand over his heart. "You fell in love with a human." Then I poked a finger playfully into his ribs. "Now stop killing my mojo, Hyde."

He grimaced. "Ugh, you're right."

"Want to know what I'm gonna do with Aidan's guilt money?" This would divert him for sure.

"What are you gonna do with your blood money?"

Aidan had insisted that I be compensated for what had been done to me. It had been decided that Nicole's inheritance would be settled on me, and I'd decided to put it to good use. "I've applied to college."

"Giving it another go, eh?" He seemed surprised.

"Yup."

"You sure that's what'll make you happy?"

"There are two things in this life I love above anything else, apart from you and Mom—animals and art. These are what make me happy."

"What do you want to study?"

"Veterinary Medicine." Art I could study in my free time with Tim. "It feels right, Tristan." I'd already decided on University Of Alaska's Juneau campus. I was really excited for my future. I'd finally found my place in the world. Crazily enough, with werewolves. More importantly, with Tristan—my place was forevermore at his side and his was at mine.

"A vet?" Tristan was beaming. "That's kinda perfect for you actually."

"Dean's pack does, after all, need a competent physician." That was, of course, until Tristan finally took his rightful place as the Yukon alpha—a notion he was starting to warm up to. Max would thank me one day. *Ha! That bastard would rather gnaw off his own tongue than thank you for anything.*

"Right! And every time Odin or I get little doggie boo-boos you can stitch them up for us."

"Watch it or I'll have you neutered in your sleep."

"That's cutting your nose off to spite your face, woman."

"True," I said, brushing my fingers down his abdomen. I halted just below his navel, skimming teasingly close to the kraken. Then, abruptly, I brought my wayward hand up to his smirking mouth. "But"—tapping his bottom lip for emphasis—"there are other parts of you that give me equal pleasure."

Tristan leaned in to kiss my neck. His hand roved around to my backside, swiftly maneuvering me so that I was straddling him. "Let's explore that thought." He instantly took full advantage of my parted lips. Then, down my throat went his roving mouth till, finally, his lips found an eager nipple.

My hands locked behind his neck. "Hmm, you're making sure I'm never tempted to neuter you, clever beast."

The sound of the *Airwolf* theme song suddenly halted his

progress lower. Tristan raised his head with a discordant jolt, nonplussed by the unfamiliar ringtone. "What the…?"

I burst into a fit of incriminating giggling.

"Did you change my ringtone?" He'd finally cottoned on to my mischief.

"Thought it was apt."

He shook his head, hauled himself out of the tub, and then headed into the house, his water tracks freezing almost instantly on the deck. By the time he returned to the tub my amusement had hardly evaporated.

"It was Melissa," he said. "The snow's coming down too hard over there, they'll try to head up here tomorrow instead."

"Is that so?" I asked with a feline smile.

"It is so." He lowered his big beautiful body back into the hot tub, eyes stalking me with preternatural hunger. "What should we do with ourselves till then?"

Without the slightest warning, I leapt bare-assed from the tub and dashed across the snow, shrieking delightedly as he gave instant chase. I knew very well how hopeless it was to try and outrun a seasoned werewolf, but I had no intention of escaping him. We ran around the yard, hurling snow at each other, oblivious to the cold. Ribbons of gossamer steam wafted off my pinkened body, and his, as we tried to outmaneuver each other.

He finally caught me around the waist, though I suspected he'd not tried very hard to catch me till now. He made short work of lifting me over his shoulder like a sack of denuded potatoes. With a little slap to my bum, he marched off into the house. Odin's head was tilted curiously to the side as we passed him by.

"Don't mind us," Tristan said to the dog.

"This isn't how Little Red Riding Hood finished," I said, upside down, admiring his powerful backside as he carried me off to do bad things to me.

He dropped me on the bed and pinned me down, eyes almost

iridescent with lust. “Depends on which variant of the story you tell—the sanitized version…or the original.”

“I can do without the sanitized version.” My answer was husky and breathless as his eyes probed mine.

They were turquoise and gold—the latter glowing like moonlight now that his wolf was so near the surface. By now, his fangs had dropped from his gums. He took his time dragging them carefully down my breasts toward my belly. He slowly kissed his way down my parted thighs. “Then you know he devours her in the end.”

I nodded approvingly. My breath shuddered from my chest and my claws raked at his back as he made good on his promise. But I was far from ready to finish quite so soon, no matter how heavenly his lips and tongue caressed me. Surprising him, I suddenly pulled away and pushed at his chest till he relented and turned onto his back for me.

My own jaws were now jagged with sharp desire as I climbed on top of him, inching my way down his torso. “And she,” I said darkly, “devours him right back.”

ACKNOWLEDGMENTS

Thank you, Alison, for rescuing this story from the rubbish bin.

To my bardic sister, Melissa, thank you for being my role model and for putting each sentence on trial for its life.

To Mom, thank you for always thinking the sun and moon shone out of my ass when I used to write you bad poetry. I love you so much.

Most importantly, to Josh for your tireless support and love. Thank you for proposing to me in a beaver on a fjord in Alaska (and thank you for not dropping the ring in the water). You are my Tristan, wolfy canines and all. I love you.

ABOUT THE AUTHOR

Jeanine Croft is an itinerant seaman turned helicopter pilot turned novelist. She currently lives in Charleston with her ball and chain (who can't decide whether he's a pirate or a pilot) and their son, Will. She's been known to have whole conversations with her characters in the shower, which isn't at all unsettling to her menfolk or the dogs. She's a lover of penny dreadfuls, fried tofu, and prefers the company of books and animals (except mosquitoes).

For more books and updates:
www.jeaninecroft.com

Made in United States
North Haven, CT
13 March 2022

17109103R00255